Romance
CULLINAN
Heidi

Cullinan, Heidi.

Special Delivery.

sy shows up, get on

NOV 1 5 2018

Sam Keller knows he'll never find the excitement he craves in Middleton, Iowa—not while he's busting his ass in nursing school and paying rent by slaving away in a pharmacy stockroom. Then Sam meets Mitch Tedsoe, an independent, long-haul trucker who makes a delivery to a shop across the alley. Innocent flirting quickly leads to a fling, and when Mitch offers to take him on a road trip west, Sam jumps at the chance for adventure. Mitch is sexy, funny, and friendly, but once they embark on their journey, something changes. One minute he's the star of Sam's every X-rated fantasy, the next he's almost too much a perfect gentleman. And when they hit the Las Vegas city limit, Sam has a name to pin on Mitch's malady: Randy.

For better or for worse, Sam grapples with the meaning of friendship, letting go, growing up—even the meaning of love—because no matter how far he travels, eventually all roads lead home.

D0925685

This book is a work of fiction. The names, characters, places, and incidents are products of the writer's imagination or have been used fictitiously and are not to be construed as real. Any resemblance to persons, living or dead, actual events, locale, or organizations is entirely coincidental.

Heidi Cullinan, POB 425, Ames, Iowa 50010

Copyright © 2017 by Heidi Cullinan
Print ISBN: 978-1-945116-12-4
Edited by Sasha Knight
Cover by Kanaxa
Proofing by Lillie's Literary Services
Formatting by BB eBooks

All Rights Are Reserved. No part of this book may be used or reproduced in any manner whatsoever without written permission, except in the case of brief quotations embodied in critical articles and reviews.

First publication 2010
www.heidicullinan.com

SPECIAL DELIVERY

HEIDI CULLINAN

This is dedicated to my husband, Dan Cullinan, because he would not let me quit writing Sam's story no matter how hard I tried. Dan, it's all for you.

ACKNOWLEDGMENTS

Thanks to Dreamspinner Press for publishing this novel the first time and for Samhain Publishing for giving it new life and letting me give it a rigorous new editing pass. Thank you as always to Sasha, who let me get away with nothing, put me through my paces and helped me clean things up while still keeping the original story the same. Thanks to my sister, Hillari Hoerschelman, for helping me with the Rio Grande Valley Spanish, and to Dan Cullinan, Catherine Duthie, and Susan Danic for beta reading and helping me iron out the wrinkles. Thank you forever to Devon Rhodes who kept me from accidentally moving the Mississippi River in the first edition. Thanks to Tom and Nina for the financial help for the trip we took west that helped me figure out where to send Sam and Mitch, and to Dan for driving through the mountains because *oh my God*, I could never. And above all, thanks to the produce manager at Wheatsfield Cooperative, whose casual comment about a deliveryman pretty much handed me the plot bunny for this story.

Thank as always to my patrons, especially Pamela Bartual, Rosie M, Marie, Kaija Kovanen, Sarah Plunkett, Tiffany Miller, Erin Sharpe, Chris Klaene, Sandy C, Sarah M, Deandre Ellerbe, Deanna Ferguson, Michele C, Jennifer Harvey, Katie M Pizzolato, Ninna, Karin Wollina, and Maija.

CHAPTER ONE

I N THE DESERTED men's restroom at the back of Middleton Community College, Sam Keller knelt on the tile, braced his hands against Keith Jameson's thighs, and broke his mother's heart.

It didn't matter that Sharyle Keller had passed away four years ago. Sam knew his mother would consider what Sam did in the handicapped stall a complete and total mockery of everything she'd ever taught him. Sam being gay wouldn't have made her upset, and she wouldn't have cared that he was about to give a blowjob at school and risk expulsion for having sexual congress on campus. What would have upset his mother was how Sam wasn't at all attracted to his partner, that to be perfectly honest, Sam hated him.

"Sex is beautiful," Sam's mother had told him. "Sex is a union between two people. Sex is a merging of souls, a holy connection. Sex is sacred, and it should only be shared with those you love."

When Sam's mother had said this, he'd been twelve and horny, but he'd also been scared to death of sex, so when his mother told him he should wait for someone who loved him, he'd nodded eagerly. Yes, he would reserve his body for those who knew the worth of it. Yes, he would learn from her mistakes. He'd signed on for it all, trusting in his mother's wisdom, wanting to be safe and wanting to please her too. After all, wasn't he lucky to have a mother who looked *forward* to meeting his boyfriends? His mother had hoped he'd want to adopt or hire a surrogate to have his child someday because she'd be more than happy to babysit. It seemed such a little, easy thing for him to promise her he would give himself in love.

However, even before he'd realized what an incredible dearth of loving male partners there were in Middleton, Iowa, Sam struggled with his vow. His mother found him gay support groups and sex-tip sites online, but Sam found the porn. He'd lost days in the images of beautiful, slender men bent in submission and sometimes degradation, and to his quiet horror, he realized this was his fantasy: he wanted to be used. He wanted to be loved and cherished, yes. But he also wanted to be *fucked*. Sometimes he didn't want it to be about love. He wanted it to be about sex, and about semen, and about not quite exactly being in control. He didn't want to get hurt, no. But he admitted to himself he wanted to come really, really close.

As he swirled his tongue around Keith's shaft and looked up at the blond boy's unshaven chin, Sam acknowledged he'd have been a lot happier if he could have found a Keith at sixteen instead of twenty-one. He'd fucked Darin Yarvin his senior year of high school, but that was nothing more than a weekly appointment to kneel on a pizza box in Darin's dirty apartment and take it up the ass. Blowing Keith flirted with so many taboos, Sam got himself off just thinking about upcoming encounters.

Keith was straight. He wasn't bi. He wasn't in the closet. He wasn't even curious. He simply enjoyed having his dick sucked as much as Sam took pleasure in doing it. He was a big, buff boy, a small-town Iowa ideal, and it was Sam's fondest wish for this ideal young man to bend him over one of the toilets and bury himself so deep inside Sam he'd see stars. Sam didn't want to kiss him. He didn't want to hold him or take him on a date. In fact, outside of arranging their sexual appointments, they didn't speak to one another. The only conversation they had was the one they were having now, where Keith asked Sam if he wanted him to shove his big fat dick into his throat, to fuck his mouth, and Sam agreed yes, very much please, and thank you.

"You like sucking my cock, don't you, bitch?" Keith would say, and Sam would nod, and shut his eyes, and let the incredible sluttiness of the experience wash over him in dark, beautiful waves until he thrust himself onto Keith as hard as Keith pushed into him, sucking so intensely he hurt his cheeks, moaning along with Keith as he cried out and exploded, hot and thick and salty into Sam's open, waiting throat. Sometimes Keith kneaded Sam's hair as he swallowed, which Sam enjoyed, but it was an unconscious gesture, and if Keith caught himself doing it, he stopped and pushed Sam away.

This more than anything else would have upset his mother, that he would know only such a fleeting bit of tenderness and from such a crude, cruel partner.

Keith's abrupt removal today had left one last trail of semen to drizzle over Sam's chin, and he wiped it away with his fingers and reached for some toilet paper. Keith watched him, but when Sam met his gaze, Keith looked away as he buttoned himself up.

Sam waited, remaining on his knees. This part was always the trickiest, and he held still, lowering his eyes, letting Keith decide when they were finished. If Keith had more abuse to hurl, he'd take it, because the last thing he needed was Keith nervous. Keith had to feel strong and satisfied and a little superior so he would want to do it again, which was what Sam wanted him to want. It wasn't ideal, but in its own way, it worked. So he waited, docile, until Keith spoke.

"You gonna suck it next Wednesday?"

Sam kept his head ducked to hide his smile, and he nodded. He held still until Keith exited the stall, and he stayed on his knees until Keith left the restroom altogether. Then he rose, adjusted his own erection in his pants, and went to the bathroom sink to wash his hands.

Sam regarded his reflection in the mirror as he lathered soap across his palms. His mother's face stared back at him, slender and pretty, brown hair tousled around large, dark eyes. The only differences were the length of his hair and the shape of his jaw and his chin, which in addition to being slightly more defined than his mother's, sported the tiniest spattering of beard stubble. In his own face, he saw the face he loved so much, the face he had assumed, naively, would be around for a long, long time. He looked into its echo now, remembering what he had done. He acknowledged what she must think of him, and his heart grew heavy.

"Sorry, Mom."

He wiped the last bit of Keith's semen from his chin and went to class.

THE PROBLEM, SAM decided later as he trudged home from campus, was that he really wanted kinky. Yes, he wanted love. He wanted to date and hold hands and make the squeamish conservatives in his northern Iowa town squirm in their twinsets. He wanted to get married. But he wanted hot sex too. *Hot* sex. He wanted to try it all, every position, every fetish. Well, not *every* fetish—a lot of them, though. He wanted an *orgy*, or at least a threesome. All the things about sex his mother had said were bad, all the objectification, all the cold, meaningless encounters—that was what he was after. He didn't know why. He only knew he wanted it.

As he wove his way through the well-manicured lawns of Cherry Hill Estates, he admitted that so long as he lived with his aunt and uncle, kinky would be hard to come by.

Uncle Norm and Aunt Delia lived on Cherry Hill Court, their three-thousand-square-foot neo-Queen

Anne sprawled over the top of *the* Cherry Hill. In the days when the development had been farmland, the crest had been lined with cherry trees. Delia, who hated mess, cut them all down and replaced them with red, green, and yellow shrubbery spaced by perfectly rounded boulders and mulched them within an inch of their uninspired lives. They were the same boring ornamentation gracing every lawn in the development, but they had one advantage—the shrubs, combined with the lack of fences, made it incredibly easy to cut across country.

Sam did this now, singing softly under his breath along with the music playing on his iPhone, sometimes pausing to pull up the texting interface and read an incoming tweet or answer a text. He sighed over Kylie Minogue's report on her next stop on her US tour, wishing he could be there, memorized the discount code from Los Dos Amigos restaurant, and with a low-grade arousal told Darin, yeah, he could swing by later tonight for a quick fuck.

When the phone rang, he checked the ID, paused his music and clicked *answer*. "Hi, Emma."

"Are you on it?" Her excitement pushed her volume so high Sam had to pull the ear bud a little ways out of his ear. "Oh my God, are you on the *iPhone*?"

Sam beamed. "It is *so cool*. I mean, the headphones have a *microphone*. I'm totally talking into it *right now*."

Emma squealed. "I can't wait to see it. You're bringing it in to work, right?"

"It's never leaving my side. Ever." He reached into his pocket and stroked the cool metal lovingly. "I have my whole music library on here. I can't believe I was nervous about getting it. It's worth every penny."

"Yeah, now all you have to do is pay for the monthly plan."

Sam winced. "Don't remind me. It's good this thing plays movies because I'll never be able to afford going to the theater again."

"You need to ask your aunt for a raise."

"Yeah, that'll happen right about the time she marches in the Pride parade." Sam hopped over a patch of foliage and veered toward the highway, the last obstacle between himself and Cherry Hill.

"So, I have something to ask you. A favor."

Sam paused in mid-step, instantly wary. "Okay."

"I want you to ask your uncle if I can rent one of his apartments."

Sam snorted and resumed walking. "You want a kidney too?"

"I'm serious. I'm tired of living in my parents' house. Aren't you? Of living with your aunt and uncle, I mean?"

"God yes. But I can't afford to move out, and last I checked, neither could you. What are you planning to pay rent with? Your biology notes?"

"I had an idea about that, actually."

The sugarcoating on her voice made Sam uneasy. "Yes?"

"I thought *we* could be roommates. Now *hold on*," she said hurriedly, when Sam broke into peals of bitter laughter. "It could *work*. Come on, admit it. It would be so fun. We get along great, and your aunt—"

"Would never agree to this."

"Would be happy to get you out of the house."

Sam ran his hand through his hair. "It's not that simple, and you know it. She hates me, hates having me living in her basement. But what she abhors above anything else is paying for me, and there's no way I could afford an apartment without Norm and Delia's help. My aunt already resents what she has to fork over for part-time classes, which is *why* I'm part-time, as you well know."

"But if it's one of your uncle's apartments—"

"It's still money out of their pockets, in their mind."

"But *listen.*"

Emma launched into another round of arguments. Sam did listen, sort of, making occasional grunts and sounds of agreement or acknowledgment, but mostly he just let her keep talking because it was easier than trying to explain that his aunt and uncle would never go for this plan no matter how she sold it. It was too bad it wasn't going to work because it *would* be great to live with Emma. It couldn't happen, not until he got his own job, which he couldn't get until he finished school, and at his current pace this might be when he reached retirement age.

He pretended anyway for Emma as he came up the last crest and onto the road. But between listening to Emma and glancing back and forth as he tried not to get hit by traffic, he almost ran smack into the semi parked along the side.

It was *huge*. The trailer was the same length as normal trailers, but the bright blue cab was an absolute monster, twice as long as the usual ones.

It also had a very nice ass sticking out of the hood.

The driver stood bent at the waist, leaning so far in the only parts of him visible were his legs and a pleasantly shaped, jean-clad backside. As Emma continued to launch her apartment campaign at him, Sam ducked behind a black Dodge pickup and headed as close to the trucker butt as he dared. Still unsatisfied from his bathroom appointment with Keith, it didn't take but a few seconds of Hot Trucker Fantasy to send all spare blood cells due south. Probably the guy had a face like the bottom of a boot, which made it all the better it wasn't visible. Sam admired his features from as close a distance as he dared, knowing later tonight he'd be imagining himself bent over a fender with strong, grease-coated hands gripping his hips and sliding back to part him before the trucker—

"*Sam.*"

Sam blinked, stumbled and jerked his attention to the phone. "Huh?"

"You aren't even listening to me."

"Sorry." Sam stepped over another series of bushes and started up the hill toward his aunt and uncle's house. "Something on the road caught my attention. What were you saying?"

"I asked if your aunt is at the pharmacy this afternoon."

"Today? You want to ask about the apartment *to-*

day?"

"Well, yeah. We could be in by the end of the month. It'd be great."

Sam vaulted the last series of bushes and fumbled with the keys to his basement entrance. God, he'd wanted a few days to plan his strategy. Maybe this would be better—get it over with. "Sure."

"*Yes.* Okay—so, I'm gonna head. When will you be in?"

"Give me fifteen minutes. That's the fastest I can manage."

"Don't be late." She hung up.

Sam tugged the ear buds out and put his keys in the lock.

The house was empty and silent. Sam moved through the immaculate den and down the hall to his room, where he dumped his backpack on the bed before falling onto it himself. He lay there for a few seconds, staring at his bookshelf without really seeing it. Reaching into the plastic crate beside his bed, he pulled out a can of sparkling water and cracked it open. He sipped at it while he surfed the internet on his phone, not quite adept at it yet but still loving the idea that he *could* do it whenever he had cell service. He played a word on his never-ending Facebook Scrabble game with Emma, tried to think of something to tweet, but then gave up, put his phone away and wandered upstairs.

Living in Aunt Delia and Uncle Norm's house was like living inside a Pottery Barn showcase, and it drove Sam crazy. As always, the opulence and waste disgusted him. To Delia, her picture-perfect home was a source of pride. Sam had grown up in a crowded, messy trailer with a mother who couldn't stand on her own after he was ten, let alone arrange knickknacks and silk flowers. Delia's house only made him lonelier.

Once in the living room, though, Sam didn't feel quite so solitary.

The urn Delia had chosen for her sister's ashes was elegant and gleaming and not at all what Sharyle Keller would have wanted, and certainly it hadn't been Sam's vote. Even so, he always felt better when he saw it, because he knew his mother was inside. He went up to her now, placing his fingers on the bottom of the urn and resting the butt of his palm against the gleaming walnut mantle.

"Hi, Mom." His fingers curled around the vase's gilded handle. "Miss you."

He never felt any weird vibes from the urn, never felt ghostly fingers caress his shoulder, no matter how long he waited for them, but it still felt good to stand here, touching the container holding the little bit of her remaining outside of his memories. The anxiety of having to ask Delia and Norm about the apartment eased, and even the shame of Keith faded a degree simply by being near her. That was the way it had always been with his mom. She fixed everything.

He stood there until he felt completely calm. Then he leaned forward and kissed the base of the ornate china. "Gotta go to work. Love you." He headed for the front door.

He reset the alarm, hurried out and locked the door before bee-lining for his beat-up Civic Delia made him hide around the side of the house behind a boxwood hedge. When the Civic took a moment to turn over, he glanced at his watch and frowned, knowing he'd lingered too long and Emma would be mad. Actually he was so late now he might be tardy for his shift. It was difficult to say whose anger made him more anxious, Emma's or Delia's.

Once he got the car going, he had to use the highway to get out of Cherry Hill Estates, and despite his lateness, Sam slowed when he saw the blue semi still parked beside the road. The driver shut the hood and headed for the door to the cab, and as Sam drove past at almost ten miles under the speed limit, he got a good look at the man's face.

Not the bottom of a boot, he acknowledged, quickly editing his upcoming fantasy. Not the bottom of a boot at all.

EMMA WAITED FOR Sam at the front of the store when he got there. Delia stood nearby at the counter sorting through a purchase order. Behind them, half-obscured by a shelf of antacids, his uncle blithely surfed the web.

Sam's uncle Norman was one of the last independently operating pharmacists in the state of Iowa. He owned Biehl Drug, a store so old it had been there since the town of Middleton was founded in 1889. By rights an independent pharmacy couldn't compete with a Walmart pharmacy *and* a Walgreens in town, but Norman had some good nursing home contracts, and to pad his income he played the stock market and rented property. He rented a *lot* of property, to the point he had a near monopoly on most of the apartments in town. Delia managed all of them. Delia managed *everything*, including Uncle Norman.

She looked up when she saw Sam, and she didn't smile, only flipped another page on the order sheet. "You're almost late."

"Sorry." Sam reached around the counter to pull out his apron and fumbled with the ties after he looped the noose of the bib over his head. "Did the truck come in yet?"

Emma's pasted-on smile strained. Sam glared at her. What, he was supposed to initiate the conversation too?

Delia continued scanning her order sheet. "Yes. It's all in the back, waiting for you." She lowered the form and gave Sam a pointed look. "The diabetic supplies are almost out, and they didn't get put on the order list. Why didn't you tell me when you checked stock last weekend?"

Sam held up a defensive hand. "I did tell you. I put a note in your in-tray."

"Well, I didn't see it. Now we're out, and you know very well Harriet Meeker will talk of nothing else at the Ladies' League as soon as she discovers it."

Sam *had* put the note in her tray, and he was about to point out if she hadn't found it, it was her fault, when he caught a glance at Emma's pleading, desperate face.

God, woman, but you owe me. "I'm sorry to hear that. Do you want me to go buy her usual at Walmart and keep it on hand in case she shows up?"

Delia waved his offer away. "Just tell me next time." She dropped the pile of mail in disgust and rubbed her forehead as if trying to grind out a headache.

Sam looked to Emma automatically for some support and found her still giving him intense *talk about the apartment already* vibes. Sam folded his arms over his chest and stared meaningfully at Emma. *No way,* he telegraphed right back. *You're starting it.*

Emma gave him one last pleading look, but when Sam shook his head, she wiped her hands on her apron and turned to Delia. "Mrs. Biehl. I had this idea, and I wanted to know what you thought of it."

Delia put down the invoice, softening a little. "Yes, Emma? How can I help you?"

"I talked it over with my parents, and we decided it's time I got an apartment. You know, for responsibility and all."

Delia smiled. "I think that's wise. Were you wanting to rent one of ours? Because I know a perfect place opening up this summer. The one above the bookshop on the hill?"

Emma's hands stopped bunching in her apron and clasped in front of her chest instead. "Oh, Mrs. Biehl, that would be great." She beamed at Sam. "Wouldn't that be *perfect* for us?"

Sam tried to shake his head in warning, but Delia's eyes were already on him, sharp as a hawk's, her smile washed away. "Us?"

Sam held up his hands. "I—"

"I thought maybe Sam and I could room together. Right, Sam?"

They both looked at him, expectant, and Sam faltered. What was he supposed to say? He felt flustered and angry. This was Emma's scheme—couldn't *she* say something?

Back in the pharmacy, Sam saw his uncle glance up from the computer.

Delia folded her arms as she addressed Sam. "How were you planning to pay your half of the rent?"

Sam felt, somehow, there was some answer he was supposed to give, something which, if he could guess what it was, would make this go right. He searched for it, he really did, but his mind was a blank, and the silence pressed on him. "I, uh, don't know." Sam looked at Emma and then at his uncle, but he found no help in either place. "I—I don't know."

Delia picked up the purchase order and resumed scanning. "When you find a roommate who can pay her half of the rent, the apartment is yours." She glanced at Sam. "Your stock is waiting."

Sam's uncle returned to his computer, and Sam turned away, feeling foolish but not really knowing why. When he headed toward the stockroom, there was no surprise at all that Emma followed him.

"What is *wrong* with you?" she demanded as soon as the door closed behind them.

Sam picked up a case of adult diapers from the pile

by the door. "Don't yell at me. This was your plan, not mine."

"But you didn't say *anything*. You didn't even try."

"You didn't give me any time to get anything ready." Sam opened the flaps of the box. "I don't *have* money. I don't know how to pull it out of my ass."

"It isn't about money." Emma pushed the box closed. "I thought you wanted this. You're always telling me how much they drive you crazy. I thought you wanted out of there."

"I do." God, he wanted nothing more. "But she's never going to agree. You heard her."

"Why do you always let her roll over you? Why don't you stick up for yourself for a change?"

"What am I going to say? What sort of leverage do you think I have? They've paid for everything for me since I was in high school. They're paying for my college. They pay for my food, and they give me somewhere to live."

"They pay for your college because they have to. They feed you because it would look bad if you starved. If J.K. Rowling hadn't made it such a mark of Cain, I swear they'd put your room in the closet under the stairs. Your mother named them your guardians, and this is the responsibility they took on when they accepted the job. You don't owe them."

Sam picked idly at the plastic wrappers visible beneath the open flap of the box. He knew Emma was right, knew he should stand up for himself, but he didn't know how to explain to her he didn't know how.

"I can't. I'm sorry. I'm really sorry."

Emma opened her mouth to launch into another lecture, but before she could, the door to the store opened and Uncle Norman stuck his head inside. "Emma, I need you up front."

"Sure, Mr. Biehl." Emma poked a finger into the center of Sam's chest. "We'll talk later."

I'm sure we will. He wasn't looking forward to the conversation already. He watched her go then pulled out his phone. He scrolled through his playlists, selected *Kylie Favorites*, and tucked his ear buds in, ready to let Ms. Minogue take all his worries away.

She hadn't cleared the first verse of "No More Rain" before the door from the front opened again. This time Delia came into the stockroom.

His aunt was a small, slight woman, but her diminutive size somehow rendered her all the more terrible. Her features were similar to Sam's mother's, but while Sharyle Keller had been as soft and cozy as a stuffed animal, Delia was as cold and un-cuddly as a china doll. Sam's mother had loved yeast and sausage and chocolate, and once her disease relegated her to a wheelchair, she had no hope of burning it off. Hugging Sharyle was a warm, soft experience. Delia ate organic salad with tofu, counted calories, and put in at least three miles a day on the elliptical machine across the hall from Sam's basement bedroom. Even if he'd wanted to hug his aunt, he'd have bruises from her bony frame.

Delia appeared unlikely to hug him now.

She nodded at the half-opened box and folded her

arms over her chest. "Were you thinking you should get paid for doing nothing in *addition* to asking for free rent?"

Sam pulled his ear buds out and started unloading the box. "Emma was talking to me."

Delia gave his pocket a cold look. "I hope that *thing* isn't going to make your job performance even worse. If I catch you surfing while you're clocked in, I'll dock your pay."

"*Hey.*" Sam shoved the package onto a shelf. "I do my job. I work hard." *A hell of a lot harder than Uncle Norman.*

Delia aimed a finger at him. "Remember, young man, I've got my eye on you."

She left. Sam made a face, murmured, "I've got my eye on you" in mocking singsong under his breath, put his ear buds back in, and hoped he could be left alone to work.

Sam enjoyed doing stock. Sometimes he did tech work behind the counter with his uncle, but he had to dress up and wear a lab coat there, deal with customers, and worst of all, put up with his aunt. In the stockroom, people left him alone.

In the stockroom, he could dance.

As discos went, shelves full of shampoo, Band-Aids, and rubbing alcohol were poor decor, but he had a wide floor to himself, and he'd long ago developed a trick of reaching into a box, grabbing a bag or bottle, and inserting it onto the shelf in time to the beat. Emma teased him, warning if his aunt found out, she'd freak, but Sam had his argument ready. Yes, he spun his way down the aisle and sang into bottles of Pert, but he was a full five minutes faster when he did it than when he didn't. He'd timed himself once to prove it.

The best of all music to stock to was Kylie Minogue, and she sang to him now. "All I See" took him through the Depends and Charmin, "Giving You Up" gave him the courage to face sorting through a case of makeup with all its tiny, tiny packets refusing to lie orderly on a shelf, and "Sensitized" encouraged him to tap his toe all the way through bar soap, shaving cream, and cotton balls. By the time "Kids" came on, he was really in a groove. After breaking down the boxes he'd done so far, he shut his eyes and boogied backward with them out the door. Belting along with the chorus as he spun, he tossed the boxes into the dumpster, swung his hips and shimmied down the wall beside the rail.

Movement out of the corner of his eye stopped him short, and he blushed as he saw a man leaning on the bumper of a semitrailer filling the alley, a trailer which was, he noted, attached to a bright blue cab. It was the same man who'd been climbing into the cab beside the road on Cherry Hill.

The man had a slow, wicked smile on his face, and he was clapping.

CHAPTER TWO

S AM TUGGED THE ear buds out and backed up against the railing. He stood on the pharmacy's loading dock, an ancient, slightly crumbling concrete structure which only sort of met the ramp of a delivery truck. The semi's trailer was docked on the opposite side of the alley at a stoop belonging to the bicycle shop, its metal ramp extended and jacked sideways to make a walkway. The driver, however, stood on the ground about twenty feet away from Sam.

"Hi." Sam gave a feeble wave.

"Hello yourself, Sunshine." The man said nothing else, just watched Sam for a minute, and when the silence went on too long, the trucker gave a rough salute against his forehead as if tipping an invisible hat. Then he pushed off the side of the trailer, climbed up on the ramp, and started unloading again.

If Sam could have placed an order for a man, this would be what he called in. The man was *ripped*. His muscular frame bulged through the thermal shirt rucked up around his elbows and filled out his jeans until they strained the seams. It was cooler now that evening was coming on, but the trucker was sweating enticingly from his exertions. He hefted huge boxes with ease and bore them away as if they were full of feathers. Best of all was when he crouched to pick something up—Sam wished he dared to pull out his phone and snap a photo of the moment before the man started to rise, his perfect, *perfect* ass presented to Sam for a private viewing.

His face wasn't bad, either. He wasn't quite a Greek god, but he was chiseled, his jaw peppered with stubble, his nose not pert and cute but not chunky, either. Good mouth. His lips weren't lush, but they weren't thin. They seemed quite luscious, in fact, especially when the man's tongue snaked out between his teeth to wet them. The only flaw the man had at all was his hair. It was ragged, too long, and dull, suggesting the man washed it with a bar of Coast and got it cut with a butcher knife every three months.

Ah, straight men, Sam thought with quiet regret.

The man caught Sam still looking at him and smiled. As the gesture became laced with invitation, Sam stilled.

Maybe not straight?

You're imagining things. Even if he's gay, this guy won't come on to a scrawny little rat like you.

The deliveryman's thumb stole up to his mouth and toyed lazily at the side of his lips, which had the effect of making Sam fill out his own jeans a bit more snugly.

"I got a camera in the front of my truck." The trucker spoke the words in a drawl so thick he practically applied it with a trowel. He jerked his head toward the front of the semi. "You could take a picture and make this last a bit longer."

Sam tried to keep his voice steady. "I've got one on the phone in my pocket."

The man planted his feet firmly on the ramp, lifted his square chin and held out his arms. "Well?"

Sam's hands were shaking, and his mind shut down all thought outside of *oh God, oh God, oh God, oh God,* but he managed to pull out his phone without dropping it, and his hand was almost stable as he fumbled with the camera function. He had no idea, though, where he found the chutzpah to lift his other hand and make a spinning motion with his finger. "Turn around."

The man grinned, rubbed his thumb across his lips and did as he was told, boldly giving Sam a front-row view of his jean-clad ass. The tiny *click* of Sam's phone shutter echoed like a gunshot through the alley. Sam felt surreal—happy, but surreal. This wasn't the sort of naughty Sam was used to. No shame at all, only *fun.* It wasn't the usual quiet, desperate sex or parody thereof. It wasn't sex at all.

Yet.

The man glanced over his shoulder. Sam's thumb, still hovering on the camera button, quickly clicked again, but he cursed his timing when the man's mouth curved into a slow, delicious grin. He frantically pushed the button one more time, but he lowered the phone without looking to see if he'd captured the gesture.

"Thanks." Sam tucked the phone into his pocket and gave what he hoped was a rakish and not constipated smile.

"Not a problem." The man didn't go back to work. He kept watching Sam, as if he didn't have a trailer full of stock to unload. Then Sam peered inside and realized he didn't see any more boxes at all. The man was done delivering.

Yet he was still here, playing with Sam. Waiting for him to play back.

Sam tried to think of a witty rejoinder, or any rejoinder, but his mind was blank, still melting down to *oh God, oh God, oh God,* his dick helping nothing by pulsing like a nuclear bomb.

"I'm Sam." He extended his hand then realized the ridiculousness of the gesture when they were standing more than twenty feet apart. He tried to turn it into a wave but gave up and stuffed both hands into the pockets of his jeans. "Hi."

"Howdy, Sam." The man eased his stance and rested his arm against one of the open doors of the trailer. "Mitch Tedsoe, at your service." Another lazy smile stole across his lips, this one so wicked it practically came with its own arrest warrant. "You need anything delivered, Sunshine, I'm your man."

I am not cool enough to play this kind of game. "You do seem to know your way around a package."

"It's all in the handling." Mitch's drawl made the last word come out missing its g. "You have to treat them careful, but at the same time, you can't be afraid to be a little rough when the occasion calls for it."

Sam was now so far out of his element he was on

another planet, but he couldn't seem to stop. It was one thing to mess with guys from school, but a total stranger? *God, yes.* He gripped the metal rail and pressed his groin against it, willing the cold iron to permeate his jeans and calm him the hell down.

"That sounds dangerous." It was a lame comeback, but his brain cells were all shutting off as his libido ratcheted up. And if he didn't keep talking, this play would end, and Sam would have to go inside and unpack more boxes of Depends.

"I'm only as dangerous as you want me to be." Mitch gave him another lazy smile. "But something tells me you could use some danger, and I bet you'd find you like it a little rough."

It was good Sam held on to the rail, because it turned out to be a handy support for failing knees. "*Hhhnnnnh,*" he said, out of vowels. He swallowed, drew a breath, and laughed, but it was shaky. "Okay. You got me."

A pair of blond eyebrows shot up. "Far as I can see, you're still up there on your balcony and I'm all alone over here. I don't got anything, Sam."

Shit, this guy was actually propositioning him? Here, in the *alley*? "Uh." Sam's hands, despite the cold, were growing sweaty. "Aren't you—uh—working?"

The man kept looking at Sam's mouth. "I could use a break. You?"

It had to be a joke. Or a mistake. Or something. Because this was the sort of fantasy Sam jacked off to alone in the dark at night. This wasn't even something he *hoped* would happen to him. This did not happen to Sam—or anyone—in real life, and it never would.

Except for right now.

Sam dropped the game and started doubting the situation out loud. "What, right here on the loading dock?"

"Naw." Mitch jerked his head toward the open door of the truck.

"Isn't it a bit cold?" Sam's voice was high and panicked. He couldn't stop looking at the open doors of the trailer. *Dark and close. And he's right. Nobody would see.* But this was a far cry from Keith in the handicapped stall. Keith he *knew.* Even Emma might not get behind this sexual adventure. This guy could kidnap him.

Yes, he could tie you up and take you with him, fucking you cross-country. Sharp, erotic images flashed across Sam's mind, and he swayed.

Mitch gave a dark chuckle. "Don't worry, I'll keep you warm."

"You're serious." Sam gripped the rail so tightly his wrists ached. "You're seriously propositioning me."

Mitch lowered himself to the ground. Sam tried not to hyperventilate as the trucker ambled over to the concrete dock of the pharmacy, tucking his hands into his jean pockets. "Come on over and play a bit, Sam. I got the bat, and you got the ball."

This was insane. "I have a bat too."

"That you do, and I would rightly enjoy getting my hands on it." Mitch's eyes were bright blue, Sam could see now, and they burned. "Wouldn't mind a taste of it, either. Wouldn't mind tastin' any part of you."

Maybe he gave in because Mitch was so close, or maybe it was because nobody had ever talked to Sam this way, or maybe, as another queen of drawl would say, it was Memphis. Whatever the reason, Sam fell victim to it, and it took every last bit of his strength to keep from melting off the loading dock and into Mitch's waiting, able arms. The promise of sex washed over him, and as if someone had thrown a switch, he calmed, aiming himself with strange serenity toward this new goal. If he did this, he wasn't going to fuck around. Not with safety, anyway. "Do you have a condom? Lube?"

Mitch's blue eyes darkened. "I'm afraid not. But there's plenty of playing to be done with the equipment we bring with us."

"You might not have noticed," Sam said, his voice only breaking a little bit, "but I'm standing behind a pharmacy."

Cats with cream didn't have Mitch's grin. "Of course there's also nothing wrong with being well-supplied. But the question is, if you go through that door, are you gonna come out again?"

"With a box of Trojans and a tube of KY in my hand," Sam promised, not so much as batting an eye. "What about you? Are *you* going to be here when I get back?"

This time Mitch didn't smile at all. "Sunshine, if you don't come out in under a minute, I'll be coming in after you."

Sam's heart slammed into his chest and then slithered down into his groin with the rest of his vital functions. "Make it two. I think I have to unpack the box."

CHAPTER THREE

SAM FOUND BOTH the condoms and KY in under thirty seconds, but he stayed inside for a beat to calm the nerves which had sprung up once he'd left Mitch's line of sight. Was he really going to do this? He knew he was, but he felt obligated to make a pretense of thinking it over. His heart pounded at his throat, and his ears rang—or so he thought they did until he realized they also sang a song, and this was when he remembered the ear buds dangling around his collar. He fumbled for his phone, stopped the music, locked the screen, and replaced the phone in his pocket.

He was going to have sex with a stranger. In the alley. While he was on shift. He clutched tighter at the box in his hand. He was using protection. Surely that counted for something.

Of course, technically, he'd just stolen the condoms.

Aunt Delia would freak if she found out. She'd fire his ass and kick him out of the house and never pay for another dime of tuition. Was fun with a trucker worth risking his future?

Sam wiped the back of his hand across his sweaty brow, taking strange comfort from the feel of cold skin brushing against heated skin. Yeah, it was worth it, because she'd never reward him for being good. He thought of all the shit Delia gave him, of her constant criticisms and lists of his sins. *You want sins, Aunt? I'll show you sinning. I'll make the devil weep, I'll sin so bad.*

He straightened, ran a hand through his hair, and opened the door.

Mitch stood on the other side of it. "Howdy, Sunshine." He grabbed Sam's belt loop and pulled him forward.

Sam drew the door shut behind him. "Hi—" he said, but then he couldn't say anything else because his mouth was occupied.

Only briefly, though—Mitch bit lightly on his lower lip, ran his tongue across it, and nibbled his way along Sam's chin to his throat, but it was enough to render Sam speechless and propel him the rest of the way into the other man's arms. *It's really happening.* He felt like an idiot, but he was a giddy idiot. Apparently an easy idiot. When Mitch's hand ran down his thigh and skirted his ass, Sam groaned and pushed back, encouraging bolder groping.

"You change your mind?" Mitch murmured at Sam's throat as his other hand slid between them to cup Sam's groin. "You want to give the neighbors a show instead?"

I want you to fuck me on Main Street, Sam wanted to say, ready to strip off his clothes himself. "No. In the trailer, like you said." He shut his eyes and tilted his head to the side as Mitch trailed his tongue along a muscle in his neck. "*Oh God.*"

"Yeah, but can you walk, Sunshine? I think if I let go, you're gonna fall off the edge. Do I need to carry you?"

"Jesus, that would be so hot," Sam murmured, not quite aware he said the words out loud until the world tilted crazily as he was slung up over Mitch's shoulder. He had just enough time to register the beautiful sight of the trucker's ass before everything shifted as Mitch scaled the railing and dropped them both to the ground.

He had one moment of uncertainty as Mitch deposited him into the trailer. Mitch had tucked the ramp away, and Sam sat, ass smarting from impact, on the cold metal floor of the half-empty truck. He was acutely aware of the darkness and the closeness of the space, of the smell of cardboard and metal, and of cold. *What am I doing? I'm going to have sex with a strange man in the back of a semi?* Then Mitch planted his hands on either side of Sam and looked up at him with wicked hunger.

Yes. Yes, I am.

Mitch pushed himself up and into the truck and slid Sam farther inside it in one motion. God, he was *so* strong. Sam had been going to the gym or lifting at home since he was sixteen, but he had nothing, *nothing* on Mitch. Maybe it was girly of him, but he loved the sense of being so overpowered by another man but of being safe at the same time.

Relatively.

He shut his eyes and let out a half-sigh, half-moan as the weight of Mitch's body pressed against his own.

He felt the rigid outline of the other man's cock, and he wished there wasn't so much material between them.

There won't be for long.

When Mitch withdrew, the loss was an ache. He turned his face toward Mitch as he nibbled his way across Sam's cheek. Sam tried to recapture his mouth, and he succeeded long enough to suck the other man's upper lip and run his tongue across his teeth. He thrilled at the shudder that went through Mitch, but when he let go to plunge deeper, Mitch drew back, rising above Sam.

He fumbled at Sam's jeans, but at his pocket, not his fly. "Something's poking me, and it ain't cock."

"Oh—that's probably my phone." Still breathless, Sam fumbled between them, shifting his hips and unintentionally—but not un-enjoyably—rubbing his erection against Mitch's. He pulled the phone out, flashed it in a quick *See?* gesture, and tossed it— carefully—aside before returning to Mitch's embrace.

Mitch enfolded him eagerly. "If I'd known I was meeting you, I'd have signed on to pick up a load of mattresses."

Sam arched his body, a move which gave Mitch better access and pressed their dicks even tighter to one another. "I can't believe I'm doing this." He clutched at Mitch's shoulders as the trucker sucked his collarbone. "Oh *Jesus*. Oh *God*."

"This your first time, Sunshine?" Mitch's fingers slid inside Sam's waistband.

"In the back of a semitrailer? Yes." Sam's breath

caught, and his stomach went concave as Mitch played against his abdomen. "And with a total stranger."

"Hey, I told you my name." Mitch teased the flesh of Sam's hip as his mouth trailed toward his ear. "You gonna let me fuck you?"

Sam wanted to point out he'd been the one to bring the condoms and lube, but hearing *let me fuck you* out loud made his brain short-circuit again. Also, speaking of condoms—he flexed his hands, lifted his head with some effort and tried to glance around. "Shit." When Mitch's hand brushed his cock in the increasingly crowded space inside his jeans, he gasped and fought for coherence. "Wait—*oh God*—lost the condoms."

"Relax. You dropped them on the dock, but I picked them up after I took us over the railing." He removed his hand from Sam's jeans, but only to facilitate his undoing of Sam's fly. "Let me fuck you, Sam."

Sam would have been hard-pressed to answer such a plea under any circumstances, but when Mitch pulled Sam's aching dick out of his underwear as he asked, it pretty much guaranteed Sam could only gurgle his reply. In the end he thrust his hips eagerly into Mitch's hand. It was apparently enough for Mitch, who stopped talking and started working his way down Sam's body. He left briefly and returned with darkness in his wake as the doors to the trailer swung shut to a crack behind them, allowing a single shaft of light to guide Mitch back to Sam.

The last bits of insecurity about what he had committed himself to fled Sam when Mitch's mouth closed around him. Darin's blowjobs, infrequent and inexpert as they were, would be intolerable after this. Mitch sucked him deep, his tongue snaking around Sam's shaft before he opened his throat and took him all the way in, until he burrowed his nose in Sam's pubic hair. Sam cried out and clutched at his head, his own exploding as Mitch moved up and down along the length of Sam's dick. Sam's hips jerked tentatively, trying to match the other man's rhythm, but just when he thought he'd found it, Mitch released him and sucked on his balls instead.

Sam opened his eyes and lifted his head in time to watch a testicle slide from Mitch's mouth. Mitch was cast in shadow, and Sam couldn't see the details, so when the hot, wet tongue ran up the length of him, Sam gasped and groaned as it pressed insistently into his slit. Then Mitch swallowed him, taking him once more to the root. Sam lay back and fucked the other man's mouth.

He came with almost no warning, feeling as if he were emptying the entire contents of his body into Mitch. He trembled in some sort of post-orgasmic convulsion, and he was grateful for it because he was sure it was the only movement he was ever going to be able to make again. He was completely, utterly spent.

They weren't even close to done.

When Mitch turned him over, Sam went rag doll, content to be positioned in whatever way Mitch wanted him. This ended up being on his knees, his jeans and underwear bunched beneath to cushion him against the cold, hard floor. When Mitch bent him forward over a box, Sam was still at full mast, hot and humming from release. His ass was bare and prickling from the cold.

With no warning at all, it was gripped by two large, rough hands. Sam shut his eyes and eased into the box, shivering in delight at how exposed he was—then his eyes opened wide as something soft and wet slide over his entrance.

Tongue. That soft and wet was Mitch's *tongue.*

He gave into the moan that came from the bottom of his balls as Mitch went at Sam's ass with vigor. *Inside.* His tongue was *inside.* He'd read about this. He'd watched it in teasing bits of free clips online. He'd *dreamed* of this. Now it was happening. He was being rimmed by a hot, sexy stranger in the back of a semi-trailer. He moaned louder and spread his knees farther apart as he lifted off the floor, trying desperately to press his ass tighter to Mitch's face, to take him deeper and deeper inside.

He was gasping when Mitch finally stopped, but only seconds later Mitch replaced his tongue with a fat index finger slicked with lube.

"You are one sexy piece of ass." With one hand Mitch pulled Sam open wider, and his finger made its first foray inside. "You gonna moan like that when it's my cock inside you?" He added a second finger, and Sam grunted, pressing back to meet its thrust. Mitch laughed, the sound low and dangerous and sexy as fuck. "Oh yeah, honey. You are a *hot* little fuck." He added a third finger as he whispered into Sam's ear, "How rough do you want it, Sunshine? Hard and fast, or slow and easy?"

Sam wanted it hard enough to send him into the next county. But he remembered the time Darin had torn him, and how fucking much it hurt, and the memory was enough to bring him back to earth. He pushed off the box enough to reach behind him and fumble with the front of Mitch's fly, pausing occasionally to lose himself in the way Mitch rubbed insistently against his prostate. He kept up his exploration until he had Mitch's dick in his hand, measuring it carefully and with some relief. Though Mitch was almost alarmingly long, he wasn't half as thick as Darin.

"Start slow," Sam instructed. "But—if you can, later—"

Mitch twisted his fingers inside of Sam's ass, making him gasp.

"Pound the shit out of you?" Mitch finished for him. Sam grunted as Mitch's fingers curled then withdrew, and Sam fell forward, trembling, onto his box.

Despite the cold, Sam sweated as he listened to the crinkle of foil. When he felt the first nudge of Mitch entering him, he opened himself as much as he could. It was different than his awkward forays with Darin, and not just because it was a different penis. Mitch was slow and deliberate where Darin was brutal and thrusting. He waited without being told until Sam was able to relax his sphincter, but once he was past that barrier, he slid still slower and slower, measuring his advance against Sam's gasps and grunts and his eventual push for more.

He was so careful Sam forgot himself, forgot everything in the world except for taking this cock deep inside his body. Mitch seemed to have turned into some sort of garden hose, he was so damned long, and Sam had visions of Mitch slithering into his belly. But after what seemed like an hour, Mitch's hips pressed to Sam's bare cheeks, and he was inside.

It was amazing. Sam was stuffed full, but not uncomfortably so, nor painfully. He shut his eyes and sank into the sensation, uncaring of the chill air, untroubled by the pressure on his knees. *So good.* The world was so good with Mitch inside of him—he didn't know if it was Mitch himself or just someone who actually knew how to fuck, or what. He'd never felt this way, ever, and he never wanted it to end. The whole world melted away, and in that moment he didn't care about his aunt, or school, or being a loser, or anything at all. He'd steal a thousand condoms, a trailer full of lube to be this full, this good, even for five minutes. It was wonderful. It was amazing. It was *perfect.*

Then Mitch began to move, and perfect gave way to a sensation which could not be described with mere words.

Slippery. Hot. Wet. And *tight*, oh God, so tight. Sam bent himself farther over the box, opening his mouth and biting the cardboard as the shudder of Mitch's movement resonated in the back of his teeth. The best was when his penis slid over Sam's prostate. It sent electricity through his veins and pumped liquid nitrogen into his system over and over again. His own dick was rock-hard, and he was moaning too, soft, breathy gasps each time Mitch moved inside him.

"How you doin', Sunshine?" Mitch's question was a guttural growl, and he punctuated it with a squeeze of Sam's ass. "You ready for something with a little more kick?"

When Sam grunted and nodded his assent, Mitch pulled back, and Sam readied himself for a more aggressive assault.

Instead, Mitch withdrew entirely and didn't imme-diately return. Sam recovered enough to glance over his shoulder as Mitch peeled off his button-down and balled the shirt into a makeshift pillow before bending down and nudging it at Sam's knees. "Up." He slid his palm gently over Sam's bare ass. "I don't want you to remember this by thinking how badly it fucked over your knees."

The gesture touched Sam, making him feel soft in-side as he lifted one knee and then the other, letting Mitch prop him onto the shirt to his satisfaction. *So much better than a pizza box.* When Mitch finished his preparations and took Sam into his arms, Sam closed his eyes and leaned against Mitch's chest, mouth open as Mitch pushed inside of him once more, and then, on an impulse that seemed to come from the bottom of his soul, he turned his face toward Mitch and captured his lips. He felt Mitch's surprise, and the saucy trucker became almost shy, his tongue darting out tentatively to taste Sam's own. When Sam would have deepened the kiss, Mitch broke away, trailing open-mouthed to Sam's ear, where he nuzzled along the edge before biting lightly at the lobe.

"I'm gonna fuck you now. You ready?"

"Yes." Sam clutched at him wherever he could find purchase. "Oh God—fuck me, Mitch."

"Hard, Sunshine?"

Sam shivered. "Yeah."

Mitch brushed his lips against Sam's cheek. "Then bend over, baby, and hold on."

It was a slow re-entry, but once Mitch pushed deep, slow was over. He pulled back, almost exiting, and then he pounded Sam, slamming Sam into the box and forcing the air from his body. The trailer filled with the *slap, slap, slap* of flesh on flesh, a sound both jarring and soothing to Sam at once.

This was sex. This was what he fumbled for in the dark, what he sought in his own fantasies and the fantasies of others—this, this searing, almost brutal claiming. Sam surrendered to it, like he'd waited his whole life for this kind of release.

Then it shifted yet again. Barely pausing, Mitch reached around Sam, sliding one hand beneath him to cradle his stomach and the other around the front of his shoulders. Mitch resumed his thrusts, but now he held Sam up and pressed him down at the same time. The switch made Sam dizzy. His breathing grew labored, and he clutched at the box as he tried to reclaim his exhilaration.

Lips brushed across the base of his neck once, and

the second time the kiss lingered. His skin prickled at the tickle of stubble and tingled at the soft, damp press of lips. When Mitch's mouth opened, Sam shuddered first at the whisper of Mitch's breath and then at the swipe of his tongue. And with that last gesture, Sam found the place he sought once more.

Sam shut his eyes. He braced one arm against the box and reached around with the other to pull Mitch's head to his neck, begging silently for him to maintain the contact. Each lick, each nibble of teeth and scrape of beard took him higher, sent him deeper into that pool of safety, a place where nothing could reach him, nothing but sex, and now because of this embrace and this strange backward kiss, Mitch. Though he had already spent himself, another pulse rose inside him. With a growl, a bite at the base of Sam's neck, and one last thrust, Mitch came inside him, and as if propelled by the act, Sam followed suit against the side of the box. They collapsed together, breathing rough, their chests rising and falling and pressing back to front and front to box. With reluctance, Mitch pulled away, running his hand down Sam's spine as he rose.

Sam remained where he was, his body still humming, mind still melted.

Another stroke, this one across the trembling flesh of his backside. "You okay?"

Sam tried to nod, but it was so much work. *I'm fantastic,* he wanted to say, but all he could manage was a garbled, "Good."

Mitch laughed quietly, and the sound made Sam

long to purr and climb into his lap. He tried to move, to do this, but all he could manage was to roll off the box. He landed on his ass, which, well-used as it was, tingled at the contact with the cold metal floor. Sam let his head loll into his arm, but he rolled his face toward Mitch and gave him a sleepy, sated smile.

Mitch reached over to tweak the toe of Sam's tennis shoe. "Much to my regret, I gotta get on the road. I have to get to Minneapolis by eight, and while you were worth it, I can't afford to be too late."

The reminder of obligation dulled Sam's glow, but only around the edges. "I should get back to work too." He bit his lip, pushed aside his insecurity and said what was on his mind. "Thank you. That was—I don't know. *Amazing.*"

"Sunshine, that was your performance, not mine."

"No. I'm never like that. Just with you, I guess." The confession felt too bald, and Sam climbed weakly to his knees and wrestled with his pants. "I mean—God, I don't know how I'm ever going to have sex again. Nothing's going to measure up."

This confession felt even more awkward, even more so as Sam saw Mitch had already refastened his own clothes and sat in a crouch near the open door. *Waiting to leave.* Sam felt a pang at the upcoming loss because he realized, as he stared at the man in the darkness who had shown him the way to great sex, that he would never see Mitch again. It was a stupid, silly thing to think, but he knew he'd miss the man more than he missed the sex.

Sam opened his mouth to say this, even part of this, but he gave up and simply reached for Mitch.

"Sam?" a voice echoed through the alley.

His heart slammed into his throat and then sank to the bottom of his stomach. *Aunt Delia.*

Mitch watched him carefully now. "Your boss?"

"Worse. My aunt."

"What's the lie we're going with?" Mitch stood and put his hand on the door. "Have I seen you run down the alley, or do I not know what the hell she's talking about?"

"You haven't seen me." Sam curled his knees to his chest and waited as Mitch climbed out of the truck.

What would he do if she caught him? He knew she was looking for a way to get out of paying for him, and now that he was a legal adult, all she needed was an excuse to give her friends as to why. Fucking the deliveryman in the back of his trailer while on the job with stolen supplies was a pretty damn good excuse, and he'd handed it to her on a platter.

Except what scared him more than anything was the realization that he didn't care. In fact, he almost wanted to get caught because then it would be out of his hands, and he'd be free.

Jesus, was he *that* fucked up?

Mitch reappeared and helped himself in again. "She's gone."

Sam climbed to his feet, but his legs were shaky. He half-walked, half-stumbled to Mitch, so focused on getting back into the storeroom he almost jumped down without saying anything else. Catching himself in time, he put his hand on Mitch's arm and looked up at the trucker's face in the late-afternoon light.

What was he supposed to say? Thank you? Before he could think of anything, he heard Delia calling his name from inside, and he decided maybe silence was best. He put his hand on Mitch's chest, stood on tiptoe to kiss him gently on the mouth, then jumped down from the trailer and scrambled up onto the dock. He lingered a moment, watching as Mitch locked the doors. When the trucker winked at him, Sam waved, pushing aside a foolish sense of loss. Then, as Mitch headed to the cab of the semi, Sam opened the door to the pharmacy and slipped as quietly as he could inside.

Emma walked into the storeroom as he entered. "There you are. Hey—"

Sam shushed her desperately, grabbed her arm, and dragged her off into the shelving. "Don't. Don't say anything."

Emma wrinkled her nose. "Sam, you smell like sex." Her eyes widened. "*Oh. My. God.* You got Keith to fuck you? And you did it *here*?"

"No, not Keith—" He heard the door open, and he clutched Emma's arm so tightly his fingers hurt.

"Sam?" Delia called from the door. "Emma? Sam?"

"Who were you with?" Emma hissed.

"Emma, she'll fire me."

"Sam?" Delia called again.

Emma raised an eyebrow. "*Who?*"

Sam realized she was in the sort of mood to dangle

him over the cliff to find out what she wanted. "A deliveryman. In the back of his trailer. *Now please, Em.*"

"Hardcore." Emma gave him a thumbs-up.

Sam was not amused. In fact, he was almost hyperventilating with panic. "What am I going to say to Delia?"

"Relax. I got it. He's here, Delia." Emma waved an irritated hand at Sam as he whimpered. "He had his headphones on so loud he couldn't hear us."

It was a good excuse. It was a *great* excuse. But the second she said *headphones*, Sam paled, and his stomach lurched, and without caring what the hell Delia thought or said, he dashed through the shelves and out the door, but by the time he got to the loading dock, the semi was already pulling onto the street.

"Oh, *shit*." Sam sank to his knees. "I forgot my iPhone!"

LATER THAT NIGHT, after a grueling shakedown from Delia and an excruciating shift of inventory, Sam snuggled into the sugar-pink softness of Emma's bed, hugged a lace-lined heart pillow to his chest, and curled into a fetal position as Emma tried to force a flask of vodka into his hand.

"It could still work out. You could get one of the smaller ones or a different generation, since they're so cheap, and replace it. Or maybe he'll call and offer to return it. I know how you are—you already have it programmed with half the Middleton phone book."

Sam pushed the flask away with the back of his hand. "I just want to lie here awhile, and then I'll go home."

Emma flopped onto the bed beside him, resting her forehead against his, and reached over to stroke his hair. "I hate it when you're like this."

Sam shut his eyes and let the touch soothe him. "I was so stupid, Em. I *am* so stupid." He paused, wallowing in his worthlessness. "It isn't only the phone. I don't know what it is. That I'm an idiot, probably."

"Was the sex that bad?"

Sam's eyes had fallen shut as soon as she started stroking, which only made it easier to replay the scene inside the trailer against the back of his eyelids. "No. It wasn't bad."

"Then why—?"

"Because I shouldn't have done it. Because it was a huge, stupid risk. Because I was so stupid I lost my brand new iPhone I saved forever to get." He buried his face into the pillow. "Oh, Em. I'm such an idiot. I don't even care. I know it's not real, but I don't care. I still want it."

Her fingers stilled, and her voice lost its soothing softness. "Babe, you've lost me."

"Being with him. With anybody, like that." He hugged the pillow tighter to his chest. "He was so…different. Amazing. I felt set free."

"Babe, that's called *good sex*. You've been settling for the freaks and losers far too long."

Sam couldn't argue with her because what she said

was logical, but at the same time he knew it wasn't just good sex. It was something about Mitch himself. He couldn't explain why. Or maybe he was delusional. Confusion tangled with guilt, making his stomach sick and his head sore.

"I shouldn't have done it while I was supposed to be working, and not with somebody I didn't even know. Not in the back of a trailer. I'm supposed to be focusing on school and working hard so I can get out of Delia's basement. I shouldn't have done that. But I don't care that I shouldn't have done it. I want to do it again." *With him.*

"Hon, it was a fling." Em resumed stroking his hair. "It's supposed to be fun, not eat you up inside."

"I know." Sam tightened farther into a ball. "It's because I'm *so stupid.*"

That earned him a slap on his backside. "You aren't stupid, you idiot."

"I just feel so...*lousy.* I can't make it make sense, Em. It all happened so fast. And then...now... I don't know. I want to go to bed and forget about it."

She kissed the top of his head—another way to make him melt. "Stay here, then, for tonight. You know my parents don't care."

Part of Sam wanted to refuse this too, preferring to sulk in the privacy of his own bedroom, but there was too great a risk that his aunt would come down to pick a fight with him. She still suspected he'd been doing *something fishy* at work, and since she suspected correctly, there was a danger when he was in this sort of mood he might actually tell her. So he stayed.

He hadn't slept over at Em's for a long time, not since those dark days just after his mom's death. She curled around him tonight as she had years ago, pressing her breasts against his back and burrowing her face in his neck, sliding her leg between his. It probably looked erotic as hell, but to Sam it simply felt safe and sweet. He loved Em's breath on his neck, the softness of her breasts, which was something he didn't say often. They were little pillows between their two bodies, and while they excited most men who got Em into bed, for Sam they diffused all thoughts of sex. If she found their snuggles erotic, he hoped she never told him about it.

She got him up in the morning and fed and dressed him. She'd put him in a pair of her sweatpants and an old T-shirt overnight, and to his embarrassment, he found Emma's mother had washed his clothes for him. He ate the bowl of cereal Emma set out for him and played nice with the parents as they asked about work, and school, and his summer plans.

"So what's the status on the apartment?" Emma's mother smiled at Sam. "I assume Emma has you roped into her scheme, as usual?"

"Temporary setback," Emma declared as she tore into her toast. "By August, Mom, you can turn my bedroom into your scrapbook room."

"It's a lot of money." Mrs. Day's voice held a warning, but it was a gentle one. Sam watched her face as she and Emma continued to spar, and it made his chest hurt. That was how his mom had argued with him, and he missed it. It wasn't fighting. It was verbal jousting, and beneath the tussle, you could feel the love.

He thought of the cold reception waiting for him at Cherry Hill, and he looked down into his bowl of Cheerios, poking the oat circles beneath the milk as he blinked rapidly and scolded himself for his self-pity.

Once he finished eating he had to go to work, but Delia was out for the day, so he spent a pleasant morning and early afternoon counting out pills and pasting on prescription labels. Even better than a shift without Delia was going home to find the house empty and a note saying she and Uncle Norm had gone with the Baumgartens to dinner and a movie and that she expected to see the dishes done and the carpet vacuumed when she came home.

Sam did the dishes and carpets as directed. Then he grabbed his keys, headed to his car, and went to the store.

He came home laden with a bottle of San Pellegrino, frozen pot stickers, and Newman's chocolate alphabet cookies. He cooked the pot stickers on the stove, did up his dishes, and took his feast to the den. After nipping downstairs to fetch his VCR tape full of this week's *Dancing with the Stars*, he tucked it into his aunt's player, grabbed the remote, and settled deep into the crevice of the couch. Uncle Norm had a state-of-the-art DVR, of course, but there was no way Delia would let him "fill it up with trash."

He'd eaten two pot stickers and had a flutter over Gilles Marini as he drew his partner close at the end of a tango when the phone rang. He groaned and almost let it go, but he realized without his cell phone, his aunt and uncle's phone was now his phone too. *Maybe it's Mitch,* his traitorous heart whispered hopefully, which was why Sam tensed and avoided looking at the caller ID as he picked up the phone. "Hello?"

"Do I need to come over with the vodka?" Emma asked when he answered. "Or are you better now?"

Sam felt even more ridiculous at his disappointment. "I'm fine. Delia and Norm are out, so I'm watching TV upstairs and eating pot stickers."

"What are you watching? Maybe I'll come over."

"*Dancing with the Stars.*"

Emma groaned. "I'm not coming over. Do you want to meet up later, though? Maybe go out?"

Sam considered his wallet. He might have a dollar, and it was weeks until payday. "No, I'll stay in. I should study."

"You aren't going to study," she pointed out.

"Okay, I won't study. But I do want to stay in."

"Are you pouting?"

"I am not pouting. I'm trying to watch quality programming. I have two week's worth of the show to get through." He gentled. "I'm fine, Em. I really am."

"All right." She sounded unconvinced. "But if you change your mind, call me back."

"I will," Sam promised. He hung up the phone and restarted his show.

Not even two minutes later, the phone rang again. He stopped the show, picked up the phone, and glared as he saw the ID.

"What?" he demanded.

Emma ignored his rudeness. "I just remembered. It's margarita night at Los Dos. Pick me up in an hour, and I'll take you—my treat."

"What is this determination to liquor me up?"

"You need some release."

Sam did a quick flashback to the trailer, feeling both a hum and a pang. "I've been released. Trust me."

"Not sex, you nitwit. Energy release. You need to cleanse your aura."

"With two-for-one margaritas?" Sam shook his head at the ceiling. "Emma, go get laid. Please."

She sighed. "I can't. Steve isn't interested." That was the part-time pharmacist Norm had hired, who was hot but so straight you could use him for a unit of measure. "I all but jumped him earlier tonight, and he actually recoiled. Come on, hon. We both need to get out. I'm worried about you, Sam."

"I'd be fine if you'd let me eat my dinner and watch my show." Sam hung up on her.

When the phone rang a third time, he was seriously pissed off.

"I told you," he said as he lifted the phone to his ear, "to go and get laid."

"I will take that under advisement," a low, sexy, and amused drawl purred into his ear. "Did you have anyone in mind, Sunshine?"

Sam dropped his forkful of pot sticker and forgot, briefly, how to breathe. "Mitch?"

"Hello, Sam. Are you, by any chance, missing a phone?"

CHAPTER FOUR

FOR SEVERAL SECONDS, Sam could do nothing but open and close his mouth like a fish.

"Sam?" Mitch called again, more concerned and less amused.

"Sorry." Sam tried to pull himself together, but all he could think was *Mitch, Mitch, Mitch.* "I—How did you get this number?"

"It's on your phone. I tried the one listed *work* but got a machine. It said Biehl, though, in the name, and this was a Biehl number, so I took a chance. Thought I'd get your boss and not you."

"It's my aunt and uncle's pharmacy. I live in their basement. Just for now," he added quickly, afraid he sounded pathetic. "Until I finish college."

"I take it our little adventure wasn't discovered?"

"Mostly," Sam admitted.

"Good." The pitch of Mitch's voice lowered. "That was a right pleasant buzz you gave me, Sunshine, all the way to Minneapolis."

Sam's face went hot. "Oh?"

"Oh yes."

Sam reached for the Pellegrino and took a big swig,

not knowing what else to say. Why wasn't he happy to get his phone back? He wasn't feeling much—maybe he was in shock. He felt drunk. He eyed the bottle suspiciously, momentarily wondering if he'd grabbed vodka after all. No, only mineral water. It was Mitch making Sam woozy and weird.

The silence stretched out. Sam cleared his throat so his voice wouldn't break. "Where are you?"

Mitch grunted. "I'm fifty-five miles from the middle of fucking nowhere, trapped in a stinking hole of a truck stop full of greasy old men drooling over magazines full of women with plastic tits while it rains like crazy outside. That's where I am."

The image was horribly clear in Sam's mind. "Sorry to hear that."

"Me too." Mitch sighed. "So, what are you doing home on a Saturday night, Sunshine?"

Sam glanced at the TV, where Gilles and his partner were frozen mid-dip. "Eating. Watching a show."

"Not out with—who was it? Darin?"

Sam went still. "How do you know about Darin?"

"He keeps texting you, wanting to know why you aren't coming over. I can assure you he has lube, and the last text promised he cleaned up his apartment and bought beer. He's also apparently very fond of the way your ass looks when it opens up. I have to say, I agree."

"Oh God." Sam shut his eyes and sank into the couch. He'd forgotten Darin entirely in the drama of Mitch and his phone. Now Mitch was reading Darin's X-rated texts? "Oh *God*."

Mitch laughed. "Sorry. They keep popping up, and I don't know how to turn them off. It took me ten minutes to unlock the screen."

Sam felt sick. "Darin isn't—Darin is—" He rubbed the side of his face, groaning inwardly. "Darin is a mistake."

"Well, I'm sorry to hear that." Mitch sounded unconcerned. "Though I admit I am curious to hear why he mentioned still having plenty of empty pizza boxes."

Sam redirected the conversation. "So why are you fifty-five miles from the middle of nowhere?"

"Stuck by a storm. Heading to Milwaukee, but I'm going to be late. It's severe weather all the way across, and I have to cover a few dicey roads. But it works out, because then I was free to try and hunt you down."

Sam put his plate on the coffee table. "Can you enjoy the night off, at least?"

"Not here. There was one guy eyeballing me, but I couldn't tell if he wanted to fuck me or punch me, and I'm not interested in either with him. But I am enjoying talking with you. So tell me, college boy. What are you studying?"

"Nursing." Sam braced himself for the jokes.

Mitch gave a low whistle. "Tough stuff. Good career, though. They will always need nurses."

"I want to do RN," Sam admitted. "I want to work in a clinic. But it's longer for that degree, which means more money and tougher classes. This semester is pretty tough, actually. I need to buckle down more, or I'm not going to pass."

"You're a smart one. I bet you'll pass just fine."

The conversation lulled. Sam dwelt on the weirdness of the entire experience, still not quite understanding how or why he could converse so casually with Mitch. He honestly hadn't expected him to return the phone. He figured it would get lost, or he'd toss it aside. He was kind of flattered Mitch would take the time to hunt him down.

It's only to bring your phone, he scolded himself. *Don't get any stupid ideas.*

"Do you know something, Sam?"

Mitch's voice was low, and it turned Sam on. "What?"

"If I close my eyes, I can still taste you."

The words hit Sam in the center of his chest. He said nothing, but he breathed a lot harder.

"I see you too." Mitch spoke so softly Sam had to strain to hear. "Such a pretty pink hole. Honey, I wish I could have spent an hour at that ass."

"*Hhhuh.*" The sound out of Sam's mouth was more a whisper of air than a word. He was aroused, but nervous too. Mitch was hundreds of miles away, but Sam felt suddenly exposed and unsafe. He reached for a pillow from the other end of the couch and crushed it against his chest.

"You liked that too, didn't you," Mitch went on. "Sweet Jesus, the sounds you made. Just thinking about the way you moaned makes me hard. Was I the first one to rim you, Sunshine?"

"No—I mean—" Sam couldn't figure out how to

answer that. Yes, Mitch was the first, but he didn't want Mitch to think he was some virgin. "Yes, but—" He remembered the way it had felt, and he lost it again. "The—the tongue—*oh God.*"

"Nobody ever tongue fucked you? That what you're trying to say, shy honey?"

Sam swallowed. The sound was audible enough Mitch probably heard it. "No."

"Such a shame. I've never seen somebody so hot for it. You need that done to you twice a day, I'm thinking." Mitch's voice dropped to a whisper. "Wish I were there to do it right now. I'd turn you over, spread those cheeks—" He gave a long, agonized sort of groan, a man imagining a forbidden pleasure. "And because I'd have time, I'd sit there a minute and talk dirty to it, because you'd moan and squirm, and your ass would pucker. I'd stare at it, watching it wink."

"*Nghyh.*" Sam gripped the phone and the pillow so tight he thought he might crush the first and tear the latter. He glanced around the room in sudden terror, as if his aunt and uncle might appear at any moment and catch him listening to someone talking dirty to him.

"Then I would lick it, Sam. I would lick your hot little hole until you were pushing back against me, same as in the trailer, and then, *then,* baby, I would spread you wider and push my tongue inside you. Way in, honey. Maybe you didn't know, but my lips were sucking at your pucker the other day, and I licked you as high up as I could. I licked you and fucked you, sweet thing, until you were mush, and then I listened to you sing same as right now. Only a lot, lot louder."

Sam *was* moaning, his hips moving too. He'd been hard since Mitch said *taste you*, and his body remembered. He could *feel* that tongue inside him.

"You wish I was there to put my tongue inside you?" Mitch's voice was so rough it was practically gravel. "Are you thinking about my tongue fucking your ass right now?"

"Yes." Sam doubled over, clutching the pillow to his chest, imagining Mitch behind him, his hands spreading Sam wide.

"Are you home alone?"

For a moment he panicked, but then he remembered Mitch was many miles away. Then he remembered he'd actually rather be in the room with Mitch. "Yes."

"I want you to take your pants off."

Sam balked. "I can't—"

"Take them off. Nobody's there to see you, and I can't do it myself. Take them off. Take off your pants. Put down the phone if you have to, get rid of everything south of your bellybutton, and let me know when you're done."

"I can't—they might come home."

"You got a bedroom, right? Go to it, Sam. Go to your room, take off your pants, and bend over. *Do it.*"

Sam did it. He couldn't believe he did it, but he stood, all but stumbled to the basement, and locked the door behind him once he was inside his room. He put the phone down on his bed. He nearly fell over, he was so nervous, but he managed to remain standing long enough to undo his button and zipper.

After shoving his jeans to his ankles, he kicked them off, letting his underwear follow. Then he took off his socks, because he felt ridiculous with them on. Above him, the TV had bailed on the VCR, and some woman cheerfully attempted to sell him dish detergent. Sam let his head fall against the bed with a shaky sigh as he picked up the phone once more. "D-done."

"Bend over the bed. Kneel on the floor and aim your bare ass at the wall."

Sam did this too. He didn't know why. He felt disconnected, floating almost. But he did it. He knelt on the floor and put his head down on the mattress, tucking his chin into his chest so he could breathe. He put the phone to his ear and let out a soft, desperate sound into the receiver.

"Suck on your finger. Make it really wet, then put it in your ass. Push it way, way, in, as slowly as you can."

Sam's hand shook as he fumbled to put his finger in his mouth. Which one? Middle? Index? He sucked both. He had never done this. He didn't understand how he was going to do this. He felt ridiculous, embarrassed, and very nervous, as if a film crew would burst in at any minute, ready to announce on the evening news that at 9 p.m. Samuel Daniel Keller of Middleton, Iowa, knelt beside his bed and stuck his own finger in his ass.

"Suck hard. Get it really wet, baby. Dripping. Yeah. I can hear you. Do it harder. *Harder.* Yeah, honey. *Yeah.*" Mitch's litany put Sam in a trance, the whole world gone except for that voice in his ear. "Now reach behind you."

Sam touched a finger to himself.

He gasped.

"*Yes*," Mitch growled. "Push it in. Push it in *deep*. Moan for me, Sam. Let me hear you sing again."

Mitch's instructions became a low, lewd litany, and Sam did everything he said. He listened to every dirty word, did everything Mitch told him to do, and above all, he made noise, because that was what Mitch wanted. He forgot about his aunt and uncle possibly coming home at any minute, and he let go. He cried out. He moaned. He felt like an animal. He *was* an animal. He fucked himself with his finger, first one, then two, and he humped his bed, all the while with the phone to his ear, grunting out his pleasure to a man many, many miles away.

This was the man he'd let fuck him against a box, a man who had made him feel slutty, wonderful and sexy. This was the man who had made him feel that and took off, leaving Sam to swim in self-recrimination. Now here Sam was, fucking himself so that man could listen.

"You're so hot, Sunshine." Mitch's breath came fast too. "God, I wish I could see you. I wish I could taste you. I wish that was my tongue inside you, or my fingers, or my cock. I wish those were my fingers, and I wish my mouth was on you, sucking you tight, letting you fuck my mouth, moaning with you, waiting to drink you when you came. I wish I were fucking you. I wish I were there fucking you right now. Fuck yourself for me. Fuck yourself really fucking hard."

"*Ohmygod,*" Sam gasped, his voice low and almost gurgling. He didn't even sound like himself. "Oh my God, I'm gonna come."

"Do it. Come for me. Come hard, and be loud. I'm underneath you, sucking you. Come in my mouth. Fuck my mouth. Fuck my mouth. Fuck me. Fuck me, Sam. *Fuck me.*"

Sam's orgasm was already building, but when Mitch growled, "Fuck me, fuck me, fuck me," it snapped, swamping him in a wave. He shouted, so loud he hurt his own ears. He shouted again, his orgasm kicking at his teeth, and then he groaned as his semen poured out of him in ropes. He shuddered, once, twice, three times, then sagged against the side of the bed as Mitch whispered soothing approval at him.

"That was so good, Sunshine—oh my fucking God, that was so good. Sweet Christ, I've never been so blueballed. I just about came right here. Boy would that be something."

Sam could barely move, and his brain still drifted somewhere above his head, but the *right here* comment snagged him back down. "Where are you?"

"I told you—in the truck stop."

Sam's eyes opened. "*In* the truck stop? You aren't in your truck? You're—you're out in the *open*?"

Mitch's wicked laugh curled Sam's toes. "Don't worry, hon. You're not the one sitting in a booth with your dick threatening to bust open your pants. That's me."

"But—people are there."

"Yeah. A bunch of dirty old men drooling at videos of women young enough to be their daughters getting come sprayed over their faces. This isn't exactly the Ritz."

Sam slid sideways until he sat on the floor. He caught sight of the mess he'd made on the mattress and winced before letting the side of his head fall to the bed. "Do you do this a lot? Talk dirty to people on the phone?"

He'd meant it as a casual comment, almost a tease, a release of his own shock at his behavior. But the tenor of the silence that came after left him uneasy.

Sam tried to backpedal. "Sorry, I didn't mean—"

"I used to." Mitch's teasing was gone, and now *he* sounded guilty. "I used to do a lot of things like that, but I haven't in a while."

But you did with me. Am I special? Sam rolled his eyes at his own idiocy. Yeah, he was so special Mitch wanted him to stick his fingers in his ass and hump his bed. "I'm so stupid."

"You aren't stupid." Mitch's voice drifted gently through the phone. "Never mind me. You're—you're a good kid, Sam."

God, he'd rather be stupid. "I'm not a kid. I'm twenty-one."

"I'm not. I'm an old, jaded man. You remind me of someone I used to know, is all. Kind of makes me feel funny."

There was no justification for the jealousy Sam felt,

but that didn't make it go away. "Some other *kid*?"

"Nope. He's an old man now too. Old Man Trouble, determined to take me to hell with him. Anyway, don't listen to me. You're sweet, baby. Sweet and sexy."

Sam felt warm and pleased, and in that moment, not guilty at all. "Thanks. You're not bad yourself."

There was a pause, but it wasn't awkward this time.

Mitch cleared his throat. "I would mail your phone, but I'm afraid it wouldn't make it. I'll be through Iowa next week. Can I see you then? Bring you your phone? Take you to dinner?"

Dinner. A date. Sam's stomach was immediately full of butterflies. "Okay."

"A late dinner, probably. I'll get to Middleton on Wednesday. That work?"

Sam felt dizzy. And elated. "Yes."

"Good. Where and when am I meeting you?"

Sam tried to think quickly. He remembered his earlier conversation with Emma and seized on the idea. "Los Dos Amigos. It's Mexican. Do you need directions?"

"I can find it. Time, Sunshine?"

Sam mentally ran through his Wednesday schedule. "Eight?"

"Eight it is. See you then. And don't string poor Darin out too long." Mitch hung up.

Sam sat on the floor for a minute, still reeling from the entire experience. He set the phone down and cleaned up, both himself and the side of the bed. He got into a pair of old sweatpants, went back upstairs, tossed the pot stickers into the garbage, and curled up on the couch, hugging the San Pellegrino bottle as he restarted *Dancing with the Stars.*

He barely noticed Gilles Marini or anybody else. He was too busy thinking of Wednesday, and Mitch.

CHAPTER FIVE

I T WAS WARM but not hot when Sam parked in the street near Los Dos Amigos on Wednesday. His car had nearly died again, this time at the stoplight on Main Street, but by some miracle it had started back up, and he got to the restaurant on time. The unseasonal chill of May was easing into hints of summer, and Sam declined to wear a coat. He'd worn, in fact, as little as possible, and made sure what he wore was *tight*. Delia had given him a pointed look, but he'd ignored her. Nothing and nobody was going to ruin this night.

Emma, surprisingly, had tried.

"The new confidence is good, and I love that you've dumped the creep-show boyfriends, but I think you're kind of building this all up in your head. It's only dinner and another boinkfest. I don't know where you're going to do it, because your aunt and uncle will be home."

"We'll work something out, I'm sure." Wasn't she supposed to be on his side?

At any rate, it was Wednesday now, and he was here, ready for the night to begin. Los Dos wasn't a big place, and if someone wanted to be nasty, it qualified as a bit of a dive. But it *was* excellent Mexican, possibly because it was run by actual Mexicans. Not that this was so novel anymore, even in Iowa, but Sam always thought it helped. Besides, the waiters were nice to him.

Mitch was at the bar when Sam came in the door, and he grinned and came off his stool to greet Sam. "Howdy, Sunshine." His smile widened when Sam blushed. Then he fished into his pocket and pulled out Sam's phone.

Sam took it from him and resisted the urge to stroke it lovingly. "Thanks." He started to put it into his pocket, but he stopped, realizing it wasn't going to work, not with these jeans.

Mitch watched him struggle, a look of appreciation in his eye. "Hmm," he said, after a lengthy perusal. Then he held out his hand.

Sam handed the phone back over. "Thanks. I won't forget."

"Me either." Mitch's eyes were still on the jeans. When he lifted his gaze at last, his lips twitched, a wicked glint in his baby blues. He nodded at the dining room. "Where do you want to sit?"

They ended up in a booth. Sam chose the one in the far corner, the one farthest from the door and cloaked half in shadow. There were only about fifteen people total in the place, but Sam felt like they were all watching him, and as much as he hated it, he worried what they thought. He'd never just gone out with a guy. He'd thought he would relish it, but so far he was too nervous.

Of course, was this really a date? It was sort of

backward when their "relationship" had officially started with a fuck in the trailer of a semi. It would have been more appropriate to simply take the phone and christen the walls of the alley with come. Yet here they were, flirting politely and having dinner. It confused Sam, and he felt shy as he slid into the booth.

Mitch was already poring over the menu. "Okay, I wanted burritos, but now I can't make up my mind. Jesus, it all looks good."

Sam's stomach growled as he scanned his own menu. Paychecks weren't until the end of the month, and he'd borrowed five bucks from Emma so he could order à la carte. "They have combination plates, and then some bigger dinners that have variety." He reached over to point out the section to Mitch. "More expensive, but you get a lot of food."

"A lot of food sounds good." Mitch squinted at the page. "Sunshine, this isn't expensive. You should see what they charge for this sort of stuff in L.A."

"You've been to Los Angeles?" Sam didn't bother hiding his wistfulness.

"I've been just about everywhere." Mitch kept reading the menu. "But I get out west a lot."

"Las Vegas?" Sam was surprised when Mitch's face shuttered.

"Not in a while, no. But I am heading west, generally, in a few weeks, after a quick run east."

"Do you go all over? All the time?"

"I do deliveries on contract, and I try to stagger them so I get around pretty much everywhere. I hate sitting too long in one place."

The waiter appeared and asked how they were doing and what they wanted to drink. It was Damario, one of Sam's favorite waiters, and Damario looked hopeful when he saw Sam. Mitch ordered a Bohemia with some relish. Sam eyed the margarita menu longingly but asked for a glass of water. Damario's expression fell. He knew when Sam started with water he'd get an order of less than five dollars and a tip of about fifty cents.

When the waiter put down the bowl of chips, Sam's stomach growled so loudly he worried Mitch had heard. He quickly scooped up a few of the chips, not even bothering with the salsa in an effort to get something into his stomach. He realized in hindsight he should have eaten a few spoonfuls of peanut butter before coming.

Sam dipped chips two at a time into the dish of salsa. "That's kind of cool how your company sends you so many places."

"I don't work for a company." Mitch waited until Sam cleared the bowl a second time before taking a more modest serving of salsa for himself. "I operate independently, one gig at a time. Sometimes I contract out for a bit." Mitch nodded thanks at the waiter as he brought their drinks. He eyed Sam's glass of water with open criticism. "Not a drinker, huh?"

"No, I—" Sam shifted awkwardly in his chair and clutched at his glass. "I only wanted water tonight, is all." He took a drink and reached for more chips.

"You travel much?" Mitch sipped at his beer. "Got a

favorite part of the country?"

"I haven't gone much of anywhere." God, he was so hungry. Had he eaten lunch? "I got as far as Minneapolis and Chicago for school trips, and when I was six, Mom took me to the Black Hills, but I don't remember much of it. Otherwise it's been Middleton with a few trips to Des Moines every now and again." He ate more chips, telling himself these would be his last for a while, but he got distracted and reached for more as he spoke. "I *want* to travel. It just doesn't work out so well."

"Why not? You got legs."

"But not money." The confession felt too bald out loud, so Sam sipped at his water and shrugged, trying to make light. "I'm busy enough with work and school. Maybe someday."

"Maybe so," Mitch agreed, and sipped his beer.

Damario came and replaced their empty chip tray, and Sam dove in before the waiter set the bowl down.

Mitch picked up his menu again. "Hell, Sunshine, I can't decide what to order. What are you getting?"

"Two tamales."

"There's a combo with tamales? Where?" Mitch frowned. "I don't see it."

"I'm not ordering a combo." Sam pointed to the à la carte menu. "There are a few dinners with tamales, though."

Mitch gave him a long, hard look. "That's *all* you're getting?"

"I'm not really hungry," Sam lied. When Mitch indicated the rapidly emptying bowl of chips, Sam fought like hell not to blush.

Mitch opened the menu to the dinner section. "Well, if you *were* hungry, what would you get? Help me make up my mind."

Sam moved his water and leaned over the booth. "Number one and number two are both really good. If you're after tamales, though, you want number six. Or eight, but eight is pretty small. Though it has enchiladas, and their enchiladas are to die for. But if you still want burritos, get number three and ask them to swap the chalupa for a tamale. They charge most people to switch, but they won't because you're with me."

Mitch ran his finger down the list of entrees. "What about this steak fajita?"

Sam's mouth started to water. "That's good too. *Huge*, though."

Damario reappeared with his pad and pen at the ready. "Are we ready to order, *amigos*?"

Mitch spoke before Sam could. "I'm gonna get the steak fajita, but get me a burrito to go too—just wrap it up in foil or something and put it in a bag." He glanced at Damario as he pointed at the menu. "Sunshine here's having number six." Sam sputtered, but Mitch ignored him and continued speaking to Damario. "What's he usually drink when he comes here?"

Damario scribbled madly and, Sam knew, trembled over the tip potentials. "My *amigo* Sam usually has a strawberry margarita. A large."

Mortification allowed Sam to find his voice. "Mitch, you can't—"

Mitch still ignored him, looking at Damario with irritation. "*Deja esta mierda de 'amigo'. No soy un pinche gringo quién te necesita besar el culo.*"

Sam blinked, speechless again. Mitch had rattled off what sounded to Sam like perfect Spanish. Damario blinked, then replied in the same tongue. Sam didn't know what he said, but Damario's tone was lighter now, less kiss-assy. Sam listened to them, ignorant and more than a little jealous.

"Why did you do that?" he asked when Damario left with the menus.

"Sorry." Mitch didn't sound sorry at all. "I hate it when they pull that *amigo* shit. I know it strokes all the white-boy egos and gets more tips, but that ain't me. I grew up in the Rio Grande Valley, and it sets my teeth on edge to be treated the same as the assholes they mock."

"I meant why did you order for me?" Sam frowned. "You're from Texas?"

"South Texas. I could spit over the border. My first boyfriend was Mexican, and he taught me his 'valley Spanish'. It's kind of a perversion of both English and Spanish, but it comes in handy sometimes." He took another swig of beer. "As for your dinner—" He pointed with his beer bottle at the chips. "I ordered for you because you're starving. I'm buying, so let it go."

"I just—It's a while to payday…" Sam gave up and hunched his shoulders over his water.

"Don't worry about it." Mitch winked at him, and when Damario returned with the margarita, Mitch pushed it in front of Sam. "Drink."

Sam did. Even with the chips, he felt the alcohol screaming through his system. He was almost glad for it, and he drank a little faster to hurry himself to the place where the tequila would take all the edges off his day. "Thank you," he said, when the alcohol softened him enough.

Mitch pulled the phone from his pocket. "I figured out how to make the music work after a bit of fiddling, but what's this about video? That mean movies? You can put movies on this thing?"

"Yes, but I don't have any loaded yet." Sam carefully took the phone from him and scrolled through the cover art. "You can get the whole internet though, anywhere. That's what I love about it. It has a GPS, and so many cool apps. And my music, of course."

"You got good music on here. I don't know half of it, but I liked it."

Sam tried not to beam, but it wasn't easy. "I get it from all over the world, from friends. I don't *mean* to pirate. But half the time you can't even get it, or if you can, it's all import and priced more than anybody'd pay. I buy a lot too, as much as I can. It evens out." He took another generous sip of margarita, and it was enough, apparently, to completely loosen his tongue. "I love my iPhone. I named her Judy."

Mitch gave him an odd look. "Garland?"

"Bernly. From *9 to 5*. The Dolly Parton movie, you know? Jane Fonda's character was Judy Bernly. My mom and I used to watch it every year on New Year's."

"I saw you had her on here too—Parton, that is. Country, pop, jazz—hell, Sunshine, you've got a whole music store." He palmed the phone and nodded approvingly at the face. "I gotta get me a Judy of my own, I'm thinking. A guy in Minneapolis showed me how to hook it up to the radio. Though, that reminds me—I about ran you clean out of battery. Poor Darin couldn't even get his texts through."

"That's okay." Sam smiled now, a little too much. He was definitely feeling the alcohol, and between it and the way Mitch's fingers kept brushing his, he felt warm and happy.

They pulled apart when Damario came with their food, and for several minutes they ate in silence. Sam was still starving, but the chips had dulled his hunger enough that, combined with the laziness of the alcohol, he could slow down and enjoy his meal. He lingered over his enchiladas, savoring the melty cheese, the shredded chicken, and the oh-so-yummy red sauce before breaking into the tamales with a quiet sigh.

"Oh my God, they're so good." Sam leaned back and let the taste roll around him. "I don't know why, but I love them."

Mitch eyeballed them critically from the other side of the booth before reaching over with his fork. He hesitated over Sam's plate, though, looking up at him silently for permission. Sam scooted the plate toward him, watching as Mitch took a bite.

"They're not bad." Mitch wiped his mouth with his napkin. "But mine are better."

"You *make* tamales?" The very idea melted Sam's brain.

"Sure. Nothing to it. Of course, mine aren't anything compared to—" He stopped short.

"To?" Sam prompted.

But Mitch only shook his head. "Little bastard pops into my head every time I'm around you, doesn't he, Sunshine?"

That comment made absolutely no sense to Sam, but something about Mitch's body language told him it would be unwise to ask, so he didn't. A strange silence came up between them, subtle but significant. Mitch retreated into his fajitas, but Sam lingered a moment, watching him eat.

"So you're heading to Chicago?"

"Yeah." Mitch still looked gruff. "In fact, to be honest, I should head out as soon as we're done here."

Sam's chin came up sharply, and his fork lowered to his plate. "What?"

Mitch cleared his throat. His face was blank, no more teasing left in it at all. "Yeah, sorry about that. It's part of the delivery to L.A., and they need the warehouse for tomorrow morning, so tonight it is. I had to push to keep my meeting with you, to tell you the truth."

It was a good excuse—valid and everything. But something about the way Mitch said it left Sam feeling funny, like Mitch was lying.

God, did he not *want* to have sex with Sam again?

What the hell had Sam said to screw this up?

Sam ducked his head, trying to hide his reaction. He felt foolish and confused. And cheated. *It doesn't matter. This was never going to be a long-term thing anyway.* But it did matter. Telling himself not to be disappointed didn't make his feelings stop.

"You all right?"

Sam startled at Mitch's comment and hurried to pick up his fork. "Oh, fine." He poked at his tamale, but he didn't eat any more.

Damario pressed for dessert or more drinks, but Sam insisted he was too full, and Mitch declared he had to get going, which made Sam's hollowed-out stomach even more uninterested in food. He tried to soothe himself, to remind himself he'd had a nice dinner, and really, he should be glad. Maybe they'd meet up next time Mitch was in town. Sam tried to rationalize his emotions, but it wasn't working.

Mitch had Damario bend down low to speak in his ear, and he pressed a twenty into the waiter's hand as he did so. When Damario rose, his expression was bright as he hurried away. He came back with a brown bag and their bill.

"I conned him into letting me have some Bohemia to go," Mitch explained once Damario left. He tossed several bills onto the table and rose. "You ready?"

Sam followed him, his heart beating a little faster. *Now he leaves.* Sam staggered in the narrow hallway and out the door, and his heart both fluttered and ached as Mitch's hand snaked out and caught his arm.

"Steady there."

When he kept hold of Sam in the alley, Sam couldn't help but lean into him, letting the touch and feel of the other man's body send an electrical charge into his own. What he wouldn't give for one last time.

"That margarita went straight to my head." *Don't go. Not yet. Not ever. Don't go.*

"Seeing's how you drank most of it before you started eating, I'm not surprised."

Sam leaned on Mitch and put his hand on the other man's stomach, feeling the warmth and firmness of him. When Mitch turned, Sam all but slid into his arms. Sam's heart soared. *Maybe. Maybe. Maybe.*

Please.

Mitch said nothing, only watched Sam's face. Sam worked hard to make his face say *Take me somewhere and fuck me.* Mitch reached around Sam's body, and Sam moved closer, thinking Mitch was embracing him. But when he let go, Sam realized Mitch had simply been putting the bag of beer into the same hand holding his burrito.

"You are something else, Sunshine." Mitch stroked Sam's cheek. Then it fell away, and nothing else happened.

Sam wanted to say, "You are too," but he couldn't speak.

They walked down the street, to where, Sam wasn't quite sure, but what he did know was this evening was about to end. Mitch had returned his phone and bought him dinner, and now they were done. Sam wished desperately he could invite Mitch to his place, to convince him he could be a little later, but he knew his aunt and uncle were home and he didn't dare. He tried instead to think of some way to extend the encounter or to make another date, but he wasn't sure how. Ask for a phone number? It seemed like a good idea, but he couldn't work out how to phrase it. Everything felt too blunt. His brain scrambled for something, anything, but he found nothing.

Mitch turned to face him. "I should head out."

"Sure." Sam did his best to sound casual, to keep the *no, no, no* he wanted to shout from echoing in his voice. "It's a long way to Chicago."

Mitch frowned briefly at Sam. "You're not quite fit to drive, though. I'd offer to take you, but I walked over here from the highway where I left my rig."

Sam brightened. "I'll walk with you."

"That's quite a walk," Mitch pointed out.

"I don't mind." Sam shrugged then ran a hand self-consciously against the side of his hair. "I'll sober up on the way."

He braced for rejection. There was somebody else. *Little bastard pops into my head every time I'm around you, doesn't he?* Who the fuck was the little bastard? Why the hell was he getting in the middle of Sam's sex life?

Fuck this. Sam put his hand on Mitch's arm. "Please?"

Mitch didn't say anything, but he touched Sam's hand on his arm. He stepped away from Sam then, but he left room on the sidewalk beside him, slowing and reaching out to steady Sam when he stumbled.

Hope stirred. *It's not over yet.* Sam wasn't sure exactly what it was he was so desperate to find, or why he had to work so hard in the first place, but he knew this was the way to it. As the night closed in around them, he let Mitch lead him down Main Street and to the west, toward the highway and whatever waited there for him.

CHAPTER SIX

"SO HOW'S DARIN?" As they wound their way through the outskirts of Middleton, Mitch reached up to his shirt pocket, patted it, and sighed. "You relieve him of his misery yet, Sunshine?" Sam winced, and Mitch laughed. "What's this—trouble in paradise?"

"Darin is no paradise." Sam was glad the darkness hid his flaming cheeks. "He's not anything. We just…" He searched for a polite euphemism, then gave up. "We fuck."

"Ah. He thought it was more than just fucking?" *Fuckin'*. He made it sound so dirty. And good.

"No. I don't want to anymore, with him." Sam shrugged. "He wants a hot hole delivered to his door." Sam clapped a hand over his mouth and stumbled. "I can't believe I said *hot hole*."

Mitch righted him casually. "You do have one, Sunshine."

His hand lingered on Sam's back, and the touch emboldened Sam. "Maybe I'll rent it out."

"If it's for sale, then put me in line for first bid." The hand slid lower. "I'll put you on retainer and take you on the road."

Sam knew a wicked thrill at Mitch's words, and an even darker rush at knowing a part of him wished Mitch were serious. He leaned on him a little.

A car drove by and someone shouted, "Sam Keller is a faggot!" as an empty beer can sailed out a car window.

Mitch kicked it with some force as it bounced against his foot. "Nice town."

Sam shrugged and tried to pretend it didn't matter. "That was Keith Jameson." Then he recalled what *else* was supposed to have happened on Wednesday. "Oh—" He clamped a hand over his mouth. "Oh God, I forgot about meeting him in the bathroom. I bet he's pissed." Sam realized what he'd admitted and glanced nervously at Mitch.

Mitch had a strange expression on his face.

"Sorry." Shame welled inside him. "I—I'm not—" How could he claim he wasn't always such a slut, when in all honesty, he was? He looked down. "I don't mean to expose myself as such a horny tart."

"Tarts are good." Mitch's drawl was thick and delicious. "You'd be a strawberry, I think."

They walked slowly now, and it was easier for him to stay upright. "Emma—my best friend—says I need higher standards."

Mitch snorted. "Hope you didn't tell her about our alley adventure, then."

"She approved. Said it was hardcore. But she doesn't like Darin or Keith."

"How about Billy or Travis or somebody else?"

"The gay scene's pretty thin around here. I wish I could get out. I wish you *would* kidnap me." He winced and rubbed at his cheek. "Sorry. Tequila makes me stupid."

"Charming," Mitch corrected. "You'll get out. You're getting your degree—that's smart."

Sam wrapped his arms around himself. "Em says I have to get through it, but sometimes I worry—college is hard for a reason. What if I can't cut it as a nurse, either? What if I flunk out before I can even try? God, I'll end up the manager of the McDonald's, and when I'm forty they'll arrest me for indecent acts with a hamburger bun, I'll be so pathetic."

"If you turn out that bad, I promise I *will* kidnap you. But you won't, Sam."

"How do *you* know? You've only met me twice."

"And had quite a phone conversation too."

"Sure. So, if I fail school, I'll sell my ass and do phone sex." Sam rolled his eyes at himself. Mitch stopped walking, and Sam did too, but the fire had gone out of him now. "I don't mean to be so pathetic. It seems to happen naturally." There was a long, uncomfortable pause, and Sam used the time to try and stare a hole in the ground in the hopes it would swallow him whole.

Out of the corner of his eye he could see the highway. They had come out on Chestnut Street, which at this point was a series of gas stations, two car dealerships, and a smattering of fast-food places. One of the gas stations was sort of a truck stop, and Sam could see several semis lined up along the side of the building. One of them had a blue cab. It was nearly over, and as usual he'd bungled everything.

"Why *don't* you leave?"

Sam frowned at him. "What?"

"Leave Middleton. Leave Iowa. Get out there in the wide world and see for yourself. Find out if you're pathetic, or if it's what people told you to be and you started to believe it."

For several seconds Sam could only stare at him. "Leave school? Leave—everything?"

Mitch shrugged. "Finish your semester, obviously. But yeah. Then go. Walk out and into something different. Don't be safe. Just go be."

"You're serious." Sam tilted his head to the side. "Is that what you did?"

Mitch's grin was rueful. "No. But it's what I wish now I had."

Sam didn't know what to do with this. Denial seemed the safest road. "I can't."

"You can." Mitch nodded to the highway. "We should keep heading on."

"But how do you know?" Sam was more unsteady now than when he'd first stumbled drunkenly out of Los Dos. "How can you look at me and know?"

He expected—wanted—Mitch to tell him he was only making conversation, or being clever, or something, anything to dismiss it. But Mitch seemed pained.

"I don't know. Forget I said anything." He picked up his pace. "Chicago is calling. Double-time, Sunshine."

Sam ran after him, lost and foolish. He knew he should shut up and make these last few minutes count, but he was rattled. He felt like he'd gone into the wrong bar to meet the wrong Mitch. Wasn't this guy supposed to be making lewd propositions and trying to feel him up under the table or do him in a bush, or something? What was with the philosophy shit?

Goddamn it, they hadn't even *kissed*.

That last thought rattled in Sam's head as they wove their way through the cars and trucks in the parking lot to Mitch's rig, and the blue cab became a lightning rod for all Sam's fears and frustrations, sucking them all in and honing them to a single point standing for everything he was, everything he wanted and would never be, and everything about to slide out of his hands. Which was probably why when Mitch turned toward him with a wry, *Well, this was fun* look on his face, Sam stopped the words before they could come out by grabbing Mitch's shoulders, pulling him down, and kissing him.

The kiss was rough and terrifying—Sam was pretty sure he'd blown everything with this insane gesture, and since he was already fucking up, he decided to make it the biggest fuckup on record. Mitch would tell people for years about the crazy psycho college kid who stuck his tongue down his throat in a truck stop parking lot, who had to be all but surgically removed from his body so he could get to Chicago on time. "He was a good lay," he could hear Mitch saying in this imagined future. "Too bad he was batshit crazy too."

But Mitch wasn't pushing him away. At first he sort of froze, but only for a few seconds. There was one more pause as Mitch clutched awkwardly at Sam's shoulders, and then, as if he'd been fishing for a gear and found it, he kissed Sam back, rough and deep.

"Up," Mitch murmured, kissing Sam once more before turning him around and pushing him into the driver's seat before following after. "In."

They fumbled their way around the gearshift and the console—Sam had a brief glimpse of a dashboard which could have rivaled the cockpit of an airplane, and then all he saw was Mitch as the truck driver shoved him against a gray curtain hanging between the driver and passenger seats. The curtain gave way, and then they were through it, and Sam fell backward onto the floor, dragging Mitch with him.

They were in some sort of room: small, but also spacious, given it was in the cab of a semi. Sam saw the black of a flat-screen television and what appeared to be a mini-fridge and microwave. *He has half an RV in here,* Sam thought, but when Mitch's body pressed to his, he didn't think of anything else, except if this semi had a TV, it probably had a bed.

"I gotta get to Chicago." But Mitch nibbled his way down the side of Sam's face as he spoke, and his hand fumbled at Sam's fly.

"Take me with you."

In the dark, he could see the outline of Mitch's face as it lifted over his head, but he couldn't read the other man's expression. He could guess it, though, when a hand kneaded gently at his hips.

"You want to come?"

The whole universe stopped as the question hung in between them. Nothing moved, and there was no sound. There was only Sam and the furious beating of his heart, and Mitch and the soft, unsteady breaths warming the air. Mitch was serious. He was seriously asking, and Sam, though angry, considered taking him up on it. He could even see it: they'd drive to Chicago and then head on south, and west. They'd ride all day and make love all night.

Together.

Except as quickly as the vision rose, it faded away.

Sam pressed a hand to Mitch's chest and stared at it. "I can't."

He wanted Mitch to push him, to drive him to saying yes the way Emma would. But Mitch didn't. He only bent down and brushed a soft, sad kiss to Sam's lips. "I gotta go."

"Kiss me first." Sam couldn't stop touching him. "Once more, before you go."

He felt Mitch's smile at his lips. "So you can leave me blue-balled again?"

I don't want to leave you at all. "Yeah."

Mitch took Sam's mouth, and Sam wrapped his arms around the other man's neck and surrendered to him. Mitch moved against him, sliding his hips over Sam's, pressing their imprisoned cocks up along one another as he delved deeper and deeper into Sam's mouth, echoing the contact above and below until they were humping one another and panting. Mitch gripped Sam's waistband, tugged hard, and they tumbled into the act they'd been dancing around all night.

"Only for you, Sunshine." Mitch coaxed Sam's hips up so he could pull his jeans down. "Only because it's you."

"We can be fast." Sam fumbled as he tried to help Mitch undress him.

"I don't want to be fast, but we'll have to be anyway." Mitch pulled back, drawing Sam upright with him. "Take off your shirt so I can taste your skin."

Sam was so hard he hurt as he squirmed out of his T-shirt, tossing it off into the darkness, crying out and arching as Mitch's mouth opened against his chest. He clutched Mitch's head and tried to aim him at his nipple. This inspired Mitch to rumble wickedly and reach up to tweak one of the tiny peaks gently before sucking the other sharply between his teeth. Sam gasped as Mitch's hand slipped down and took his dick in possession, stroking it several times before letting it go, rising and pushing Sam to the floor.

He made quick work of Sam's shoes and his already half-removed jeans, and then, when Sam was naked except for his socks, opened his legs wide, lifted his ass high and sucked on the inside of his thigh. Mitch remained clothed, which Sam found highly erotic. Sam aimed his hips toward Mitch's mouth, gasping as those lips dragged down to the juncture of his thighs and his waiting cock.

The sex this time was a blur. A lubed finger entered

Sam, and he held his legs against his body, spreading himself as Mitch entered him. He gave over to the sensation of being fucked, to being with Mitch, of letting go so much he was practically a rag doll. The Technicolor explosion in his head built as the other man thrust, and once he'd come, it took only a few strokes to bring himself along after.

On the cold, metal floor of the semi, with Mitch still pressed inside him and with a pool of cooling semen on his naked stomach, Sam was, for one moment, complete.

Then Mitch pulled away, and it was over.

He pressed a kiss to Sam's face. "Oh, Sunshine." Another kiss, this one lingering on Sam's lips. Rising, he gathered Sam's clothes and handed them to him.

He also passed over a paper towel, which Sam used to clean himself. He stumbled into his clothes, feeling heavy and sad, and a little angry. Not at Mitch, but at something. He couldn't name it, which angered him even more. When he was dressed, Sam stood and faced him. This couldn't end, and yet it was about to. Sam felt tongue-tied and lost, unsure of what to do now.

It was Mitch who acted—he reached for a pad of paper up by the driver's seat, and after scribbling something on a page, he handed it to Sam. "In case you ever decide to put out that lease." He was teasing, but there was a gruffness about him that left Sam aching all over again. Sam took the paper, pocketing it with an almost wooden nod. Mitch helped him over the captain's chairs to the door and handed him his phone.

"You sure you're gonna be okay walking?" Mitch looked doubtful. "I could drive you near home at least."

Sam shook his head. "I'll be fine." He tried to smile but gave up and kissed Mitch one more time softly on his lips. "Thanks."

"Bye, Sunshine." Mitch closed his door.

The semi pulled onto the road and onto the interstate.

Everything felt surreal as Sam watched Mitch go, as he walked to his car, which only faltered twice before starting. He drove home slowly, playing echoes of the evening over in his mind, but by the time he reached Cherry Hill, it almost seemed like a dream.

It did become a dream once he went to bed. He dreamed of Mitch kissing him, Mitch pressing inside him, Mitch smiling at him. He woke hard, aching and ready to cry.

I should have gone with him. Sam didn't know how he could have, but as he woke that morning, all he knew in life was he should have gone with Mitch, no matter what the consequences.

Mitch was gone. It was too late.

SAM WENT THROUGH the next few days in a zombielike state. Twice he almost called Mitch, but he couldn't think of what to say. He ignored Darin entirely, and when Keith caught him in the hall and asked him what the fuck he was doing, Sam ducked beneath his former bathroom buddy's arm and went to class.

Sam didn't care about anything. He felt wrong and empty, except when he lay in bed. There he felt raw and hurt and terrified. Not even a visit to his mother's urn could make these feelings go away, and he couldn't understand why.

The night before school term ended he lay in bed with Judy clutched in his hand, stroking her side as he stared at Mitch's contact information typed so carefully on the screen. *Come get me,* he wanted to say. *Come back, and take me with you. I don't know why I want you, but I do, so please, please come get me.*

Sam didn't call him. He went to bed, and the next day, as he knew he would for the rest of the summer, he got up, got showered, and went to work.

Except when he got there, Delia waited for him, one hand on her hip, the other resting at her side. She held something black and small inside her hand, her fury radiating off her in icy waves. "Where were you the day you unloaded stock? The day you asked me to give you a free apartment? Where were you *really* when I called for you?"

Sam stilled. Something told him the wrong answer would send him to hell, but the trouble was, he didn't know what the right answer was. He fished for a safe response and settled on Emma's lie. "I was in the shelves, and I didn't hear you."

Delia's smile was tight as she lifted whatever it was she held. "No. You weren't."

Sam frowned, then froze as he got a good look at what she held in her hand.

It was a security tape.

CHAPTER SEVEN

"W HAT—" SAM'S VOICE broke, and he swallowed to try to right it. "What's that?"

"Security footage. I borrowed it from the bike shop. I knew you were up to something in the alley, and this morning I realized I could find out exactly what by checking the tape." Delia didn't smile, not even in triumph. "I *watched* it. I watched it, Sam, and I was nearly *sick*."

Sam wasn't feeling so good himself. But Mitch had shut the door. What had they done outside? What—? He took a step backward and glanced around, wondering who else was witnessing this little scene. There were no customers—Delia would never do this in front of *customers*. Steve, though, was in the pharmacy, and Sam could see from the temp pharmacist's expression he listened to every word.

Delia took a step closer to Sam. "What did you do in that trailer? With that *man*?"

Sam's face was hot, but his blood was cold. Honestly, he wasn't sure how much longer he could stand upright. "I—I—" He couldn't manage anything else. This was his worst nightmare come true.

This was about to taint the best thing that had ever happened to him.

Delia tucked the tape under her arm. "You make me *sick*. Utterly, completely *sick*. Carrying on with that kind of man not just while you were at work, but in *my* shop, right there where anyone could see you. I only hope no one else has seen this. I shudder to think what a laughingstock you would have made of me."

Sam took another step back and ran into a display of books. He reached out to right it but only sent books tumbling to the floor. What was he supposed to do? What was he supposed to say?

Delia didn't seem to think he should say anything because she kept talking, and every word was a knife. "Your mother. Your poor mother. Thank God she's not alive to see this. It's her fault for encouraging you, but I'm glad she can't see what you've become."

That's not fair, Sam wanted to say, because it wasn't, to judge him for one incident. But *he* knew what else he'd done, and how much more he wanted to do. He hated Delia for invoking his mother, but he couldn't argue with her. He stood there, taking it, feeling small and miserable and dirty, not knowing what to do or say. He waited for her to finish, to throw him out, so this could end.

"Quite obviously," she went on, "you won't get paid for that day. I'd love to fire you for it, but that gets me nowhere, only gives you more time to plan your whorish little escapades."

Sam blinked. "You—you aren't kicking me out?"

"Oh, I'd love to. But how can I? I promised your mother I'd get you through school, even though we both know you're never going to amount to anything when you finish. *If* you finish." Delia stared at the ceiling, as if she couldn't stomach the sight of Sam any longer.

"Delia, I'm sorry." He really was.

"Go. Leave. I don't care what you do with yourself today—just go." She leveled her gaze at him. "But you'll be at the house tonight, at six sharp. You'll be there, and you'll do whatever your uncle and I say. There will be nothing more of what I saw on this tape. Do you understand? Nothing like this ever again, or so help me, I *will* throw you out, promise or no."

She turned on her heel and stalked toward the office. Sam watched her go, too numb, too horrified, too defeated to do anything else. It wasn't until a customer came through the door that he was able to move.

He left his car at the pharmacy and walked aimlessly all the way to the north edge of town. A text came through on his phone, but he didn't look at it, only reached down and turned off the ringer inside his pocket. He walked on and on and on, barely making sure cars weren't coming before he crossed the roads.

He ended up in a cornfield.

It was June, so the field was already planted, full of neat and orderly rows of corn sprouted as far as the curve of the earth would allow him to see. The ground was black and rich, and the corn was bright green. It looked so good, so right, so full of promise.

It made Sam sad.

I promised your mother I'd get you through school, even though we both know you're never going to amount to anything when you finish.

He'd known Delia hated him, but he hadn't known she'd already written him off. *Never going to amount to anything.* The words kept ringing in his head, pealing the bell of his damnation.

It's her fault for encouraging you, but I'm glad she can't see what you've become.

Never going to amount to anything.

You make me sick. Utterly, completely sick.

Never going to amount to anything.

He sat there for hours, so full of shame he didn't know how he'd ever rise again. It would only get worse. She'd yell more tonight, and his uncle would be there too. Thank God he and Mitch *hadn't* done anything outside the trailer—she was grossed out by the touching and kissing. What if she had seen the rest?

But it was so good. It was better than anything that's ever happened to me.

Sam buried his face in his hands, let out a shuddering breath and held himself there, palms over his eyes, thumbs in his ears, breathing, and breathing, and breathing.

When he was able, he pulled out his phone to check the time and turn the ringer back on. It was four o'clock. He had two hours until judgment day. Oh God, he'd rather die. He scrolled through his texts, saw Emma had left four and a voice message too, but he couldn't deal with her right now. He couldn't talk to anyone, possibly not ever again. He couldn't—

Sam frowned at a phone number he didn't recognize at the beginning of a text. He pushed it warily to bring up the message, and then he sucked in a sharp breath.

Hey, Sunshine. Headed past your exit, and I thought of you. Hope you're having a great summer.

Sam's hands trembled as he reread the text. He checked the time stamp. *1:15.* Mitch had been here—in Middleton.

Come back.

The next thing Sam knew, his fingers moved over the keypad.

Shitty summer. Shittiest ever. He shut his eyes until he had himself under control, letting out an unsteady breath as he finished. *I should have gone with you.*

For some reason, *this*, not anything his aunt said, broke him, and he put the phone on the grass beside him and buried his face in his knees.

His phone chirped out a few bars of Kylie's "Fever" to let him know he had a text. Sam lifted his phone from the grass with shaking hands.

I can swing back and pick you up.

Another text came through.

You want me to?

Sam heard nothing, saw nothing, and knew nothing but the small, luminescent screen in his hand and the four beautiful words staring up at him. In a dream, he slowly punched in four characters, and "send."

Yes.

Then he added, a little more quickly,

Please?

His whole body ached as he waited for the reply. It came in under a minute.

Meet me at the DeSoto truck stop at 8. Call me if you have any trouble.

Sam clutched at the phone, staring at the message and trying to digest the enormity of what he had done.

Another text came through.

Will you be okay until I get there?

Sam typed a response. *Yes.* Then he added, with shaking hands, *Thank you.*

He could almost hear the reply echoing in his head with Mitch's thick, sultry drawl.

Anytime, Sunshine. Anytime.

NO ONE WAS in the house when he arrived, but Sam still moved through it like a thief, his heart pounding so hard he thought he'd have an attack. When he got to his room, he forced himself to slow and run a steady circuit through his possessions. He lingered a long time at the bookshelf, hesitating with some anxiety over his comics. In the end he left them all, but he felt sick knowing there was a good chance Delia would sell them, or worse still, throw them away. He'd have to have Emma keep them safe.

Emma. He pulled out his phone then put it away. No. She'd talk him out of this. He'd call her once he was on the road.

Should you be talked out of this? Sam shoved the voice of reason into the bottom of his backpack with the rest of the clothes inside. He had to go. He had to do this, to try.

In the end, from his room he only took toiletries and clothes, stuffing his backpack until it nearly burst, but when he was done, he went upstairs. He was terrified every second of hearing the key in the lock of the front door, but the sound didn't come, and he forced himself to calm. He had a half an hour left. Plenty of time.

He dropped his backpack with a weighty thud in a chair in the living room and hurried into the kitchen. He returned with an empty plastic food container in his hand, which he opened as he approached the small, lavish urn on the narrow shelf. With great care, he set them both down on the brick before the fireplace, opened the urn, and dumped the contents into the plastic tub.

He was *not* leaving without her. Sam's hands shook while he poured, as he worried that *now* he would feel the ghosts, and they would beat him and pin him to the floor and send him instantly to hell for messing with his mother's ashes, but nothing happened, and once he sealed the container shut, he felt calm. Sam recapped the urn quickly and placed it back on the mantle.

To get the container into his pack, he had to lose two T-shirts, and these he stuffed into the bottom of a decorative, wide-mouthed vase in a corner because he was now so panicked about getting caught he didn't want to take the time to run downstairs. His need to get away had become acute urgency, as if the whole universe were about to press on him and keep him in place, to trap him in Delia's clutches forever. At this point he didn't care if it were a real or imagined threat—he didn't want it to happen, period.

Sam hefted his backpack onto his shoulder and left.

He drove through the development onto the highway and headed south toward Desoto. He was going. He was *gone*. His panic abated a little. This would work. He was really leaving. He was actually doing it, and it was going to *work*.

Fifteen miles out of town his car died.

Sam stared at the dashboard, letting the loud silence fill his ears. He tried to start it several times—he got out and opened the hood, looking for something obvious, but he wouldn't have known what to do with it even if he'd found something. It all seemed like car to him. He tried several more times to get the engine to turn over, but it wouldn't budge, and now it was clearly flooded too.

Was this a sign? Was *this* his mom interfering, stopping him from doing something completely stupid?

It *was* stupid. This was crazy. This was insane. Stupid, reckless, and *he* was stupid and reckless. He couldn't keep his car running, and now he was skipping off with his alley fuck? What the hell did he think he was going to prove? He should go home.

Never going to amount to anything.

You make me sick. Utterly, completely sick.
Never going to amount to anything.

The doubt rose higher, crested, and then suddenly it was gone, beat down by an unexpected lightning strike of anger.

He wasn't going back. He wasn't *ever* going back.

Sam sorted furiously through his pack, taking more and more out of it until it was light enough to haul without breaking his back. He got out of the car, locked it, and headed south, texting madly as he went.

My car died on 965, he typed to Mitch, *but I'm coming on foot as fast as I can.*

It was three miles to the exit, which was nothing by car but might as well have been ten miles when he was running with a backpack strapped to him. He stopped when his text message chimed, but he growled in frustration and stowed it when he saw it was only Emma. He didn't have time for that now. He had to go. He had to get there, because he'd missed his destiny the first time. He wasn't going to let it slip away again.

When he stepped into a rabbit hole on the side of the road and twisted his ankle, he went down in a cry of anguish, realizing he could never cover this distance, not in time, acknowledging destiny would in fact brush past him once more. As he sank into the dirt and grass and the cold bit through his sheen of sweat, he turned his face to the sky, and when his view became blurry, he let the tears fall.

The sun was setting in the west, and it was so bright Sam could barely look at it. It cast the road in brilliant orange-red light, making the shadows of the road signs and fence posts so long they seemed to go on forever. It glared over the rim of the world, over the last hill that Sam could see, where, just beyond his vision, the interstate wound its way to Omaha and on toward Denver. He could see the tips of the signs advertising the truck stop where Mitch waited.

Sam got up, put his pack back on his shoulders and limped on.

Somehow he got to the top of the hill, and though he still had another half a mile to go, he could see the truck stop in the distance. He searched madly for the blue of Mitch's rig, but he couldn't see it. It was getting dark fast, and by the time he arrived at the overpass it was almost completely dark. He pulled out his phone and saw it was five minutes past the time Mitch had appointed. Surely he'd wait a few minutes? Sam hurried over to the other side of the building, but though he scanned the lot, there was no blue semi there.

He circled the property twice, but Mitch wasn't anywhere. *He wouldn't leave me,* he tried to reassure himself, but panic bit him, and his stupid tears threatened to come back. He pushed them away and headed to the ramp, setting his jaw in determination. No. Mitch wouldn't leave. He *wouldn't.*

Though it probably wouldn't be a bad idea to call and check where he was.

Sam actually had his cell phone in his hand when he heard the unmistakable sound of a big truck braking and shifting gears. Looking up, he saw a great hulk of a semi coming down the hill toward him, heading onto the overpass, lights blazing. It was huge. It was beautiful.

It was blue.

CHAPTER EIGHT

T HE SEMI CAME to a stop in the middle of the road across from Sam, and Mitch leaned out the window.

"I about drove into Middleton to look for you." Mitch's voice was gruff. "Where the hell did you get off to?"

"I went down to the truck stop." Sam nodded over his shoulder at the brightly lit set of buildings. "Must have missed you when I was around the back." His breathing came short and winded, and his ankle still smarted a little.

Mitch is here. He's going to take me with him.

Mitch jerked his head at the passenger door. "Well, come on—get in."

Sam shifted his pack as he rounded the front of the rig, but he didn't take but three steps before his ankle made him stumble. Whatever adrenaline had carried him down the hill and around the truck stop twice had run out. He had to all but drag his foot as he moved across the road, and it was a relief to climb up on the running board and haul open the heavy door to let himself inside.

"Why didn't you sit still if you were hurt?" Mitch frowned as Sam settled into the passenger seat. "Why didn't you call me?"

Sam pulled his right leg up, wincing as he did so. "I don't know. I was trying to get here in time. Sorry."

Mitch started to speak but stopped himself. "I gotta get this thing out of the middle of the road." He shifted gears, and the truck moved.

He'd done it, Sam realized. He'd gone with Mitch. They were going. West. He was going west, with Mitch.

Mitch wound them around the truck stop and toward 965 and the on-ramp. "Are you serious, Sunshine? You're coming along? All the way to L.A.?"

Sam only hesitated a moment. "Yeah. If that's okay."

Mitch fixed his attention to the road as he drove the rig. Sam kept quiet, watching at first with trepidation and then awe as Mitch maneuvered through the maze of vehicles and obstacles within the parking lot. When an SUV darted out from behind another rig and blocked their path, Sam gasped and shut his eyes, but Mitch got the truck stopped, regrouped, and then aimed for the interstate.

"I don't know how you drive this." Sam looked around at the expanse of road they occupied as they approached the on-ramp. "Do you ever hit anything?"

"I try not to, but let me tell you, it's usually some other asshole who pushes me into it." Mitch grimaced at the taillights of the SUV as it zipped onto the ramp. "As somebody who has personally put 250,000 miles on the U.S. Interstates in the past five years alone, I'm here to tell you, if the road belongs to anybody, it's the big rigs, bringing everybody their big-screen TVs and cheap toilet paper and produce off the boat from Brazil. Not to mention the damn cars people drive recklessly, trying to get us all killed." He let his shoulders relax. "Sorry. Trucker's soapbox. I'll do my best to keep it to a minimum."

Sam said nothing, only watched as Mitch put the rig onto westbound I-80. Sam paid attention to the way Mitch merged, using his mirrors, downshifting and pacing himself to make his way into the traffic safely. There weren't many vehicles on the road, but the one car in the right-hand lane didn't get over when Mitch approached, not until Mitch was almost on top of him, and when the guy finally moved, he also honked and tossed Mitch his middle finger.

"Not if you were the last guy on earth, buddy." Mitch shifted gears a few more times and settled into his seat, glancing at Sam. "So."

Sam fought the urge to wriggle uncomfortably. "I guess you're wondering why I'm here."

Mitch shrugged. "Sure, but you don't have to tell me anything you don't want to."

"You'll bring me along, just like that?"

"Yep." Mitch kept his eyes on the road.

Sam considered this. There had to be a catch. "I don't have money. A little, but not—"

Mitch held up a hand. "I don't want your money, Sunshine."

Sam studied Mitch's profile for a few minutes, trying to read him. He looked good, backlit by his dashboard. Sam realized it was just the two of them, so close, and it would be this way the whole time. They'd be together all day, and all night.

Heat spread through Sam's body, but he wasn't embarrassed. "I won't mind paying...other ways."

To his surprise, Mitch didn't give him a wicked grin and a dose of innuendo. Instead, his hands tensed on the wheel. "You don't have to pay me anything."

Now Sam was embarrassed. "Sorry." He turned his face away to stare out the passenger window.

Mitch sighed, a ragged sound. "Sam—" He shifted in his seat. "Shit. I didn't mean—"

"No, it's my fault." Sam tucked his feet up so he could hug his knees to his chest. "I'm just...edgy. I can't believe I'm doing this. I feel pretty stupid."

"You aren't stupid. If you left, it wasn't for anything but a good reason."

Sam buried his face in the valley of his knees. "I couldn't stand to hear about how depraved I am anymore."

"This your aunt?"

"I live with her and my uncle. I have since I was fifteen, when my mom got sick. She had cancer. Pancreatic cancer." He picked at a loose string at the seam of his shoes. "She had multiple sclerosis too. It started when I was little, and it was bad by the time I was ten. She was evening out, working to keep herself strong, and we were going to be okay. Then, boom.

Cancer." He pulled the string until it broke. "She was gone."

Mitch let the silence hang a minute. "You been with your aunt and uncle since?" Sam nodded. "But you're an adult now—surely you could move out?"

"I don't have any money. I can't get loans for school, and it takes years to earn enough on my own before I can get them. It's a tax thing. My uncle claimed me because they were my legal guardians for a year. That's all it took. With my mom alive just one more year, I'd have qualified for every need-based scholarship available. Under Uncle Norm's income, I qualify for nothing. So they pay, but not much, and only part-time. Which is why it takes forever."

"But you work."

"Yeah. For *them*. Half of what I get goes for room and board, and the rest I need for books and gas and clothes and sanity. It took me forever to save for my phone, and it's killing me to pay for the plan." He realized without a job it was going to be impossible. What would the phone company do, he wondered, when he couldn't keep his contract?

"That's a shit deal. They owe you better."

Sam shrugged and resumed picking at his shoe. "They paid my mom's bills. They took me in."

"Sounds like that's what they owe your mom." He shook his head. "Well, you're rid of them."

Sam rested his cheek on his knees and looked out the window. "All I can think of is how I would have been better off working the full three years until I could be declared independent and would have qualified for aid on my own." He hesitated before letting his darkest regrets come out. "Maybe if I'd taken the time, I might have realized I didn't want to be in nursing."

"You don't?"

Sam shrugged. "I don't know. Maybe. I think I got into it out of guilt because I wanted to help people, same as other people helped my mom. I thought I'd enjoy it, but it's mostly a lot of horrible grunt work. I don't want to wipe ass in a hospital. I don't want to work insane crazy overnight hours for years until I can get into a decent schedule. Health care is good, and it's a steady job, but—" He sighed. "I don't know."

"You're young. You got time to figure this stuff out."

Sam bristled. "I'm not that young. Anyway, how old are you? Eighty?"

Mitch lifted an amused eyebrow. "Thirty-three."

Okay, that *was* a lot older. "I suppose you think I'm some stupid, whiny kid."

"You're attached to that word, aren't you? Stupid. Is this a gift from your aunt, or did you take it on yourself?"

Sam didn't answer, not knowing what to say.

When Mitch spoke again, his voice was softer. "For what it's worth, I don't think you're stupid, and I don't think of you as a kid. If anything, you're too damn old for your age. I know middle-aged men who fuss less than you. How about you give yourself a break, Sunshine? You took a pretty big leap, coming away with me. Yeah, there are a lot of unknowns, but you're smart, and you don't have anything to lose. Let yourself live a little."

Sam let this sink in as much as it could. "I do have some money saved." Guilt backwashed, though, and he had to add, "I should save it for fall tuition."

"You don't know yet where you're going this fall," Mitch reminded him. "If you're going anywhere at all."

"This economy is so bad. It's stupid to goof my way through the summer when I could be working, even if it is for Delia. It's stupid. *I'm* stupid."

"If you say that word one more time, I will pull this rig over and paddle your ass."

Mitch sounded serious, and Sam wasn't quite sure what to make of that. He chose his next words carefully. "It's not smart to waste money or time."

"But if you're headed down the wrong road, you're wasting more time and energy than if you stand still awhile and try to sort yourself out. Except in your case, heading down the road is what counts as standing still. You said yourself you've never traveled, not really. Well, there isn't anything like changing your environment to change your mind, or at least to give you some decent perspective. You don't know something until you've stood outside it and looked at it objectively. Come see a sliver of the world with me, and I promise you a few months on the road will change your life completely."

Sam couldn't decide if changing his life completely was exciting or terrifying. "I can't go with you for months."

"Then come for whatever time is right for you. How much money you got saved, Sunshine? You got enough to buy yourself a one-way plane ticket home?"

"I do."

"Good. Then you keep it tucked aside, and everything else is on me. You've got your exit if you need it, but other than that, you're enjoying a side trip out of your usual life."

Sam balked. "You can't do that."

"I can, and I will." He gave Sam an arch look. "Would you care to tell me I'm stupid?"

Heat in those blue eyes caught Sam up, and he nearly said the word to see if Mitch was bluffing. "Why are you doing this? Why would you do this for me, if not for sex?"

He hadn't meant it to come out so blunt, and he waited for Mitch to get angry, but Mitch shook his head. If anything, he seemed guilty.

"No, Sunshine." He wiped his hand over his mouth. "I wouldn't do that."

"But—we *are* going to have sex. Aren't we? Sometimes?"

Now Mitch smiled, staring out at the road as if he were undressing it. "Oh, I have no objection to that." He flicked his thumb absently against the wheel. "Let's put it this way: I like you, Sam. I want to help you. I want to be the guy who, when you look back at this summer years from now, you think of as the friend who helped give you the space to figure out who you really are." He winked. "If you think of me as a damn fine lover too, I will not be put out in the slightest."

Sam considered all this. It was surreal, what Mitch offered, which was probably why Sam could answer. "I wouldn't have minded being your whore."

Mitch's easy, sultry smile fled so quickly Sam blinked. He didn't understand how he kept doing this, saying things that upset Mitch. He panicked and started babbling.

"That's what she called me. A whore." Sam swallowed. "I shouldn't want to be one, I guess, even with you."

Mitch could not look at him long, but he did so as frequently as was safe, and he studied Sam's face carefully. His own expression was unreadable.

He poked around in the dashboard for a few minutes, searching for something beneath the papers and wrappers there, but he eventually gave up.

"Do you say that," he asked at last, "because if I made you pay your way in ass, then it would put you off the hook for such a big decision, or because you get off on the idea of doing whatever I tell you, of having your body be at my command?"

Sam thought about this. "Both."

Mitch's thumb caressed the wheel for several minutes. The road was completely dark now except for the semi's headlights, making it seem as if the whole world were gone as the silence stretched on and on and on.

"Sorry," Sam said at last. "I don't mean to be awkward. We don't have to—"

"It's not." Mitch looked at Sam. "You really want to play with me?"

Sam was glad it was so dark, because his face had to be scarlet. "Not if you think it's gross."

Mitch's laugh was velvet. "Oh, I don't think that at all." He rubbed his chin, still staring ahead at the road. "Okay."

Sam's heart beat one hard thump against the wall of his chest. "Okay?"

"Yep. So long as you want it, so long as you get it's a game, that you can call it off at any time, I will take payment from you for your portion of this trip in ass and other acts of submission and general sluttiness." He tapped his thumb on the wheel. "But it's a *game*, and it only goes on so long as everybody is having a good time. You got that?"

Sam nodded, trying not to look too eager. "Yes."

"The thing is," Mitch went on, "these games need a safe zone. You need to give me boundaries, and you need to give me a word."

"Word? You mean a safe word? Is this BDSM?" His voice went up on the end of the acronym.

"From your tone there I take it bondage isn't your thing?"

"It's the sadomasochism part I'm not wild about." Sam attempted to buck up a bit. "I don't know about bondage. I've never done it."

"What have you done? Because I will tell you, I've done quite a bit." It was weird, but Mitch looked chagrined, guilty. Then the look was gone. "Where are you coming from on this, Sam? Talk to me."

Sam did a mental review of his sexual practice. It didn't take long. "I've only been with a few guys. Nobody who ever meant anything. You know about Darin. There were a few others, but they were just one-night fucks or guys I sucked off at school. Usually straight guys." Sam hesitated. "I liked the way it made me feel. Vulnerable, but powerful too."

"I already know you get off on direction and talking dirty." There was heat in Mitch's tone now. Sam wondered if Mitch was getting hard talking about this. He knew he was.

"And I know you want it a little rough," Mitch added. "But what about games? If I tie you up, will you freak out?"

Sam had the sudden image of Mitch binding his hands behind his back and spreading his legs open. His voice was hoarse when he spoke. "No. But—I don't want to hurt."

"What about exposure? You want this game only between us, or will you get a kick if I let other people see you're doing what I tell you? Nobody who would hurt you," Mitch said quickly, when Sam gave a quiet squeak. "Nobody who would make you feel bad about it."

Sam's head still reeled. "Maybe."

When Mitch next spoke, his words held strange, unreadable weight. "What about more than one partner? Would—would you enjoy that?"

Yes, I want that so much I hurt. But there was the odd tone in Mitch's voice again, and Sam couldn't tell if this was something Mitch wanted, or if it was something he didn't. Sam hunched in his seat, wondering if he'd bit off more than he could chew.

Mitch glanced at him and grimaced. "Sorry. I'm going too fast."

You want this so much. Don't fuck it up by being shy. "I like it when you make me do things, tell me what to do. When you tell me to take off my pants and touch myself or take off my clothes." He dared a glance at Mitch. "I like having sex with you. I feel *free* when you tell me to do stuff. It's so dirty, but with you it's okay." He stared out the windshield. "It'd be hot if you…made me do stuff for other people. It's embarrassing, and I have no control, but I do. You're *making* me be sexy, so it's not my fault." He blushed. "Never mind. This is stupid."

Mitch remained quiet for another mile. Sam worried he'd broken everything already. But as they came up over a hill near a rest stop, Mitch said, "Safe word. You didn't pick one."

Sam blinked and tried to think. "Violet."

"Favorite color?"

"Character. From *9 to 5*."

"Good. Remember Violet, then." He aimed the semi toward the rest stop. "I believe I promised you a spanking if you said that word again."

"Wait—*wait*." Sam held on to the dash as Mitch pulled into a parking spot. "You can't be serious."

"Oh, I'm very serious." He locked the doors and undid his seat belt as he faced Sam. "Stand up and strip that ass bare."

CHAPTER NINE

*H*E'S TEASING YOU. Sam told himself this, but as he sat frozen in his seat, watching Mitch's rigid jaw, it was a hard line to buy. Sam breathed shallowly, as if to keep from being noticed by too much movement. After a minute or so, his hand hurt, and he realized this was because he held the seat belt strap so tightly it cut into his skin.

"You remember your word?" When Sam kept blinking, Mitch added, "Your *safe* word?"

It took work to force the word out. "Violet."

"Okay." Mitch pointed at Sam. "Get your ass over my knee."

No, Sam wanted to shout, but he couldn't, and what was weirder, he undid his seat belt and stumbled around the console and headed for Mitch, moving as if he were in a dream.

"Take off your pants." Mitch tugged at Sam's T-shirt. "This too. Take it all off. Right now, Sam. *Do it.*"

Sam had been ready to argue until the gruff command to *do it.* For some reason this inspired him to reach for the hem of his shirt, pull it off and toss it onto the passenger seat. He fumbled with the fastenings of his jeans because Mitch stared at his waist, and the look made all Sam's blood run south. But when he pushed his jeans and underwear down and his phone started to tumble out of his pocket, Mitch leaned forward, steadied him and caught the phone in one motion. He put Judy into a small compartment in the dash before nodding at Sam's jeans. "All the way off. Socks too."

Sam undressed, dick hardening as he did so, which amazed him because a large part of him wanted to run. This was beyond stupid now. This was crazy. But oh, God, it was the most sexy thing he'd ever done in his life.

He'll stop if I say the word.

Or would he?

Hesitating with his sock in hand, Sam looked Mitch in the eye. "Violet."

Immediately, Mitch softened and touched his arm. "Too fast, Sunshine?"

Sam let out a breath, a two-ton weight off his chest. "Just testing."

Mitch stayed where he was, watching Sam's face. "So you want to keep playing? Because we don't have to, if you don't want to. It's okay. We can go slow."

"I don't want to go slow."

Mitch's mouth turned up in one corner. "You're ready to take your punishment?"

Sam nodded.

"You want me to spank you for saying you were stupid?"

Sam hesitated. Then he nodded again.

Mitch arched his eyebrows. "Say it. Tell me what you want."

Sam did not want to say it. He wanted it to happen to him, but even as he thought that, he realized it wasn't fair. He swallowed and tried to hold his head high. "I—I want you to...to spank me. Because I'm stupid."

Mitch made a noise in the back of his throat that sounded disturbingly like a growl, and the next thing Sam knew he pitched forward toward the dash. He stopped at the last second, arms rigid against the panel of instrument readings or whatever they were, a knee on his stomach and another under his thigh. His bare ass stuck high in the air.

"Say it." Mitch's voice was tight and angry. "Tell me you're stupid."

"I'm stupid," Sam said without hesitation and more than a little sass.

Mitch spanked him.

It was no gentle tap, but a smart *slap* against Sam's bare buttocks, and it came with an accompanying smacking sound echoing loudly in the cab. Sam cried out, the sound half-recovery, half-outrage, and he tried to wriggle away.

Mitch held him in place and spanked him some more.

The sting from the first blow started to radiate, and when the second one came down, it amplified the first, and by the third Sam worked harder to get away. The more he struggled, the more firmly Mitch held him down, and by the time Mitch finished the seventh slap,

Sam had learned to hold still and breathe.

After the tenth, Mitch stopped and rested his palm on the globe of Sam's now acutely smarting ass. "Would you care to say it again?"

No, Sam would not, because he did not want to be spanked anymore. Yet there was a tightness inside him now, an anger fueled by all the hurt and shame and confusion he'd felt all day, and—well, he was stupid. "Yes," he snarled. "Because I am. I'm *stupid*. I'm stupid, stupid, stupid, *stupid—ah!*"

The spanking resumed. It hurt from the start and with more than a little sting. *Violet,* Sam thought, but even as part of him wanted to end this, the part driving only cried out—and in a move making him feel utterly, utterly like a whore—he arched his ass up higher toward the striking palm. By the tenth strike Sam's ass was on fire, but the burn was spreading, and his cries had become moans.

"And now?" Mitch asked, as calmly as you please. But Sam could feel Mitch's erection poking at Sam through the jeans. He was enjoying this. A lot. If he was a whore, Mitch was too.

Good.

Sam shuddered. "I'm stupid. I'm so stupid." He shut his eyes. "And I'm a whore. I'm a slut."

Mitch's laugh was a shiver of dark pleasure. "Oh, but, Sunshine, you aren't stupid." A finger slid down the tingling crack between his cheeks, and he gasped as Mitch's hand closed gently around his balls. "You can be as slutty and whorish as you want, and it will never make you stupid."

Sam's arms had been rigid against the dash, but when Mitch stroked him, they went slack and weak. "I do stupid things when I'm slutty."

"You're awfully slutty right now with your bare ass all red while you hump my hand. You can make this stop any time, but you don't. You're running off with me to God knows where, and you all but begged me to make you my little sex toy on the way. Do you think that makes you a whore?"

Sam was, indeed, humping into Mitch's hand, because it was stroking his cock. "Yes."

"Do you want to be my whore, sweetheart?"

Lust, hot and thick, shot through Sam's body. "Yes."

"Are you stupid, Sam Keller?"

Sam hesitated.

Mitch's finger pressed at Sam's hole. "I'm enjoying this. I'm feeling pretty slutty myself. Am I stupid?"

"No," Sam replied, no hesitation at all.

"Turn your head to the right."

Sam did.

Mitch pressed his fingers gently against Sam's lips. "Open."

Sam complied, opening his mouth like a baby bird, shuddering when Mitch slipped two fingers inside. "Suck."

Sam did, shutting his eyes as he remembered the last time Mitch had ordered him to do this. Except then Mitch had been so far away. Now he was right here.

And these were *Mitch's* fingers.

Sam sucked hard, running his tongue around Mitch's fingers, knowing very well where they were going to end up, and he wanted it, oh *God* but he wanted it. Slutty? Whorish? He could give Lady Gaga a run for her money. He loved it. He didn't feel dirty, at least not in a bad way. He had, as Mitch had pointed out, nothing to lose.

Mitch pulled his fingers free, and Sam put his head down, spreading his legs without being asked, his dick aching at the thought of what was about to happen. But though Mitch's finger pushed at his entrance again, it didn't enter.

"Are you stupid, Sam?"

It's a game, the still-functional part of Sam's brain warned him. *A test. If you say yes, he'll smack you. If you say no, he will stick those beautifully wet fingers up your ass.* Sam wanted the fingers. He'd lie if he had to, to get those fingers. But apparently the part of him willing to lie was the same part that wanted to run, because it still wasn't driving.

"I don't know," Sam whispered.

The leg beneath his belly shifted, but instead of spanking him, Mitch brushed his day-old beard and a faint, damp touch of lips against Sam's spine. Sam shivered, going soft, bending his shoulders forward. Even his erection let go a touch.

Slowly, Mitch's finger pushed inside him.

Sam rode those fingers even as he loosened himself—he'd gotten good at this part with Darin, who rarely took any time to prepare him at all, and he'd had to learn how to ease an entry or be ripped apart. Or go without sex, and given the three options, it had seemed best to learn how to open himself so well the Titanic could have entered him. All this was unknown to Mitch, of course. Sam could feel Mitch's surprise and his pleasure as he easily added a second finger and finally a third. With just spit for lube, it was a bit tricky, Sam had to admit. But if he had any skill in bed, this was it, so he forced himself to relax further, pushing his ass up, impaling himself on Mitch's fingers.

Mitch groaned, and so did he. Then Mitch's fingers began to move, and Sam let himself fly away.

Within a few minutes he gasped and cried out, but he also lost his grip on the dash. Mitch did his best to hold him up, but then he swore, and the next thing Sam knew he was being turned over with Mitch's fingers still inside him. He marveled at this shift for a second, trying to figure out how the hell Mitch had done it, but when the fingers started fucking him again, he was lucky to remember to breathe.

Mitch supported him still, but now he was able to cradle Sam into the crook of his shoulder and his elbow as Sam melted, Mitch holding him up when his head lolled. He threw Sam's right leg over his business arm, and Sam had his foot pressed into the driver's side headrest, which also managed to expose him to Mitch's fingers at maximum-slut angle. Except after flailing with his left leg, which couldn't hang to the floor and couldn't get purchase on the edge of the seat or Mitch's knee, he kicked it up in the air, and Mitch grabbed his calf with his left hand. Then, by God, he was well and truly trussed. Slut City, and his ass was the busy inter-section.

It was fucking glorious.

"Open your eyes and watch."

By Mitch's command, Sam did, lifting his head groggily and staring through the sexual haze at his exposed body. He was a sea of white flesh across Mitch's jeans, except for his cock, which bulged red—almost purple now, actually, dark hair nested around it. At the apex of his thighs was Mitch's hand, large and strong and framed by the blond fur on his arm as it thrust three of his fingers over and over inside of Sam.

"Oh God." Sam trembled as he took himself in hand. "*Oh God.*"

"You're so hot, Sunshine." Mitch's teeth grazed his lobe. "Inside and out. Hot and tight. Come for me, Sam. Come now, right now, hot and naked in my arms. Come on, sugar. Come on. Come on. Come on."

Sam didn't know how to categorize the sounds he made now—cries, grunts, and something more. Some-thing guttural but oddly musical. He sang, a strange, surreal song only he and Mitch could understand. The pressure built inside him, not just in his groin but in the back of his brain. Before he came, the explosion reso-nated inside him, and he turned his face into Mitch's neck. When he came, he bucked, almost launching himself out of Mitch's arms, but Mitch held him down, and he held himself in place by sucking at Mitch's skin. When it was over, he let go, both of his now-very-sticky cock and Mitch's throat. Sam saw the red, angry mark he'd left there. The warm semen ran over his fingers, his stomach, his thigh.

Sam sagged into him, spent and sated.

Mitch's laugh was a rumble reverberating in his chest. "Feel better?"

Sam managed to grunt. The next thing he knew, the world tilted as Mitch stood and carried him through the curtain and into the cab.

Moving around in the dark, Mitch shifted Sam in his arms as he pushed and pulled at things and at one point appeared to be tugging at part of the wall before placing Sam tenderly into bedlike softness.

"If I'd have known I was picking you up, I'd have washed the sheets."

Sam's ass throbbed and his dick purred, sending waves of contentment through the rest of his body. Mitch moved in the darkness to the other side of the cab, where he first washed his hands and then wet a cloth which he brought over to Sam to clean him too. Sam lay there, letting him, too blown away to do anything else.

"I gotta drive us on a ways into Nebraska." Mitch stroked Sam's hair. "You okay?"

Sam leaned into Mitch's stroking fingers. "Yeah."

Mitch tousled Sam's hair affectionately before lifting away. "You go on and sleep. You look like you could use about eighty winks at least."

Sam didn't know what to say. Despite his Grand High Slut performance, he was too shy to tell Mitch what a great time that had been. Mitch hadn't even gotten off. Too moved to do anything else, Sam turned his head and placed a soft kiss on the inside of Mitch's wrist.

Mitch's hand trembled, and he stroked Sam's lips with his index finger—which smelled of musk and soap—before pulling away.

"Good night, Sunshine."

Sam watched him go through the curtain, and as the truck rumbled to life and Sam slipped into the darkness of sleep, he prayed he wouldn't wake to find out this was nothing but a dream.

THERE WAS NO forgetting for Sam, however, that he was indeed running away with Mitch. After a few hours of deep sleep, he woke still stowed in Mitch's bunk, and after that he wandered in and out of slumber, dreaming strange dreams he couldn't recall once he woke, tucked naked into the narrow bed with the diesel engine rumbling all around him. But late into the night, he dreamed Aunt Delia screamed at him and chucked bananas at his bright blue umbrella while he shouted *Violet* at her. Then the dream was gone, the engine had stopped, and a large, warm, Mitch-scented body climbed into bed beside him.

The bed was narrow, and Mitch was a large man— by rights they shouldn't have fit at all, but Mitch maneuvered them into place, and soon Sam nuzzled into Mitch's naked back, his own pressed against the rear wall of the cab as Mitch tucked the blanket around them. Mitch fell asleep without so much as a word, and after a few minutes, Sam joined him.

He woke in the morning with his head on Mitch's shoulder, his leg thrown over Mitch's body, his arm around Mitch's waist. Mitch's left arm was wrapped around him, holding him close, and his hand rested on Sam's bare ass. His other arm lay across Sam's own.

Sam had never been this close to anyone, ever, except for Emma and his mother, and never had he lain quiet like this with a man. Darin fucked him but never held him, and while his few forays to clubs had gleaned a few close-held dances, never had anyone wrapped their arms around him and simply kept still, let alone slept. Lying tangled with Mitch was something new. This embrace was more than the lost shelter of his mother, more than the familiar reassurance of Emma, more than the erotic whispers of his fantasies. More what, he didn't know. All he knew was that being held by a man transcended all those other embraces, taking him to a place so pure and wonderful Sam would do about anything to keep it.

Mitch stirred, groaned, and slid his hand up over Sam's shoulder to sleepily tousle his hair. "Mornin', Sunshine." His hand fell away from Sam to land on his own hip as if it were too heavy to hold up any longer. "What time is it?"

"I don't know," Sam said, but Mitch was already lifting a watch from the floor beside him and looking at it.

"Six thirty. Gotta rise and shine." Mitch pressed a quick kiss on Sam's forehead. "Get dressed, hon, and I'll feed you."

Mitch untangled himself from the sheet and got out of bed, and Sam indulged in a moment's regret they weren't going to start the day with more sex. He hadn't eaten since breakfast the day before, though, and as soon as he was aware of this, it was all he could think about. He rose to hunt down his clothes.

The darkness of the cab gave way to the full brightness of morning light as Mitch pulled back the curtains separating the sleeping area and the dash. This was not only a bedroom, though: it was also the kitchen area, and when Mitch stepped inside a space hidden behind a tall and narrow door, Sam saw it was also a bathroom. Across from it was a sink, a fridge, a microwave, and a TV. As he fished his underwear and jeans from the floor, he craned his neck around and saw he'd been right in his assessment the night he'd walked Mitch to the truck stop: he really did have an RV back here.

Sam eventually found all of his clothes and started climbing into them. He dismissed the day-old underwear, and after a moment's debate and glance at his pack on the other side of the cab, decided to go commando. It wasn't something he did usually, and his jeans felt odd as they brushed against his bare ass. He was extremely careful about zipping, and he finished as Mitch came out of the bathroom.

"Your turn." Mitch pointed behind him. "Or you can wait until we get inside. I'm due to empty it before we take off, and I'll fill the shower too."

"I'll go when we're inside, if that's okay." Sam wasn't sure he could pee with Mitch on the other side of the door. When he glanced at Mitch's neck and saw the bright red hickey there—a hickey Mitch showed no interest in hiding—Sam stuffed his hands into his pockets, abruptly sheepish.

Mitch headed to the front of the cab and climbed out the driver's side door. Sam hung back, not sure if he should follow or use the passenger door until Mitch waved him forward. He helped him down, giving Sam a thrill when Mitch didn't only assist him but indulged in subtle groping as well.

"How's your ankle?"

Sam had forgotten about it, which he thought was a good sign. He took a few steps, and outside of a faint twinge, it was perfectly fine. "It's good."

Mitch skimmed his hand down Sam's back before nodding at a long building across the parking lot. "Come on."

They were at a truck stop again, and this one seemed large enough to be considered a small village. They'd parked in what could only be described as a sea of semis, and all around them were canopies for fueling stations, garages advertising repair, and other buildings which might have been warehouses. Several fast-food companies had logos on the outside of a large main building, but there was also a bold yellow sign reading RESTAURANT, and it was there Mitch headed.

"Where are we?" Sam caught sight of himself in the

reflection of a semi's chrome fender and hurried his fingers through his hair. "Colorado?"

"Not quite. I got too tired to push over the border. We're in North Platte, Nebraska."

Sam didn't know where that was exactly, but he knew it had to be farther than Omaha, so this was foreign territory to him. He craned his neck around the sides of trailers, trying to catch a glimpse of the landscape, but so far it looked the same as Iowa.

"Bathroom is that way." Mitch pointed to his right as he headed left toward the hostess stand. "You want me to order you some coffee to get started?"

"Sure, thanks." Sam hurried away. He hadn't felt that urgent when he was in the cab, but now the need to piss was rather acute.

The urinals were crowded with men larger, dirtier, and grimmer than Sam wanted to face, so he chose a stall instead, and as he took care of business, he contemplated the strange new chapter in his life.

This could, he reasoned with himself, be a good thing. He trotted out all Mitch's arguments, adding one of his own: on this trip, he could be himself for once. He could do anything he wanted, within legalities and reason, and no one would talk about it at the bank or, more importantly, bring it back to the makeup counter at Biehl's. He could slut out all he wanted with Mitch, anywhere and anytime, and he wouldn't be judged. Even if someone gave him trouble along the way—well, they'd move on just as quickly, wouldn't they? This little segue from real life would be nothing but win.

Sam returned to the restaurant nervously, aware this mental declaration was an invitation for the universe to sic some big badass biker on him or worse. Outside of a few looks, however—some appreciative, some derisive—he returned to Mitch's table without any incident of note.

Mitch glanced up at him from his newspaper, smiled briefly and continued reading.

"Their eggs are a little off here, but if you get them in an omelet, you don't notice so much." Mitch looked up long enough to nudge a menu at Sam. "Eat up, because it's nothing but snacks until we're done unloading in Denver."

Sam opened a menu. "What are you hauling, anyway?"

"Scrap metal, though it's an odd kind. This guy in Chicago collects it, and a company in Denver buys it and turns it into recycled stuff. They have some arrangement going, and I got in on it. They're one of my bridge legs from Midwest to west." His finger slid down a column and tapped a small square of text. "My original L.A. order fell through, but I think I may have found the next leg. Order for me, will you?" Mitch pointed to an item on Sam's menu before reaching into his pocket for a small cell phone. "I'm going to try and get us a load for Old Blue."

"Old Blue?" Sam arched his eyebrow over the top of his menu.

"My truck." Mitch gave him a wry grin. "You name your toys, and I name mine."

Sam smiled and returned to choosing something to eat, because he was seriously going to expire if he didn't get food soon. As he scanned the breakfast items, he listened to Mitch chatting amiably with someone on the other line, sometimes drifting into Spanish. He didn't so much as pause when the waitress came.

The waitress looked at them oddly.

"Hi." Sam pointed to the menu. "I'll have number three and an orange juice." He glanced at Mitch and bit his lip. "I forgot what it was he said he wanted."

"I know what *that one* wants." The waitress folded her pad and left.

Sam frowned at her, wondering what had crawled up her ass and died. He glanced at Mitch, wanting to share a shrug to diffuse her attitude. To his surprise he saw Mitch watching her retreat, looking red-faced and guilty. He didn't seem angry or even affronted, just guilty, especially when his eyes darted to Sam.

He cleared his throat and looked down at the newspaper again as he resumed his conversation.

Putting that weirdness out of his mind, Sam did a quick survey of the restaurant. There were a lot of people present, mostly men, but there were some women too. There were two families, but they were closed off, dealing only with themselves. None of the women were alone, sitting instead with men who either had ball caps with unruly hair or big bushy beards, or both. Almost everyone in the room was overweight.

No one smiled either, which seemed odd to Sam. Everyone was grim, solitarily eating their breakfast or conversing seriously at the counter or urging children to eat up so they could get on the road. Some of the other truckers watched Sam the same way the waitress had, and it started to irritate him. He glanced down at himself, but no, he wasn't flaming out or anything. He didn't necessarily *look* gay, no more than usual. Sam and Mitch simply sat there, not even touching hands.

I know what that one wants. Sam caught the waitress's eye as she came through. The look she gave him was decidedly dirty and homophobic.

Sam rolled his eyes. *Stupid rednecks.* He vowed not to think of them anymore.

Mitch was charming up whoever he was speaking to, promising them "*Si,* I can do that, *no hay problema,*" and mentioning figures in some sort of negotiation. It went on for a long time until at last he hung up.

Mitch cupped his hands around his coffee. "They're cutting back same as everyone else. So I lowered my rate, and then I lowered it again. They're going to call and check on a few things, so hopefully it works out."

Sam sipped his coffee. "What is it?"

"A custom fencing company in Cortez. I used to carry parts to and from them regularly, but they've stopped calling, and they switched to another, cheaper carrier." Mitch pointed to the paper. "But then I saw that company went out of business. The run will barely cover gas, the offer I floated to them, and they never have a full load. I might be able to get a long load for Phoenix from Denver. Maybe." He rubbed his chin. Abruptly his face shuttered, and Sam followed his gaze to see the waitress coming toward them with a serving tray. "Ah-ha—here's food. Good, because now more than ever we need to get going."

The waitress behaved now, possibly because Mitch radiated some serious fuck-off vibes. Sam wanted to ask more questions, but Mitch shoveled food into his mouth, so Sam said nothing and ate as much as he could. He didn't finish, and when Mitch pressed him to eat more, Sam held up his hands.

"I warn you, it will be a long time before another sit-down." Mitch reached into his back pocket, pulled out his wallet, and handed Sam a pair of twenties. "Go on to the other side and get some snacks. I'm out of everything, so get what you want. Grab me a big liter thing of water, a bag of whatever pepper jerky they got, and a pack of Winstons."

"Winstons?" Sam repeated, taking the twenties.

"Cigarettes." Mitch threw more bills on the table and rose. "I'm gonna go dump Old Blue's toilet and refill the water and gas and such. Sorry, but we're gonna have to skip showers this morning. You can catch one on the road if you like."

"Okay." Sam stood awkwardly with the wad of twenties in his hand, watching Mitch stride purposefully down the aisle of the restaurant to the outside door.

He wandered over to the convenience store at the other end of the hall from the bathrooms, trying to remember the list Mitch had given him. Cigarettes, but he'd get those last because they were behind the counter. He hadn't seen Mitch smoke before. It depressed him a little, but he told himself to get over it. He got the jerky and the water, and he wandered around trying to decide what else Mitch might want, but mostly he got distracted.

Sam had been to a few truck stops, but not many, and never one like this—it was as if he'd stepped into an alternate universe. The convenience store was almost a Walmart—you name it, this place had it. It had a lot of souvenirs too, mementos of Nebraska which Sam couldn't imagine anyone would want, but some things were out-and-out odd, like clocks fashioned from segments of trees, varnished and sporting a painting of Elvis or Reba McEntire on the face. Stylized Native American stuff abounded, as well as paintings of wolves. Kitschy decorative pieces in glass and ceramic and crystal decorated the shelves, figurines of fairies and unicorns, cute little boys and girls kissing, and cows and pigs playing poker.

Then there were the Butt Buckets.

At first Sam thought they were some sort of gay joke, but no, they were serious. The thing was a container for your cigarette butts, which also extinguished them or something. There was a spit bucket too, and Sam shuddered when he saw the container looking suspiciously like something you were supposed to pee in.

Tall racks housed political stickers and American-themed items, and along a far wall boasted a selection of porn that would have made Darin weep, even though it was all straight. Portable DVD players were for sale, as well as CB radios. Sam wondered if Mitch had one.

Eventually Sam tore himself away from the cabinets of oddity and forced himself to shop. He got a couple more off-color glances from truckers, but he ignored them the same way he ignored the stares he got in Middleton. He ended up at the cash register with a bag of Cheetos, a few microwavable meals in tins, a half-gallon of milk, a loaf of bread, and a jar of peanut butter. He did a few more searches in vain for mineral or sparkling water, settled for something flavored instead, and checked out.

Mitch had Old Blue parked in a new place, and the hood was open on the cab. The whole front of the truck was angled forward like a cracked nut. Mitch was engrossed in his work, so after a quick ogle of his ass, Sam slipped into the cab, put away the groceries, and sat on the unmade bed as he tried to decide what to do.

He donned fresh underwear and put on deodorant. He brushed his teeth at the sink, and he straightened the bed. He poked around in the cupboards, hoping for something dirty or interesting, but mostly he found Mitch's clothes, a bag of kitty litter, and a lot of papers. A DVD player sat in one cupboard, and on top of it he found several hardcore porn videos.

Sam examined them, taking a tiny peek into Mitch's sexual world. There were several twink videos and some college-set ones too. The underlying theme, though, was bondage and domination. And threesomes or more.

Well.

Sam closed the cupboard, aroused and slightly

nervous, and continued on his search. He discovered an old laptop and an emergency flare, and most important of all, an outlet. Sam grabbed his backpack and fished inside for the cord to his phone. He'd begun to fear he'd left it behind, and then his fingers brushed the length of cable. The cord had nested around the plastic container he'd buried at the bottom of the pack. Carefully, Sam took them both out.

For a few minutes he sat with his mother's ashes, holding the container in his lap and stroking the top of the lid. *You didn't leave everything behind,* he scolded himself, and the little voice was right. He turned the tail of the cord over in his hand, realizing in this day and age you couldn't fully run away, not really. Delia wouldn't be upset, not yet, not any more than normal. She'd think he was out. She'd still be angry. Em would be worried, but not frantic. But by the end of the day, they would both start to worry, and when they inevitably crossed paths and realized neither of them had seen him—then things would get interesting. They'd also start calling.

Sam cradled the container of ashes higher on his chest, leaned over it, and sighed.

What he wanted, he admitted, was to have an adventure peppered with almost nothing except what he'd had with Mitch last night. He wanted a James Lear novel: near to constant episodes of sexual encounters strung together with a bit of mystery, and maybe, for window-dressing, some self-discovery. He wanted to have woken up this morning to Mitch suggesting sex.

He wanted to have sex now. He wanted to be coerced into strange sexual acts with him while on the road for the benefit of passing drivers who would also be gay, and should their escapades lead to encounters at rest stops, all their witnesses would be disease-free. He wanted a fantasy, in short. He wanted escape.

That was what Mitch had sold him, yes, but maybe it had only been a game last night and Mitch was bored already because Sam was too tame. He tried to tell himself Mitch was doing actual work today and there would be sex later, but this thought upset him more. He wanted to be Mitch's sex toy, yes, but he wanted to be so irresistible Mitch did little else but him. He didn't want to wait patiently in the passenger seat until Mitch had a free moment. What sort of adventure was just following him around, fetching groceries? Was this all it would be?

God, he was nothing but an ungrateful bastard. He should go home if he was going to be no better than a whiny four-year-old.

He opened the lid to the ashes with a trembling hand and stared into them, and when a tear surprised him by rolling down his nose, he let it fall into the gray silt.

"Mom," he whispered, "I know he said not to say it, but I feel really stupid."

He wished—oh God, he wished some soft breeze would blow up from nowhere, some subtle touch to let him know she was there. *Just a tiny bit of magic,* he pleaded to the ashes. He prodded them gently with his finger, as if this would spur something.

Nothing happened.

When the door opened, Sam startled, almost spilling the ashes. He did lose a few, but he scooped them up and put them in the container as best he could. He found some still on the floor once he closed the container, though, and he worked to gather them into his fist as Mitch stuck his head around the driver's seat.

"Hey—you said you've never been to Nebraska, right?" Mitch grinned and jerked his head toward the door. "Come on."

Sam still had the ashes in his hand, but Mitch was watching, so he clutched at them and hurried out, keeping his mom tight in his grip as Mitch helped him down, grope-free this time. Once they were on the ground, Mitch took hold of his elbow and led him with a purposeful step toward a ditch around the back of a maintenance building. As they cleared some grass, Sam realized it wasn't a ditch at all.

It was a river.

"This is the Platte." Mitch gestured at the water. "Well, okay, this here's the south fork. A bit east is where the North and South Platte meet. They feed into the Missouri River, which in turn empties into the Mississippi." He looked out across the water, and Sam watched his face. Mitch appeared pleased. "They followed this river on the Oregon Trail and the Mormon Trail, and the interstate winds along beside it. So when you travel down this road, you're going the same way so many people went before you, all heading west, to hope."

Sam stared at the river, not knowing quite what to say to this. It was a pretty speech, but it seemed odd coming from take-your-pants-off-and-bend-over Mitch, and he didn't know why Mitch had delivered it to him. So he stared at the water, and he found, actually, the river was soothing. He could hear the noise of the truck stop behind him, and the interstate beyond, but here at the river he could hear birds too, and the whisper of a breeze in the grass, and the soft sound of the water as it wound its way slowly to the Gulf of Mexico. Something small eased inside Sam, a drop of water on a hot day, but for that moment it was enough.

He remembered the ashes still in his hand, and before he could think too long about what he was doing, he extended his arm, opened his palm, and let them go, watching the powder drift into the weeds and the water. The ease he'd known vanished with that release, though, and he wrapped his arms around himself.

Mitch's shadow fell over him, and the trucker touched Sam lightly on his shoulder. "Ready to go, Sunshine?"

No, Sam wasn't ready. He didn't want to keep going, because he felt awkward and ridiculous, and he was sure he was going to regret his impulsive decision to run. But he looked out at the water, imagined a small bit of his mother now sailing south, and said, "Sure."

CHAPTER TEN

THEY REACHED DENVER by early afternoon.

Sam enjoyed the drive. Mitch let him pick all the music, and after starting with safe pop artists, he eventually wandered into more of his favorite British indie bands and on into country. When Mitch seemed to genuinely enjoy everything he played, Sam put it on shuffle and let the wild, weird eclecticism that was his musical taste carry them westward.

Settling in his seat with his feet on the dash, Sam watched the landscape change from the river valley of North Platte to the scrubby plains of eastern Colorado to the Rocky Mountains rising before him like gods lifting their heads on the horizon. At first Mitch had to point them out to him because Sam focused on the landscape, wondering where the hell all the trees had gone, and it took him several seconds to figure out the dark shapes ahead were not all clouds.

"Cool," he'd said, but he felt a little let down. He'd thought somehow the mountains would be bigger. They did grow, slowly—and then he got out a map. Shouldn't they be in Denver by now, if the mountains were that close? Then he realized how far the mountains still were away. "*Shit,* how *big* are they?"

Mitch smiled. "That was the reaction I wanted. Now imagine you're in a covered wagon traveling for weeks."

Fuck. Sam sank into his seat. "I would be staying in Denver, thanks."

"And now you know why Denver is there."

Sam regarded Mitch for a moment, noticing the light in his eyes, the sudden eagerness in his posture. He'd smoked several Winstons on the way into Colorado, appearing agitated and almost bored, but now he looked excited, as if he were happy to be where he was going.

"You wouldn't have stopped in Denver, would you?" The thought of pioneer Mitch was attractive. "You'd have hiked over the mountains like Grizzly Adams."

Mitch shrugged, but he still smiled. "I'm not much of a naturalist, and I have no desire to meet wild animals, so probably not. I'd have helped lay down the rails and saved up to ride the first train, though. Mostly I enjoy traveling. Seeing things. Learning."

Sam went back to watching the mountains come closer and closer. He could see the snow on the tops of some of the tallest peaks. "Will we drive into them at all?"

"If this deal comes through, yes, to get to Cortez. Quite deep inside them, in fact."

Sam tried to imagine the mountain roads, but he honestly couldn't wrap his head around the idea. He assumed they would drive between the peaks in some winding valley. It would be fun to look up at them from so far below. "I hope you get the deal, then."

The warehouse where Mitch took his load was on the southern side of the city, but it was out in the open, the mountains still visible in the distance. Sam offered to help unload, but Mitch shooed him into the cab. "Sit tight. Watch some TV. Stay here."

Sam didn't want to watch TV. He felt edgy, and bored, and nervous. He pulled out his phone and stared at it. Knowing he had to face it sometime, Sam called Emma.

At first she didn't believe him.

"That's funny," she said, when he told her he was in Denver. "Seriously, where are you? Your aunt has called me twice."

"No, really. I'm in Denver, with Mitch." He told her about driving off, about his car running out of gas. "Actually, I need to get my car off the road. Would you mind?"

"What the *hell*? Sam—you are *seriously* in Denver? You ran off with your alley fuck? *Why?*"

"I was mad. Delia—" He bit his lip, not knowing how to explain this. "She knows about Mitch. What we did in the alley. She said all sorts of crap, Em, and she promised to make my life hell."

"So you ran off with a stranger?"

She made *stranger* sound like *axe murderer*. Sam hunched further into himself. "It just sort of happened. I texted Mitch, and I guess he was close, because he said if I got to the truck stop, he'd pick me up." Okay, this sounded crazy out loud. His hand tightened on his phone. "So…I went, and…" He gave up. "Emma, don't be mad."

"Mad? Sam, I'm *scared*. Who is this guy? God, am I going to read about how they find your mutilated body in some ditch?"

"He's the guy from the alley—you thought he was okay then."

"Yeah, when he was a casual lay. Sam, do you even know anything about him? What if he's some sort of pervert?"

Sam started to say Mitch wasn't, but he remembered the porn and faltered. He was starting to feel a little sick, and he didn't care for it. "I shouldn't have called."

"Why didn't you call me when this happened?" she demanded, now sounding hurt as well as angry. "I would have taken you in, you idiot."

"What, forever?" Sam's stomach hurt. "Forget it, Emma. I'm sorry. I'll be fine."

"Come home, Sam." She was pleading now. "Get on a plane, and I'll come get you. You can come and stay with me. I'll talk to my mom, and we'll find a way to get the apartment. We'll find you some other job, and we'll find a way to get you tuition for the fall. *Come home.*"

Sam didn't know what to do. He'd felt good today, mostly, but there was the awkwardness from earlier in the morning and the fact that Mitch had yet to so much as wink at him since breakfast. Should he go back? Was Emma right? He looked out at the mountains, which appeared more and more ominous.

"Sam?"

Emma sounded worried. Sam jerked himself out of his fear reverie. "I don't know. I don't know."

"Then come back."

The door to the cab opened, and Sam startled guiltily. "I gotta go," he said, and hung up. He turned to face Mitch, ready to explain. Mitch appeared unconcerned—in fact, he seemed quite happy.

"Sunshine, get your dancin' shoes on because we are going to party. I got the fencing load to Cortez—for my *full* rate, and I don't have to start off until morning."

"Oh?" Sam tried to sound happy too.

"And I got Fuzzy to lend me his truck, so I can show you around town." He pointed at the curtain. "Go on—get yourself a shower, if you want."

Sam did, so Mitch showed him how to use the shower, and the toilet, which Sam was distracted by for a moment marveling how, really, you could use both at once, if you wanted. He hurried through his ablutions. Mitch apparently *did* wash his hair with bar soap, and Sam had to climb out wet and fish his own shampoo and conditioner out of the pack. He fussed and primped as much as he could with limited supplies. When he exited the cab, Mitch, who had been leaning against the front fender as he smoked and sipped at a Mountain Dew, narrowed his eyes appreciatively as he stubbed out his cigarette.

"You look damn fine, Sunshine."

Sam smoothed his hand self-consciously over his

hair. "I should have packed a blow dryer."

"We'll stop at a Walmart on the way." Mitch squeezed Sam's butt as he came past. "I won't be long, honey, and then we'll go eat. Go on inside, though."

Sam would rather have stayed outside, but he didn't want to argue, so he followed him in. Mitch wasn't long, technically, but Sam spent the whole time Mitch was in the shower pacing back and forth in the tiny space, alternately glancing out at the mountains and toward home. By the time Mitch came out, *Sam* wanted a cigarette.

He settled into his seat while Mitch dressed, trying to be polite and not ogle, but he wished he hadn't resisted when Mitch finally appeared. He looked *good*. He was much the same as he had appeared before, except more scrubbed, and his eyes were bright. He wore cowboy boots, and he had on a cream-colored button-down, but his jeans were the same faded blue. Sam's only complaint was that Mitch's hair would look a lot better once it dried and got messed up again. Mitch didn't seem to care, though, eagerly herding Sam out of the cab and toward a beat-up brown pickup truck near the side of the warehouse.

They did stop at a Walmart, where Mitch made Sam pick out a hair dryer, and more food and drinks too. They didn't have any sparkling water, only the name brand San Pellegrino, which while it was Sam's favorite wasn't very economical. When Sam tried to stop at one, though, Mitch put four more in the cart. They poked through the clothes but didn't get anything, and after paying, they were back on I-25 and heading into downtown Denver. Mitch gave him a small tour as they drove.

"They have this mall that's closed to all traffic but a shuttle bus, which is nice. The Mint is here too. They hold a Grand Prix race through the downtown once a year, though I've never been here for it. And they have the stadiums, of course. Anywhere in particular you want to see?"

"I don't know." Sam rubbed his arms. Emma's warnings kept swirling in his head. "Wherever. Whatever."

"Are you cold?" Mitch started to roll up his window.

"I'm fine." Sam put his hands in his lap.

"Hungry? You only had that peanut butter sandwich for lunch."

Sam thought if he tried to eat he would throw up. He might anyway. "No, thank you."

Mitch's concern faded to tension, which was just as well because Sam wasn't exactly calm. God, he felt so stupid.

After a while Mitch cleared his throat. "Do you…want me to take you to the airport?"

Sam shut his eyes, hung his head, and drew his knees up onto the seat. "No," he murmured. *And yes.*

More silence. Sam was dimly aware they were driving through a residential area now. God, he *should* go home.

"How about," Mitch said after a while, "we go somewhere and have a drink?"

"Okay." Sam kept his body tucked in tight against itself.

Mitch turned the truck around at a boulevard and headed into the downtown, and all the while Sam sat swimming in chaos. He tried to lose himself in a sense of history, to imagine he was on some wagon train, but he kept coming back to how ridiculous he felt, and how childish, and how he wished he were already drunk.

He was momentarily distracted as they parked in front of what could only be a gay bar, given the rainbow signs hanging in the windows, and he felt a little better, thinking it would be nice for a change to go into one of these places with a partner. Then he remembered how stupid he was being with Mitch, and he fell back into his awkwardness as he followed Mitch through the door and up to the bar.

"Two tequila shooters," Mitch said to the bartender. He turned to Sam. "What for a chaser?"

Sam's head swam. "I don't…" He bit his lip. *So stupid.*

"A beer," Mitch answered for him, and he picked something random off the tap.

"I'm sorry." Sam flattened his hands on the top of the bar so they'd stop shaking.

"Drink." Mitch shoved the shooters at him. "Then we'll talk."

Sam downed the first tequila shot and gagged.

When he'd recovered, Mitch took his hand and turned it over, exposing his wrist. "You're supposed to lick it." When Sam stared at him in confusion, Mitch lifted his arm and aimed Sam's wrist at his mouth. "Lick, Sunshine."

With only a moment's hesitation, Sam's tongue stole out to lick his own skin. When Sam tried to withdraw, Mitch shook his head. "More."

Sam licked again, more slowly, and heat built inside of him, especially when Mitch lowered his arm, salted the wet spot, and brought it back to Sam's mouth.

"Lick the salt off."

Sam did, making a face all the way until Mitch pressed the second shot glass into his hand.

"Drink."

Sam did, and as he lowered the glass, Mitch came at him with a wedge of lime, which he tucked gently into Sam's mouth.

"Suck."

Sam did, shutting his eyes against the tang and the watery way the two shots of tequila made him feel. When he opened his eyes, Mitch took the lime out of his mouth, pushed his beer at him, and nodded to the bartender and said, "Two more, and a second Coors."

"I can't do two more," Sam protested, but he did so weakly. He felt calmer. Maybe this was the answer: stay drunk.

"One of them is for me." When the bartender brought back the next round, Mitch put one glass in front of Sam and the other in front of himself, licking Sam's wrist before salting it. By the time he sucked the lime, Sam's dick pulsed, not hard but getting there, and when he did another shot, chasing his lime juice away with a swig of beer, he felt much better than he had when he'd come in.

Mitch, though, looked worse. He stared into his beer. "I'm sorry."

That threw Sam. "What?"

Mitch took a long drink before answering. "For yesterday. Last night. I went too fast. I tried not to, but I did, didn't I?"

Sam frowned, thinking the tequila must have already made him too fuzzy. "Fast? You mean the...spanking?"

Mitch nodded grimly. "And what came after. I'm sorry if I scared you. I'm trying so hard not to screw this up. You were just so..." his fingers tightened visibly on his glass, "...hot."

"Scared me?" Sam couldn't believe this. "No, you didn't scare me. Not until..."

"Yes?" Mitch leaned forward. "When did I scare you?"

Sam blushed, partly from the alcohol but mostly from a complete panic over how he was supposed to answer this. He couldn't very well admit he'd been nervous after Mitch *didn't* fuck him.

Mitch watched him intently. Sam's face was beet red now, and he knew the bartender was listening. "I was scared when you stopped." He stared at the top of the bar, into the empty shot glasses. "I thought I'd done something wrong. I probably did." Sam's face burned so hot it felt distended. He looked up at the bartender. "Can I please have more tequila?"

The bartender grinned and grabbed the bottle. Sam gripped his beer, let out a sigh, and drained the rest of it.

When he set his glass down, another shooter sat in front of him. The bartender winked. Wincing inwardly, Sam bent over and pressed his forehead to the top of the bar. He stilled at a gentle touch at his neck, and he shut his eyes and exhaled when Mitch brushed his lips against Sam's ear. "Are you telling me you weren't scared off, but upset because I didn't do *more* to you?"

"You know," Sam said to the top of the bar, "if you want to have them leave me a bottle and give me a quiet corner, I could stay here for a few hours, get insanely drunk, and then you could pour me onto a bus."

"Sunshine." Fingers slithered through his hair.

The next thing Sam knew, Mitch hoisted him upright by the collar of his T-shirt. Sam watched his wrist lift from the table, but when Mitch turned it over and applied his own tongue to Sam's pulse, Sam lost the little air left in his lungs. Sam kept his eyes on Mitch's as the other man salted Sam's skin before licking it off. He caught Sam's finger and thumb as well before drawing away, and he kept their eyes locked as Mitch tipped the shot into his mouth before reaching for a lime. When Mitch sucked hard on the fruit, Sam had to close his eyes, the intensity of the moment and the volume of alcohol in his system more than he could take.

Mitch tossed the spent lime into the bowl with the others and pulled his wallet out of his pocket.

"We're leaving?" Sam asked, confused and a little

concerned.

"We're taking a walk." Mitch pushed several bills toward the bartender. "We'll be back."

"We'll be waiting for you," the bartender said as Mitch slid a hand around Sam's waist and took hold of his ass.

CHAPTER ELEVEN

S AM FELT NERVOUS but hopeful, fairly sure there'd be sex now. He was loose enough thanks to the tequila to not care about much else. Mitch took them past the truck to the street, where he discreetly held Sam's arm as they angled toward a park. Once there Mitch aimed them at a bench, and they both sat down. Mitch leaned his elbows on his knees and stared at the ground. Finally, he spoke.

"So." His fingers rubbed over each other before lacing together to still the nervous movement. "I guess we need to talk."

"Okay," Sam said, drunk, lost, and confused.

Mitch held himself rigidly in his posture. He seemed so nervous, and it was odd to watch. "I had it all worked out in my head how I was going to take it nice and slow, and then the next thing I knew I was offering to spank you, and then—my God, Sunshine." He ran a hand over his face.

Sam felt somehow he was missing something important. "That's…okay. It was different, but I liked it."

This did not console Mitch. He rocked on his heels, ready to vault off the bench, but then he stopped and stared down at his hands as he twined his fingers together between his knees.

"I told you I used to…do stuff. Kinky stuff. It ended badly." He puffed his cheeks full of breath and blew the air out. "I don't want this to end badly too."

Sam didn't either. But he didn't understand how being all awkward was going to help. "What happened?"

"There's this guy. The one you remind me of. We used to…do things. We traveled together." Mitch's fingers tangled. "We were real good friends, but we fucked it up. Bad. And we did it by letting games get away from us."

The *little bastard*. It had to be. Sam didn't like this guy, because whoever he was, he not only clearly had Mitch's heart, but he'd left it way out of Sam's reach. Sam fidgeted. "I don't get what you're trying to say, Mitch. Do you want me or not?"

"I want you, but I don't want to screw it up. I don't want to scare you."

Sam sensed he walked on thin ice. He was missing something here, and if he didn't get a handle on it, he'd go under. "So what is it you think is going to scare me?"

"This isn't going to work."

Sam didn't know if Mitch meant this conversation or this relationship. "Tell me."

Mitch's expression was both wooden and tortured. "I was good all day, and you were skittish."

"But that was *why* I was skittish. I thought you were going to have me fuck myself with a dildo or something while you drove, and then you sat there and smoked and told me about the goddamned river."

Mitch's eyes flickered with heat.

Sam's heart kicked. "*Would* you have wanted me to fuck myself with a dildo?"

"That would have been a little distracting," Mitch admitted, but his voice was husky.

"Then what *would* you have done?"

Mitch tapped his thumb against his leg, and when he spoke, he was careful and deliberate. "I wanted to fuck you when I woke up. I wanted to turn you over and lick you, and eat you out, and I wanted to fuck your mouth."

Sam felt hot, but in a very different way. "Well, you should have."

"I also wanted to tie you down and spank you. I wanted to make you squirm, and groan, and then I felt you stroking my chest, and I shelved the idea because I didn't want to fuck things up."

"Mitch, this doesn't make any *sense*. I know I must be stupid, but I don't *get it*," Sam cried.

He gasped as Mitch grabbed him roughly by the shoulders.

"I have fucked up every relationship I've ever had. I tried so many times, but he always got in the way, and he was *right*, but I keep hoping with you—" Mitch cut himself off. "If you *were* stupid, if you *were* some idiot twink I didn't care about, I would seduce you and fuck you all the way to Los Angeles. I would take you to sex clubs and tie you up to the bed while I drove, and I'd fuck you with a vibrating plug until you begged me to pull over and do you myself. I would make you kneel on the floor and I would fuck your mouth and tug your hair back so I could watch my cock slide in and out."

Sam's head swam with the erotic scenes Mitch painted, and he couldn't for the life of him imagine why Mitch thought they were bad. But Mitch kept talking, and Sam began to understand.

"I would fuck you until we were bored, and then I'd let you go. But I *like* you. And I don't want to fuck it up. And I would—I would *fuck it up*, because I always do. Once you put sex into the picture, I don't know how to behave."

He seemed so nervous, so scared, so un-Mitch, and between this and the tequila, the world spun. Sam could feel the threads between himself and Mitch stretching, ready to break. He knew he needed to do something, but in his own way, he was as fragile as Mitch.

God help him, but Sam was turned on. *I would make you kneel on the floor, and I would fuck your mouth and tug your hair back so I could watch.* He shivered and laid a hand on Mitch's thigh. But he didn't—couldn't—look him in the eye while he spoke.

"So you can either be my friend, or my lover, but not both?"

Mitch's hands clenched. "I don't know, Sunshine. That's just it. *I don't know.*"

Sam considered this, trying to find reason when all he wanted to say was, *For crying out loud, fuck me.* Wasn't it *smart* of Mitch to slow down? Shouldn't Sam be glad? Grateful? What was wrong with him, that all he could feel when Mitch said he was afraid of using him was that he wished he'd hurry up and do it?

The weirdest part was, he *did* care for Mitch as a friend. He cared for him a lot. Couldn't Sam simply be his traveling buddy?

It took every ounce of control to keep from screaming, *No.*

Sam's hand, still on Mitch's thigh, kneaded nervously as he spoke.

"I meant what I said last night. I want—I want to be a whore, but I'm scared. Not of you. Of me." His hand tightened on Mitch's leg and held it like an anchor. "I found your porn. The ones about twinks and college boys. I got all…hot, because I thought, *I want him to do that to me.* Then I felt slutty and ashamed. I didn't want you to think of me that way. Well—I *did*, but I felt ashamed for wanting it. Maybe you'd sneer at me and shove me away when it was done, because how could you not?"

"Sunshine." Mitch put a hand in Sam's hair. "Never, Sam. Never."

"Then what's the problem?" Sam tried to meet Mitch's gaze, but he couldn't manage it yet, and so he slid his hand up Mitch's side instead, pressing his palm flat against his shirt, feeling his body move as he breathed. "I'd understand if you had to treat me like that. I know it—" He shut his eyes. "I know it's awful to want the things I want, but I don't…mind, if you have to look down on me for it. No, it really is okay," he said, hurriedly, when Mitch's hand tightened on his shoulder. "I mean—it's why I let Darin fuck me and why I sucked Keith off in the bathroom. They aren't nice after, but it's okay."

Except as soon as he said that, he knew it wouldn't be okay, not with Mitch. It was fine with Darin and Keith because they didn't matter.

Mitch mattered.

Mitch leaned forward and pressed a kiss to Sam's forehead. "I will never, ever be disgusted by you, Sam. Ever." It felt like a vow.

Sam shrugged, bowing his head to hide his discomfort. "Then I don't understand the problem."

Mitch said nothing, and they spent several minutes in uncomfortable silence. He kept unconsciously massaging Sam, and it relaxed him and eventually allowed him to speak.

"Last night was good." Sam relaxed a little as Mitch continued to touch him. "I loved what you made me do on the phone that day too. I loved how I felt during and after. I loved the trailer. I loved it all. I loved being held down and how you told me to watch. I even liked the spanking. It was weird, but okay too. Maybe not every day, but maybe…sometimes."

Mitch nuzzled the top of his head, and Sam fought against shutting his eyes, realizing for the first time they were in a public place. No one was watching, though— people passed, and some glanced at them, but most looked hurriedly away. Their bench was far off the path, so they had to be more a distant blurry set of figures than anything.

Sam let his eyes drift shut, his breath catching when Mitch's hand slid over his ass. "The trouble is I don't know exactly what I want. I mean—this is good. It'd be okay if, for example, if you m—" He swallowed before forcing himself on. "Made me undo my pants and touched me. Right here, in the park."

His face flamed, and he felt almost sick with shame, especially when Mitch said, "That would get us arrested." But then Mitch squeezed his ass and added, "Unbutton your pants, Sam."

"You said—" Sam stopped talking when Mitch's hand tightened again.

"I said to unbutton your pants."

Eyes wide and scanning for police, Sam reached down and slowly undid the fastening of his jeans.

"Unzip and pull your cock out so I can see it."

Sam didn't have to work much to pull himself out, as he was so fucking hard he was already peeking above the elastic. "I thought you said we'd get arrested?"

"If I started tugging at you, yeah. But this, nobody can see." He brushed his lips over Sam's hair. "How you doing?"

"Nervous," Sam admitted. "But...good."

"Nervous why?" Mitch pressed. "Nervous like you don't want to do this?"

"Just...nervous." He looked down at himself. His dick was there, pink and vulnerable, the smooth round head exposed. Sam shivered. "Nervous because you think I'm—" He bit his lip and shook his head. He'd been about to say *easy*. "I thought it was supposed to be girls who felt this way. I'm so stupid."

"I warned you about calling yourself stupid," Mitch said, his voice dangerous.

"Oh." Sam's face flushed. Mitch's hand on him stilled, and he pushed into it. "More...spanking?"

"I don't know. That didn't seem to teach you much." Mitch's hand slid up and dipped inside Sam's waistband. "But we'll deal with that in a minute. I'm thinking someone told you sex was slutty and slutty is bad. And I don't think you have to be a girl to feel that way. Your parents tell you this?"

"No. Well—I don't know who my dad is. Mom—" He tried to figure out how to explain his mom without making her sound bad. "She wanted me to be happy. She wasn't against sex, but she didn't want what happened to her to happen to me. My dad was a fling. She said she felt so cheap and so bad after, and she never wanted that for me. She wanted me to be loved. She always told me how beautiful sex could be, and how I should only do it with people who loved me. But it doesn't work like that. To be honest, I don't want it. It sounds boring. Sometimes I don't want it to be pretty at all. If she knew the sort of shit I did, what I want—" He broke off and leaned into Mitch's shoulder.

The wind picked up, making him cold, but it also teased the tip of his penis, reminding him it was exposed. It made him hard again. So did Mitch's hand, which kneaded his bare skin, pulling the flaps of his jeans back with the motion, further exposing the outline of his erection. "So...if I tell you I want to play a game with you tonight, if I want to make you feel slutty, then take you to Old Blue and have some kinky sex, am I going to push you too far?"

Sam wiggled so Mitch's fingers slipped into the crack of his ass. "What kind of kinky sex? Wait—slutty *before* we go back to the truck?"

"There's a sex shop down the road." Mitch's finger teased between Sam's cheeks. His voice was unsteady as he added, "For this game, I would need some supplies."

Sam had to work to keep from reaching for himself now, he was that aroused. "Do you want to tie me up?"

"Not until we get to the rig." Mitch's thumb brushed against Sam's ass. "But then…yeah. Maybe."

"What—" Sam swallowed. "What would you do before?"

Mitch spoke carefully. "I'll put some toys on you and in you. Then take you to the bar for a while and get you nice and relaxed."

Sam clutched at Mitch's thigh. "*In* me? Like a…plug?"

"I was thinking beads. If that would be okay."

This was such a strange conversation, like they were alternately wrestling and yielding and then getting up to shake hands. "It sounds…slutty." He licked his lips and forced himself to add, "In a good way."

"You sure?"

Mitch's finger probed him, and Sam imagined Mitch sliding something up inside him, keeping it there while the bartender watched. "I—I think."

He pressed his face into Mitch's shoulder. Could he

do this? Compared to Mitch, everything that had come before had been fucks in the dark.

All the more reason to do this.

"Yes." Sam was breathless but not hesitant at all.

Mitch squeezed his ass once more before pulling his hand out of Sam's jeans. He brushed his thumb along Sam's now-weeping penis. "Button yourself up then, Sam, and we'll go shopping."

SAM HAD EXPERIENCED the sex shop in Middleton, and he hadn't much cared for the experience. Part of this was because he'd been terrified someone would recognize him, but most of it was because Emma giggled the whole time. She'd picked up gelatinous dildos and aimed them at him, and she'd mused about strap-ons and asked him which of the fur-lined handcuffs he'd choose. He knew she dismissed everything as silly toys, but some had actually turned him on, though others scared him. He'd never gone again.

The Denver shop Mitch took Sam to was not the Pleasure Palace of Middleton, and Mitch wasn't giggling. In fact, his first move once they were within the doors was to put his arm around Sam's waist and slide his hand into Sam's left front pocket, pinning him to Mitch's side.

Mitch aimed him at a display case. "The way this game goes is you pick something, and then I pick something. If I pick something that scares you, use your word."

"What about if I scare you?" This didn't come off as coolly as Sam intended, because he was dazzled by the rainbow display of dildos in front of him.

"That's not possible. I will tell you, though, if I think something is a bad idea."

That seemed fair. Sam started scanning items. "Okay—so, one each?"

Mitch's hand stroked his hip from inside the pocket. "Oh, I thought four or five. Hell, Sunshine, you could talk me into a cartful of toys, but I figured you'd want to start out small."

Five? Sam picked up a shining dildo that appeared to be made of glass and found, actually, it was. Then he saw the price and had to work not to drop it. When he picked up a few other interesting items, he couldn't seem to find anything that wasn't outrageously expensive, especially when multiplied by five.

Sam couldn't take it. "It's too much money."

Mitch leaned in and nuzzled his temple. "I don't give a damn. Think of it this way: do you want something cheap shoved up your fine little ass?"

This was a fair point, but the price still bothered Sam. Four or five things each at this rate would be more than a semester's worth of textbooks. *Do I really want to do this?* When Mitch had said they would play a game, he'd thought he meant sex. Why did they need props? What was wrong with cocks and mouths and hands and asses? He could do fine with nothing more than some fruit-scented lube.

Mitch stroked him a little more openly now, and

that was pleasant, so Sam settled in and tried to get comfortable. He glanced around nervously at the other patrons, frankly marveling no one came over to stop them from making a public display. Almost everyone in the shop was male and with other males, and the women present were generally with other women. There were a few straight couples, but here they were a minority.

Mitch nudged him. "Choose, Sam."

Sam wasn't sure what he was looking at. Oh yes. Dildo City. So many different shapes to shove up one's ass. He found he preferred the colored ones as opposed to the fleshy ones, which resembled dismembered penises too much for his taste. Beyond this, they all looked like dildos, and he pointed at a random purple one. "That."

"Ah," Mitch said, in a careful way that made Sam self-conscious, and he tried to withdraw. Mitch held him fast and picked up the dildo with his free hand. "Here's an important lesson, Sam. This one's for ladies only. You'll notice it doesn't have much of a base." Sam frowned, not understanding, and Mitch mimed a few thrusts. "Gets slippery with all that lube, and it might get sucked inside."

"Oh God." Sam took the dildo from him and laid it hurriedly back down. "I don't know which one. I don't know one from another."

"Well, then why didn't you say? Here, let me give you a tour."

Mitch led Sam through the whole section, explaining various dildos and vibrators and plugs, debunking the mysteries of the shapes and angles. Self-consciousness quickly gave way to simple excitement, both academic and sexual. After some consideration, he chose a medium-sized orange one that had a slight curve at the top and a nice wide base.

Mitch picked it up and led Sam to another wall. "Now for mine."

This section was full of silicone beads strung together and rippled dildos tricked out in the same rainbow of colors and of varying sizes. Mitch's eyes were all for the beads, though. Sam had heard of these, but he'd never used them, or really even seen them. They didn't seem too daunting. "Okay." He reached for a blue string of the middle size nearest to him.

"Not quite." Mitch picked up a wicked-looking black number near the top. "This pick is mine." But he handed the beads to Sam, letting him inspect them. "Unless you want to veto?"

Sam ran his finger over the fattest bead through the package, but he wasn't concerned. It wasn't as fat as the dildo he'd chosen. He shrugged. "It's okay."

Mitch smiled and tucked it under his arm. "Next?"

This isn't so bad, Sam thought, and spent the next ten minutes wandering happily through the store, occasionally asking Mitch what things were. He didn't linger long at the riding crops, and he was quietly nervous when Mitch fingered some rope, remembering what he had confessed earlier. He scanned everything, and finally, not knowing what else to choose, decided to be a little daring and picked up a cock ring, once Mitch assured him they didn't hurt. After asking for advice on kind and size, he selected a plain, non-vibrating silver one.

For his next selection, Mitch picked a pair of leather cuffs with a short chain between them. Sam wasn't sure about them but didn't voice a complaint.

He assumed they were done, but when they turned down the next aisle, Sam stopped short at the product all but leaping out at him from the top shelf.

Actually there were two of them, both the same thing except one was packaged for men and women and one was marketed at men and men. Frankly Sam thought the men were having more fun, but both couples were going at it with the submissive partner on all fours, and both fuck-ees were being held up by a sort of strap around their abdomen as their lover pounded them from behind.

"Oh," Sam said, and he couldn't seem to manage much else.

Mitch massaged Sam's hip. "Looks good to me. Is that your choice?"

"I thought we were done." Sam couldn't stop staring at the faces of the men.

"Do you want this, Sam?" Mitch asked patiently.

Sam considered lying, and at first he tried to talk himself out of it. Shame rose up and choked him out of nowhere. *What am I doing here buying sex toys? What am I thinking, wanting a strap for Mitch to hold me up with so he can fuck me deeper?* Except he really, really wanted that strap. He couldn't speak, and so he nodded, his face as red as the anal plug on the shelf below.

Mitch picked the strap up wordlessly and reached for a package beside it which read, *vibrating thong*.

Sam laughed. "Seriously?" But Mitch only waggled his eyebrows, and after determining Sam didn't object, added it to his pile.

Mitch steered them toward the movies, and here Sam felt a little more comfortable. He decided this was actually a pretty smart way to explore sexual ground without anyone feeling awkward. He twitched at a title mentioning a golden shower and was relieved to find Mitch didn't seem interested, either. He saw one of the college-boy videos Mitch had in Old Blue, and Sam took a moment to inspect it more closely. It did look pretty good, he decided, except all the sleek young men were apparently having sex with one another, which was less exciting than he'd thought. But when he saw one called *Hot Truckers 2*, he waved it at Mitch.

"Interested in replacing me already, huh?" Mitch teased, but he put it in his pile. When Sam protested he didn't have to get it, Mitch held up a hand. "No, see, now I get to pick one."

Sam went quiet, waiting to see what Mitch would choose.

He took his time, inspecting everything, but in the end he went back to where the college-boy videos were and picked up one called *Twink Kink*.

Sam took it from him, inspected it, and glanced at Mitch. "You like them, don't you? Twinks."

Mitch watched Sam carefully. "You don't look pleased."

"Well, I guess *I'm* one. But I always wonder if I'm being made fun of when someone calls me that. Like I'm vapid."

"I'd ask if you want me to put it back, but there's not much to be done about the others you already saw."

"I guess that's it. Because if there's all this wall of stuff, and *this* is what you pick over and over again, and if this is what I am...well, now I feel kind of hot."

"That you are." Mitch indicated the video. "Well?"

Sam shrugged. "Sure."

They browsed a little longer, laughing at some of the titles, getting aroused at some of the suggestive poses on the covers. Then Sam went around the corner.

He'd found the BDSM section.

The straight porn was mixed in with this, which he certainly didn't need to see, but there was also a small gay section, and in a way, these videos were scarier than the heterosexual versions. Men and women were bent over, spread open, and tied up in the pictures on the covers.

Was this what Mitch was into?

Some catalogs sat stacked under a sign reading SPE-CIAL ORDER ONLY. Sam picked one up, opened to a random page, and gasped.

"Walk before you run, Sam." Mitch tried to take the catalog from him, but Sam turned away, so scared he was cold but also unable to stop staring.

Spreaders, they said. He didn't understand them

exactly, but what he saw was a woman bent over, her ass exposed and her legs wide apart, held there by an iron bar, her hands cuffed and attached to the same. He saw another woman with a bizarre smile upon her face as she lay on a bed, spread-eagled. Then he saw the man.

The man had no visible face because the picture showed only his upturned ass and gaping, shaved hole. His ankles were spread over a foot apart, his hands clamped to the same bar as his legs. There was a lock at the end of the bar. The man knelt, completely shaved, his pale balls hanging down as he waited, one assumed, to be fucked.

Sam made a strangled sound and gripped the sides of the catalog.

Mitch tore it out of his hands, almost literally. "Don't scare yourself."

Sam could still see it, the image burned forever on his brain. "Have you done that?"

"What—used spreaders, or BDSM in general?" Mitch put the catalog back, but he fussed with it after, and Sam knew Mitch was avoiding his gaze.

"Both." Sam watched Mitch's hand tighten on the shelving, and he had his answer. He felt queasy. "You—you're *into* that?"

"No. Whatever's going on in your head—fuck no, I'm not into that." Mitch ran agitated fingers through his hair and groped for the packet of cigarettes in his shirt pocket, but he put his hand down, acknowledging in frustration he couldn't smoke here. "Look, Sam. This isn't what I need to do to get off."

"But you *do* get off on it. You have, in the past."

Mitch grimaced. "Sometimes."

Sam turned to the toys—clips and gags and cuffs and weird things that screwed in. "I don't get it. Why would you want to *hurt*?" *Why would you want to hurt me?*

Mitch held up a hand. "I'm not a sadist. But I know people who are, and I know plenty of masochists too. It probably sounds strange to someone not in the Scene, but it works for them. Everybody's into something different. Everybody has different limits. And that's okay."

Sam could appreciate this in an academic way, but he felt frustrated because Mitch wasn't addressing his own interest in the subject. Sam took the catalog from him, holding the image of the bound man in front of Mitch's face. "Would you want to do that to me?"

Mitch quickly shifted his eyes to the ceiling, looking as if he wanted to push up one of the tiles and climb into the ductwork.

That's a yes. Sam tried not to be disappointed. "But *why*? I don't *get* it—what about it is hot? Please, Mitch—tell me, so I can understand."

Mitch kept his eyes averted, but Sam could see him sifting carefully through possible explanations. "It isn't *necessary*. It isn't something I *need* in you, or in anybody. But if you let me strap you down and make you so helpless, if you found helplessness fun and if you trusted me *that much*—" He shut his eyes briefly, and Sam thought he saw Mitch suppress a shudder. "That would be hot."

Sam turned the magazine around and tried to view the photo with new eyes. He was surprised to find that, if he worked at it, he could change his point of view. This image, a pale, faceless man held down on a white background as if any monster could come by and fuck him at a whim, was scary as fuck. But when he imagined this with Mitch, in a close, cozy room, maybe with a fireplace, with *his* body strapped inside, his eyes shut as Mitch touched his skin—well, that was different. If it was Mitch gripping his hips and probing at his back door, preparing him, getting ready to fuck him as Sam lay there, bound and bent over, unable to stop him, capable of neither encouraging or resisting, as submissive as he could possibly be—

"Oh." Sam swayed a little, bowled over by the image, and his hands trembled. *Oh.*

Mitch took the catalog away. He looked gruff and highly nervous. "I don't *need* that, Sunshine. There are a lot of ways to show me you trust me. There are a lot of things I find hot. I love spicy food, but I wouldn't want to eat it for dinner with you if you didn't like it too."

Yes, but would you go and eat it with someone else? How the hell that could matter when Sam offered himself up as a plaything for strangers as Mitch watched, Sam couldn't explain. But then he remembered the other man, the one Mitch had traveled with: the ghost between them. Had Mitch done these things with him? Was that what had gone wrong? Or was playing like this what had hooked him so badly that even when Mitch was with Sam, he couldn't seem to forget this other guy?

Mitch took his hand and leaned forward to brush a kiss against Sam's hair. "Let's go back to the bar."

Sam stopped brooding and looked up sharply. "Not to Old Blue?"

"Not yet." Mitch winked at him. "I have a plan."

They headed to the register, and on the way they passed the rope display which had unnerved Sam earlier. He thought of the spreaders, of the other man who had used them with Mitch.

Sam took a deep breath, and then he picked up a package of purple nylon cord.

Mitch saw this and raised an eyebrow.

Sam did his best to play it cool. "I decided you wouldn't hurt me, so there was no reason to be worried."

Mitch touched Sam's cheek then picked up a package of nylon ankle cuffs. "So I *don't* hurt you."

The bill would have paid for one of Sam's classes.

"Don't worry about it." Mitch hauled them both down the street toward the bar. Once in the parking lot, however, he hustled Sam into the truck instead. As soon as the door closed, he said, "Take off your underwear."

Sam felt a little self-conscious but also very horny, so he did as he was told. He worried other people would see as he knelt on the seat, but then Mitch's lips landed on his butt, and he forgot there was a world beyond the truck. Once Mitch had him gasping, cold lube made him jerk as Mitch's finger entered him.

Something else entered him too.

"What—?" He gasped as it went inside him.

"Beads." Mitch pushed another one in.

They were getting bigger, and Sam would've sworn they were ringed with fire and half a mile wide. They weren't balling up because Mitch slipped his finger between beads and straightened them. Sam could feel the things in his teeth. By the time Mitch pushed the last one in, Sam started to pant.

Mitch slapped his rump and told him to sit down and put on the underwear.

"You're going to leave them *in*?" Sam cried. He sat down. At least he tried to. "Oh God."

"Underwear." Mitch spoke calmly, but Sam could hear the arousal in his voice. He *enjoyed* this.

Sam wasn't sure. In the end Mitch had to help him, because every time he sat he squirmed.

"I think we need to put your cock ring on you." Mitch helped Sam into his jeans. "You won't make it five feet without it, I don't think."

This was how Sam ended up arching off the seat, hands on the dash and the window as Mitch wrestled the metal ring first onto his penis, and then, as Sam moaned, over his balls.

"Too tight?"

Sam shook his head.

"Good."

Mitch put his hand in Sam's underwear and fussed with something. Then he withdrew.

"What did you do?" Sam wriggled as something

small and flat pressed to his perineum.

"Something for later." Mitch grabbed his hand. "Come on."

CHAPTER TWELVE

THE BAR WAS busy now, but Sam barely noticed because he was so focused on the fact that if not for the cock ring, he'd have come in his pants two steps out of the truck. He felt as if his hips were undulating, and maybe they were, because every step he took sent the beads rolling around inside him, rubbing against his prostate, heightening awareness of his anal canal and quite possibly his colon. The beads and their sensations left him horny, and if he'd been alone, he would have jerked himself off. But if he got too hard, the cock ring tightened and eased his erection back down.

Mitch got him a drink, and Sam sipped it absently, too busy exploring the sensations inside him. As he leaned on the bar, pretending to listen to the bartender's conversation with Mitch—which was once again about trucking and whether or not Mitch could set the owners up with some deliveries on the cheap—he swayed his hips slightly, keeping up his internal friction, and at the same time this movement inspired Mitch's hands to slide up and down the sides of Sam's body.

Sometimes, when Sam wiggled too much, Mitch pushed his pelvis into Sam, and Sam would arch with him enough to show he yielded, but not enough to move away. After a while Mitch stroked him, first his hips, then the outside of his groin, and his stomach, and while never breaking stride in his conversation with the bartender, his hand slipped forward and traced the outline of Sam's dick, stealing down occasionally to tease the unyielding metal of the cock ring. Sam let his head fall against Mitch's chest, opening to him. When Mitch's erection pressed against his jeans, he swam away on the sensation, thinking he would be quite content to stay this way forever.

"If the two of you ever decide to sell tickets, be sure to let me know, and I'll be first in line."

The voice was unfamiliar and came from Sam's right—Sam turned in Mitch's arms, blinking as he came out of his sensual trance. A balding middle-aged man smiled at him with an expression that was both friendly and carnal.

Sam frowned. "Tickets?"

"To your show." The man's eyes ran down Sam's body to his groin, where Mitch fondled him.

Abruptly, the spell was over.

Embarrassment flooded Sam, blood flowing from his erection to his face. But even as he tried to retreat from the attention, a small voice inside him tried to stop him. *He's not mocking you. He's enjoying you.* Sam couldn't decide, though, if this was good or bad.

Mitch hadn't acknowledged the man when he'd spoken, but as Sam went from yielding to wary in his arms, he turned from the bartender to the stranger.

"Can I help you?" His tone suggested he'd be helping the man out of his sight if he didn't care for the next words that came out of his mouth.

The balding man held up his hands and gave Mitch a *no-harm-meant* smile. "Admiring the pair of you, that's all." He stuck out his hand. "Leon Baines. I haven't seen either of you in here before. Are you new in town?"

"Mitch Tedsoe. We're passing through." He accepted Leon Baines's hand and gave it a perfunctory shake before withdrawing.

Leon seemed ready to order Sam for lunch. "And the lovely young man? What's your name, honey?"

"Sam." He felt steadier now, but he was still unnerved by Leon's blatant sexual attention.

"A pleasure to meet you, Sam." When Sam didn't offer his hand, Leon took it himself, lifting it carefully, sliding his fingers over Sam's in lieu of the polite handshake he'd given Mitch. When Sam did not pull away from his touch, Leon all but purred. "Oh, but you are *delightful*, my dear."

Sam glanced up over his shoulder at Mitch, who had resumed his conversation with the bartender. But Mitch wasn't entirely focused on the man behind the bar. His eyes would slide to the right occasionally, enough to take in what went on beside him. When he caught Sam watching him back, Mitch's gaze shifted to Leon before moving to Sam, and then he raised an eyebrow. Sam held still, confused. Mitch's mouth played at a smile before he bent down and whispered in Sam's ear. "Play if you want to, Sunshine." He returned his focus to the bartender.

Sam glanced at Leon, who leaned an elbow against the bar. Leon transferred Sam's hand there as well, where he continued to make quiet love to it as he spoke. "So where are you from?"

"Iowa." Sam kept his focus on his captive hand.

"A *farm boy*."

Sam glared. "I've never even been on one. A farm, I mean," he corrected quickly, realizing his mistake too late.

Leon was too wrapped up in his fantasy to pick up the accidental bait. "So wholesome and sweet. And *strong*, and lithe. Look at those beautiful muscles." His fingers traced the outline of Sam's biceps, looking at them as if he'd like to eat them, or at least lick them.

Sam was not exactly aroused by this, but he wasn't appalled by it, either. Mostly he was surprised. No one had ever ogled him before—well, Mitch had, but somehow he was different. This was the way Darin looked at him, as if Sam were a piece of meat, but there was an appreciation in Leon's gaze he didn't quite know what to do with. Sam realized it was the attention he was attracted to, not the man. He didn't know what that meant, and he turned in refuge to his drink, which to his dismay was empty.

The next thing Sam knew he had another drink. It was the same thing Mitch had gotten him, something fruity and sweet that went down way too easy.

"So where are you headed, Iowa boy?"

Leon moved closer now, and somehow Sam slipped sideways into Mitch. Mitch stroked Sam's left hip, and Leon rubbed Sam's right thigh with his knee. When Sam wiggled, the beads tickled his insides. He clung to his drink and tried to keep hold of himself.

"We're just traveling." Sam clutched at the bar when Leon's knee nudged him again. "With Mitch. I'm traveling with Mitch. He's a semi driver."

"Lovely." Leon didn't sound as if he cared at all. He ran his hand over Sam's hip. When Sam stared at him fuzzily, Leon angled toward Sam's cock. Sam gasped, tensed, and at last Mitch noticed what was going on.

He wasn't outraged as Sam expected. He only stared calmly at Leon, who stared back, his hand still poised over Sam's fly. Mitch nodded at Sam's groin. "This man bothering you?"

Leon gave Sam a look that somehow conveyed innocence and wickedness all at once.

Sam swallowed hard. "Um."

Leon smiled up at Mitch. "I was about to ask if Sam wanted to come meet a few of my friends."

Mitch ran his hand across Sam's shoulders. "Well? Do you want to go?" When Sam tossed an *Are you high?* look at him, he laughed. "I think that's a no."

"The both of you come, then. You've talked business all night. My friends all own businesses. If you're looking for merchandise to carry, you might find some at our table. I can put in a word for you."

Mitch's hand still stroked Sam's shoulder. "It's up to Sam."

Sam stood on tiptoe to reach Mitch's ear. "You did see he was pawing me?"

"I did. You seemed to enjoy it. Was I wrong?"

Even half drunk, Sam could hear the hesitation mixed in with the casualness of Mitch's question. He remembered their discussion before, of his own insistence he wanted to try things a little kinky.

Mitch had let all this happen *on purpose.*

Sam glanced over at Leon, who winked. Sam bit his lip.

"I won't let anything happen to you," Mitch promised. "Nothing you don't want. I'll watch you the whole time, no matter where you are in the bar. I'll keep you safe, Sam."

Sam leaned into him. "Okay."

They crossed the bar, Leon carrying Sam's drink and Mitch leading Sam with his arm around his waist. Sam's throat felt dry, though, and since Leon had his drink, he stole a sip from Mitch's glass on the way. Sam glanced up at Mitch in surprise. "You're drinking plain Pepsi."

"Can't keep an eye on you if I'm not sober enough to pay attention. Also, we'll need to get going in no later than an hour, and I need to drive us across town."

It was weird how this more than anything made Sam feel safe, and he smiled as Leon took them to a table and introduced them to the three men seated there. It was a curved booth, and everyone shoved over to let the newcomers sit down. Leon tried to maneuver Sam between his friend Craig and himself, but Sam held tight to Mitch, which landed Leon at the end of the semicircle.

Leon hadn't been joking: his friends were all local businessmen, and Mitch chatted them up, asking who their carriers were and what they charged. To Sam's relief, Craig, who sat beside him, looked bored.

"I hate it when they talk business," he murmured to Sam.

Craig was younger than Leon, and a lot more handsome, and a lot less smarmy. He seemed attracted to Sam too, which Sam enjoyed.

Sam stirred his drink with its straw. "What do you want to talk about?"

Craig shrugged. "Anything else. TV. Movies. Music."

Sam beamed. "What sort of music?"

"The usual. Pop, mostly. Some jazz. A little electronica. Have you heard the new Imogen Heap album? It's absolutely gorgeous."

Sam tilted his head to the side and regarded Craig with as much seriousness as his succession of fruity drinks would allow. "Who do you prefer: Kylie or Madonna?"

Craig winced. "How can you ask? It's impossible to choose." But he tapped his finger against his beer and considered the question. "Madonna. Oh, don't give me that look," he scolded when Sam made a face. "You're a puppy. If you'd lived through Blond Ambition, you'd think differently."

"Did you go to that concert?"

"No. I was ten. But I remember watching the show on HBO and wishing I could. I've caught every tour live since Drowned World, though."

Sam sighed wistfully. "I love Kylie. I about died when I heard she was coming to the US, but I couldn't get tickets."

Craig's smile was evil. "I went."

Sam clamped a hand on his leg. "*Oh my God.* How was it? Amazing?"

Craig's eyes danced, and he leaned in close to whisper, "Sweetheart, it was *magic.*"

"Tell me." Sam clutched Craig's thigh. "Tell me all about it, *please.*"

Craig did, detailing every song and sequin, speaking softly into Sam's ear, and as the story wound on, his hands wandered over Sam. The toe of his shoe stroked Sam's calf. All the while, Sam kept his hand on Craig's thigh.

Craig leaned in and nipped Sam's ear. Sam shuddered.

With a low laugh, Craig did it again. "Is your boyfriend going to beat me up for this?"

Sam glanced at Mitch, who remained deep in conversation, but when Sam turned toward him, Mitch put his hand over Sam's, the one resting on his own thigh, and he squeezed.

After squeezing back, Sam returned his focus to Craig. "I—I think he likes to watch, actually."

"So you're a little kinky, are you? Very nice." He sucked briefly on Sam's earlobe. "You guys looking for a third?"

Sam had a sudden vision of Mitch holding him to his chest, watching while Craig kissed his way down his stomach. He sucked in a breath but found he couldn't answer.

This didn't seem to bother Craig. "You're sweet. Sexy, but shy." Beneath the table, Craig ran his hand over Sam's knee and gently hooked Sam's leg over his own. Sam dug his fingers into Craig as the other man's fingers traveled up his thigh. "Play with me?"

Sam could only nod.

As if from a great distance away, he remembered there were other people at the table, and he sat up, opening his eyes to let them dart warily around the group. Mitch spoke to the two across from him, something about rates per pound, and they listened intently, but Leon watched Craig and Sam with interest. Mitch's hand slid over Sam's leg closest to him, and as Craig moved higher, Mitch did too. Sam squirmed, realizing what was coming, but even though he tried to stop it, his fondlers met in the middle over Sam's swollen groin, and Sam's hand served only to hold them there in emphasis.

Sam stilled, and so did Craig and Mitch.

Mitch lifted his eyebrows slightly. Then he smiled, the tiniest upturn of lips, and with terrible slowness, Mitch caressed first Sam's hand, then Craig's. Then Mitch stroked Sam's rigid erection.

Now it was Craig who shuddered. He leaned forward, his free arm resting on the table as he spoke to the two men. "Tell Mitch about this new design you're testing," he suggested. "Maybe he can hook you up with a supplier."

As the men spoke animatedly, Craig appeared interested, but all the while his hand danced with the other two beneath the table. His fingers tangled with Mitch's and Sam's, and he ran his thumb down the ridge of Sam's tortured dick. Then, still pretending to listen to the conversation, he undid Sam's fly. Sam flinched, but he didn't stop him, only clutched at Mitch's hand.

Mitch placed Sam's fingers on the zipper, closed Sam's thumb and forefinger around the tip and forced him to pull it down. Then he reached inside the strange underwear, pulled Sam's erection out, found Craig's hand and nudged his fingers toward the bottom of Sam's shaft.

Sam melted into a slouch as the two men stroked him in a strange concert, completely ignoring each other above the table as they worked together below it. Their ministrations made Sam wiggle, which aggravated the beads. Sam was so hard he thought he would explode. He ached, not only in his groin but in his shoulders, and his legs, and in his belly. He was exquisitely aroused, more than he'd ever been in his life. But he was also embarrassed to be found out, and so he kept quiet, letting the men torture him, letting them send him out to sea on a thick haze of lust.

Then his balls began to tingle.

At first he thought he was just that turned on, but then he realized, no, something literally buzzed there, something small and focused. It pulsed, sometimes buzzing hard, sometimes soft. Just when it was about to drive Sam out of his mind, it would fade away, but then it would return without warning. It was the underwear, he realized. Sam clutched at Mitch, who pressed something small and smooth into Sam's hand. It had a button. Sam clicked it, and the buzzing stopped. Mitch took it back, and the underwear buzzed again.

Vibrating underwear. That had been the little something Mitch slipped inside, some control to make the underwear rock and roll. Apparently it had a remote.

The hands on Sam became more insistent, and the buzzing came more frequently, and Sam started to thrust his hips against the onslaught, half trying to escape, half trying to encourage them. His eyes darted from the businessmen to Leon, the former of whom were too engrossed in business to notice, and the latter who watched Sam openly. Leon met Sam's eyes, and Sam found he could not look away.

Craig found Sam's cock ring, sliding his thumb along it, and Sam bit his lip to keep from crying out.

Leon glanced at his watch. "Goodness. Will you look at the time? Ten thirty already."

The two men who had yet to realize what was going on beneath the table startled almost in unison. "Oh, no. Honey," one of them said, turning to the other, "we'd better get home."

"We have your card." The other man smiled apologetically at Mitch. "We'll be in touch. Good to meet you." When Sam looked up at him through a haze of alcohol and arousal, the man faltered, then laughed. When he rose, he winked. "Enjoy your evening, Craig." Then they were gone.

Craig kept a firm grip on Sam's penis, making Sam's eyes roll back in his head. "I'll see you at work tomorrow, Leon." Craig's fierceness made Sam shudder. When Leon started to object, Craig added, "I'll do the Peterson project for you, if you leave."

Leon hesitated, then swore as he rose. "You're a horrible bitch, Craig. They were *mine.*"

"*Were* being the operative word." Craig leaned forward to nibble at Sam's neck. Leon swore again, but then he was gone.

The buzzing increased, and Sam gave up, tipped his head against the booth and let out a cascading sigh.

Craig nuzzled his way down Sam's neck. "My apartment is a block from here."

The words kicked heat into Sam, but fear too, and the latter won out. He dug his fingers into Mitch's arm. Craig licked his way down Sam's throat, but Sam kept his eyes on Mitch, who bent toward him.

"Violet," Sam whispered.

Mitch's face softened, and beneath the table, he firmly pushed Craig's hand away. "No, thank you."

Craig seemed disappointed. "Ah. Maybe we can find somewhere a little more private?"

Sam averted his eyes, still clutching Mitch's hand.

Mitch stroked Sam's thigh. "Do you want to leave?"

Sam didn't know. He was horny but also confused. His panic stemmed now from not knowing what he wanted, let alone how to vocalize it.

"Talk to me, Sam," Mitch said. "Tell me what you want."

Sam shut his eyes and leaned against Mitch's sleeve. "I don't know."

"Do you like this? The three of us playing?"

Playing. Everyone kept saying that, as if they were talking about swings and merry-go-rounds. Sam let out a breath. "Yes, but—it's a little too…much." He shivered as Craig's hands returned to his groin. "But I don't want it to stop, either."

"Do you dance, honey?" Craig's hand slid up Sam's arm. "We could all go out on the floor together and dance."

Sam looked at Mitch for guidance, but then Craig's thumb flicked against the tip of Sam's penis, making him moan.

"There's a place off to the side that will be perfect." Craig tucked Sam inside his underwear and zipped but didn't button him. He leaned over and kissed Sam's cheek before tugging at his hand. "Come on."

Craig led Sam out of the booth, and Mitch followed. Once they were standing, Mitch held on to Sam's waist, his thumb hitched into Sam's belt loop, for which he was grateful because it kept his undone pants from falling down. They wove between the dancers, moving far to the back of the room to a dark corner by the stage, where they slipped into the space behind a large speaker. Once there, Craig took Sam by the hips and smiled as he pulled them together. He moved, his hand snaking to Mitch's waist, drawing him closer as well. Mitch came willingly, pushing up against Sam's sliding waistband.

They danced mostly with their hips as hands went everywhere and heat built inside of Sam. Mitch didn't do much, just held him and stroked, but that was fine, because Craig more than made up for him. No one could see them, not with the crowded bodies on the floor or the huge speaker blocking them, but neither were they alone. Sam felt safe and highly aroused. When Craig took Sam's cock out of his pants, Sam let him, and Mitch held his arms, pulling Sam's hands up to lock them behind his neck so Sam's fingers were tangled in Mitch's wiry hair. As the music pulsed around them and arousal carried him away, Sam closed his eyes, tipped his head back, and surrendered.

Craig kissed his way down Sam's throat, his hands working with intent at Sam's dick. Mitch had his hands beneath Sam's shirt, stroking the flexing tautness of Sam's belly, but he dipped down, tugging at Sam's waistband to expose Sam's whole cock to Craig's hand. Craig nuzzled Sam's cheek and stole a swift kiss from his lips.

Mitch grabbed Craig by the back of the head. Sam watched, dizzy with lust, as Mitch bent around him and took Craig's bottom lip between his teeth.

Then Mitch let go and pushed Craig to his knees. Sam watched, spiraling out of his head as Mitch's hands guided Sam into Craig's mouth. Craig looked up, and Sam looked down, mesmerized by the sight. Mitch's hands slid Sam's pants farther down, stroking the smooth globes of his ass as Craig swallowed Sam, taking him to the root, his lips closing over Sam's cock ring. The ring tightened as Sam's erection swelled.

He tugged at the back of Mitch's neck, trembling as Mitch's fingers slid to his cleft. He gasped when Mitch found the cord to the beads. He cried out when Mitch pulled, pushed, and turned the handle. He froze as he saw Mitch watching him with dark intent. Sam's lips parted as Mitch tugged again on the beads. Then, gaze still on Sam's face, Mitch slipped a finger in alongside them.

Craig sucked him, Mitch fucked him, and Sam slid away, staring up at Mitch's face until he couldn't see anything, his eyes glazed by lust. Mitch's thrusts pushed him deep into Craig's throat, and the music drowned out his cries as the two men used him. He opened to them, right there on the dance floor, and let them.

Sam came abruptly, his hips bucking almost violently against Craig's face as his fingernails dug into Mitch's neck. He shut his eyes and tried to pull himself to Mitch's mouth to silence himself, but Mitch moved away, and so he nestled his throat instead, burying his scream into Mitch's pounding jugular, against the fading hickey he'd left there the night before. When it was over, he shuddered, convulsing for several seconds before sagging, depleted.

Craig rose, hands skimming up Sam's sides before catching Sam's face. He glanced at Mitch, paused, then kissed Sam sweetly on the cheek. Pulling back, he planted a kiss on Mitch's mouth as well, though Mitch kept his lips firmly closed.

"Please." Craig gave Sam's penis a gentle squeeze as he tucked him into his pants. "Come to my apartment. I swear I'll be good."

Mitch refused before Sam could object. "We've got to get going." He pulled his finger out of Sam and did up Sam's jeans.

Craig seemed disappointed but not surprised. He pulled his wallet out and handed Mitch a card. "If you're ever in Denver again." With one last touch of Sam's cheek, he was gone.

Mitch pocketed the card and took Sam's hand, leading him out of the bar into the parking lot.

CHAPTER THIRTEEN

T HEY DROVE IN silence to the warehouse.

Sam sat carefully, the anal beads now even more irritating after his orgasm, the cock ring heavy against his tender balls. He found he could not look at Mitch and took refuge in watching the city pass by. However, he startled out of his reverie when Mitch swung abruptly into the driveway of a fast-food restaurant. "I forgot to feed you. You want a cheeseburger?"

Sam nodded and touched his stomach absently, abruptly hungry.

Mitch ordered him two and got the same for himself. He tossed Sam his order, and after wolfing his food down in the parking lot, he drove them back to the warehouse, keeping his hands rigidly on the wheel. Sam ate all of his food, but the silence had him worried. He wondered if he'd done something, but he was so confused by the back and forth and the sheer madness of everything they'd done that he couldn't manage much of any reaction, except that he was tired and glad he was with Mitch.

When Mitch parked the truck, he didn't take the keys out of the ignition. In fact he didn't make any move to leave the vehicle, only sat gripping the wheel and staring straight ahead.

"I'm okay. I swear." Sam rubbed his greasy fingers nervously along his jeans. God, was it always going to be this awkward? When would either of them learn to let go?

Mitch glanced at Sam. "You seemed…upset when we left."

Sam started to pull his legs up onto the seat but stopped when it aggravated his insides. He rested his cheek on the back of the seat instead, looking at Mitch's arm rather than his face. "I wasn't. I'm not." He forced his eyes up. "I'm overwhelmed is all."

"I shouldn't have had us go back to the bar, after the shop." Mitch sounded wretched. "I should've brought us here."

God, Sam was *tired* of this. "You didn't want to. You wanted to tease me. I wanted that too."

"This is everything I ever did wrong with a man coming back to haunt me all over again." Mitch rubbed his hands over his face.

What am I supposed to do? What am I supposed to say? Sam tried to draw his knees up, but as soon as he moved, he jerked and hissed.

"What's wrong?" Mitch reached for him in alarm. "Did you get hurt?"

Sam blushed. "The—beads. I'm so sensitive now."

Mitch pulled the keys out at last. "Come on, then. We'll go to the rig and take them out, and then I'll leave you alone."

Sam put a staying hand on his arm. "I don't want you to leave me alone."

Mitch looked at him, and they sat frozen in the dark, silent truck. *Tell me what you want.* That's what Mitch needed him to do, except Sam didn't want to have to say it. He didn't want to hear out loud what he wanted, but Mitch needed it. Mitch needed it a lot more than Sam needed to not feel awkward.

"I want you to take me into Old Blue, and I want you to do things to me. I want you to use the things you bought on me. Every last one of them. I want you to..." Sam's breath caught, and he had to shut his eyes. He made himself keep going. "I want you to m-make me show myself to you, and I want you to f-fuck me." He swallowed his fear and pushed on. "I was upset after the bar because I loved it so much. Because it felt so good to have you watch. Because it was so dirty and awful to do all that with a stranger. Because it was hot and it was wonderful, and it's everything I've always been afraid to be. It's difficult for me to believe someone actually wants to see me that way. But when I stop being afraid, I know it's okay, because it's you." He opened his eyes and looked over at Mitch, more vulnerable than he'd ever felt in his life. "I feel safe with you."

Mitch stared at him for a long time, his face unreadable in the dark. Then he stroked Sam's cheek with a single finger. It smelled musky, and Sam realized it was because it had been inside him. He shivered and pressed a tentative kiss against the digit.

Mitch stroked Sam's face. "I don't want you to be

afraid of me."

"I'm not." Sam took the musky tip of Mitch's finger into his mouth. "Can we go inside?"

Mitch nodded and opened the door.

Sam brought the bag from the sex shop, and they walked side by side without touching all the way back to Old Blue. Once inside, Mitch disappeared into the bathroom, and Sam stood in the darkened cab, trying to decide what to do.

He fiddled with his phone until music played softly. He chose Kylie, needing comfort, but he put on *Impossible Princess*, because he needed edgy and extra sexy. When Mitch came out, he smiled shyly and took his turn in the bathroom. He removed the cock ring and put it in his pocket, but when he started on the beads, he heard Mitch call him. He hesitated, but left them alone and opened the door.

Mitch grabbed him, hauling him out of the bathroom, and pinned him to the floor.

Sam flailed, more from surprise than anything, but when Mitch's hands were on his clothes, he stopped and helped him, sitting up and pulling his shirt over his body as Mitch tugged ruthlessly at his jeans and underwear until he was naked. Before Sam could get his T-shirt over his wrists, Mitch trapped it there, tangled and bunched, and he pushed Sam's hands high above his head. Something thick and rough slid around first one wrist, then the other, and when he tried to pull his arms back down, they were stuck fast. He heard the metal scrape of chain. *The cuffs,* he realized. *The cuffs with a chain between them.*

He was bound.

Mitch was on his knees now, and Sam watched, his erection thickening as Mitch fastened the nylon cuffs to his ankles and looped the rope though them. Lifting Sam's legs one at a time, Mitch snaked the cord through something in the ceiling before bringing it down to truss up Sam's other leg in the same manner. When he finished, Sam's ass barely touched the floor, and his legs were open in an obscene V, his bead-filled ass gaping beneath his swollen dick. *Too much,* he wanted to cry, but that was the fear talking. Lust rose, higher and faster than the fear, and he heard his own confession from the pickup echoing in his ears.

It's okay to do this, to be this slutty, Sam told himself, *if Mitch wants it too.*

Mitch stood, surveyed his work, then looked at Sam. His gaze was full of question. But there was lust, too, and want. He enjoyed what he'd done to Sam. He liked the idea of what was coming. He didn't think Sam was a dirty whore.

He thought Sam was a *beautiful* whore.

"Please." Sam strained against his bonds with a terrible sort of pleasure. "*Please.*"

"Please what?"

Sam struggled, thrusting his hips into the air. "Please do something to me."

"Something slutty?"

"*Yes.*" Sam's eyes stayed on Mitch's waist.

Mitch's hand slid over his own groin. "Give me an

example."

Sam licked his lips. "Take off your pants, and put your cock in me. Please."

"Where in you, Sam?"

Sam shuddered. "In my mouth."

Mitch unbuckled, unfastened, and undressed. Sam's mouth went dry as Mitch straddled him, knelt, and nudged his penis past Sam's lips.

Sam engulfed it, moaning as he sucked, opening his throat, watching the rough tuft of blond hair until he had to close his eyes because his face was buried in it. When Mitch pulled Sam's head back, Sam held still, letting Mitch thrust inside him, almost choking. Mitch grunted and gasped, and then he simply fucked Sam's mouth mercilessly, taking away Sam's breath until Mitch spent himself inside. When Mitch withdrew, Sam coughed and winced around his tender jaw as he struggled to swallow Mitch's load.

Mitch knelt beside him and took Sam's face in his hands.

"I don't want to go too far with you." Mitch stared down into Sam's eyes with a fear greater than anything Sam had felt in the bar. "I don't want to hurt you. I don't want—"

To lose you. Sam could hear the unspoken words, could see them in Mitch's eyes, even in the dark. Sam nuzzled his hand.

"I want to go too far," Sam whispered. "With you."

Mitch caught Sam's mouth, teasing him into a kiss. Sam shut his eyes as Mitch kissed and licked at the spunk around his mouth, his lips, and then stole inside, kissing him deeply.

After breaking the kiss, Mitch moved to Sam's exposed anus, and Sam watched as Mitch tugged at the cord. Sam fought and bucked and struggled against his bonds as Mitch removed the beads, one by one, and when they were all out, he gasped as Mitch pushed his finger inside, sawing slowly in and out of him.

"You're so hot inside, Sunshine. So hot and tight." Mitch lifted Sam's ass, spreading his cheeks wide, enjoying the view. He played with Sam awhile, opening and closing him, fingering him until Sam bucked and begged and pleaded to be fucked.

Mitch took out the dildo Sam had chosen, smeared it with lube, and pushed it inside of Sam with one stroke, burying it to the base. Sam arched and shut his eyes, waiting for the thrust. But Mitch only teased him with it, turning it around inside him, spinning it, until Sam nearly wept with need. Mitch only smiled, saying nothing, and continued his torture.

Eventually Mitch withdrew the dildo, untied Sam's restraints, and carried him to the bed. Sam kissed him, trying to urge him into engagement, but Mitch only turned Sam around, pressing his own erection into Sam's back as he drew Sam to his chest. He didn't touch Sam's penis, but he stroked his chest instead, and his nipples, and his neck.

Sam was so aroused he ached. He strained against Mitch, making pleading sounds, but Mitch quieted him with kisses and more tender strokes. "Give me a minute,

Sunshine."

Sam didn't want a minute. "*Mitch.*" He bucked.

Mitch's hand closed tight around the base of Sam's shaft, not hurting him, but it was the cock ring all over again. "A minute, Sunshine."

Sam stilled as best he could and gave him one.

Mitch kept his hand on Sam's dick, but once Sam had calmed, Mitch briefly caught his mouth, then simply held him. Despite Sam's arousal, the embrace was so sweet, so peaceful, that Sam calmed. It was so good to be held, such a strange juxtaposition to the hardcore scene they'd just finished. Sam felt soft inside, so soft it was almost dangerous. *I would do anything for him. Anything.*

He stilled a little more, eager but also apprehensive to see what *anything* would turn out to be.

Something brushed his ass, and Sam startled. When he realized it was a cold finger-full of lube, Sam shifted and opened for Mitch in anticipation of what was to come. Mitch nipped at Sam's shoulder and hip, and Sam, wordless and half-hypnotized, lifted his ass into the air as he pressed his face into the pillow.

Something slid beneath his belly. *The strap*, he realized, and let his body soften, opening to Mitch as he thrust. It was a silent, wicked fucking, slow and thorough, Mitch grinding his hips against Sam, nudging his thighs wide. He pulled Sam tight to his pelvis with the strap, until Sam couldn't move at all, and his cries went higher and higher as Mitch's cock went deeper inside him.

"What's too far now, Sam?" Mitch thrust roughly as he spoke. "What do you need?"

"Come inside me." Sam gripped the sheets. "*Now, Mitch. I want—almost hurt—deeper—oh.*"

His cries poured out on a sigh, and he nearly came, but Mitch came first, shuddering as he pushed into Sam. When he let go, Sam fell to the bed, and Mitch collapsed on top of him. Before Sam could recover, Mitch rolled them over, slipped the strap around Sam's leg, put the handles in one hand and yanked Sam's legs apart.

He encouraged Sam to stroke himself, then tucked his other leg to the side, opening him until Sam felt himself gape. Mitch tickled at Sam's anus. Then he hauled back and slapped it.

The sound rang out through the cab, and Sam cried out as Mitch slapped him again and again. The pain shot through Sam but the pleasure did too, until he bucked and wanked and grunted as he watched Mitch spank his tender hole. When Sam tensed, Mitch jammed his finger deep, caught his mouth and kissed him as he came.

Was it the alcohol making Sam spiral so high, so far, so totally beyond any control he'd ever known? Was the buzzing inside him because he was, in all honesty, quite drunk? Was that why he'd behaved with so much abandon? Was that why he'd not only let Mitch use him this way but encouraged him?

Or was this what he truly wanted, and Mitch had only brought it out of him?

Mitch lowered them to the bed and drew Sam to him, spunk and all. "We'll buy new sheets tomorrow." Mitch kissed him, and Sam shut his eyes, shut off his thoughts, and sank into those loving arms.

CHAPTER FOURTEEN

I T HAD BEEN a wonderful, incredible night, but when Sam woke the next morning, he immediately wished he were dead.

Mitch wasn't in the bed beside him, but Sam could hear him moving around. Every scrape and shuffle echoed in his aching head, and he groaned, falling back into the pillow.

"Need the toilet?" Mitch called, and Sam grunted in reply.

Mitch pointed at the mini kitchen. "Water's in the fridge. Aspirin's in the cupboard. I gotta go get this rig loaded." He came close to the bed and touched Sam's hair. "You gonna be okay?"

Sam tried to nod, but it hurt too much. He gave Mitch a thumbs-up instead, rolled over into the pillow and did his best to go to sleep.

This proved impossible, however, as every time he drifted off there would be another bump and scrape from things being loaded into the trailer. Eventually he gave up and made a twenty-minute project of getting himself to the toilet, where he emptied first one end and then the other. He rested for some time with his head on the lid before cleaning up both the room and himself with a shower. By the time he got dried and dressed, Mitch was peeking his head through the curtain.

"You gonna be able to ride okay?" he asked, when he got a good look at Sam's green face. Sam nodded carefully. "Good, because we're leaving in ten minutes. You need us to stop anywhere on the way out? Need anything? Something to eat? Peppermint, maybe?"

Sam considered for a minute. "Gum?"

"Can do." His eyes flickered over the bed. "And spare sheets."

Sam blushed, remembering the crust of semen he'd washed off himself in the shower, remembering how it got there.

Mitch cleared his throat. "Any regrets, now that it's morning?"

Flashes of touches, glances and sensations played across Sam's mental screen. "Only the alcohol."

Mitch studied him a moment. Then he nodded, appearing satisfied. "Get ready to roll then, Sunshine."

They were on the road in less than ten minutes, in fact, though they stopped almost immediately at a strip mall along the way where Mitch ducked into a budget store and came out with several changes of sheets, four packets of gum, Pepto-Bismol, and two Starbucks cups. Sam held up his hands at the cup Mitch pushed at him, until Mitch showed him the tea bag hanging from the side.

"Peppermint." He set it in the holder nearest Sam's seat and pointed to the bag on the floor between them.

"There's peppermint candy, too, in there with your gum. In case."

"You're a believer in peppermint, I take it." Sam sipped the tea, feeling a bit steadier after.

Mitch shrugged as he pulled his seat belt across his body. "Gives me comfort, I guess. My mom gave it to me when I was little. Seemed it fixed about anything."

Sam rooted the sack of hard candy out of the bag. "It was spearmint with my mom. She didn't care for peppermint."

"Oh." Mitch seemed disappointed. "You should have said—I would have gotten that instead."

"No—I hate it, especially now. The smell of spearmint Life Savers makes me think of my mom lying there rasping in her bed."

Mitch grimaced. "No spearmint, then."

Sam unwrapped a piece of candy and popped it in his mouth. He offered a piece to Mitch, who declined.

"How old were you again?" Mitch asked. "When your mom passed? Seventeen, you said? So you were out of school?"

"I was a senior in high school, but between her being sick and my being so upset after, I dropped out and started over the next fall, which was why I didn't start college until I was twenty." He propped his feet on the dash and slouched a little in his chair, looking out the window as the interstate led them into the foothills. They'd driven for half an hour, but they still were quite some distance away from the mountains. "My aunt put me in counseling, which upset me at the time, but I'm glad for it now. I should probably go back. Sometimes I'm still angry Mom had to die." He ran his finger down the glass of the window. "She fought MS almost my whole life, and then cancer killed her. It felt like God cheated. And that he was really fucking mean."

Sam retreated into silence, sipping his tea and sucking his candy as they wound into the foothills at last, distracted by how much they seemed like mountains.

"My mom ran off when I was eight," Mitch said, out of nowhere. Sam looked at him, surprised, but Mitch kept his eyes on the road, except when he was reaching for his coffee, and even then he only glanced at the console. "Went off with some guy she met at a bar. She puts it better now, said Dad hit her, but I didn't know it then. I only knew she was gone."

"Jesus. *Eight*?" Sam tried to remember himself at eight, and couldn't. The only thing he could think of was crushing on David Duchovny while his mom watched *The X-Files*. He hadn't worked out at eight that the tickle in his tummy when Mulder took off his shirt was a sexual response, but it didn't stop him from holding his penis tight in his bed as he replayed the scenes in his mind. Other than this, though, he remembered eight years old as innocent and happy. Hell, he'd still believed in Santa, at eight. "That's…young."

"Fucked me up a bit, I'll admit. Though I don't remember being sad. Just hollow and confused. Was sure it was something I'd done, but she'd always been so nice to me, like she really loved me." He rubbed at his mouth. "Don't know why I said all that."

"No." Sam shifted in his seat to better look at Mitch. "I mean—I don't know. It feels good, talking about my mom, and I like hearing about your past too." He realized it might not be the same for Mitch and faltered. "But if you'd rather—"

"No, I want to hear about your mom. I want to hear any stories about you. It's just, not many of my stories are good."

"Oh. Well, if you don't—"

"—but I don't mind telling—" Mitch said at the same time. He stopped and tossed Sam a rueful smile. "If you don't mind listening."

"I enjoy listening. To whatever you want to tell me."

They made their way through the foothills, taking turns sharing stories from their lives.

"My mom loved irises." Sam slouched down in his seat and angled himself sideways so he could watch the mountains rising around the road. "She thought they were the most beautiful flowers, but my aunt hates them. Says they don't bloom long enough and leave boring foliage. Well, all my mom ever wanted was a garden full of irises, but first we lived in a trailer next to guys who always trampled the tiny patch of green we had, and then we lived with Aunt Delia and Uncle Norm. So Mom never had her garden of irises."

Mitch frowned. "That's a bummer."

Sam held up a finger. "I did the next best thing, though. The last year she was alive, I made her a mini one. I took a big plastic tub, those storage bins, you know? I filled one with dirt and iris rhizomes in the fall, watered it and prayed like hell until spring. I kept it behind the garage so my aunt wouldn't find it, and by some miracle the flowers came up. So I dragged the tub over to the house and parked it under my mom's window so she could watch them bloom."

This made Mitch laugh. "Awesome."

Sam grinned. "It was. She *loved* it. She cried and clapped her hands. She spent the whole month they bloomed, I swear, sitting at the window and looking at her flowers. My aunt went nuts, because they were eight or ten different colors, and here was this damn Rubbermaid in the middle of her yard, and the neighbors asked about it, and she didn't know what to say without making herself look bad. Oh, God, she hated it. She hated *me* for it. But she left the tub until the blooms went away, and she promised Mom she'd plant them in a real garden in the fall."

"Did she?"

Sam shook his head. "Mom was too sick to notice anything by then. I was going to plant the tub again anyway, but she—" Sam stopped and took a drink of tea. "I had some at her funeral, and they burned them up with her when they cremated her."

"That's the container you have in your pack, right? What you let go at the Platte River? That was sweet. You gonna do it the whole way?"

"I don't know. I hadn't thought about it. I had those in my hand because I spilled them and was cleaning up when you called me out. It seemed right, though."

"Well, if you ever want to stop, say the word. I'll

keep my eye out for irises, for sure."

The offer made Sam feel warm and eased some of the sadness speaking about the irises had brought up. "Thanks."

Mitch cleared his throat. "So. Your uncle, was he sort of your dad? Didn't you say you don't know your real dad at all?"

"No idea who my dad is. I think my aunt might know, but she won't tell me. But no, Uncle Norm really isn't the dad type. Anyway, he's not the dad I'd have wanted. He sat there reading the paper until they got high-speed, and he's been on the computer ever since. Never asked about anything I was doing, only told me to pass the potatoes."

Mitch grunted, but it was commentary enough.

Sam picked at the seam of his jeans. "I always wanted a dad like Emma's. God, he took her everywhere. Still does. They go on *dates*, they call them. They head out together every week, and if money is tight, they take a walk. When she was a kid, he went with her to every Disney movie, every ball game. She rolls her eyes at that now, but I watched it growing up and ached. It wasn't what they did together. It was the way he looked at her, as if everything she did was beautiful and amazing."

Sam stopped picking at his jeans and rubbed his hands over them instead. "It's not that my mom didn't pay attention to me, or love me, or tell me I was great. And I don't feel I was cheated because I didn't have a dad. Okay, I do a little, but it's deeper. Like, it would have been nice to have a guy to explain a wet dream.

Somebody who actually knew." He sighed. "I don't know."

They drove a few miles in silence. They were heading into the mountains proper now, always traveling on an incline, and Sam started to wonder if they would drive on a slope all the way to Cortez. Mitch had downshifted and went a lot slower now, and Old Blue worked harder. A few cars languished by the side of the road, steam billowing from beneath their hoods. Sam glanced at Old Blue's nose worriedly, but the semi seemed fine, so far.

"My dad wasn't Emma's dad." Mitch kept his eyes firmly on the road. "Or even your uncle. Mine was…pretty nasty."

Sam didn't know what to say to this, so he waited, watching as Mitch tapped his thumbs on the wheel.

Finally, Mitch reached for his Winstons. "Hit me a lot, especially after my mom left. But mostly he was good at making me feel like shit. Called me names— loved to call me faggot, which scared the shit out of me because I was starting to think maybe I was one, and I thought, shit, how does he know? So I worked damn hard not to be a faggot, which, to my shame, means I was terrible mean to boys I thought were gay."

Sam had no idea what to say, so he said nothing.

Mitch put a cigarette between his lips. "There was this one guy. God, he was so sweet and shy. I wanted to kiss him and touch him. Scared the piss out of me, so I bullied him. I was such an ass to him. I think he dropped out of school because of me. I tried to find him later, when we were adults, but I couldn't." He lit the cigarette and took a long drag. "Pretty sure if I die and try to get to heaven, poor Gary Ingall will be standing in front of the gate, and I won't be able to go in for my shame." He smoked for a minute. "But all I knew was I had to make sure I didn't drive my dad away too because he was all I had left. Eventually I grew enough brain cells to figure out he wasn't worth killing myself over."

Sam let this swim in his head and realized, had he and Mitch gone to high school together, Sam would have been the Gary Ingall. The thought was sobering. But they couldn't have gone to school at the same time. "Thirty, you said you were?"

"Thirty-three." Mitch grimaced. "Old man."

"That isn't old." Though it was, Sam acknowledged, a significant difference to his age of twenty-one.

"Dead and buried in gay years." Mitch patted his stomach and looked down at it in disgust. "Old, flabby, and out to pasture. Still don't know how the hell I caught you. You should have run off with Craig from last night. Or somebody even better."

Sam balked. "I'm not running off with a guy I met for two hours in a bar."

"But the trucker from the alley is fine, is he?" When Sam stammered, too embarrassed to reply properly, Mitch sighed, put his cigarette into—God, there it was—a Butt Bucket, and reached for another. "Sorry, Sunshine. I don't know to quit when I'm ahead."

But he'd put the bee in Sam's bonnet, as his mother

would say, and Sam sat for a few minutes trying to work out why it was okay to run off with Mitch but why he didn't want to play around with Craig outside of the bar. "I wouldn't have run off with you that day in the alley. It was so…unexpected. Then you returned my phone. I mean, it was nice. Really nice. You seem safe all around. But not in a boring way. And you bought me dinner, and—and—" His face was so red it was hot. He tucked his legs against his chest. "Oh, I don't know."

Mitch studied him thoughtfully, as much as he could while still driving. "So it wasn't about how I look at all? I could have been bald and fat?"

"Well—I guess—I don't know, honestly." How did they get on this subject? How did he get out of it? "I *do* enjoy how you look." *Big and strong.* "I—I guess it's more how you look at *me* that attracts me." He put his hands on his cheeks. They were searing. Sam tried to think of how to deflect this conversation. "What about you? What attracted you to me?"

Mitch drew on his cigarette before answering. "The way you were dancing."

"Dancing? I wasn't—" Sam stopped, remembering how he'd boogied down as he tossed the boxes into the dumpster. He blushed anew. "You liked *that*?"

"I did." Mitch sounded serious. "You were so damn happy. And cute, sure, but mostly happy. And then you looked at me, and I could tell you wanted me—that glowing, happy, handsome guy wanted *me*." He shook his head before drawing on his cigarette. "I didn't stand a chance."

Sam reveled in this for a moment, not quite knowing what to say. He remembered another of Mitch's comments, and it cast a pallor Sam couldn't ignore. "You said I reminded you of someone. Is it that guy you traveled with?" Mitch's smile predictably faded, but Sam didn't let himself back down. He wanted to know. "Did he make you happy too?"

Mitch was quiet for a few seconds. "Yeah. But in a different way, Sunshine."

Tell me about him, Sam thought but couldn't say, because he wasn't sure he was ready to hear. He was too afraid he'd find out he could never keep up. But it killed him, not knowing about this other guy. There was no denying he still affected Mitch. Sam only had to hint at him, and Mitch shut down.

Sam gave up. "Sorry." He slumped in his seat. "I shouldn't have brought it up."

"Don't worry about it," Mitch said, but he still sounded gruff to Sam.

"We can talk about something else." Sam's cheeks heated. "Or you can stop and get me a bucket of ice to stick my head in."

"Sure thing." Mitch started to angle the truck toward a small gas station on the side of the road.

Sam sat bolt upright in his seat. "I was kidding!"

Mitch grinned. "Getting diesel, honey." He put out his second cigarette and nodded at the building. "You want anything to eat, now that your stomach is settled a bit? This place makes decent breakfast burritos. I could grab you one. Or do you want to come in and poke your head around?"

Mitch tensed even as he made the offer, and Sam remembered the last truck stop. But his legs were getting sore from sitting. "I'll come."

They were in a sort of basin surrounded by mountains, and the gas station, while clearly catering to truckers, was tiny when compared to the behemoths littering I-80. It was also much, much colder up here than in Denver, and Sam hurried inside to escape the wind. He used the restroom then met Mitch at a small counter where a polite woman served them breakfast burritos. She gave them no dirty looks whatsoever. Sam stuffed his burrito with sausage, egg, and green pepper, whereas Mitch filled his with beans, meat, jalapenos, and salsa, splashing hot sauce on top. They ate standing at the counter, Mitch surveying the magazines and notices.

A few truckers did give them odd glances, but Sam decided not to care. Mitch, he could see, did care, and hurried through the rest of his food.

"I gotta give Blue a systems check before we head on." Mitch started toward the semi. "You want to stretch your legs some more, or hang out inside?"

Sam, already huddled against the wind, nodded to the cab. "I'll go back to Blue."

Was it Sam's imagination, or did Mitch seem relieved? "TV might work, but the satellite's iffy up here." He glanced sidelong at Sam. "Course, there's quite a video selection."

"I could watch the twink video, sort of preview it

and see if they're kinky enough for you."

"You do that." Mitch slid up beside him and took a good, hard hold of Sam's ass. "Be sure to give me a full report."

Sam's blood hummed from the exchange when he got in the truck, but he didn't break out the porn. Instead he unplugged his phone, tucked himself into the corner of the bed, and tried to find the internet.

His signal was horrible, and there was no 3G, so he gave up reading his email and called Emma.

"Thank God," she said when she answered. "So, are you coming home?"

Sam watched out the window as Mitch checked dipsticks and cables. "No." He felt easier as the rightness of his answer permeated him.

"What? You're not coming home *ever*?"

"I'm not coming home *yet*." Sam toyed with the cord to the headphones. "I'll come back eventually, Emma. I'm fine." Mitch caught his eye and smiled, and Sam waved. "In fact, I'm really good."

"You do sound better," Emma acknowledged reluctantly. "God knows you deserve a vacation. Do you need money? Because I have some—"

"I don't need money. I'm okay. I'm fine."

"You have to text me every day. If anything goes wrong, *anything*—"

"If anything goes wrong, I'll leave him, and I'll call you first."

"Okay then." Emma sounded slightly mollified. "Take care of yourself, Sam, please. It's so lonely without you here."

It felt good to hear. "You should go ask Steve to console you. Tell him how worried you are about me."

"Actually, he's the one who told me something happened with Delia. He called me. Totally blew me out of the water. He's pissed at her too. We talked for an hour. He was like a different person. I wish he would let go in other, more sexual ways. I want the man in my goddamned bed."

Sam remembered how cautious Steve always was, how he'd kept himself quiet while Delia shouted, but he also thought of how he'd called Em. "Maybe you should call him more."

"I can't have sex with him over the phone," Emma snapped.

"You might be surprised. Think of it as foreplay."

"Sure, I could tell him he's sexy and that I want to grab his ass." Emma sighed. "I *wish* I could. But then he'd think I'm a whore. Maybe that's it. Maybe he's heard I'm easy."

God, did they *all* suffer from this? "I think if he thought you were easy, he'd be in your pants already. I know he's not gay, so that's out. I can't think of any other reason for a guy to say no to you."

Emma blew him a kiss. "Miss you, Sam."

Sam blew one back. "I miss you too, Em."

"Then come home."

"I will," he promised. "Just not yet."

Once he hung up, he sat in the seat awhile, staring at the mountains. He played a few games, then gave up and watched the sky, thinking. The mountains were snowcapped, rugged and beautiful. Sam felt quiet, sated, and safe.

When the silence pressed on him, he scrolled through his music, finally selecting a mellow playlist that still had some Kylie on it. He realized they'd driven all the way from Denver in total silence, except for their talking. He couldn't think of the last time he'd been so happy *not* listening to music, especially in a car. He and Mitch weren't awkward with each other anymore, either.

Things were looking up.

Mitch climbed into the cab, rubbing his hands on a rag. He nodded at Sam as he saw him hooking the iPhone up to the stereo. "Ready to go?"

"Ready." Sam settled in, the music wrapping around them as Mitch pulled Old Blue onto the highway and into the mountains once again.

CHAPTER FIFTEEN

THE ROAD THROUGH the mountains was absolutely beautiful.

Mitch had warned it would take all day to get to Cortez, but Sam never loved a long drive more in his life. He snapped several pictures and even took a panoramic photo, but he knew none of the images came close to capturing what he saw with his own eyes. It was as if the world were smaller and bigger at once: the mountains made everything seem crowded close, but the sky expanded bigger than he'd ever seen it above his head. The towns they passed were charming, small and tucked like spare change into whatever corners they could fit. There were ranches, real honest-to-God *ranches*, with cowboys and everything. Wide, clear, rushing streams followed the road, their waters nothing like the mucky, muddy rivers back home. There were no irises, but Mitch did stop beside a large patch of columbine, which Sam was sure his mother would have loved. He dusted them liberally with her ashes.

The one thing Sam could have lived without were the winding roads.

Most of the time the highway was simply bendy, but

as the day wore on and they snaked deeper into the mountains, the roads became narrower and higher against the sides of the peaks they climbed. Mitch pointed out the tree line to Sam, the place so high in elevation not even the evergreens could survive. Apparently the atmosphere was too thin. Sam was impressed by this, but in an increasingly less favorable way as that line crept closer to his own elevation.

"*We're* okay, right?" He stared worriedly up at the bare rock and snow. "I mean—we can breathe long enough to pass through?"

"Don't worry, Sunshine. There will be plenty of air."

Sam tried to take reassurance in Mitch's confidence, and he told himself that *obviously* they would not build a road so high travelers couldn't breathe, but he found he nurtured a quiet panic the higher they went. They were in a national forest now, and while there were still homes and towns, they were fewer and farther between.

Then they passed a sign reading, WOLF CREEK PASS AHEAD: TRUCKERS CHECK YOUR BRAKES.

Sam turned to Mitch in alarm. "The sign—Did we—?"

"Did my brake check in Del Norte." Mitch caught the look on Sam's face, and his expression changed to surprise. "Sam—honey, are you okay?"

"Fine." Sam tightened his fingers against his armrest.

But if he'd thought the road was winding before, he soon realized he hadn't seen anything until now.

The road *climbed* the mountain, weaving back and

forth like a ribbon along the side of a cake. It had no rail. Oh, sometimes there was a little metal suggestion, but mostly a sheer edge led abruptly into hell below. Rocks dotted the side of the road, several of them boulders. One was as tall as Old Blue. Signs advised motorists in all caps to WATCH FOR FALLING ROCK.

Mitch drove slowly now, keeping all his focus on the road and his driving as he shifted gears and watched gauges. They climbed higher and higher, weaving first one way and back the next, sometimes hugging the side of the mountain, sometimes the edge. As they went higher, Old Blue went slower, and slower and slower. Sam looked out the window and saw not only the tree line a short walk up the side of the peak, but snow on the ground all the way up through the brush.

"Here's the top." Mitch started shifting again, and Sam saw the same slope they had climbed open up in reverse before them, felt the weight of the rig pushing them from behind. As Mitch fought it off with gears and feet, Sam sank into cold, paralyzing terror.

Was that a burning smell?

Was that smell the *brakes*?

Sam swallowed hard, but his throat was almost too thick and tight to do so.

There was a moment of strange, white silence and even whiter light, and then Sam heard a voice as if from far away. It became louder and sharper, and suddenly he was back in Old Blue, and they were pitching slowly down a mountain road, Mitch shouting at him.

"*Sam.* Jesus—Sam, are you okay?"

Sam pushed some words out of his throat. "Mitch—I—" Terror swept him up, and he couldn't say anything more.

Mitch shifted his gear, and the grinding sent Sam into shivers. "Sam, are you hurt, or are you scared?"

Sam stuttered through a few attempts of saying he was scared, then gave up on the letter S and regrouped. "Not h-h-hurt."

Even through his terror Sam could see Mitch's body sag in relief. "Okay, Sam, relax. I have done this road more times than I can count. Sunshine, I have done the Red Mountain Pass in winter—this is a fucking cakewalk by comparison."

Sam tried to nod, not able to process what Mitch was saying but liking the sound of his voice. He tried shutting his eyes, but it was too easy to imagine the truck sliding off the edge. He fixed his gaze on the ceiling, but he could see the side of the mountain rushing by in his peripheral vision. Looking straight on was out, because that was what had sent him into hysterics in the first place.

"Stay with me, Sam," Mitch called, and Sam turned toward him as if he were a beacon. He felt calmer instantly, partly because it was Mitch, strong and sure and solid, but also because while the view beyond him was the valley, it was the higher part, and it wasn't swooping by but drifting. Sam could pretend they weren't separated from death by little more than the pressure applied by Mitch's feet.

Sam relaxed a fraction. "I'm sorry."

"You should have told me you were scared." Mitch remained focused on the road, but he glanced at Sam when he could. "I could have explained it to you."

"I—" Sam swallowed the metallic tang of more fear. "I feel it pushing. The truck."

"It's a heavy load, and this is a steep grade. In a car it isn't such a big deal, but I'm kind of a short train. I can't stop suddenly. So I have to keep Blue going nice and slow and steady. But I know how, Sunshine. There isn't much in the world I'm truly good at, but this I will confidently tell you I am."

To prove his trust, Sam took another look at the road. The winding parts were getting a little longer, but strange gravel ramps occasionally ran up the side of the hill, sometimes with huge yellow barrels at the end. "What are those?"

"Runaway truck ramps. *Don't go green on me, Sam.* They're for safety. In case of emergency."

In case the brakes fail. Sam turned away from the road and back to Mitch. "Have you ever had to use one?"

"Once," Mitch admitted. "On one of my first mountain runs. Didn't do a brake check, and didn't quite get the idea of how hard I had to work to keep my rig under control. But never again. Not one time since. Rigs go over the Continental Divide on all manner of passes, all day every day. You might as well worry about being hit on I-80 in Nebraska. Possible, but not probable, and it's a risk you take along the way."

Sam kept his eyes on Mitch.

Mitch remained calm and steady. "Don't think about it. Think about something else."

"Okay." Sam tried. But nothing came to mind.

"Ask me questions. Anything."

Sam tried to think of something. "What's the kitty litter for?"

"Kitty litter?" Mitch frowned and then laughed. "Oh, in the cupboard. For winter, on the ice, if I get stuck."

Sam's hands tightened on his seat. "There's snow now."

"It's okay." Mitch kept gentling him, his voice soothing and easy. "It's okay, Sunshine. I swear. Forget the questions. Tell me more about your mom. Tell me what she'd tell you right now, if she knew you were taking your first trip west after all these years."

Sam tried to imagine his mother, sitting in her chair, listening. "She'd think it was great." His gaze fell to Mitch's arms and legs, not the window. "She'd say, good for you, Sammy."

"Hope she wouldn't be too upset by your escort."

Sam smiled. "She'd like you."

"Were you out to your mom?"

"Oh yeah. She was in PFLAG and everything, until she got cancer." The memory warmed Sam. "I told her when I was ten, not realizing what I was doing at the time. I was staring at a boy on the playground, and Mom wheeled over. I remember being so caught up in him, like it was a spell, and then Mom asked if he'd hit me or made fun of me, and I was so shocked she'd think such a thing that I said, 'No, Mom—I wish I could kiss him.'"

"And what did your mom say?"

"Nothing, for about ten minutes. Then she took me to the store and had me pick out my favorite ice cream and anything I wanted for sundaes, which was awesome because that *never* happened. I always had to pick one thing and only the brand on sale. So I picked *everything*. I made the most disgusting sundae ever, with four kinds of ice cream and five kinds of sauce and ten cherries, and ate it with a huge whipped-cream grin as Mom sat across from me at the kitchen table and asked me if I thought about kissing boys a lot, while she ate my sundae along with me."

It was good, talking about his mom. Sam smiled as he went on. "I was a little nervous, but then she passed me more fudge, which somehow made it okay, so I said, yeah, actually, a lot. She asked if I wanted to kiss girls too. She seemed so calm, and so I told her, no, only boys. She asked what I enjoyed most about boys. That threw me, until she said her favorites were big, strong men—what about me? I didn't know, so I said I liked that too, but I remember feeling good, like it was okay."

Sam relived that moment, the sun filtering through the dusty curtains of the trailer, his mom hunched over the Formica table, smiling as they ate together. "When we finished our first sundaes we had seconds, these slightly more sane. She asked if other boys at school knew I wanted to kiss them. I said, no, and she told me that was fine, but when I wanted to let people know how I felt, to tell her, and she'd be happy to help me figure out what might be the best way. So we finished our ice cream, and when I went to bed, I lay there a long time, looking up at the ceiling. Finally I thought, well, I guess I'm gay. Then I went to bed."

When Sam finished, Mitch glanced at him, his expression warm and happy. "I like your mom."

Sam smiled. "Me too."

Mitch nodded at the road. "We're down, Sunshine."

Sure enough, the road had evened out into a regular decline now, and ahead Sam saw the edges of a town. He let out a breath and sagged into his seat as Mitch drove on.

When he pulled off at the side of the road, though, near a small store, Sam remembered how stupid he had been up on the pass, and when Mitch unbuckled and stepped over the console toward the curtain, Sam stood as well and held out his hands.

"Mitch, I'm so sorry," he began but lost the rest of his apology as Mitch took Sam's face in his hands, brought his mouth down, and kissed him.

Sam stilled, then melted, sliding his hands up until he found Mitch's shoulders. He hung on as Mitch opened his mouth over Sam's, and Sam answered the kiss with the same intensity of passion. Every thought, all his fear, and most of his brain cells fled at the touch of Mitch Tedsoe's tongue against his own. He made soft sounds in the back of his throat, and he kneaded at Mitch's shirt, digging for his skin. He pressed his body into Mitch's, feeling his heat, his strength, but his softness too. It was headier than anything Sam had ever known. Sam gave himself over to this wonderful new moment, marveling at himself, at how he seemed to know the right blend of aggression and submission, fueling the kiss, reveling in the way Mitch's hands stroked the sides of his face and the taste of his mouth.

When they broke apart, it was Mitch who pulled away, nuzzling Sam a bit until he let him go, and after one last squeeze of Sam's hand, Mitch parted the curtain and headed toward the bathroom. When he came back out, he was quiet, which suited Sam fine because he didn't know what to say.

They stopped that night in Durango, making a sort of camp in a parking lot near a warehouse Mitch knew the owner of, and after a picnic of microwave meals and snacks from the cupboard, Mitch settled in with a Bohemia and Sam with a bottle of mineral water. Lying twined together on the brand-new sheets, they broke in the porn.

They started, at Mitch's suggestion, with the truckers.

It was disappointing. The production was low budget, and they wasted too much time on bad plot. The sex was good but kind of stupid, as it mostly had a truck in the background. The truckers didn't look like any of the truckers Sam had seen at all. It was just some guy fucking another guy in front of a fender, or getting a blowjob, or doing really gross kissing that should have been hot, but all Sam could think of was the kiss after the pass, and these didn't compare. The only thing exciting about the movie was the way Mitch's hand skimmed over his hip.

"I clearly don't know how to pick porn." Sam craned his head back to look at Mitch. "Let's watch yours."

Mitch brushed a kiss across Sam's forehead and disentangled himself to comply with Sam's request.

Twink Kink was a lot better. It started with a young man with a slight build, smooth chest, and dark hair walking alone through a neighborhood at night. Two men appeared out of nowhere, kidnapped him, and took him to their sexual dungeon, where they stripped him naked and had their way with him, which after a few moments of protest, he completely enjoyed.

Sam did too. Not just because it was hot, but because their play mirrored what was on the screen. When the kidnappers ran their hands over the boy's body, Mitch's hands roved over Sam's chest and beneath his shirt to stroke his skin. When they attached nipple clamps to the boy—well, first, Sam flinched, and then he gasped as Mitch took first one of Sam's nipples and then the other between his fingers. When they tied the captive's hands above his head, Sam lifted his own without prompting and let Mitch pin them.

Soon he was naked and writhing in Mitch's arms, gasping and arching and crying out along with his counterpart on the screen. When the twink's torturers untied his hands and sent him to the floor, holding their engorged dicks before his mouth, Sam slid down Mitch's body and fought with the fastenings of his jeans.

In the end he managed to get them off and took Mitch in his mouth, not looking up so he could shut his eyes and imagine he was the twink in the video with two strangers forcing him to act on his own lust. He nursed on Mitch until he tugged at Sam's hair. Then he shifted to Mitch's balls, sucking one, then the other, and then took both into his mouth before pushing gently on Mitch's thighs and sliding down to his perineum. Then, riding along with the gasps of the boy on the screen, Sam went all the way down.

He'd never had his mouth on anyone here. He told himself not to be nervous or paranoid of germs. Still, he gave Mitch's anus one quick swipe with the sheets as a sort of consolation before pressing his thumbs along the edge of Mitch's opening. Bending his head, Sam pushed his tongue into Mitch's heat.

Mitch's reaction was heady. Even that small touch sent him shuddering and reaching for Sam's head. With a fistful of Sam's hair in his hand, Mitch pushed Sam's face right into his pucker. It felt good to have Mitch be the one panting and shaking after Sam had practically melted down the side of the mountain. Sam forgot his hesitation and gave over, laving first in a circle, then poking, then circling again before pulling Mitch's cheeks apart with his thumbs and inserting his tongue. *Warm.* It was hot and soft, and Mitch trembled around Sam's tongue, pushing it out, but when Sam spread him, it opened for him. All the while Sam worked, Mitch clutched at him and made frightening, beautiful sounds. Sam lost himself in poking and licking and pressing, until suddenly Mitch shouted and seized, and then he pulled Sam back up, through his legs, over his stomach, and toward his face.

He kissed Sam roughly, his hands trembling as he thrust his tongue into Sam's mouth with more force than Sam could prepare for. Then he withdrew and turned Sam over, pinning him to his sticky chest with one arm, his other hand reaching down to stroke Sam's dick. Up on the video screen, the twink was tied to a bench, and he grunted and gasped around two cocks, one in his mouth and one in his very red ass.

Mitch put Sam's hand on his own still-swollen dick, urging him into a masturbating rhythm before letting go and running his hand between them. As Sam continued to stroke himself and watch his counterpart get fucked on the screen, Mitch slipped a semen-slick finger inside him.

"*Oh.*" Sam lifted his legs and spread them when Mitch reclaimed control of his cock with one hand as the other moved inside of Sam.

He masturbated Sam slowly, a sort of punishment that went along with the torture the kidnappers gave the twink on the screen. They stopped fucking him and started flogging him, swatting him first with a paddle and then a crop. Sam thought the twink should be screaming, but he only moaned, clearly having a gay old horny time. He was eager, too, as they untied him and mounted him on one of the attackers who'd positioned himself on the floor. As Sam watched, the other man came up from behind him, and then—

"Oh God." Sam's chest heaved as he realized what was about to happen. "They're both—*both—at once?*"

"Would you want that, Sunshine?" Mitch twisted a finger inside of him. "Would you take two dicks at once?"

Sam shuddered. *No, no, no. It would hurt.* But he watched the agonized rapture on the twink's face onscreen and remembered how it felt to have Craig before him and Mitch behind him, and he shivered. "Yes."

The next thing Sam knew, he was on the floor, on his knees, cold lube sliding into his ass. He felt the dildo pushing at his entrance.

Lust flipped immediately over to fear. "Mitch, I—"

Mitch squeezed his hip in reassurance. "Not tonight. But something close."

The dildo drove into Sam, and he moaned. When Mitch pushed him down so he sat on his own legs in a fetal position, he went, turning his cheek to rest on the floor as Mitch took first one arm and then the other and tucked them beside Sam's feet. *Like the spreader.* Sam gasped as Mitch forced his legs apart, shoved two fingers in alongside the dildo and began to fuck him.

It wasn't a double fucking, but it was quite a lot, and it was different, and it was lewd and hot and very slutty. Sam made a symphony of incoherent noises before coming violently against the steel floor. He lay panting and twitching as Mitch gave him a few last pumps, withdrew, and gathered Sam in his arms, drawing him toward the bed.

The television was off, the cab was dark, and the night was silent around them as Mitch held Sam in his arms, cradling him to his chest, placing soft kisses on Sam's eyebrows. After a while he stilled, and then, with almost no warning, Mitch went to sleep.

Sam watched him in the shadows. He thought of all that had happened that day, of how he had woke hung over in Denver, driven into the mountains, panicked on the pass, and was now here, sated and safe in Mitch's arms. He felt so far from home, as if he were on another planet, except when he looked at Mitch's face. When he saw Mitch, he knew he was home.

His feelings swelled inside him, a joy and sorrow at once, a terror more intense than any mountain pass. Sam shut his eyes and placed a tender kiss in the center of Mitch's chest.

CHAPTER SIXTEEN

M ITCH, SAM WAS starting to realize, always woke early. He stirred at five, and by five thirty he'd dressed, eaten, made coffee in a pot Sam hadn't even known he'd had, and was trying to get the internet on his laptop.

"Stay in bed," he told Sam when he sat up.

Sam fell onto his pillow. "Checking your mail?"

"Looking for jobs. Trying to, anyway." He grimaced and shut the laptop. "Can't get a signal, though. No free or pay Wi-Fi. Only bad thing about the mountains."

Sam pointed at the front of the cab. "Get me my phone." He took it from Mitch, poked around a bit then handed it to him. "Slower than dial-up with no 3G, but it's internet."

"How do I use it?" Mitch asked, mystified, and Sam crawled to the floor, dragging the blanket with him as he leaned against Mitch and showed him.

Mitch was pleased. "Thanks, Sunshine." He ruffled Sam's hair and looped his arm around his shoulders, gently pinning him in place while he used the phone to surf.

Sam watched, groggy but comfortable. "Where are

we going today?"

"That's what I'm trying to suss out." He rubbed his thumb along Sam's naked shoulder absently as he waited for a page to load. "I thought somebody might have a load for Phoenix, but there's nothing." He frowned. "Just loads to Vegas."

"Oh?" Sam perked up.

Mitch continued to frown. "I'll find one somewhere else. If I take a load to Phoenix, I *know* I can get something to L.A. right off."

After several minutes of searching, Mitch swore. There was nothing to Phoenix. Only Vegas.

"We can make it quick, I guess." He rubbed his jaw. "It might be okay."

Sam tipped his head at Mitch. "Why don't you want to go to Vegas?"

Mitch pursed his lips. "Bad memories."

That wasn't all, Sam could tell. This was the same look he got when Sam said the wrong thing, or when they got too kinky. This was what always tied Mitch up inside. Suddenly, Sam knew. "It's him, isn't it? The guy you keep talking about. He's in Vegas."

Mitch pressed his lips tighter together. "Don't worry about it."

Sam tried not to. He slipped out of Mitch's hold and climbed to his knees, taking the sheet with him until he was at the bathroom, where he gave up and dropped it. He used the toilet, splashed water on his face, pausing to glance in the small mirror posted over the mini sink. He needed to shave—he actually had a tiny bit of beard. He stroked the whiskers, wondering if he had time to deal with them. He touched his chest too, rubbing at the few wiry hairs there, thinking of the smooth-skinned boy in the video.

He thought of the nameless, faceless man in Vegas who kept getting in his way.

Sam ran wet fingers through his hair, doing his best to tame the mess, and went out into the cab. He hesitated a moment, retrieved his sheet and went back to the bed, where he tried to gather enough courage to speak.

Eventually he did, and he headed back up to the front of the cab to deliver his announcement. "I want to go to Vegas."

Mitch glanced up at him, wary. "Why?"

Sam lifted his chin. "I want to meet him. This guy."

Mitch's expression didn't just shutter, it went cold. "No."

"Then tell me about him. Tell me what went so wrong. Tell me, so I don't do it too."

"You will *never* be like Randy."

A name. Sam latched on to it, a precious bit of treasure. "Tell me about him. Tell me about your past, Mitch. Tell me, please."

"No." Mitch rubbed at his cheeks. "Don't do this, Sam. Leave things be."

I can't. He keeps getting in the way. Or something did. Sam had to know. He had to understand.

But what would he find out?

Sam rose, taking his sheet with him, heading for the coffeepot, not because he wanted some but because he had to move. "I shouldn't have brought this up. It was a stupid idea."

He yelped when Mitch grabbed him, and the air went out of him as he came down into Mitch's lap. Mitch took his face in one hand, holding it in place as he regarded Sam with a stilted expression. He ran his thumb over Sam's cheekbone, but he didn't say anything.

Sam tried to turn away, but Mitch held him fast. "I'm sorry—" He stopped talking as Mitch kissed him. He melted immediately, opening for him, sliding his hand up his arm. But as quickly as it had begun, the kiss was over.

"I'll take you." Mitch stroked the side of Sam's face in a tender gesture that made Sam jump. He lowered his hand, chastised. "Try and keep an open mind, okay?"

Sam pulled back. "Open mind? About what?"

"Just generally open."

Sam pushed down a queasy sensation in his belly. "You're freaking me out, Mitch."

Mitch tweaked Sam's nose. "Good." He handed Sam his phone and climbed to his feet. "So. I'll call the place here in Durango that has a load, and we'll see what we see."

They ended up having to go to Cortez and backtrack to Durango, because instead of a load straight to Vegas, Mitch got one going via Flagstaff, and it was bigger, so they had to dump their Cortez load completely first. Sam was embarrassed when he found out Mitch had done this partly so Sam wouldn't have to go over the mountains again.

"I would have been able to handle it," Sam insisted.

"I don't want you to hate the mountains. Give your-self a few days to recover." Mitch shrugged. "Anyway, I thought you might want to see the Grand Canyon."

Sam sat up. "Seriously?"

"Has to be quick," Mitch warned, "and can't be at the main viewing areas. But if we come in from Camer-on, you can watch it open up, and hop out at one of the smaller points."

Trying to forget the awkwardness of Vegas, Sam focused on the wonder at hand. The Grand Canyon. He hadn't even considered that would be an option. Anticipation made him bouncy, distracting him until Mitch angled the rig toward the warehouse drive.

"I'll help you load." Sam undid his seat belt.

Mitch put out a hand to stay him. "You can't."

"Mitch, I'm a stock boy. I can lift things."

"It's regulation. Has to do with insurance and labor laws." Except Mitch looked guilty as he said it, and in that moment Sam was convinced Mitch kept him inside on purpose.

Hiding him.

Sam wished he hadn't thought of that. "Well—can I do anything to help in here?"

"Hang loose. I promise I won't be long."

Sam fell back in his seat, watching as Mitch climbed out and started talking to the manager or whatever you called the guy who ran the warehouse. Sam picked up his phone and scrolled through the archaically paced internet awhile before giving up and tossing his phone aside. He put some new coffee on. He ate a peanut butter sandwich. He picked up his phone again, sent a text to Em. He poked his head out, saw they were ready to load and decided to take a shower. Mitch had refilled it in Cortez and drained the toilet. Sam had tried to help with this too, but Mitch had sent him with a list and a wad of twenties to the grocery store.

I'm the little woman. Sam shut his eyes beneath the spray.

Keep an open mind.

Sam attempted to avoid thinking about what that might mean, but as he toweled his hair and slipped into his now not-very-clean jeans and his last clean shirt, it was difficult to think of anything else. Dramatic scenarios crept up like dandelions no matter what he did, and the more he tried to mow them down, the thicker they came back. It wasn't just this Randy guy. By the time Mitch finally came into the rig, Sam was a small and quiet wreck. He helped Mitch tidy things up and put the coffeepot away, but once they were on the road, he only lasted about twenty miles before his dark thoughts returned.

"Are you married?" Sam held his breath as he waited for the answer.

Mitch startled so bad he spilled his coffee. "What the fuck?" He replaced the cup in the holder and shook the liquid off his hand. "No, I'm not married."

Sam nodded tersely. That was the worst one. "Drug runner?"

Mitch gave him a long, strange look. "Sam?"

"I want to know what it is I'm supposed to keep an open mind about."

Mitch's posture eased at once, but not completely. "Jesus. You're barking up the wrong tree, Sunshine. And you watch too damn much TV."

"Then *what is it*? I'm going crazy."

Mitch didn't answer for almost a minute, opening and closing his mouth. He looked terrified. "Give me a little bit to figure out how to word it?"

"Okay." Sam settled into his seat to wait, but several miles went by, and Mitch didn't say anything. *He isn't planning to,* Sam realized, and felt frustrated, then angry, and then simply tired.

The landscape changed rapidly. They were still in the mountains, though the terrain was a lot more rugged, and the vegetation was starting to thin. Mitch pointed out some mountains in the distance and told Sam they hid the ruins of cliff-dwelling houses, and that there were in fact a lot of Native American artifacts in this area. "You can hike in a lot of the preserves."

"Have you ever?" Sam asked, but Mitch shook his head.

"Wouldn't mind, someday."

After this they lapsed back into silence.

They drove through the backside of some city—Sam lost track of where they were—and into road construction which made Mitch swear under his breath as he had to balance Old Blue on a narrow shoulder near a drop that wasn't very big, but still significant enough to make Sam feel a bit sick, and after a few miles when Mitch suggested he go lie down, Sam did. Though he didn't mean to, he slept, and when he woke, he came back to the front of the cab, looked out at the landscape and stopped short.

"What—what is this?"

"Desert. We've entered the Navajo Nation. You missed Four Corners while you napped, I hate to tell you."

"But there aren't any cactus, or anything. There's *nothing* here." Sam sank into his seat, wide-eyed and shaking his head. "It looks like a wasteland."

"Now you know why the government didn't mind giving it to the Navajo."

Sam couldn't stop staring. There was *nothing* around them. Nothing at all. Occasionally a sad, solitary trailer appeared far off near a crop of rock, no road from the highway leading to it, and often no car visible either. Even fueling stations were rare. All Sam saw was miles and miles of desert with the occasional rock formation. Sam almost wished for Wolf Creek Pass, which while terrifying, was at least beautiful and less lonely. He wondered if he had cell service out here, but he was afraid to check.

It was a two-lane road only, which meant they sometimes got caught behind slow vehicles. However, they were often the vehicle people backed up behind before passing on a straight, flat stretch.

"This isn't Arizona jurisdiction," Mitch said when Sam commented on it. "If we get picked up for speeding, it will be by Res cops. While I don't begrudge them their attitude, I don't want to feel the brunt of it. It'll add some time, but we won't find any trouble, either, if we go the limit."

Sam could hardly argue with that, but it did make for a long, barely bearable ride. Mitch only stopped once, and that was to use the bathroom and take a walk around the outside of the rig. He'd had a cigarette while he was out there, and he had another one back inside the truck. Once he put it out, he turned down the music.

Mitch kept his eyes on the road even though it was nothing but a straight line all the way to the horizon. "The thing is, I used to be a different kind of person. You saw a little of it in Denver, especially when we were at the bar."

Sam almost grinned. "Is this the sex stuff? Because—"

"Let me get this out." He reached for another cigarette and took his time to light it and inhale. "You don't seem to care so much that I'm older than you. But it matters, because in the years between when I was your age and now, I did a lot of stupid shit." He took another drag. "And I did a lot of it in Vegas."

With Randy, Sam added silently.

"If we don't run into anybody," Mitch went on, "it won't matter. But if we do—" He flattened his lips and tapped out some ash. "Hell. I knew I couldn't do this right."

"Mitch, I don't care—"

"Well, you should. Even if you don't, I do. I see how you look at me, Sam, and I know what you're doing, and it makes me feel like hell. Maybe that's why I'm different with you." Mitch took another drag, and his hand wasn't entirely steady. "You can't understand because you're so young. And don't tell me you're not that young. You are. I was pissy too when I was twenty and people told me I had a lot to learn. Then I hit twenty-seven and knew what they were talking about."

"I'm twenty-one." What was he doing that made Mitch feel like hell?

"Yeah. That's worse, because now you're legal in every way, so you think it's over: all you have to do now is crack the nut of the world, and it's yours."

How the hell did all this become about him, Sam wanted to know? He tried not to be angry, because that seemed to be what Mitch expected. It wasn't easy. "So tell me how I look at you that makes you so upset, and I'll stop."

"Like I hung the moon," Mitch said bitterly.

"How rude of me." Sam turned his face away. It was all too close to the bone, and it hurt, puncturing the perfect moment when Mitch had held him after the pass. He picked at his sleeve. "I suppose now you'll tell me I've made you into some fucked-up father image."

"Shit," Mitch murmured. "I knew I'd screw this up, which was why I didn't want to talk about it."

"Well, if you're going to think of me as some stupid kid, I wish you would have let me off in Denver, or never picked me up at all." Sam's chest hurt more with every beat of the conversation. "Though since you kept fucking me, *you're* the sick bastard." Unless he thought Sam was throwing himself at him. Sam drew his knees to his chest and buried his face in them.

"I don't think of you as some stupid kid." Mitch spoke more harshly than Sam had ever heard him speak. "But yeah, I am a sick bastard."

Sam was too overcome by his own emotions to know what to say. He felt guilty, and angry, and mostly confused. Nothing Mitch said made sense. It explained nothing whatsoever about why he was supposed to keep an open mind in Vegas, and it didn't tell him anything about this Randy.

The desert felt even wider, empty, and more desolate.

They stopped at a place that called itself a trading post, and Mitch fueled the rig again. He encouraged Sam to get out and walk around, and the place did seem interesting in a horribly kitschy tourist sort of way. But Sam only shook his head and stayed where he was.

"I'm not going to leave you here," Mitch said quietly.

"I know that," Sam shot back.

"Go on," Mitch urged him. "We got another hour before we get to the canyon. I'll meet you inside. I want to check things over, but I wouldn't mind poking around a bit too."

Sam went, but he didn't enjoy himself, even though it was the wonder of the truck stop mall on crack. He'd never seen so many souvenirs in one place, some of them tacky, some of them beautiful. There was a restaurant too, and somewhere apparently a hotel. They sold hats, mugs, Native American dolls, fudge, stuffed animals, magnetic rocks, and jewelry. It was wild, weird, and wonderful. Sam didn't care, because all he could think about was how things had gone so wrong with Mitch.

It was right about then Sam found a selection of beautiful blue-glass items. They were so delicate, so intricate. They were full of rainbows—little pots and vases and plates fashioned out of glass. He picked up a tiny chest, inspecting it more closely. *Mom would have loved this.*

Despair shafted him so fast Sam almost dropped the glass trinket on the floor. Replacing the chest with blurry vision, Sam went outside and sat on a bench to wait.

He startled when someone sat beside him, and his chest hurt as he realized he was almost upset it was Mitch.

"Here." Mitch handed him a package of foil. "It's a Navajo taco."

Sam started to say he wasn't hungry, but he smelled the meat and was immediately starving. He opened the foil and frowned. "It doesn't look anything like a taco."

"No," Mitch agreed, opening one of his own. "But it's good."

It was, Sam conceded, as he ate. It was also huge. He barely finished half of it. Even Mitch couldn't finish all of his.

"You can save it if you want," Mitch said, "but I'll warn you, they're not so great the second go-round. Bread gets all mushy."

Sam tossed the remainder of his away.

Mitch held out a small white box. "I got some fudge. You should try it."

"Not hungry." Sam headed to the truck. Mitch followed, and they walked in silence, Sam more miserable than ever. As he stepped onto the running board, a sharp wave of regret hit him, and he stopped.

"I need to go back inside." Without waiting for Mitch to respond, Sam all but ran to the trading post, heading toward the rainbow glass.

The chest was expensive, almost so much he had to forget it, but when he looked at it, all he could see was his mom. When he touched it, he swore he could feel her. It was probably his fancy, because after all these years of wishing, this was the closest he'd ever come to an after-death connection, and he knew he was emotional now and likely to invent things to comfort himself. Still, he would take what he could get. He kept the tears that threatened at bay, letting her wash over him, so grateful for it now. He knew even if it were twice as expensive, he'd be purchasing it. He picked it up, cradled it carefully, and headed to the register.

Mitch caught up with him on the way, and Sam stiffened when Mitch reached for his wallet.

"No," Sam said sharply, then forced himself to soften. "I'm getting this myself." And he did, using his credit card, consoling himself by pointing out he hadn't spent so much as a dime of his own money so far. Of course, if he left Mitch, that would soon change. He shut the thought down, watched the brilliant rainbow-filled blue glass disappear beneath the protective wrapping the clerk put it in, then carried it as if it were the most fragile of eggs all the way to the cab.

Once he was inside, Mitch took it from him. "I have a safe place for it, if you'll let me put it there."

Sam let him take it. They were quiet as they got on the road. They wound now deep into the Navajo Nation. After about half an hour, Mitch pointed off into the distance.

"That's the start of it. Watch the ravine."

Sam did, underwhelmed at first, but as he kept his eye on the crack in the earth and the miles continued to go by, it grew larger, and larger, and larger, until he was sitting forward in his seat, eyes wide.

"Keep watching," Mitch said.

The road changed, and as soon as there was forest, a sign announced they were in the Grand Canyon National Park. Mitch slowed at a station to pay a vehicle fee, and then they climbed a hill. The forest deepened, and Sam sat back, amazed.

The trees were tall, and beautiful, and so close to the road. He couldn't see the canyon anymore, but the trees were enough—they were the only thing to see, but as opposed to the desert, here Sam felt comforted and safe. He gasped in delight when Mitch slowed Old Blue and pointed to a huge elk walking away from them on the side of the road. Sam fumbled with his phone and tried to take a picture, but all he got was a closeup of the animal's ass.

The traffic was thick now, some cars pulling off to lookout points. Mitch stayed on the road until they were a ways in, at which point he pulled Old Blue into a parking lot and killed the engine.

Sam stared.

Mitch's hand brushed his. "Come on."

The Grand Canyon was beautiful. It was huge, it was—it was beautiful. There wasn't any other word. The rocks opened before him in layers of more colors than he could count or name, a whole world, and when Mitch indicated a small structure in the basin beside the river, Sam realized *how* far down those things were, and how big the canyon was, and he was amazed all over again.

Mitch motioned to him. "Come down to the rail and get a better look."

Sam went, but he grew cautious as he made his way down the rocky stairs to the railing, and once there, he didn't go up to it but hung back a little, holding his arms around himself as he took in the sight below.

Mitch came up beside him, and for a long time they stood there, drinking it in.

"I'm so sorry, Sunshine."

Sam said nothing because he didn't want to talk about it, not here, not now, maybe not ever.

Mitch put his hand on Sam's shoulder. "I fucked things up pretty good, and I'm sorry."

"I don't *want* you feeling sorry for me." Sam tried to

pull away.

Mitch held him fast. "I'm sorry for *me*." He caught Sam's chin and lifted it, but Sam kept his eyes down.

"Take me to Phoenix. I'll get a flight home from there."

"*Sam.*"

"Or Flagstaff," he amended hurriedly. "I'll get a bus or something."

Mitch grabbed Sam's face with his whole hand and tipped it up hard. "I'm not leaving you anywhere." Sam flinched, and Mitch softened, but he still held on to Sam. "Goddamn it, Sunshine. I fucked up. Don't do this."

You made me feel so awful, Sam thought but couldn't say. He felt ridiculous—here he was at the *Grand Canyon*, and he wasn't even looking at it. He couldn't though, not with Mitch making him crazy, and he pressed his hands onto Mitch's chest to push him away. But when he did, his feet slipped on the rock, and he cried out. When his attempt to steady himself caused him to slip even more, he stopped pushing at Mitch and started pulling at him, trying to right himself.

Mitch's arms went around him, drawing him close. Sam lifted his head, dizzy and lost, looked at Mitch's face, saw it coming closer, and shut his eyes as he opened his mouth to meet Mitch's kiss.

It was full of the anger and hurt between them, and Sam fought back until he felt the metal of the rail behind him, and then he stopped, yielding, too conscious of the edge to fight. The kiss gentled, and Sam's hands flexed against Mitch's shirt.

Mitch broke the kiss but kept his lips close to Sam's, nuzzling him as he spoke. "Do you want me to take you to Phoenix? Do you want to go home? Or do you want to come with me to Vegas?" His hands clutched at Sam's waist. "Whatever you want, Sam. I'll do whatever you want."

Sam kept his eyes closed and held on to Mitch, but he felt as if he were suspended over the canyon behind him. "Do you want me along?"

He felt a panicked thrill as Mitch's hands grew tight against him. "Yes. And no. But not because I don't want you."

"Because of what you think I'm going to see about you," Sam finished for him, and Mitch nodded.

"Why I'm such a bastard is because I *like* the way you look at me. I don't want—" He broke off.

"I want to go with you."

Mitch brushed a kiss against his mouth. "All right."

He turned Sam around, and they stood there at the rail for some time, Mitch's arms around Sam. Occasionally Sam caught other viewers gawking at them, some in distaste, but he ignored them and tried to hold on to this fragile peace between himself and Mitch. But all too soon Mitch squeezed his hip and said, "We should keep going."

At the truck, Sam went straight to the cupboard, picked up the plastic container, and returned to the rail. He stood there, this time alone, watching with strange feelings rolling around inside him as he let go of another handful of his mother's ashes, watching them drift on the wind down into the canyon below.

CHAPTER SEVENTEEN

S AM FELT A little better as they headed through the rest of the park, which took quite some time to navigate, especially as they hit heavy traffic around the main viewing area and Old Blue caused even more congestion. But soon they left the park and the forest behind. The ragged desert was over, and after a while they came to a town that didn't seem quite so desolate as the ones they'd passed in the morning.

"Williams, Arizona," Mitch said. "We're going to backtrack now to Flagstaff and then head to Vegas. Should be well under our deadline for arrival."

Flagstaff was nicer than Sam had suspected it would be, and after the desolation of the Navajo Nation, it was almost odd to see thick nests of houses and interstate. He tucked his feet onto the seat and watched it go by, calmer than before, but still quiet. When Mitch stopped at the warehouse, Sam didn't offer to help. His thoughts drifted between the desert and the canyon, sometimes teasing him with the memory of Mitch's embrace. Vegas loomed like the gates of hell in his mind, and when Mitch returned, Sam could tell it was the same for him too.

The awkwardness was back. Sam was so tired of it he didn't try to relieve it.

Mitch cleared his throat. "You want to stop somewhere to eat?"

Sam shook his head. "We have all this food in here."

"Well, yeah, but I thought—" Mitch cut himself off. "If you'd pass me my jerky, I'll eat while we go."

"I can make you a sandwich," Sam said, more testily than he meant, and then he let his shoulders fall as Mitch nodded curtly in reply.

They ate and drove in silence.

It was night by the time they turned off the interstate onto Highway 93, and the landscape changed, no longer the comforting forests of Flagstaff or Williams. The desolation wasn't as bad as what they'd seen in the Navajo Nation. The road was two-lane and narrow, and though the road wasn't too high above the desert, it was bordered by metal rails whenever the road dropped off too steeply for a vehicle to make it unscathed, which was a great deal of the time. Sam settled in as best he could, wondering how long it would be until he saw the city lights, wondering, too, if he still wanted to see them.

A soft rain began to fall, and Sam watched the windshield wipers slide back and forth until his eyes fell shut and the long day lured him into sleep.

A sharp bang woke him. The truck lurched and shook, and Sam held white-knuckled to his seat as Mitch swore and pulled it over to the side.

"Hold on," he said, and then he was out the door and into the rain, leaving Sam sitting there alone. When a *thunk* reverberated through the truck, he held still, but when it came again accompanied by a vicious, muffled curse from Mitch, he opened the door and climbed out.

The rain came down harder now, and in the distance lightning flashed, illuminating the canyon around them, making it seem alien and foreboding. Sam squinted into the rain and stumbled along the truck, avoiding the rail marking the abrupt edge of the road as he headed to Mitch, who stood at the side of the trailer, his body rigid.

"*Two* blowouts. I checked the goddamn tires, but there must have been something in the road. We're fucked." He slammed his hand into the trailer and kicked the tire in front of him, which when the lightning flashed, Sam saw was ragged and torn. Both that tire and the one behind it were totaled.

"Can't we change them?"

"Not unless you can hoist up eighty tons." Mitch kicked the tire again. "*Sonofabitch.* I'll have to call service, but at this hour they won't come until morning, not out here. And the load will be late. *Fuck.*" He pushed off the trailer and ran a hand through his wet hair. "I'm blocking the road too. I'll have to set out hazard signs."

Sam stepped forward. "Let me help."

"Get in the cab." Mitch turned away.

"Damn it, Mitch." Sam reached for him. Mitch growled and shoved him, knocking Sam backward, making him stumble in the mud and rain.

Sam hit the rail and screamed as he went over.

It was a ditch, not a canyon, but as he fell he saw the mountain edge, the canyon, and the night sky all at once. He hit hard, knocking the scream and his breath out of him. He tasted blood and dirt, and his whole body hurt. As a final kick in the pants, the rain drove sharply into his eyes and mouth and ran into his nose until he choked.

When Mitch grabbed him, though, he cried out with what little air he had left in his lungs, and kicked, and pushed, and the more Mitch fought to take hold of him, the more Sam fought back, scraping his arms and his head against the rocks, kicking up mud and pushing into Mitch's chest.

"Fuck you." Sam tried to kick him in the shin. "Fuck you, Fuck you, *Fuck you.*" He felt the sudden urge to cry, so he shouted more, kicking until Mitch pinned him with his body, holding his head down with a palm pressed against his forehead.

"You're going to cut your fucking head open. God-*damn* it, Sunshine." The lightning flashed, lit Mitch up, and his body pressed into Sam.

Sam pushed into him, and to his surprise, Mitch shuddered.

"Fuck me," Sam whispered.

When Mitch's eyes darkened, Sam thrust his pelvis, taking hold of Mitch's waist and grinding into him. "Fuck me." He tugged on Mitch's waistband. "Fuck me right here, Mitch. *Fuck. Me.*"

He half-expected—half-wanted—Mitch to refuse him, and he was ready to be angry. So when Mitch's mouth came down over his own, Sam opened up and gave him his anger, letting the tender feelings he'd crushed that morning return as nothing more than dark lust. He tried to be empty, hateful, but he couldn't quite manage it, and he worked as hard to keep from crying as he did to keep Mitch from seeing.

"Fuck me," he cried, when Mitch's mouth trailed to his neck. He lifted his hips and helped Mitch pull down his jeans and his underwear. He felt rock and mud against his ass. "Fuck me. Please. *Fuck me.*"

He held up his legs, drawing them back as Mitch pushed on them, bending down to spit on him. He groaned when Mitch worked it in with his fingers, opening him. Sam kept shouting, then fumbled for Mitch's pants, gasping in relief when he freed him. Sam rolled over, pulling himself apart with his hands. But when Mitch pushed into him it was too tight, too dry, and he cried out again, this time in pain. Even so, when Mitch withdrew, he tried to keep him there.

"Get in the truck," Mitch growled, and when Sam didn't move, Mitch stood, scooped Sam up, and hauled him over his shoulder.

Sam's pants were down, so when Mitch slapped him on his ass, it was bare, and the blow was loud, cracking like the thunder booming out around them. It stilled Sam for a second, mostly out of shock, but he soon began fighting, all the way to the truck. When Mitch tossed Sam inside, he pressed him into the seat, and when Sam started to wriggle away, Mitch held him down with one hand before spanking the ever-loving shit out of Sam's bare and wriggling ass with the other.

These slaps were harsh and angry, and instead of arousing Sam they made him swear, shout, then silently cry. But they kept coming, mixing with the rain that came in through the open door, the mud from the ground, and the rocks embedded in his skin. At some point they all rolled together into something new, something hard and erotic. Sam shook, begging incoherently.

When the blows stopped and Mitch pulled his legs apart, he sobbed, but when Mitch hesitated, he only opened himself farther, and when Mitch licked him, he sighed and sank into the seat in surrender. He pushed back, humping, moaning, begging, until as suddenly as it had all begun, it ended.

Mitch slapped him a last time on his ass. "Go on inside."

Sam went, shaking, his ass burning, his arms and head aching, his whole body bruised and muddy and slightly bloody, but he throbbed through it all, making him feel strange and a little sick. He peeled out of his clothes, washed his hands and sat on the floor, naked, and didn't move.

When Mitch returned, he pulled out his phone and placed a call to a service station. Then, for the first time since Sam had started riding with him, Mitch turned on his CB.

"This is Blue, sitting on 95 heading north into Sin City. Anybody got their ears on?"

There was a silence, then static, and then a faint

voice said, "Roger, Blue. This is Razor Baiter. What's your pleasure?"

"Nothing," Mitch replied. "I let go a pair of alligators here, and I'm downed. No granny lane, and no shoulder, either, so keep your eyes peeled."

"Ten-four, Blue," Razor Baiter said. "You need a 10-34?"

"I'm called in, thanks."

"Blue?" This was a new voice on the CB, and Mitch stiffened at the sound of it. "Well, well, Old Man. Here I thought you were dead. You headed for the dice, are you?"

Mitch's whole body tensed as he replied. "I'm dropping off then bundling out for L.A., Skeet."

"I'll look for you." Skeet's voice flowed like wicked silk over the crackling CB.

"I see you up ahead, Blue," Razor Baiter said. "Can I leave anything for you? Bottle of Jack? Couple of girly mags to keep you company?"

Skeet laughed. "You're a green apple, aren't you, Razor, if you're offering that to Blue. It's a good buddy he's after, but knowing him, he's already got himself a buffalo. Ain't that right, Old Man?"

"Spread the word about the bubble trouble, boys. This is Blue, over and out."

Mitch snapped off the radio without listening for a reply. Then he locked the doors, killed the engine, and climbed back toward Sam.

He lifted him up and nudged him into the shower, and he stayed there while he turned on the spray, aiming it at Sam. Sam let Mitch lather him, rinsing away the mud, dirt, blood and rocks, and then he let Mitch lead him over to the bed. He lay there, silent, while Mitch took a shower of his own, and he didn't move, not even when Mitch came and sat beside him naked on the bed. Mitch's hand rested on his bare ass, and Sam's heart kicked a beat when Mitch spoke.

"I've picked up guys before."

Sam opened his eyes and stared at the wall, listening.

"I've picked them up at truck stops, and by the side of the road. I've taken them to the next town or across the country. I used to do it a lot, so much that when other truckers saw me, they'd call out on the CB, asking if Old Blue had somebody along to blow his horn. Because I'd pick them up, and I always fucked them." He stroked Sam once, then pulled his hand away. "And I did it with Randy."

Sam held still, not sure he wanted to hear this.

"What you said to me that first night in North Platte was pretty much what I always did. I played games with them. The games got kinkier and kinkier as the years went on. Eventually Randy got into the act too, the two of us riding together and picking guys up, and the games got more and more wild, and more intense, and then, finally, somebody got hurt."

"Hurt?" Sam echoed.

Mitch blanched. "Not—Jesus. Not *hurt*. Just feelings." He grimaced. "But it was ugly, and it tore me up. I swore we were done, and we were. I never picked up anybody again, not for two years." His hand on Sam's hip stroked sadly. "Until I picked you up."

He pulled away and faced the front of the cab, bending forward to rest his elbows on his knees.

"I'm not a real nice guy, Sam. Not usually. I'm gruff, and I'm rough, and I don't have many friends. I get in more fights than conversations. The only time I'm charming is when I want a job or want to fuck somebody, and even then I think it's probably a dubious claim. It's why I do cross-country drives, and why I don't turn on the CB anymore except for what I just did." He sank forward deeper onto his knees. "When I take you into Vegas, if I take you around for more than a drive through town, we're going to run into people I know, who know what I am. When they see you, they'll think you're one of those boys. My special deliveries, they called them. But you aren't that, Sunshine. You *aren't.*"

Sam turned over and faced Mitch, who sat blue-shrouded and miserable in the dark. "What am I, then?"

"Damned if I know." He ran a hand through his hair. "You scare the shit out of me, Sam, and the way you keep looking at me cuts me up. I know it's my fault, and I keep trying to fix it, but I broke it, didn't I? So you might as well know the truth. What I did to you, what I almost did there in the rain, when I hit you, knocked you down, over the *edge*—" He broke off.

"You didn't hit me on purpose."

"I about died when I realized what I'd done." Mitch trembled. "And then there I was, fucking you raw—

shit."

Sam pushed up onto his elbow, then winced because it hurt. He lay back down and reached for Mitch. "I told you to do that. I begged you for it."

"You're not them." Mitch looked almost sick. "You aren't them, but I keep making you that way."

"Mitch, I wanted you to fuck me. It hurt, but I didn't want you to stop. I wanted it. I've wanted everything you've done to me."

"You're not them," Mitch insisted angrily. "You're not *him.*"

"Will he be there? Randy?"

"That was him on the radio."

Sam glanced at the front of the cab, as if an echo of the man might still be there. It had been a mistake to come. He wished they could leave. If the tires weren't blown, Mitch would go. This was his fault, for insisting.

Yet if they didn't face this, nothing would ever be okay.

What's there to be okay? a dark voice inside him whispered. *What sort of future outside of more fucking do you think the two of you have?*

Sam shifted uncomfortably on the bed.

Mitch sank forward so far his head was nearly between his knees. "I'm too old for this."

Sam tugged at Mitch's bare arm. He realized Mitch wore only a towel, and that he himself had on nothing at all. "Lie with me." He tugged again. "Come lie with me, Mitch."

Mitch came, reluctant, and Sam wrapped the sheet

around them, pushing away the towel so they were pressed skin to skin. He kissed Mitch's chest, his neck, and his mouth, coaxing him open, stealing inside as his hands roved over the other man's body, shaping it, feeling it. He explored Mitch's arms, his sides, his pecs, and his belly, moved on to his hips, and finally, his cock. Mitch stroked him back and kissed him, but though the heat built up between them, it never crested, just kept a slow, steady burn, until they both grew weary and simply pressed their foreheads together, their hands slowing to gentle skims, until they stopped entirely.

They lay silent in the dark, waiting for morning, listening to the thunder and the rain as the storm played out across the desert.

MITCH'S TRANSFORMATION BEGAN with the arrival of the service truck.

Once again Mitch was gone when Sam woke, except today he came into consciousness to the sudden banging that turned out to be the huge portable jack hefting up the end of the trailer before Mitch and the tow truck driver wrestled two new tires into place. Sam hurried into pants and took his shoes and T-shirt with him on the way out the door, eager to be out of the unsteady vehicle. This was his first mistake.

The tow truck operator saw Sam first. Sam was so barely dressed his pants weren't even buttoned, and he gave the tow truck driver an awkward wave as he hopped on the rocks to put on his shoes. The man gave

Sam a disgusted look and returned to tightening lug nuts on the first tire. When Mitch came around, he saw Sam and flinched.

Sam tugged his T-shirt over his head and tried not to notice. When the jack shifted and the trailer shuddered, though, he hopped the rail he'd fallen over the night before, putting some distance between himself and the vehicle. But he didn't get twenty feet away before Mitch saw him.

"Careful, Sam," he called out. "There's scorpions and snakes out there."

Sam yelped and headed to the trailer.

"See you had some takeout from pickle park," the tow truck driver remarked as Sam went by.

Mitch's grip on his wrench fumbled as he aimed it at the next nut. "Sam's a friend." Mitch's tone suggested the conversation should end now.

The mechanic snorted. "Yeah, I bet he's a real good buddy."

For some reason, this made Mitch even angrier, and for a horrible moment Sam thought Mitch was going to use the wrench on the guy. But he said and did nothing, and Sam hurried around to the front of the truck, where he remained out of sight, trying not to think about how badly he had to piss. When they lowered the trailer, Mitch came up front to the cab.

"Get in," he said, and Sam did quickly. He headed straight for the bathroom, and while he was using it, the engine started, and Mitch took them off toward Vegas. Sam washed up, came out, dithered a moment, then unplugged his phone from its charger and surfed. It took him a few minutes, but he found a Wikipedia entry for CB slang. He looked up buffalo and pickle park, and more by accident than anything, good buddy, which apparently didn't mean what it used to mean from the 80s' trucker movies.

Ah. Sam plugged the phone in, grabbed a mineral water from the fridge, and headed to the front of the cab. He sat down, drank a little, then decided this would be better faced head-on.

"You know," Sam said, as carefully as he could, "it's not like it's a lie."

Mitch glanced at him, still ruffled. "What's not?"

"What they said about me on the radio, and what that guy said. You didn't pick me up at a rest stop, but surely a truck stop is close. And while I'm not exactly a prostitute—"

"It's not the same."

"Well, it's splitting hairs, from where I sit. I don't care."

"*I* care." Mitch glared at him. "It's not what you are."

This was last night's argument again, and it was dangerous territory. *Am I your boyfriend, then?* He couldn't ask that, even though he wanted to, because it felt ridiculous, especially after yesterday.

Sam propped his feet on the dash and retreated into his bottle of water. The endless desert gave way to small mountains cropping up in the distance. "This is why you kept me in the cab all the time when you loaded and unloaded. You didn't want anyone to see me."

Mitch didn't take his eyes off the road. "Yes."

Sam's hand tightened on his bottle. "Fuck. I'd rather be known as your piece on the side than your great big secret."

"You're not—" Mitch cut himself off and reached for his cigarettes.

"I'm not a secret? I'm not your *buffalo* or your *good buddy* or your *pickle* thing, whatever they called it? What the fuck *am* I?"

"You're Sam." Mitch lit his cigarette.

"This is so fucked." Sam threw up his hands. "What the hell *do* you want me to be?" Sam gestured at the city beginning to open up before them, just the start of the suburbs. "Why did you bring me here? Do I have to hide the whole time in Las Vegas too?"

"I don't know." Mitch put out his barely smoked cigarette and lit another one.

Sam swore, unbuckled his belt, and headed through the curtain, ignoring his first entrance to Las Vegas entirely.

He got into the shower as Mitch pulled off the road and toward the warehouse. Sam took his time, doing his hair and primping, swearing at his lack of clean clothing. He needed a washer and a dryer. Climbing into his mud-caked jeans, he stuck his head out the driver's side window and glanced around, hoping to see a Walmart or somewhere he could buy something different to wear.

"I knew they were wrong."

A familiar voice drifted up at Sam from below. Sam looked down, surprised, and found a dark-haired, wiry, slightly greasy man wearing a black T-shirt, black jeans, and black motorcycle boots leering up at him. "I heard the rumor Mitch had cleaned up his nose, but it's good to see some things never change. What's your name, honey?"

Sam felt somehow he should be embarrassed, but this guy was so outrageous he couldn't manage it. "My name's Sam."

Then the puzzle pieces clicked, and even before the man spoke, Sam knew what he was going to say.

"Good to meet you, Sam." The man's face lit up in a wicked grin. "My name is Randy."

CHAPTER EIGHTEEN

THE LITTLE BASTARD, standing in front of him after all this time. This was Mitch's Randy. The man who kept fucking up Sam's life.

Sam tried not to let his nervousness show. "Hello."

The man laughed, a deep belly rumble that tingled Sam's insides. "You're a pretty one, Sam. You and Mitch heading to the Watering Hole after he unloads?"

"I have no idea." Sam glanced down at himself and suppressed a shudder at the sight of his pants. "I hope to hell we're heading to a laundromat, or a mall."

"I can take you shopping, baby. You climb on down here, and we'll take a little ride."

This wasn't so bad, actually. Randy was more over the top than scary, so far. "I don't even know you, except you're the guy from the CB last night, the one who made Mitch mad."

"Oh, I usually do," Randy agreed. "But yeah, that was me. Why don't you come down, and we'll see if I still have my touch?"

"I'm not going anywhere with you." Sam was almost enjoying this. "I'm waiting for Mitch."

"Come on," Randy teased. "He ain't *that* good."

Sam lifted his eyebrows. "You know this from experience?"

Randy's eyes danced. "Yep."

It was a blow, but he'd walked into it. Of course they had experience. This was the guy Mitch was still hung up over. Sam attempted to cover his sensitivity with a shrug and a boast. "Well, *I* think he's that good. So the answer is still no."

Randy seemed amused. "Aw, baby, you're a *pet*. Well, why didn't you say?"

Pet? Sam frowned at him. "I don't know what you're talking about."

"He give you a name? A nickname?"

Sam could sense the trap rising up around him, but he didn't understand it. He kept quiet.

His silence only egged Randy on. "No? Well, that was usually my specialty. I'll call you Peaches."

"Sam?" Mitch called out.

Sam felt guilty even though he had no idea why, his blush deepening at the sight of Mitch. His lover's face was wooden as he glanced back and forth between Sam and Randy.

Sam ran his fingers through his hair. *Don't let this go weird. You can do this. Show him.* "Mitch, I'm out of clothes. I need a washing machine, and probably something to wear in the meantime."

"I'll give you something—" Randy started to say, and Mitch turned on him, going from wooden to furious in half a second.

"Randy, you stupid fuck." He waved an angry hand

at him. "Goddamn it, why the hell are you here?"

"Looking for you, you big faggot." Randy punched Mitch mildly in the arm. "I like your boy. Bring your shit to the house, and we'll play while we wait for the wash." When Mitch started swearing again, Randy only grinned. "I got your bike in the garage, if you recall. Unless you plan on running Blue bobtail around town?"

Mitch rubbed his neck, looking nervous. Sam didn't know if he wanted to kiss him or hit him. There was something else there too in Mitch's expression, and as soon as Sam saw it, he wished he hadn't.

Longing. Sam saw longing.

Sam turned to Mitch, too tired to keep this up. "I don't care where we go," he lied. "I need to have clean clothes, like, yesterday."

"Get the dirty stuff and toss it in a garbage bag. Bring anything you want to have around with you for the next few days."

"We're staying that long?" Sam asked, surprised and a little afraid.

"I have no fucking idea." Mitch stalked off.

Sam rolled his eyes, then ducked inside and started to pack.

He had most of the dirty clothes in a garbage bag and was trying to decide if he should bring something for Mitch or anything to eat when the door opened. He held up a pair of jeans and glanced over his shoulder. "Mitch, do you want—Oh," he said, when he saw Randy standing there.

Randy gave him a lewd grin and a wave. "Just came

to help you, Peaches."

Sam tried to look busy. "I think you came to piss him off." *And scare me.*

"Oh, that's an added benefit." Randy leaned against the bathroom door and ran his eyes up and down Sam's body. "Baby, you are sex on legs."

"And you're really gross." Sam tossed his iPhone charger into his pack.

"You've got sass. That's good. Mitch's boys usually don't have sass."

"I'm not his boy." Sam added a pair of Mitch's underwear and socks to the charger. *According to him, anyway.* "And I'm not a *pet*, either, whatever the fuck that is."

"Seriously?" Randy stood straighter. "You two aren't fucking?"

"Seriously, you can go wait outside." Sam debated on the bag of jerky, then tossed it in too.

"Naw, he's too pissy about you, and you're the little lady in here packing up his shit for him. You're a pet."

"Hey." Sam turned on him with a fierce smile. "You know, I don't need laundry after all, so why don't you get the fuck out."

Randy held up his hands and whistled low. "Baby, put the gun down. Jesus, maybe the two of you aren't fucking, if you're both this uptight."

Sam bent down to the fridge, poking for more mineral water. He took out a yogurt too, and a spoon. He packed the water, but he grabbed a spoon and ate the Yoplait.

"We keep fighting." He regretted his confession instantly, but he was unable to stop talking now that he'd begun. "Since Durango."

"Shit—you been with him that long?"

"Since Iowa." Sam ate more yogurt. "Fuck. Forget I said anything. You're only going to be an ass, I can tell."

Randy looked stunned. "I'll be damned. You *aren't* a buffalo, are you?"

Sam was really starting to hate the word. He tossed the yogurt in the trash and his spoon in the sink. "Go away, please."

"Seriously." Randy was earnest now. "Are you two—together?"

"I have no idea." Sam zipped the bag shut and did one last check around the cab. Had he packed the right stuff for Mitch? Should he have even bothered? He glanced at the bathroom, thinking about his shampoo, but Randy blocked the way. He shouldered the pack. "Fine. If you won't leave, I will."

But as he tried to walk past, Randy grabbed him by the arm. Sam stiffened and fought him. Randy's hand closed over Sam's crotch, and Sam froze, half in terror, half in a sort of shocked arousal.

"Peaches." Randy nuzzled Sam's neck with the scruff of a beard, and Sam shivered and got hard.

Randy felt the shift, too, and groped him boldly. "I'll give you five hundred dollars if you let me take you off right now and fuck you."

The eroticism of being held captive and fondled by a stranger was washed away by those words, which hit

Sam like a bucket of cold water. He wrenched himself away, and Randy laughed. But just as he got ready for an angry retort, Randy held up his hands, and something in his smile caught Sam.

"You aren't a hooker, Peaches. But you are somethin' sweet. Now I get why the pair of you are so funny." He ran a finger down Sam's cheek, and Sam flinched, but only after he remembered that was how he should react. Randy chuckled. "Oh, baby, this is gonna be an interesting couple of days, I can tell that now."

Sam pulled away, and when Mitch came into the cab, Sam was torn between relief and panic, almost running into him in his efforts to get away from Randy. "I packed for you. But I don't know if I got the right stuff."

Randy laughed, and Mitch glowered at him. "Whatever you brought is fine. Let's go."

Randy pinched Sam's ass as he left the cab, and he grabbed it when Sam jumped. "Real interesting," he whispered, then slapped Sam's rump and stepped out into the parking lot.

CHAPTER NINETEEN

RANDY DIDN'T FLIRT with Mitch, which was what Sam feared. No, Randy flirted with Sam.

At first nothing happened. Three feet from the rig, Sam remembered his mother's ashes, and once he had them, Mitch drove Old Blue to wherever it was he would store her for the next few days. This left Sam with Randy, and that was when the game began.

"Come on, Peaches." Randy put his arm around Sam's waist and led him in the opposite direction. "Let's run away quick before he comes back."

Sam detached himself and put significant distance between them. "Are you going to do this the whole time?"

Randy grinned. "You make it too easy and too fun." He didn't grab Sam again, only spun his keys on his finger and smiled to himself as he nodded toward the beat-up pickup that made the one in Denver look like it had come from the showroom floor.

"Do all truckers only drive pickups when they aren't in a rig?" Then Sam realized his assumption. "Wait—you *are* a trucker too, right?"

"Yeah, though I do other things too. Not all truckers

have pickups, no, but after riding up that high all the time, it's hard to go crawling around on your belly." He opened the door with his key, slid across, and unlocked the other for Sam.

It was a bench seat, but Sam quickly realized when Mitch was inside, they'd be crammed close, and he could only imagine what Randy would do. He lingered in the doorway, wincing at the sun. "Hotter here than in Colorado. A lot."

"You've been in the mountains, so yeah, this is gonna seem pretty warm. Nights still get cool, though."

"Not in Iowa. It stays muggy and hot all night."

"Well, with you there, I'm sure it does." Randy patted the seat beside him, leering. "Get on in here, baby, and let me get to know you better."

Sam didn't move. "Are you always like this? Seriously?"

Randy said nothing, only patted the seat again. Sam stood there until Mitch came. When he slid across the seat, Randy grabbed his thigh, squeezed it fast, then leaned over to murmur in Sam's ear. "Peaches, I get much, much better than this."

As they drove through town, Randy pointed out this or that landmark, feature, or interesting historical or cultural tidbit, and Sam leaned into Mitch. Mitch draped his arm across Sam's back. Randy teased Sam, and through him, Mitch. Every time he reached down to shift, Randy's hand deliberately caressed Sam's knee, and Sam frequently had to push it off his thigh. Mitch saw it all, and every time he did, his hand tightened on

Sam's shoulder. It was so over the top Sam thought it had to be an act, that Randy was deliberately being the biggest asshole he could possibly be, but Sam couldn't quite figure out why. He had no idea why Mitch was so quiet either. He'd complained for a few minutes, but now he sat rigid, as if he were waiting for the inevitable, horrible end.

Finally, Sam decided he'd had enough.

"Interesting as this is," he said after Randy had taken them by their seventeenth wedding chapel, "I'm not kidding about needing to do laundry."

"Oh, we're going shopping, Peaches." Randy's hand drifted briefly to Sam's thigh, departing again before Sam could remove him. "Almost there too."

"My name is Sam." He moved his legs closer to Mitch.

Randy said nothing more as they drove down the street. Mitch lit a cigarette.

Sam saw a lot of porn shops and seedy bars and more than a few disreputable people eyeballing them as they drove. When a car backfired ahead of them in traffic and Sam stiffened in surprise, Mitch's arm tucked a little closer around his shoulders, and he bent down to brush his lips against Sam's temple. "It's okay, Sunshine. I got you."

Randy pulled into the parking lot of a dirty place that said DISCOUNT CLOTHING, and Sam stuck close to Mitch as they got out of the car and headed into the store.

He'd thought the place was a sort of thrift store, but

once inside Sam saw it was more of a clothing warehouse. Everything was new, and some of it quite stylish, but it was shoved onto racks and shelves in no particular arrangement, either by style or size. Sam tried to find jeans, or any kind of pants really, but after five minutes the only thing in his size he'd come up with was a pair of dress pants. They were nice, but at home he'd have nowhere to wear them. He searched on, wishing Randy would've taken them to a Walmart so he'd already be changed.

Randy appeared over the top of a rack of clothing and passed him a pair of folded jeans. "Here, Peaches. Try these."

Sam peeked at the size, which was exactly right. "Yeah, these are—" He opened them up, letting the legs fall down to the ground, and he turned to Randy, glaring. "How about a pair *not* covered in holes?"

"You said yourself it was warm," Randy pointed out. "Built-in air conditioning."

"Free advertising too." Sam poked his fingers through the gashes underneath the seat.

"How about this. You try them on, and you show Mitch."

"I'm not buying something this impractical." Sam pushed them back at Randy.

"You actually are from Iowa, aren't you? Here, then—you try the jeans on, and if Mitch likes them, *I'll* buy them."

"You're not buying anything for me." Sam glared at the jeans. "I'd look like a hooker."

"Yeah, figured you'd enjoy that part." Randy passed another pair over. "Here. A more sensible pair for your Iowa side."

These, Sam noted, had no holes, but they did have chains at the pockets and were splattered decoratively with paint along the cuffs, seams, and on the butt. After peeking at the price tag, he decided if they fit okay, he'd keep them.

The dressing rooms were on the far side of the store and were little more than sagging curtains over a wall of shakily piled boxes. Randy ushered Sam inside and handed him the jeans one at a time. He also stayed at the gap, clearly intending to watch Sam get undressed.

Sam hesitated over the button of his jeans. "Where's Mitch?"

"Outside having another cigarette." He made hurry-up motions with his hand. "Come on. Let's see what you're packing, Peaches."

It was something about Randy's voice, Sam decided, as instead of demanding Randy get the hell out of his dressing room, Sam simply undid his jeans and pushed them down over his hips, averting his eyes so he couldn't see Randy watching. When Randy murmured appreciatively, Sam's ears burned, but he kept getting dressed, looking at the floor, boxes of stock making up the walls—anything but Randy's face. *Mitch wouldn't leave you with him if he wasn't safe,* he tried to tell himself. Except he was pretty sure nothing about Randy was safe.

Neither, he thought, sucking in a breath as he

tugged the waistband into place, were these jeans.

Randy wolf-whistled. "That's the stuff, baby."

Sam ran his hand self-consciously over the leg and then the ass. "I can't get them—you can see my underwear."

"You are the funniest combination, Peaches, of prude and slut. The answer, of course, is to wear different underwear, or none at all." He pulled open the curtain and motioned to Sam. "Come on, let's go show your honey."

Sam wrapped his arms over his belly as he followed Randy. He felt the breeze blow across his legs at every step, and he was suddenly conscious of every other patron in the store. Most didn't look at him, but the few who did made him feel even more naked. When Sam balked, Randy grabbed his hand and dragged him the rest of the way, up to the front window where Mitch stood staring out at the street while he smoked.

Randy rapped on the window. Mitch turned. Randy spun Sam slowly, his hand lingering on Sam's hip. Mitch's face was closed off, but his eyes gave him away. He liked the jeans. He nodded curtly and took another drag, but he kept his eyes on Sam's bottom half.

Randy chuckled. "Still think they're impractical?"

Sam headed for the dressing room. "I need to try on the other pair."

Randy didn't come along and watch, to Sam's relief. The jeans fit well, and Sam hated to take them off and put on his dirty ones, but he did, and carried the lot to the register. He gripped the ripped pair tightly, fighting a silent war with himself, but in the end he decided to get them too, and handed the clerk his credit card.

It was refused.

Sam flushed a deep, terrible red, a blush that worsened when the clerk wouldn't hand his card back. "But—that's *mine*. Why—?"

Randy peered over his shoulder. "Did you call and tell your bank you were traveling? Sometimes they put a hold on them if you don't."

Sam had not. "Give me my card," he said to the clerk, fumbling for his license. "See? It's me." He let out an audible sigh of relief when she handed it over, but he balked when Randy passed her his credit card instead. "*No.* I'm not getting them."

This seemed to amuse Randy a great deal. "Baby, come on." He presented his card again.

Sam shoved him harder. "You aren't buying them, and if you do, I'm not wearing them. I'm not your *baby*."

"What's going on?" Mitch asked, coming up behind him.

Sam averted his gaze. "I had trouble with my card. It's got credit, but I guess I should have called and said I was traveling. It's no big deal. Let's go, so I can wash things."

Mitch pulled out his wallet.

Randy shook his head. "I already tried that."

Mitch held Sam's gaze and gave the clerk his own card.

"Mitch," Sam protested, but weakly. He didn't want

him to do this, but he wasn't going to refuse him the same way he had Randy.

"Let me do this, Sunshine." Mitch waved the card in front of the clerk, who watched Sam a little longer before acquiescing and running the charge.

Mitch collected the bag too and carried it all the way to the truck.

"So," Randy said, as they crossed the parking lot. "Sunshine, is it?"

He spoke casually, but from the way Mitch stiffened, Sam knew it had significance.

Randy grinned, triumphant. "I told you, we always name the pets."

"*You* did." Mitch sounded angry. And guilty.

"You agreed to them." Randy raked Sam up and down with his gaze. "Nope, you really are Peaches, not Sunshine."

"It's not like that." But Mitch didn't make eye contact with Sam as he said it, and suddenly the nickname which had made Sam feel so cherished and tender didn't anymore.

Randy seemed pleased with himself. "How about a quick stop at the Watering Hole?"

"I still need to change my clothes." Sam tried not to think about being a pet. But it was impossible. *Is that all I am to him? Why does he look so guilty?*

"I've been burning the candle at both ends," Mitch said. "I need to crash for the afternoon."

"Even better." Randy slung an arm around Sam's shoulder.

Sam dislodged him, moving himself closer to Mitch as a result. Mitch surprised him by putting his arm around Sam's waist. Sam started to stiffen, but Mitch squeezed him gently, and the gesture diffused Sam. He relented and sagged against him.

Randy watched them, frowning. "I ain't buying it yet," he said, in a different tone than Sam had yet heard him use. Less snarky, more…stern.

"Nobody's sellin' you anything, Skeet," Mitch replied with a lightness that eased Sam. He wished he knew what the hell was going on.

"I meant to pay for those." Sam spoke quietly so Randy wouldn't hear as he and Mitch waited for Randy to unlock their door.

"This isn't your mama's glass chest. Only a few pairs of jeans." Mitch leaned close, so close his lips brushed Sam's ear as he spoke. "I call you Sunshine because when you smile, the sun comes out."

Sam shut his eyes, the words a balm he hadn't fully let himself acknowledge he needed. He remembered what Mitch had told him about the alley, about him looking happy, and all his doubts washed away. He brushed a kiss against Mitch's lips. When he pulled away, he caught Randy watching them. Randy seemed surprised and wary.

"Speaking of jeans." Mitch squeezed Sam's ass. "I'm looking forward to seeing you wear yours. Especially the ones with the holes."

"But they show my underwear," Sam protested, as he opened the door.

"Wear the pair I bought you."

Cue the blush. "I didn't bring them."

Mitch's grin was wicked as he urged Sam into the truck. "I did."

CHAPTER TWENTY

THE DRIVE TO Randy's house didn't take long from the neighborhood where they bought Sam's jeans. After a quick stop at a gas station to pick up beer and some more cigarettes for Mitch, Randy took them down a series of streets until he pulled up behind a small, plain but decent-looking house. He parked in the drive and killed the engine. There wasn't much of a yard, and it was done up in gravel and scraggly cactus rather than grass. But inside it was cool, and while it was shabby, it was cleaner than Sam would have expected.

Mitch, who had hauled in the bag of dirty laundry, a smaller bag of his own, and Sam's jeans, deposited them in the middle of the living room and collapsed on the couch.

Randy came in after him and gave him a withering glance. "Mitch Tedsoe, I was so looking forward to your mess."

Mitch, keeping his eyes closed, flipped him the bird. "I gotta crash. My room still there? Or did you finally rent it out?"

Randy snorted. "That was an idle threat to get you to come back, as well you know. Though I'll admit I've used it more and more for storage."

"So long as you didn't store anything on the bed, I'm good," Mitch murmured.

"A little, but we can shove it off easy enough." Randy picked up Mitch's bag and extended a hand to him. "Up, Old Man."

Sam watched them go, feeling much a third wheel as he hovered in the entryway and the pair of them moved down the hall. He spent a moment wondering how exactly he was supposed to behave, then decided, *fuck it*, and grabbed the shopping bag and headed in search of a bathroom. He found one in the hallway and changed, skimming out of everything and putting on his new jeans—the paint-splattered ones—and brought the dirty clothes out to sort with the others for the wash. He upended the entire garbage bag on the floor, sorted out light from dark and separated the sheets into their own pile. He put the darks back into the bag and the lights and sheets into two piles as unobtrusive as possible by the wall to the kitchen. He found the washer, started the first load, and when he still found himself alone, wandered down the hall to see what the hell was going on.

He stopped and listened as soon as he heard his name.

"Sam is a good kid. Don't fuck with him." Mitch sounded half asleep already.

"I'd like nothing better than to fuck with that hot little piece. Same as always, Old Man."

There was a groan, and it startled Sam. It was

a…pleasured sound. He dared a peek around the corner and startled anew at what he saw.

Mitch was naked down to his briefs, lying face-down and sprawled on the bed, which wasn't even on a frame. It was a mattress and box springs in the middle of the floor. Randy straddled him, fully clothed and sitting on Mitch's ass as he massaged the other man's shoulders, but he also rotated his own hips in a sensual motion. As Sam watched, Randy reached back, caressing Mitch's thigh and sliding his fingers toward the hem of Mitch's briefs.

Mitch bucked, and Sam ducked into the hall, his heart heavy.

"Knock that shit off," Mitch said, a little less groggily. "He's gonna see you, and I don't need you making this more complicated than it already is."

Randy snorted, and Sam heard a muffled slap of flesh, which he suspected was Randy's hand against Mitch's ass. "You old goat. You're serious, aren't you?"

"I'm not fucking kidding, Randy. Leave him alone."

There was a pause, which felt heavy to Sam, but that could have been because he was bowing under the weight of everything he heard, his emotions bouncing between hope to fear to betrayal to euphoria, sending him in an elliptical orbit of confusion.

"Let me take the two of you out tonight." Randy's voice was oddly gentle. "I want to watch you interact."

"No, you want to fuck with him, and with me."

Randy's laugh was a guttural purr. "Oh yes. But first I want to watch."

"We are not putting on a fucking show for you."

"See, I think that's where you're getting it wrong. But I'm not sure yet. I need to study this a bit more."

"Shit," Mitch murmured. "Leave him alone until I'm awake. Try and be a nice person for one damn afternoon."

"I'll be *very* nice to him." Randy winked. "And to you."

There was another silence, and then another moan, and a wet sound that sounded far, far too much like kissing. Sam wanted to look but didn't dare. He went to the kitchen, but he didn't know what to do or how to behave. He wanted to cry, and he wanted to shout, and he wanted to stop them or at least make sure they weren't doing what he was afraid they were doing. In the end, he stood against the counter, dying a little as every minute passed.

"Hello."

Sam whirled around. Randy stood in the archway between the living room and the kitchen, looking smug. Sam clenched his fists at his sides and wished he could hit him.

Randy grinned. "Oh, Peaches, you're cute, that's what you are. Relax. He's not going to fuck me, not with you here. Not *without* you, anyhow, but I'll admit I'm probably dreaming even then." When Sam sputtered, Randy leaned on the archway and folded his hands over his arms. "I know you were standing there listening, because I saw your shadow, and I know when you left because it moved. And you'd damn well better not plan on playing poker in town, baby, because you don't have the face for it." At the fridge, he pulled out two beers, holding one out to Sam. "Here. Sit. Drink. I'll make you some food, and we'll talk."

Sam took the beer with some reserve. He sat at the table and held the bottle for a long time, watching Randy open the fridge again and take out hamburger, tomatoes, cheese, and a carton of eggs. After a while Sam opened the beer, but he still didn't drink it.

Randy cracked an egg, slid the yolk into a bowl, and tossed the shell into the sink. He didn't turn around. "Ask, or you'll drive yourself crazy."

Sam *hated* him. "What am I supposed to ask?"

"Anything. The four million questions you have would be a good place to start."

Sam glowered at his back. "Like you're going to give me honest answers."

Randy shrugged. "Sometimes I will. And for every question you ask, I get to ask you one too." He cracked another egg. "See? We both win."

Sam watched him stab the spatula into the ground beef for a few minutes, then gave in. "Were you kissing him?"

Randy paused, clearly both amused and surprised. "Yes."

Sam's jaw tightened. "Did he kiss you back?"

Randy laughed. "Peaches, you suck at this game, you know."

"*Did he kiss you back?*"

Randy returned to his ground beef. "Yes, he did.

And then I blew him, and he came in my face, and he told me to tell the skinny bitch in the kitchen to fuck off, because he'd have no other."

"You're an ass." Sam shoved the beer away.

"And you're not very smart, for a college boy." Randy continued to poke at the frying meat. "You weren't listening, if you heard our conversation and could still ask if he kissed me back. Either that or you think far more highly of my seduction skills than he does, in which case I will be happy to bend you over the table."

Sam startled and moved reflexively toward the wall. Randy turned in time to catch the movement and looked pleased, but in a strange way.

"Yeah, you're a puzzle, aren't you, little man? The question is, how to best figure you out?"

"How did you know I was in college?"

"The neon sign on your forehead. You have a look about you that says you've been poking your head under the hood. I see too many of you running around this town. If you weren't in college, you damn sure studied something a lot."

Sam gave in and reached for the beer. "I'm in school for nursing. But it's taking a while." He took a drink. "It's not going real well, either."

"Not what you thought it would be, or harder than you imagined?"

Sam considered this. "Both." He scraped his thumbnail against the label on his beer. "It's taking so much time. And I'm tired of having no money and no life. Sometimes I don't know if it's going to change when I'm through, either." He shook his head. "Then I figure I'm a stupid whiner and should shut up and go study."

"It isn't stupid to make sure you're aiming yourself in the right direction. You only get one spin on the blue ball. Make sure it goes the way you want." He salted the ground beef. "How'd you meet Mitch? Rest stop or truck stop?"

"The alley behind my aunt and uncle's pharmacy." When Randy glanced over his shoulder again, it was Sam's turn to be smug.

"No shit?" Randy sounded surprised. "So you, what, struck up a conversation?"

Sam tried to think of how to describe it. "In a way."

Randy rolled his eyes. "He fucked you."

Sam lifted his chin. "And this is funny?"

"It's a relief. So he fucked you. How'd you end up on the road with him? You left school and went?"

"No. I accidentally left my phone in his trailer, and he called me, and then he came back to return it, and we had dinner, and then—"

"Then you ran off with him?"

"No. Then he left."

Randy put down the spatula and turned fully around. "And you didn't have sex with him again?"

Sam blushed. "I thought I got to ask questions?"

Randy waved him aside. "In a minute. This is huge, here. Did you or did you not have sex with him—what, dinner in a *restaurant*?"

"Yes." Sam was getting testy. "It was nice."

"So he calls you, tells you he wants to return your phone, and then has dinner with you." Randy gave him a look that said this was the tallest tale he'd ever heard. "Then gave you a peck on the cheek?"

"Okay, there was a thing in Old Blue after. And there was the phone sex. But everything else, yes."

"*Phone* sex?" Randy turned off the burner, grabbed a chair, and straddled it. "Start over, and this time don't skip shit."

Sam did, reluctantly, editing as much as he could, not wanting to tell any of this at all, and yet somehow he couldn't resist his confession. He gave Randy the bare bones of their alley encounter, the phone call, the dinner, and what came after, and then he explained how everything had gone south with his aunt, and how he'd texted Mitch.

"He said to meet him at the truck stop near me, so I did, and here I am," he finished.

Randy watched him, eagle-eyed and dubious. "And you've been fucking your way across the west, have you?"

Sam folded his arms and glared. "How did you meet Mitch? How long have you known him?"

Randy blew him a kiss before returning to his stove. "Since 1997. You know, when you were in grade school. We met at a truck stop outside of Houston." He tossed Sam a smirk. "I was his first hustle."

Sam hated, *hated* that answer. "So you're lovers?"

Randy snorted. "*Lovers.* Fuck no. Have we fucked?

Yes, and in more ways than your corn-fed mind can imagine. But we never were and never will be *lovers*." He poked hard at the once-again-sizzling meat. "Jesus."

Sam felt as if the weight of the whole Rocky Mountains had lifted off him. "Then why are you riding me so hard?"

Randy's voice switched to a purr. "Peaches, I would be more than happy to ride you hard."

Sam hated the shiver that voice and those words gave him. He retreated into his beer, peeling at the label again.

"What's the kinkiest thing you've ever done?" Randy asked.

Sam was done with this game. "I'm not answering that."

"Sure you are. I'll answer it too. Mine is that I blew a frat boy in the middle of a hotel hallway while another one ate an ice cream cone out of my ass." When Sam choked on his beer, Randy laughed. "Damnedest thing is, it was only last week. So. Your turn, Peaches."

Sam considered the question, more for his own curiosity than because he intended to answer Randy. "Well, it depends on your criteria. Do you mean it had to feel dirty, or what?"

"Kinky. Like, you were doing it, and it felt really, really bent, but you loved it anyway." He poked at the meat. "I want to see what my boy's learned over the past two years."

Sam let his sexual history roll past him in a swift, erotic home movie. Yes, the kinky stuff was with Mitch, but the hell he was going to tell any of that to Randy. Then he remembered Darin, and the time he couldn't decide if he wanted to fuck or watch the game. "You won't be learning anything, because it wasn't with him."

Randy turned around. "Oh, do go on."

Sam raised his eyebrows, only blushing a tiny bit. "Getting fucked from behind during the entire last quarter of a basketball game while I knelt on a pizza box. He used my back for a plate, humped me in time to the dribbling, and slapped my ass every time his team scored."

"Spanked you?" Randy's eyes danced.

"No, it was more of a tease. Just a slap. It was so disconnected, like I wasn't even there."

"And you got off on it?" Sam nodded reluctantly, and Randy clapped. "Peaches, honey! Well, that's one big question answered."

Sam was afraid to ask what question Randy meant. "Why do you call me Peaches? Is it the pet thing?"

"Partly. I call you Peaches because your ass is a very nice pair of them."

"You haven't seen my ass," Sam pointed out.

"True. Why don't you stand up, drop your jeans, and let me find out?"

Sam flipped him off.

Randy blew him another kiss and went back to cooking. He cracked one more egg before reaching for a whisk. "So. We've got domination and humiliation so far, which is a nice start. I assume you like it rough too. Performance, though. That's going to be the real cliffhanger, I can see it already."

"What the fuck are you talking about?"

"Your sexual preferences." Randy beat the eggs violently. "So, what's the answer? You get off on the idea of being fucked in front of somebody or not?"

Sam sputtered. Randy kept beating the eggs patiently, as if he hadn't asked a question so personal even Sam wasn't sure of the answer.

"Shy boy," Randy said wistfully, and picked up the frying pan. He reached for a strainer, poured the meat into it, and rinsed. "So, asking you if you'd do a threesome is out?"

Sam got up from the table, suddenly shaky. "I'm going to switch my laundry."

But Randy's questions haunted him as he pulled the clothes from the washer and put them into the dryer. *You like the idea of being fucked in front of somebody?* His hand shook as he handled the clothes. He remembered Craig and what had almost happened, what could have happened, if he'd said yes. He acknowledged how much he'd wanted it.

Sam swallowed against a dry throat. Why was Randy asking him all this? Wasn't it Mitch he wanted? This had to be some kind of trick. Some kind of test. Randy was clearly trying to get rid of Sam, so if he admitted that, he'd tell Mitch, and then—

He felt a warm hand on his back, pushing him down, and then another one on his hip as it pulled him roughly against Randy.

"The pizza fuck went something like this?" Randy

pushed his groin into Sam's ass. "Oh, wait—you said you were on your knees."

Something pressed into the backs of his knees, and Sam gasped as he went down, falling onto his hands to brace himself. He cried out weakly, and he shut his eyes as Randy ground into him, his hand at Sam's neck, keeping him in place.

"Please." Sam shut his eyes, fighting to keep from going slack. "Please—don't."

The hand at his hip skimmed up to stroke the base of his spine. "See, people think it's easy to fuck with somebody's head, but it isn't. You got to really watch them. Because right now it's hard to tell exactly if this scares the fuck out of you because you hate it, or because you're afraid I'll find out you love it."

Sam shuddered, the pleasure-fear ratio quickening at the thought of being discovered. "Please—*please stop.*"

But Randy kneaded his hip now, pushing what was clearly an erection against Sam's jeans, and his own dick hardened in answer. Then Randy's hand snuck around toward it, and Sam yelped and fought. He ducked and rolled away. Randy caught him and held him flat on his back. Grinning down, he took Sam's erection roughly in his hand.

"And the answer is you're afraid I'll find out you love it."

Sam tried to knee him, but Randy dodged. "*Fuck you.*"

"I'd enjoy that very much." Still smug, Randy gave

Sam one more knead before rising to his feet.

"Leave me the fuck alone." Sam struggled again.

Randy made a moue with his lips and sidestepped Sam's foot. "Make it worth my while, Peaches." He pointed at Sam's crotch. "Show me your goods, and I'll be a saint until Mitch gets up, I swear."

"Fuck *off*." Sam climbed to his feet.

"What I'm wondering is if you're submissive for Mitch or if you'd respond to anybody. My money's on anybody. And I think that's why you're so scared."

Sam *was* scared. He edged toward the kitchen.

Randy blocked him with his arm, and Sam froze, looking to the floor. Randy chuckled. "Oh yeah. I bet you're real fetching in a pair of handcuffs. Better yet, tied up and bent over a bench."

"*Stop*." Sam shrank into the wall.

"Show me your cock." Randy didn't touch Sam at all, but Sam felt as if he'd been caressed lewdly. "Take it out and let me see it."

Sam aimed for the washer, but Randy trapped him with his other arm. He shut his eyes. "*Let me go*."

"See," Randy said, still maddeningly calm, "that's the thing. You want me to let you go, when all you have to do is duck under my arm or shove me, and you're gone. You want to be here."

"You'll grab me if I try to go." Sam's throat was dry, his teeth aching. He kept hoping Mitch would burst in and beat the shit out of Randy, but he knew somehow that wasn't going to happen. He told himself Mitch wouldn't leave him with someone truly dangerous, but it wasn't easy to believe now, standing here. His erection, already going soft, faded away to nothing, and he shrank into himself, closing down.

Abruptly, Randy was gone.

"And that's too far." Randy's seductive tone was gone. He backed away, holding up his hands, then bent to finish putting Sam's laundry in the dryer. Sam watched him, stunned, scared, and confused. *Run,* he thought, and imagined himself tearing through the kitchen, down the hall to Mitch, shutting the door, and crawling into the bed beside him. Hiding, being safe. Except he could also imagine the smirk on Randy's face if he did that.

All of a sudden, he was furious.

"You *son of a bitch*," Sam said, and rushed him.

Randy rose from the dryer, and when Sam hit him, he slammed the other man into the front of the machine. Sam grabbed Randy's hair, yanking it roughly. "You *fucking son of a bitch*. What the *fuck* do you think you're doing?"

Randy went limp in his arms, eyes still wide with surprise, and as Sam glared down at him, they twinkled. "See, *that* is the right sort of question, Peaches." When Sam looked at him in confusion, he wriggled his pinned arm free, reached around, and calmly as you please, unzipped himself and pulled down the waistband of his briefs to reveal a thick, hard, bulging, and uncut erection. For a stunned second, Sam stared down at it. But when he felt his own body begin to respond, he let go as if scalded and retreated toward the kitchen.

"You," he said, voice shaking, "are seriously fucked

up."

"Everybody's fucked up, Peaches." Randy zipped himself up again and shut the door to the dryer. "Go on and get your whites, why don't you, and we'll get those started too."

"You've got to be fucking kidding me. You think I'm going to fall for that twice?"

"Oh no. I'm done baiting you." Randy held up a solemn hand. "No, Peaches, I'm serious. I pushed you too far, and if you tell him about that, he will punch me out, and then you two will be gone, and it's all over. I'm an angel from here on."

Sam faltered. "*What* is over?"

Randy winked at him as he headed into the living room, where he picked up the rest of Sam's laundry. "Sam, you just got more out of me than you deserve. You're not getting that too." He came through, dumped the whites into the washer, started it up, and returned to the kitchen, patting Sam's shoulder on his way by. "Sit. Drink. Ask me questions. Nice, boring things, like what I do for a living or where I come from, or how I love living in Vegas. I'll make you an egg casserole, we'll eat, and everything will be fine."

Sam watched him cook for a few minutes, trying to decide if he should run, hide or hit him again. In the end, he sat down. "Where are you from, Randy?"

"Detroit." As Randy poured the meat in with the eggs and added the cheese and other ingredients, he kept talking, and Sam leaned back in his chair and pretended to listen.

CHAPTER TWENTY-ONE

MITCH SLEPT FOR three hours. Sam spent the first two edging around Randy and doing laundry, and for the last one he slept beside Mitch, partly to escape Randy, who seemed ready to cause more trouble, and partly because he was tired too. The room was warm, though, with sun beating against the curtains and the air conditioning only sort of working in there, so Sam stripped down to the buff before sliding in beside Mitch, who grunted, rolled over, and drew Sam to his chest before falling back to sleep.

When Sam woke, Mitch was already awake, kissing his neck as his hand moved to the part of Sam that hadn't needed consciousness to come to life. Sam moaned softly as Mitch stroked him in earnest, and when they both reached a fever pitch, Mitch turned him over and drew their cocks together in his hand, masturbating them until first he and then Sam came.

"We're hell on sheets." Sam smiled as he settled, sated, against Mitch's shoulder.

Mitch traced lazy patterns on Sam's arm. "Randy give you any shit while I was out?" When Sam didn't answer, Mitch's hand fell away. "Fuck. I should have known better." His fingers drifted up, teasing tentatively at Sam's hair. "You want us to get out of here?"

"He's your friend." Sam kept thinking how Randy had admitted they were also more. "You haven't seen him in a long time."

"You ever think there might be a reason for that?"

Sam lifted his head to look at Mitch. "Then why did we come here at all? Why didn't you tell me no?"

"Fuck if I know." Mitch shut his eyes and fell back against his pillow. "It's always this way when I come to Vegas. Starts everything up again. Makes me feel crazy."

"Vegas or Randy?"

"They go hand in hand." Mitch tucked his arm behind his head and stared up at the ceiling. "Randy and I traveled together for years. We worked the same company, and we pooled our earnings. Randy bought this place, and I bought Old Blue. We did long runs together all over the country, taking turns driving. We got into all kinds of trouble. I get itchy feet, and Randy gets homesick. He loves Vegas. He loves wild parties and lots of people. I like open spaces. It got bad toward the end. So we split. You're kind of witnessing the awkward reunion."

Sam lay there for a minute, digesting all this.

Mitch's hand tightened briefly on his arm. "How long, Sunshine? How long are you gonna stay on the road with me?"

Sam faltered. "I—I don't know."

"Another month? Another week? Another day? When do you want me to look for a job heading east?"

He stroked Sam's shoulder. "Or don't you want to go back?"

"I have to eventually." Sam stared across the room at a pile of boxes balanced precariously on top of an old computer monitor. "All my stuff is there. I have bills, and—well, I guess at some point I'll have to go back to school. Or drop out. Or something." He swirled his finger in Mitch's chest hair. "But I think I'll go. To school."

"In Iowa."

"Well—yeah. Since it's where I live."

There was a long, heavy pause.

"You wouldn't…maybe move somewhere else?" Mitch's tone implied he was carefully avoiding land mines.

Sam's heart beat faster. What was Mitch asking? Why was he asking it? "Well," he said, even more carefully than Mitch, "that would depend."

"On?"

"I need to finish school. If I could go full-time this fall, I'd be done by next December. After that, I could go anywhere. But in other states I'd have to pass the nursing boards. Which isn't such a big deal, just more money."

More silence.

Sam looked out across the landscape of Mitch's chest, running his fingers into the wiry hairs and down toward his stomach, teasing the lingering beads of semen pooled around his abdomen. "I guess that's real life for you. I can't expect every day to be a vacation."

Mitch said nothing, only continued to stroke Sam's hair.

Sam skimmed his fingers down and rested them on Mitch's hip. "I can probably go another week or so."

"I'll keep my eye out for something heading to Chicago." Mitch's fingers grazed Sam's ear. "What do you want to do, until then? Somewhere else you want to see? Or have you had enough of the road?"

I want to stay with you. Sam shrugged. "I'm flexible." His finger swirled around Mitch's bellybutton, making sticky circles. "I don't want to fight anymore."

Mitch snorted. "We shouldn't stay here, in that case."

Sam stared out across the room. He felt oddly numb, but behind it there was a great deal of sadness. *This is going to end.* Something told him being on the road again was only going to amplify this. Maybe it would be easier here with Randy reminding him he was only something different to pass the time, a buffalo after all.

"We can play it by ear." Sam slid his leg alongside Mitch's beneath the sheets.

The door to the bedroom opened, and Sam and Mitch scrambled to get out of the way as Randy launched himself headlong at the center of the mattress.

"Skeet," Mitch growled, tugging the sheet up over Sam's middle. "You are a fucking menace."

"What do you expect, if the two of you are going to stay in here all afternoon and party without me?" Randy rolled over, his eyes boldly raking Sam's naked body, especially his belly. "I see Peaches already had his shower."

Mitch pulled the sheet higher, subtly wiping at the semen on Sam's skin as he did so. "Don't you have a job or something?"

"Off today." Randy's grin showed teeth. "And tonight. What do you say we show your little cherub a night on the town? We can do the mild version tonight, but let me pull some strings at work and maybe tomorrow we can get into something serious to carry us into the weekend."

"Where do you work?" Sam felt moderately safe in the circle of Mitch's arms, even if Randy eyed him as if he were a Vegas buffet.

"I do short runs for a company operating out of Vegas, but I work distribution there too. I play prop, and sometimes I tend bar at the Hole. Which"—he leaned over to slap Mitch's leg—"we need to get you to, now that you're conscious. People will want to say hi."

"I don't think that's such a good idea," Mitch said, but Sam thought he heard some longing in his voice.

Sam turned in his arms. "I don't care where we go. I mean, it'd be fun to see the Strip at night, but even a cab ride would be enough."

Randy looked horrified. "You cannot come to Vegas and just take a cab ride."

"Sam, going anywhere with this idiot is going to land us in trouble," Mitch warned.

Now Randy was angry. "What, you don't come home for two years, and you give me your laundry while you take a nap, and that's all I get?" He sneered. "Well, I guess you haven't changed."

Mitch tensed, and Sam held up a hand. "Hold on, both of you. Mitch, I'd love to meet your friends. Or your enemies. Or whatever. A night on the town sounds fun. I've never done that before, except in Denver with you." Mitch's eyes softened, reflecting remembered heat, and Sam blushed before turning to Randy. "You're insane, but I bet you're fun. If you can stop trying to scare me off every ten seconds, I'd be open to a night out with you." When Randy lifted an eyebrow at him, Sam folded his arms over his chest, resolute. "Yes, I know you'd rather have Mitch to yourself, but I'm here, so just cope."

"I'm not trying to scare you." Randy leaned on one elbow and gave Mitch a leer. "*He* knows what I want. And I know what *he* wants."

Mitch glared. "Fuck off."

Randy blew him a kiss and slid closer to Sam. "A night out sounds fun. We'll get dressed, go to the bar, hit a buffet for dinner, and see the town." He touched Sam's clavicle, tracing the line of it to his sternum. "Maybe we can catch a show. Who do you want to see, Peaches?"

His finger traced the planes of Sam's chest, and they all watched, hypnotized. Sam felt the touch like an electric charge, especially when Mitch didn't say anything, just watched too, his fingers tightening slightly on the sheet over Sam's stomach.

Sam swallowed, trying not to shiver as Randy's finger strayed near his nipple. "I—I don't know. Anything is fine."

"I thought you looked flexible." Randy's finger skirted the dark ring of his target. "Something edgy, I think. Off the Strip."

His fingers splayed, five points resting on Sam's chest, spanning the nipple. The fingers moved, grazing it, making it form a tentative peak. Smiling at it, Randy flicked his finger again. Sam twitched, but otherwise didn't move. Mitch's hand flexed, and Sam's breathing quickened, but otherwise he gave no reaction.

Randy stroked the nipple more regularly until it was a prominent, pink and hardened bud.

"We could go to the Stratosphere." Randy rotated his thumb over the sensitive area. "You haven't been up the tower, Mitch, since they put in the rides."

"Sam doesn't like heights." Mitch's fingers slid lower down Sam's belly, pulling the sheet with them. They teased the tip of Sam's erection, and Mitch pressed his hips forward, letting Sam feel his own.

Randy's thumb joined his fingers, and he pinched Sam's nipple gently. "That's a shame. We'll have to think of something else to do all three of us can enjoy." He pinched again, and Sam shuddered. "What do you say, Sam? What should the three of us do?"

Sam couldn't breathe. Randy gently tweaked his nipple, felt Mitch close his hand over Sam's erection beneath the sheet and simply held still, letting the men touch him. The tension between them was so tight it bounced, but Randy slid beneath it, his entry point

Sam's nipple.

Then Randy leaned forward, pinched the nipple firmly once more and licked it.

Sam gasped as the tongue darted out, pink and fat, and he shuddered as it scraped over his flesh. Behind him he felt Mitch swell.

"Randy," Mitch growled, but it was difficult to tell if he spoke in anger or desire.

"Shh." Randy licked again. Sam shut his eyes and pressed helplessly into Mitch's hand. "See? He's into it." He licked a third time, laving him openly, and Sam gave up and cried out.

"Mitch," he called, and arched toward Randy's mouth.

"Sunshine." Mitch's voice was low and rough. "Do you want him to stop?"

No, Sam thought, but couldn't bring himself to say.

"Such sweet little buds," Randy whispered, his other hand grazing Sam's stomach. "Let me play with him awhile. You like to watch, Mitch. Watch this."

Sam cried out as Randy's mouth closed over his nipple, sucking the small bud into his mouth. His fingers dug into the mattress as Randy teased the sensitive flesh with his teeth, then opened his mouth over it and flicked lewdly with his tongue as his hand trailed down over Sam's stomach, seeking out the sticky residue. Then he continued farther down, teasing at the nest of curls around Sam's erection.

Sam held himself back, too afraid to let go. What did Mitch think of this? What would this do to them?

He tried to turn to look at him, but Randy sucked, and Sam convulsed. Mitch's hand tightened tentatively on his hair as Sam's other hand gripped the edge of the sheet. Mitch's cock, hot and hard, pressed between the juncture of his legs, against Sam's aching balls as his hand grazed Sam's thigh. When Mitch hesitated, Sam knew Mitch wanted to open him, to give him to Randy's waiting hand. Sam wanted it too. He wanted to yield, to be exposed, to feel both men's hands on him.

I want this, Sam admitted to himself, and he let his body go slack and pliant, waiting for Mitch to take him over the edge.

But Mitch's hand went up, not down, and it shoved Randy gently but firmly away. "Give us a minute, Skeet."

Randy lifted his head, a protest ready on his lips, but whatever he saw in Mitch's eyes stilled him. He shut his mouth, and to Sam's surprise, without so much as a saucy comment, he left.

Mitch rolled Sam onto his back and leaned over him.

His expression was strange. He seemed sad and eager and…something else. Resigned? Yet also hopeful. He was a strange, un-Mitch-like mix, and it confused Sam even more.

"Sunshine, do you want to do this?"

"I don't know." Sam lowered his eyes to Mitch's chest, his face heating. "Maybe?"

"We've been dancin' around this for a while." Mitch stroked his cheek. "I'll admit, you open up like a flower,

Sam, when two men touch you. But I don't—I don't want you to get hurt."

"I don't know. I can't—I can't do it with just anyone." Sam flushed deeper. "I don't want to make things awkward for you."

"Having sex with you is not awkward. And I will admit, I'm open to the idea of...sharing. I want to do this with you. But not if it's going to hurt you. And Randy—" He wiped his mouth. "Randy's a bit fucked up. You sure you want it to be with him?"

Sam didn't know that either. He worried about what Randy was doing, about his jealousy. But what right did he have to be possessive? Randy would stay in Mitch's life. He wouldn't.

"We can get an escort," Mitch suggested, skimming his hand up Sam's hip. "It doesn't have to be him."

But Sam knew it did, somehow. They could bring in anybody to be the third, but Randy would still be there, forever between them. *Finish this,* he told himself. *Finish this, one way or another.* He lifted his face and looked at Mitch. "I want to do it."

Mitch nodded, but Sam couldn't read anything on his face as he kneaded Sam's hip. "We'll go slow. You can back out at any time. I'll keep him in check. You decide, Sam. You make all the rules. I won't let anything happen you don't want."

When Mitch bent down to kiss him, Sam opened for him, both his mouth and his body, and he let himself go, praying he hadn't made a terrible, irreparable mistake.

THEY STARTED AT the Watering Hole.

This was a small bar not far from Randy's house which while not strictly gay, at the very least didn't mind what way the patrons' fences swung. Or maybe they just didn't mind Randy. Everyone in the bar knew him and either greeted him with a lusty shout or a glare over the top of their drinks. The bartender served up a draft for him automatically, and Randy accepted it with some pride, clearly enjoying his position in this public court.

They recognized Mitch too, and his reception was different. It was a man at the end of the bar who saw him first. "Mitch Tedsoe!" he called out, and embraced him. Others soon followed, but there was no bellow of welcome for him, only quiet nods and subtle waves. Whispers flew as he crossed the room. Many people ogled Sam as well. As Mitch predicted, they regarded Sam with either derision or leers. As much as Sam said he didn't care, he found that, actually, he did.

Randy returned to where Mitch lingered and took his hand, tugging him farther into the bar. "Come on, Old Man, and say hello."

Mitch held back, but Sam nudged him forward. "You go on. I'll sit here and get something to drink." Frowning, Mitch reached into his pocket. Sam held up a hand. "I have money."

Pulling out his wallet anyway, Mitch pressed a twenty into his hand. "Shut up and take the money, Sunshine." After a gentle caress of Sam's wrist, he followed Randy. Sam sighed and shoved the money into his pocket before heading to the bar.

The man who'd greeted Mitch raised his glass in silent toast to Sam and nodded to the empty stool beside him. "Come take a load off, sugar, and I'll buy your first round."

Sam sank into the chair, but he stuck out his hand as he did so. "Hi. I'm Sam." *Please don't treat me like a back-alley whore.*

The man unwrapped himself and sat up, extending a long, beautiful dark hand to engulf Sam's. "Tyke." He gestured to the bartender. "What are you drinkin', Sam?"

"Um—" Sam glanced quickly toward the taps, but he couldn't see them. "Just a beer. Blue Moon would be nice, if they have it."

They did, and Sam soon sipped at a tall pint with an orange in the bottom as he sat with Tyke, watching Randy and Mitch make their way around the bar. In the background, club music played, and Sam tapped his toe a little as he drank and soaked up the atmosphere.

"So the circus is back in town." Tyke grimaced. "I thought those two were finished for good, but I guess not."

"You know both of them?" Sam tried not to sound too eager for information.

"Ain't nobody in here doesn't know about them. Used to be the best show in town, to sit here at this bar and watch those two carry on. Sometimes they were fightin', sometimes they were neckin', and sometimes both. Of course, the best shows were when they brought in a third party." He gave Sam a look up and down. "That gonna be you tonight, sweetheart?"

Sam said nothing and retreated into his beer, but he suspected his ears were red.

Tyke snorted. "Shit. Well, luck to you."

"I'm not one for putting on a show."

"Don't matter. Randy will make sure you do." Tyke watched as Randy waved his arms and told a story to a group of men at the far wall, while Mitch stood by, reserved. "You came in with the big one, didn't you? You with him? Or did they pick you up together?"

"I've been traveling with Mitch."

"Oh, one of *those*." Tyke motioned to the bartender. "Joe, couple of tequilas over here, huh?"

Sam shook his head. "Um—thanks, but I'll stick to beer."

"Sugar, you're gonna need at least three shots of something, if you're tangoing with those two." He grimaced, still watching Mitch and Randy. "If you're with Mitch, that means Randy's on your ass. He's either trying to scare you or steal you. And trust me, sweetheart, it will be one or the other."

"But Randy said he wasn't interested in Mitch," Sam protested. "I mean, I think he wants to sleep with him again, but he doesn't—"

"That boy don't know what he wants," Tyke said with some disgust, "except that he wants the big guy. He doesn't exactly want to fuck him, but he sure does love fucking *with* him, and I mean that in every sense of the word. They don't sit well together, not for long, and something always blows up when they hook up, but they keep coming back."

"They do?"

"I was here for their last one two years ago. Mitch came in with a boyfriend. He wasn't going to pay any attention to Randy, he said. They were over for good." Tyke picked up his tequila, swirled it, and set it down before reaching for the salt. "By ten, the three of them were in a booth, the boyfriend's legs hooked over their knees, eyes rollin' back in his head. By eleven he was out in the alley getting it from behind by Randy. By midnight they'd taken off. Mitch got really drunk, and when Randy came back at two, gloating, Mitch punched him out cold. They had to take Randy to the hospital, and by the time he got out, Mitch was gone."

Sam stared across the room, able to imagine this scenario all too clearly. Then Randy caught him looking, winked, and Sam retreated into his beer. When he put the glass down, Tyke pushed the tequila in front of him, and the salt, and Sam licked his wrist. Once he knocked the shot back, Tyke handed him the lime, but as his hand came away, his fingers lightly stroked Sam's wrist.

"You want to blow off these losers, baby, and come party with me instead?"

Sam took the lime out of his mouth, stared at the bar a second, then gave in and laughed. When Tyke raised an eyebrow, Sam reached for his beer. "I have been hit on more in the past four days than in my whole life."

"That's just sad." Tyke pushed another tequila at him. "Where you from? Kansas?"

"Iowa."

"Shit." Tyke licked his wrist and took the salt from Sam. "Wait, they got gay marriage in Iowa, don't they?"

Sam drank the shot and reached for a lime. "But it didn't do much for my dating stock."

"Well, come on then, babe—let's go party. Let those two fuck each other up." Tyke's hand slid up Sam's thigh. "Let *me* fuck *you*."

"Mitch is my ride home." That felt too crass, too unfinished, so he made himself say the rest. "Also, I like him."

"Fuck." Tyke nodded at the bartender. "Joe, this poor boy's drinks are on my tab tonight. It's the least I can do."

"*No.*" Sam stood, pulled out his wallet and produced the fifty he'd tucked behind his library card. He handed it to the bartender. "That's for *his* drinks, and mine, and Mitch's and Randy's." He lifted his chin. "If you take credit cards, I'll cover their tabs at the end of the night too."

He hadn't tested his card after reactivating it, but he figured the odds Mitch would let him get away with paying were low anyway. What mattered was right now, where Tyke and the bartender and several other strangers looked at him, impressed. Either that or they thought he was crazy.

Whatever they thought, he felt good, and when the song shifted and Bananarama's "Twisting" started to play, he turned to Tyke. "Dance with me."

Tyke pulled back. "Fuck no, you aren't dragging me into this bullshit."

"I'll let you grab my ass." Sam delighted at the dark light he saw pass over Tyke's eyes.

"You'll let me grab your dick." Tyke rose, taking Sam into his arms. The bartender grinned, reached over to a knob on the wall and the music got louder. Tyke led Sam to the dance floor, sliding his body against Sam's own, spinning him so they were back to front, his hands traveling down Sam's sides, his hips, his thighs and— with everyone watching—made good on his threat.

Sam lifted his arms, laughing, and wrapped his hands around the back of Tyke's neck as he let the man lead him in an undulating dance. He ignored Randy, who looked surprised, focusing instead on Mitch, who was difficult to read. He paused, still moving with Tyke, but he kept watching Mitch, waiting for any sign this was too far and he should stop. But Mitch just watched, and then slowly gave him a tiny, sensual smile.

Randy came toward him, and Sam knew Mitch wouldn't be far behind. *Here we go.* Sam shut his eyes and surrendered himself to his dance with Tyke, knowing it wouldn't last long.

But Sam did dance awhile with Tyke, all the way through the song, in fact, and when it was over and several of the patrons applauded, it was Randy who clapped the loudest. It was Randy who took his arm, slid his hand to Sam's hip, and led him by his belt loop to where Mitch chatted with old friends. He kept Sam at his side, his hand on his back, his butt, and his body in general, which Sam saw was quietly noticed by everyone.

Sam worried about what Tyke had told him, and for the sake of their audience he kept himself unresponsive, but this only emboldened Randy, which in turn aroused Sam. Humiliation—that's what this was, what he was into. As he stood smiling and pretending to listen to the conversations around him, Randy fondled him openly and Sam bounced between reveling in the sensations and worrying the next thing he knew he'd be tied up in some S&M dungeon with a tail sticking out of his ass and a ball gag in his mouth while men peed on him.

Because he'd read about this sort of thing, and he knew what he was doing was turning into a *sub*. Subordinate. Submissive. Someone who wanted people to do things to him, to shame him, to punish him. It sounded fine, maybe exciting in theory, but when he saw some of the sites about submission—and worse, read the free online porn—he lost all his taste for it. He didn't want to call Mitch Master or Sir. That was just weird. Fine for other people, but he'd feel stupid saying it to Mitch. But that was where the safe-word thing had come from. He'd figured that out. So Mitch must have been into this, or at least knew about it. Sam didn't want to be in "the Scene".

He didn't want a collar. The tying up was okay. The kinky sex was absolutely fine. And he wanted to do whatever this was they were doing with Randy, though it was probably the stupidest thing he'd ever done. It

was hot. It felt good. It felt dangerous. It was a dangerous man groping him and displaying his possession
against Sam's will, in front of Mitch, whom he actually
wanted. Sam was an object, a thing to Randy, little more
than a walking sex toy he could turn on whenever he
wanted.

It felt so, so good.

So good, in fact, that he had to break off what
Randy was doing to him or risk humping the edge of
the table or at the very least crying out in breathy gasps.
Randy and even Mitch, he suspected, would love that,
but this was more performance than he was willing to
give. Murmuring an excuse, he stumbled across the bar
toward the bathroom with as much grace as he could
manage, which wasn't much at all. He did return Tyke's
salute on his way into the hall. Once he was inside the
bathroom, though, he went to the corner, pressed his
hands to the cool concrete block and sank wearily
against it as he waited for his erection to go down.

When someone put a hand on his shoulder, he
nearly leapt out of his skin, and he got ready for more of
Randy's molestation. "Just give me five fucking
minutes," he snapped, but when he looked up, it wasn't
Randy behind him.

It was Mitch. Chagrined, he started to back away.

Sam grabbed the front of his shirt, hauled him into
the corner and kissed him. "I thought you were Randy."
He nibbled at Mitch's lips before diving in again. "Oh
my God, Mitch, I'm going to come in my goddamn
pants."

Mitch laughed, low and wicked, thrusting his tongue deep into Sam's mouth before sliding his lips down his chin and neck. "I can take care of that." He unbuckled Sam's jeans.

"Not here," Sam protested, but Mitch was already on his knees, and Sam's erection, leaking precome, was in his hand and headed for his mouth.

"Wish you would have worn the ripped jeans." Taking hold of Sam's thighs, Mitch swallowed him down.

Sam came immediately into Mitch's mouth. He twitched for several seconds after, pumping helplessly as Mitch lapped at him before zipping Sam away. He wiped at his mouth as he rose, looking pleased with himself. "Having a good time, Sunshine?"

With a strangled sound, Sam collapsed against him. "Oh my God, it felt so...lewd, standing there, letting him feel me up. I mean, he *grabbed my cock* once, right through my jeans. He had his hand down the back of my pants. He had his *finger in my ass*. Right there, where anyone could see." He shut his eyes and nipped at Mitch's buttons. "Mitch, am I depraved?"

"In the most beautiful, wonderful way." Mitch kissed the top of his head. "Come on. Let's go fuck with his head some more."

CHAPTER TWENTY-TWO

"**H**OW WAS I fucking with his head?" Sam asked as Mitch led him back into the bar.

"You stood so still. You didn't react at all, and then you ran."

"I reacted. Trust me, he knew. He felt, anyway."

Mitch patted Sam's ass. "Keep up the good work, Sunshine."

Sam followed Mitch to the booth, where Randy sat in the place where Mitch had been. He started to rise, but Mitch shook his head. Randy did look uncertain, Sam realized with surprise. He seemed even more confused when Mitch nudged Sam over to sit beside him.

"So you're from Iowa, are ya?" one of the guys said as Sam settled in. "Hawkeyes, or Cyclones?"

"I'm not one for sports," Sam admitted. "Though I always thought it would be pretty to live in Ames, so Cyclones, I guess."

"I'm from Sioux City. Born and raised. Moved out here ten years ago because I got sick of the snow. But I did like goin' to Ames for the football games. Especially the Iowa/Iowa State game. God, those games were a good drunk." He elbowed Mitch. "Usually could convince some of the frat boys to give you a piece too, if you played your cards right."

The idea of introducing himself to frat boys for a fucking both excited and terrified Sam. He reached for his beer and found it had been refilled.

"You go to Iowa State?" the Sioux City man asked.

Sam set his beer down. "Middleton Community College. I'm studying nursing."

It was a little depressing that even at a table full of gay men, this still garnered snickers, though he quickly learned it wasn't the usual mockery when a man on the other side of Randy asked if he was giving free physicals later. Sam blushed and sank deeper into the booth.

Randy stroked his thigh.

It was a tentative move, which had Sam feeling wicked realizing he'd managed to unnerve a man he'd started to think was part goat. So Sam decided to encourage Randy, opening his legs and giving him a quiet invitation to continue. It was a lot easier now that he'd had some release, but when Randy's hand slid between his legs, cupping him, he still reacted, though thankfully not as strongly.

Sam looked across the table. Mitch watched, and his gaze inspired Sam to be even more open to Randy's daring fingers. His eyes were all for Mitch, though, reveling in the way *he* watched so boldly, clearly knowing what was going on underneath the table, enjoying it as much as Sam. He remembered the way Mitch nudged him at Randy, giving Sam to his friend.

The memory made Sam shudder.

Randy leaned over and nuzzled Sam's cheek. "You doin' okay, Peaches?" When Sam nodded, Randy purred and lowered Sam's zipper. Sam didn't move, not until Mitch's foot nudged his own. Randy glanced across the table at Mitch, his expression wicked as he deftly pulled Sam's half-rigid cock from his underwear.

"You're a little under the weather," Randy murmured, stroking him. "Don't tell me I'm doing something wrong."

Sam kept watching Mitch. "Huh-uh."

"Scared?" Randy licked Sam's ear.

The toe of Mitch's boot ran up the inside of his jeans, and Sam shut his eyes. "No." He tipped his head back to give Randy better access to his neck.

Randy's hand on Sam's dick was suddenly a little tight. Sitting up, Sam saw Randy narrow his eyes at Mitch, who wore a smug expression. Randy let go of Sam and swore under his breath.

"You whore," he said, whether to Sam or Mitch it wasn't clear.

Mitch offered up a mocking kiss before turning to Sam. "You ready to go have dinner on the strip, Sunshine?"

It had been a long time since Randy's egg casserole, which hadn't digested well with how much the laundry incident had unsettled him. Sam nodded, fastened his pants and took one last drink of his beer before rising with Mitch out of the booth. Randy came too, but he didn't touch Sam anymore as he and Mitch said their goodbyes to their friends, not until they were heading out the door, and there he did nothing more than grab Sam's elbow. "You let him get you off in the bathroom."

Mitch tossed his keys in his hand with a joyful twist.

Sam rolled his eyes. "Well, you know the rules. You only get so long at the piñata, and then someone else gets to try."

Randy laughed, but Mitch sobered. "Sorry, Sam. I don't mean to make you a game."

Sam squeezed his arm. "I don't mind," he said, and he warmed when Mitch smiled at him.

Mitch drove, leaving Randy free rein with Sam, but he was much less aggressive. He still smarted, apparently, from being bested, and was seeking a new course of action. But Sam thought maybe he respected Sam more too. *Maybe this will work, and I won't screw them up again.* He encouraged Randy's hand higher on his thigh.

They parked in a garage and headed up the Strip, letting Sam gawk and point at the lights and the sights. He saw the Luxor pyramid, and the castle of Excalibur, and the mini New York City. They ate at the buffet at the Mirage, then stopped at the Paris casino and gambled a little, but after losing five dollars in less than three minutes, Sam refused to play anymore, preferring to sit on Mitch's knee and cheer him on, until he too gave up, and they went to find where Randy had gone.

"I can't believe you lost forty dollars that fast, and you don't care," Sam said, still shaken by the thought as he followed Mitch across the casino floor.

Mitch shrugged. "Randy will make up for it. But

speaking of money—" He pulled a fifty out of his pocket and handed it to Sam. "I believe this is yours."

Sam stared at the money. "Is that the money I put down at the bar?"

"I gave you money." Mitch tried to stick the bill in Sam's pocket.

Sam backed away, getting angry. "I wanted to buy my own drink. And I bought Tyke's too." When Mitch caught his hands and forced the bill into his jeans, he fought him, torn between his rage and his reluctance to make a scene. "*Mitch!*"

"You need to save your money for school." Mitch shoved the money in place and let him go. Sam sputtered and reared back to give him some sass, but Mitch walked away, calm as you please, leaving Sam little choice but to trail along behind him, quietly steaming. When they came to the blackjack table where Randy played, Sam went to the other side of Randy, keeping himself as far away from Mitch as possible.

"Uh-oh, trouble in paradise." Randy sounded pleased. He kept his eyes on the table as the dealer laid down his card, then raised a finger to indicate he wanted another.

Sam watched the card come down. Randy held up his hand, sat back and waited, first as the other player went over and then as the dealer went over twenty-one as well. Randy clapped his hands once and looked with satisfaction at the cards.

"Peaches, you bring me luck." He scooped up his chips.

Mitch nodded at a set of tables across the room. "Figured you'd be playing poker."

"Warming up, warming up." Randy stood, put an arm around each of their shoulders and glanced between the two of them. He did a double take at Sam. "Peaches, what happened?"

"Leave it," Mitch said, which only made Sam angrier.

He slid his arm around Randy's waist. "So, you're good at gambling?"

"I'm not bad," Randy said, clearly indicating he thought he was pretty fucking good.

Sam reached into his pocket, pulled out the fifty and held it up. "Win something with this for me."

Randy appeared puzzled, but when he caught Mitch's glower, he laughed. "Okay. But what do I get for it?"

"Well—" Sam didn't know. He didn't care. He only liked seeing Mitch not so sure of himself. "The money?"

"I don't *want* the money, honey." Randy trailed his hand down Sam's back. "What do I get, Sam, if I double this for you?"

His hand teased at Sam's waistband, his thumb lifting up Sam's T-shirt to scrape against his skin, and the motion bled the last of Sam's anger out of him. "I—I don't know. What do you want?"

"Shit." Mitch unhooked himself from Randy and turned away. Sam saw him reaching for his packet of cigarettes.

"Peaches, Peaches, Peaches," Randy said, "you are

so much fun. What do I want? Oh my. The possibilities. Let me think."

Sam swallowed as Randy's fingers slipped into his waistband. It was a given he'd be offering some sort of sexual act. "I—" His voice broke, and he cleared his throat. "I could give you a blowjob."

"Boring." Randy's fingers wedged between his cheeks. "I want this, honey. Your ass."

Sam stiffened. "I'm not going to let you fuck me for—"

"Not fuck," Randy corrected, and caressed Sam's cheek. "I want to lick it."

Heat slammed into Sam. "For h-how long?"

"How long did you give Mitch in the bathroom?"

Sam blushed. "A minute and a half?"

"I want five." Randy nodded at Mitch. "And he watches."

That, actually, had been the only part Sam worried about: being alone with Randy. "Okay. What do I get if *you* lose?"

"What do you want?"

Sam had no idea. He tried to think of what Randy had that he wanted. Anything sexual would please him, and he wasn't sure he wanted to ask for that anyway. He bit his lip, trying to think.

"I won't lose, just so you know." Randy unhooked his arm to pocket the fifty. "How about if I lose, I teach you to play poker?"

"If you lose," Sam said, "you have to answer any questions I ask for five minutes. Answer them *honestly*."

"Deal." Randy tucked his cup of chips into the crook of his arm and rubbed his hands together. "Now. Who's dealing tonight?"

It took Randy several minutes to choose a table, and when he finally sat down, he was serious in his play. Sam stood behind him, not really understanding the game. Before he could even pretend to understand what was going on, it abruptly concluded.

Randy lost.

"Patience," he said, unconcerned, when Sam gave him a look of surprise. "Poker is about the pot, Peaches. Besides, I'm still warming up my hands." He leaned close and added, "I'll be sure to have them nice and toasty before I collect."

Sam retreated behind the chair and didn't shrink away when Mitch came up beside him.

"What'd you bet?" he asked, as they watched the dealer pass out new cards.

Sam leaned in close and whispered to him. Mitch gave a quiet grunt that could have meant anything, and Sam added, "But you have to watch."

Mitch's lips quirked in a small smile. He leaned forward and clapped a hand on Randy's shoulder. "Win big, Skeet." He rocked on his heels, settling in to watch.

Randy did. He took the next hand, and the one after that. He lost on the third but not by much, and then he won three times in a row. He picked up his stack, held them up near his shoulder without turning around and said, "That's one hundred, Peaches."

Sam blushed as he stared, hypnotized by the neat

stack of chips. They might as well have been a dildo, for their effect on him. But then they vanished, and Randy set them on the table.

"Double or nothing." Randy motioned to the dealer. "I'm in for another."

"All at once?" Sam cried.

"That's not how you play poker," Randy said, but he wasn't mocking. "No worries, baby. I'll get you your money."

Randy's long fingers curled over the edges of his cards, his body posture relaxed as he continued to play. He won his hand, pushed out more chips, and won the next too. He lost two after that, but the next pot was huge, and he won it, and after the next hand, when Randy won again, a huge grin split his face.

Randy rose, nodded to his fellow players and scooped up his chips. Then he kissed Sam on his cheek. "Time to collect."

Sam rubbed the spot on his face that he'd kissed. It felt electric. "What—*now*?"

"That's right." Randy glanced at Mitch, and for a minute it was the poker game all over again. Whatever went on in their stoic exchange, it ended when Randy turned away in disgust. "Double bluff. I should have known."

"What?" Sam's heart hammered so loudly it echoed in his head.

"I think we can find a place down the hallway on the second floor." Mitch jerked his head toward an escalator.

Randy snorted and pulled Sam against him. "You can't let him win all night, you know."

Sam tripped over his feet as they led him away from the floor. "I don't even know what you're talking about."

Randy grimaced and nodded at Mitch, who all but ran to the escalator. "If I'd have known how badly he wanted to watch, I would have insisted he not."

"I wouldn't have agreed." Sam caught the eye of several people they passed, wondering what they'd think if they knew he was about to go off and let someone lick his ass to satisfy a bet. While his boyfriend watched.

"Yes, I know." Randy pursed his lips. "I'm losing my touch, I think."

"We're seriously going to do this *in the hotel*?" Sam felt they'd strayed from the important detail of this scene.

"Know just the place." Mitch sounded cheerful as he hopped onto the bottom stair of the escalator.

Oh my God. Sam looked at them both. "You've done this *before*?"

"Yes," Mitch answered, but at the same time Randy said quietly, "Not quite like this."

CHAPTER TWENTY-THREE

T HEY LED SAM to a bathroom.
It was a single stall far, far at the end of a hall, situated near a ballroom which at the moment wasn't being used. The way to it was dark, and from the look the security guard gave them, they weren't the first ones to consider the out-of-the-way room's potential alternate uses. But Sam soon learned he'd misunderstood, because as soon as Mitch pressed some money into his hand, the guard smiled and left.

"In you go." Randy hustled him inside. Once the door closed, he pushed Sam into the corner by the mirror. Behind them, Sam heard Mitch set the lock.

Randy's hands were on Sam's waistband, and his fly—Sam gasped softly as his jeans and underwear slid down his hips. He shut his eyes, hot and cold at once, completely terrified as Randy's hands—warm as promised—grazed tenderly over the bare cheeks of his ass.

"Ten minutes," he said silkily. "Start the clock, Ted-soe."

Double or nothing. Sam felt slight pressure on his butt as Randy knelt and settled his knees on the floor.

Sam opened his eyes and caught sight of Mitch in the mirror, saw him leaning lazily against the door, his eyes intent on Sam's bare ass. Doubt swelled up suddenly in Sam, swamping any remaining lust.

"They are a fine pair of peaches, Peaches." Randy traced his finger down Sam's crack.

Sam shivered. *Wait,* he tried to call, but his throat was too dry to speak. He licked his lips, swallowed and tried again. "Wai—"

Randy parted his flesh, pressed his tongue to Sam's hole, and Sam's speech got lost on a low, helpless moan.

Wet. Sam pressed his forehead into the juncture of the mirror and the wall, curling his fingers into tile and glass as Randy's tongue ran up and down the length of him. He licked lightly at first, and then came at Sam with fierce pressure, pushing against his anus, wiggling until Sam gasped, flexed, then gave way and let him inside.

Mitch is watching. Mitch is watching this happen to you. The thought sent Sam into a terrifying orbit, and he searched for Mitch in the mirror. He stood on the other side of the room, arms folded. The only thing about him that had changed was his face, and as soon as Sam was aware of it, he couldn't look away.

Mitch wasn't angry. Mitch was...something. Aroused wasn't the right word. That implied something nicer than what Sam saw. Mitch looked like Sam felt when he indulged in really dirty porn. This was what Sam felt without the guilt. This was a man watching raw sex and liking what he saw. It had nothing to do with

Sam, though as soon as Sam thought this, he knew that wasn't true, even before Mitch's eyes lifted, caught Sam's, and the tenderness came back.

You okay?

No words, but Sam heard them all the same, and they were enough. He relaxed a little, nodded imperceptibly and shut his eyes, sliding into the sensations Randy gave him.

And Randy was definitely giving him sensations. Sam sank into the corner, trying to find the counterpoint within himself to what he'd seen in Mitch's face. It felt so good, what Randy did, and part of him—most of him—was turned on because this was nothing more than a lost bet. He let Randy do this because Randy wanted to use him, both for his own pleasure and to get a rise out of Mitch. The part of Sam that had spent the last ten years feeling guilty for wanting this screamed, and it took him away from full release. So as Randy licked and thrust and wiggled his tongue up, down, around. and inside Sam's ass, Sam pressed his cheek to the mirror and fought for breath as he battled to keep his shame at bay.

A hand touched his shoulder. Mitch stood beside him now, watching him intently. Sam let out a ragged breath and reached for him. Their fingers met at the edge of the sink, and the contact eased Sam. He shut his eyes and floated, the heat of Mitch's fingers burning the shame away.

That is, until he felt a sharp slap against his ass.

It was Randy's hand, and it came over and over until Sam released Mitch and glared at him. Randy glared back. "*My* ten minutes." He pushed Sam toward the wall and fell to his work once more.

"Actually," Mitch said lazily, "the time is up."

Sam and Randy groaned in unison, and Mitch laughed.

Randy slapped Sam's ass again, lightly this time. Then he kissed the dimple at his pelvis. His voice was shaky when he spoke. "Okay. You two are going to give me five minutes alone."

Mitch's eyebrows shot up. "Really?"

"Not for that." Randy sank onto the floor, leaning into the wall. He ran a hand over his face. "Just to recover. Jesus, Peaches, the noises you make could make a man come in his pants. Please tell me I am fucking you later." Sam, who had been trying to fasten his jeans over a burgeoning erection, faltered. Randy rolled his eyes. "Please tell me I am fucking *somebody* later. Or that someone is fucking me. Or jacking me off. Or sucking me off. Or *something*?"

"I think we can arrange *something*." Mitch led Sam out of the bathroom.

Once the door closed, he drew Sam into his arms, pressed him against his own erection, and kissed him hard.

When they broke away, they were both breathless, and they touched each other with tender caresses at complete odds with the crude game they'd just played.

Mitch squeezed Sam's hand. "You only have to say stop, and it's over. I still remember your word. And if you can't say it, hold up two fingers."

"I'm okay," Sam said somewhat reflexively, but as he curled closer to Mitch's chest, he realized, actually, that he was.

The door to the bathroom opened, and Randy appeared, agitated and disheveled.

"There's no point in waiting five minutes," he growled. "Can we go home and fuck now?"

Mitch looked wicked. "We haven't even made it to the Bellagio. Sam would love the fountains."

Randy narrowed his eyes at him and at Sam. Then, with no warning whatsoever, he put his hand boldly to Mitch's crotch. Sam gasped in surprise, Mitch winced, and Randy grinned.

"Sure, we can go to Bellagio." Still smiling, he tightened his grip on Mitch's dick. "And I hope they turn as blue as your goddamned rig, you fucker."

He strode off down the hall, and Sam and Mitch followed, but despite Randy's sense of victory, Mitch smiled too. In fact, Sam didn't know that he'd ever seen him happier.

THEY WALKED TO Bellagio, Sam gawking at everything along the way until they finally came to the huge, arcing sprays of water in front of the casino. As the water danced to the music, Sam simply stood there and gaped. When Mitch put his arm around him, he didn't think twice, just leaned against him and settled in to watch.

It was about then things started to get weird with

Randy.

"I'm thirsty," he declared abruptly. "Let's go to Krave." Before anyone could object or even agree, he grabbed Sam and dragged him in the direction from which they'd come. By the time they arrived at the bar, everyone was thirsty, and Sam was ready to collapse into a booth. He barely had a sip of his drink before Randy took it from his hand, passed it to Mitch and hauled Sam onto the floor. "Dance with me, baby."

Sam tried to glance at Mitch, but he couldn't see him. "Randy—" He gasped as Randy gripped his hips and ground them against his own.

Sam gave in and swayed to the music. He had to admit it was fun to be out in the middle of so many men, dancing with someone clearly determined to get into his pants. He wrapped his arms around Randy's neck and let him hook his thumbs in his waistband. "Does Mitch ever dance?"

Randy slapped him on the butt. "Will you stop thinking about him for two seconds?" Then he paused, noticing the way Sam jumped at the slap. "Hmm. So you want a bit of slap with your tickle, do you?"

Sam wished he could have ingested more alcohol. "A little."

"You let Mitch spank you?"

"I thought we weren't talking about him."

Randy pressed his hand on the globe of Sam's ass. "This is spanking. It's very different. Did you let him?"

Sam nodded hesitantly. "Twice."

"And you liked it?"

Sam nodded again.

Randy moved them to the music, nibbling occasionally at Sam's neck. "I want to spank you."

Sam didn't know what to say, so he didn't say anything. But he thought about it. And thinking about it made him hard. "We'll ask Mitch."

Randy's breath was hot at Sam's nape. "It's your ass, Peaches. You make that decision."

Sam shook his head. "I'll do it, but I'm asking him if he wants me to first."

"He'll want you to."

"I'm still asking him."

They danced a little longer. The song changed, and Sam wanted to go sit down, but Randy wouldn't let him. And once the music started up, Sam didn't want to go either.

"Bananarama *again*." His hips swayed of their own accord. "God, I love this song. I love this whole album."

Randy looked bemused, but Sam ignored him and danced in earnest. He slipped out of Randy's arms but didn't go far, because when he got to the chorus, he spun around and pressed his back to Randy, humming along as he put Randy's hands on his hips and got serious with his boogie.

Randy nuzzled his neck, sliding his hands over Sam's body as he moved along with him.

"Mitch doesn't dance." His lips tickled the flesh of Sam's ear.

"That's too bad." Sam arched into him, snaking his hand up over the back of his head.

"You're not quite as bashful as you were before." Randy continued teasing his ear.

"You had your tongue in my ass," Sam pointed out. "It's hard to be shy after that."

"I want a lot more in your ass." Randy darted his tongue briefly into Sam's ear.

Sam shuddered and threaded his fingers into Randy's hair. "Maybe. Let me take this slow. I've never done it before."

"Peaches, you have had sex before."

"Not with two at once. Not—not fucking. Not all the way." He thought of the twink video, of the double penetration, and he faltered. He couldn't let himself think about that.

Not yet.

Randy's hand closed tightly on Sam's hip. "Then how about just you and me?"

Tyke's warning from the bar came back in a rush. *He'll try to scare you or steal you.* Sam pushed out of Randy's arms and faced him, arms over his chest.

"No," he said with more emphasis than he'd ever given the word in his life. "Does he mean that little to you, that you have to take everything he has?"

He was ready for Randy to argue, but if anything he went still, and for a second, Sam did too, not even aware of the music. Randy seemed…lost. "He has you, does he?"

Now Sam did blush. "I didn't mean—" He looked away, his heart hurting. "I have to go home, before too long. And he knows that. I'm having a good time. I like him. But I don't know how it would ever work with us long-term." His chest tightened further, and in a panic, he brushed the thought away. "I need to go get my drink."

Randy grabbed his arm—gently—and held him there. "I'm sorry."

The sincerity of his words caught Sam. "It's okay." Sam wasn't sure what he was accepting an apology for, but something told him this didn't happen often with Randy.

Randy held out his arms. "Finish your song?"

Sam hesitated a moment, then let Randy arrange his arms around Sam's neck. "I do need to get my drink, after." Sam relaxed into the dance and began to sway. "I wonder if they'll play Kylie?"

"Do you have a favorite song?"

Sam gave Randy an affronted look. "There isn't just *one.*"

"One you want to dance to?"

Sam considered this. "If I got to pick anything? 'Made of Glass'. But it's kind of a rarity. They won't have it here."

The song finished, and they went to the table where Mitch lounged sipping his beer, waiting.

"Need to go out for a cigarette?" Randy slid into his chair, sounding oddly hopeful to Sam.

"Nope." Mitch squeezed Sam's knee. "Have fun?"

Sam tipped his beer to his lips and took a long drink. "I love dancing."

"I remember," Mitch replied, and Sam smiled, feeling warm.

Randy rose. "I'll be right back." He disappeared into the crowd.

Sam watched him go. "Is he okay?"

Mitch watched him too. "Not sure. What'd you two talk about on the floor?" When Sam shuttered, he sighed. "I already know he tried to get you to have sex with him alone, so if that's what has you worried, let it go."

"How—?"

"Because he's Randy." Mitch took Sam's hand and stroked it. "What'd he say?"

Sam ran through the strange exchange that had been most of their conversation before he remembered the part he needed to tell Mitch anyway. "He wants to spank me."

Mitch's face changed, a shadow passing over it that reminded Sam of the bathroom at the Paris casino. "And what do you want?"

"I want to know if you mind."

Leaning forward, Mitch kissed Sam on his temple. "Sunshine, I am never going to care. I don't care who you fuck. Even Randy. You can fuck anybody you want to without me. Just tell me about it, so I know."

"But I don't want to fuck anybody without you," Sam protested, and Mitch smiled.

"I know."

Sam met Mitch's gaze, and for a minute he forgot he was in the bar, in Vegas, or even on the planet. Then, as if from far away, he heard the music. His eyes widened, and he gasped. "Kylie!"

Randy appeared, triumphant. "They didn't have the one you wanted, but they did have 'All I See'. Will it do?"

Sam laughed, dropping Mitch's hands. Randy held out his hand, beaming wickedly, and Sam rose, going eagerly to him now that he had things settled with Mitch.

Randy lifted an eyebrow at his best friend. "Want to go have your cigarette now?"

Mitch settled into his chair. "I like to watch."

Randy faltered, but Sam grabbed his hand and dragged him to the floor. "Come *on*. I want to dance."

THEY DID DANCE, until the music paused for an amateur strip show, which they all enjoyed, Sam especially when Mitch leaned over and said he thought that was a good idea for later. He kept imagining he was the one up there, taking off his clothes for the crowd. He knew he wasn't ready for it in real life, but it was still fun to pretend.

He ended up on Randy's lap at some point, which meant before long Randy's hands wandered over him, and after a few more drinks, he tugged at Sam's T-shirt to remove it, and Sam let him. Randy slipped his hands into Sam's waistband, undid his pants, and soon Sam's T-shirt was a flimsy camouflage for the hand job Randy gave him right there in the middle of the bar. Sam tipped his head against Randy's shoulder, watching

Mitch watching him be fondled. Mitch's eyes had gone dark, and Sam realized at the house things would get even more interesting. The thought made him harder, and he forgot people were probably watching, forgot that technically if the bouncer caught them they'd be in big trouble, and he made soft, breathy sounds as he closed his eyes and let Randy take him away.

"I'm going to slip out and have a cigarette," Mitch said, "and then we can go."

Sam, much as he enjoyed what was happening to him, wanted to go now. But when he suggested to Randy that they follow him and let him smoke on the way, Randy shook his head.

"'I'm going to have a cigarette' is Mitch code for 'I need to think'. Unless he's driving, he makes sure he does it alone most of the time." Randy traced his tongue along the outside of Sam's ear. "A lot of the time it's because he's nervous. Right now, I think he's planning."

"Planning?" Sam's belly flexed as Randy's hand cradled his balls.

"What we're going to do with you." Randy's finger moved lower, teasing at Sam's entrance. "This has all been a warm-up to the big game, Peaches. You're going to be the plaything of two men. You ready, baby?"

If Sam were more ready, he'd blow up. "You—you've done this a lot? Taking home a guy, and sharing him?"

Randy's tongue explored Sam's ear. "There's a difference between taking home a guy from a bar and someone like you, who we know. A trick is just a fuck.

But with you, Sam—shit, honey, we've been fucking you, and each other, all night." His free hand stopped tracing Sam's nipple to stroke his hair. "Head games. Jockeying to see who's on top—metaphorically, but I suppose technically too."

"Who won?" Sam let his legs fall farther open so Randy could reach him better.

Randy's chuckle made his body tingle. "You did, Peaches."

Sam frowned. "But I didn't want to win."

"I know." Randy nipped at his nose. "That's what's throwing the game."

Why did it have to be a game at all? "I want—I like when you guys tell me what to do. When you do things to me."

"Then that's what will happen."

"But—"

"Open your legs and hook them over my knees."

The command in Randy's voice caught at Sam. He gentled and complied. When Randy's finger pressed against his hole, he bit his lip and relaxed as Randy carefully entered him.

"If I had lube," Randy whispered, "I'd push harder into you. I'd fuck you right here for everyone to see." Sam gasped, and Randy sucked briefly on his earlobe. "If people asked what I was doing, I'd tell them. I'd ask them if they wanted to watch." His finger pressed a little deeper. "You'd lie here, sprawled like a whore, and you'd let them." He kissed Sam's cheek and his jaw with lewd, wet kisses that left his skin damp. "You want that, don't you, Peaches. You want to be my whore. You want to be a whore for Mitch and me together. You want us to use you, all night. You want what we did in the bathroom at the Paris and you want it to keep going. You want us to make you feel dirty, don't you, Sam?"

Sam, who had been lost since *sprawled like a whore*, gasped open-mouthed against Randy's neck. "Yes."

"Then we're going to give it to you." Randy thrust into Sam. "He's coming back now, and we'll go to the house. Open your eyes and look at him, and let him see what you want. He knows where my hand is. Show him how much you love it when he sees you being used."

They were all the right words, all the secrets Sam had written on the darkest parts of his heart, but that only made it all the more terrifying to lift his head, open his eyes, and see Mitch coming toward them. He wanted to be apprehensive, to hold back, to not let him see, but he knew Mitch wouldn't let him see his lust until he saw Sam enjoyed it too. So he did his best to let go, to do what Randy told him and let Mitch see, let him see what Randy's masturbating did to him, what it made him feel, to let him see how dirty and depraved he truly wanted to be.

He saw the dark light in Mitch's face, saw his own lust, his own depravity, feeding off Sam's.

Randy's finger stilled and left him, and then his hand tucked Sam into his pants and did up the fly.

They led Sam out together, which was good because he was in a complete sexual coma. He was still without his shirt, vulnerable and naked and therefore even more turned on as they wove their way through the crowd, Mitch in front, Sam in the middle, Randy at the rear. Sam felt the eyes of others on him sometimes, and he wondered if they knew, if people sat at tables thinking, *those three will go have sex now.* He wondered if people cared. He thought about Middleton, or tried to, but his hometown and all the guilt and shame it telegraphed were far away in so many ways. It didn't matter, not now. Nothing mattered. Only this.

The walk to their garage was long, and Sam felt even more naked walking shirtless on the street. He let himself be aware of people they passed, saw their judgment, their appreciation, and their indifference. Even when he saw a group of men make faces and mouth *fag* at him, he didn't fear, not with this crowd, and not with Randy and Mitch around him. Especially with Mitch. He worried a little as they went into the garage, worried the men would follow, but they didn't, and the next thing he knew Randy nudged him into the truck. But Randy didn't follow. Instead, he stood at the door and said, "Take off your pants."

"What?" Sam stilled halfway across the seat.

"Your pants," Randy repeated. "Your jeans. Take them off. I want to molest you on the way home."

The thought of riding through Las Vegas naked while Mitch and Randy fondled him, fully clothed, was heady. But his mind raced ahead and found the flaw. "The parking ramp attendant will see. I can't."

"Put your shirt over your crotch." Randy made a hurry-up gesture. "Come on, Peaches."

Sam turned to Mitch, who regarded him impassively. "I can't," he whispered.

Mitch said nothing.

Randy took hold of Sam's belt loop.

"*Violet.*"

Mitch's hand came across the seat, staying Randy's. "That's a no."

Randy blinked. "Good to know." He let go of Sam and slid in beside him. Mitch did too.

Sam's heart beat in his ears as Mitch pulled out onto the street. He hadn't thought about it, he'd simply shouted, and he still reeled from that while the others easily accepted the end to the game. Sam was relieved but confused. Were they done? Had he wrecked it? He shifted in his seat, feeling awkward and remorseful.

Randy watched him. "Is this his first time using the safe word?"

"Just once before," Mitch confessed.

This seemed to flummox Randy. "Have you played that tame?"

Mitch took a second to answer. "Sam gets off on a different kind of domination. Some humiliation, yeah, but inside his own head. He doesn't want it from other people."

Sam quieted at this, rolling the words around in his mind. They were true. He'd just never thought of it that way before.

Mitch was talking again. "Though, yeah. Mostly, we've been tame by your standards, Skeet."

Sam turned to him. "You didn't need to be. I—I

would have done more. I will too."

Mitch rubbed his chin. Then, with some reluctance, he reached for his cigarettes and lit one before he answered. "I was being tame for me."

"Oh." Sam felt shame creeping up like a frost.

"No, Peaches. That's my fault." Randy sank into his seat. "Well, what now?"

Mitch smoked a little and shrugged. "That's up to you."

Randy made a bitter noise through his nose. "Please. I'm not in charge."

They were speaking in some sort of code, and it was driving Sam crazy. "What's going on?"

Mitch said nothing, only continued to smoke. Randy sat quietly at first but finally swore under his breath. "Fuck. Fine, but if you want your five minutes of honesty, you pay for it. I'll swap you your previously mentioned blowjob for some answers."

Sam thought it sounded kind of fucked, but he wanted to hear this. Plus, sex would get them out of this weirdness and back to where he wanted to be. "Okay."

Randy stared out the window as he spoke. "What's going on is that the last few times Mitch and I did this, it went badly. He started liking the third guys we introduced, and I fucked it up every time."

"It wasn't exactly that." Mitch flicked his cigarette ash out the window. "I made some of my own mess. And we rigged the outcome by the guys we were picking. They couldn't handle it, and we knew it."

"Oh, so you tell me all this now, after I've stewed in

my own guilt for two years?"

Mitch shrugged. "You had some of it coming."

Randy seemed somewhat chagrined. "Fair point."

This was still confusing, but definitely more interesting. "So what did you guys do to them?"

"Same thing as you," Randy said. "Took them out, fucked with their heads, brought them back, fucked their asses."

"What did you do that was weird?" Sam turned to Mitch. "Why don't you want to do it anymore?"

Mitch said nothing, just kept smoking.

"Because if he has to choose," Randy said reluctantly, and with no small amount of disdain, "he'll choose 'emotional connection over kinky sex'. That's a direct quote."

Sam tried to digest this, but it didn't make sense. "But—Mitch, when we met, the first thing you did was fuck me in the back of your trailer."

Mitch pushed the spent end of the Winston out the window and reached for another one. "I thought you were asking *him* questions."

"I want to know whether or not we're about to blow everything up."

Randy snorted. "Well, see, you're a conundrum. You're both. You're kinky and emotional at once. But how far, with both? What will happen to you if we take you too far? Will you hate him? Will you decide you like me better?"

"No," Sam said emphatically.

Randy sighed. "Yes. But you still might reject him, if

he's the one who takes you too far. And he doesn't want that."

"You can shut up anytime, Randy," Mitch growled.

"Did you ever think, Old Man, that maybe we'd have encountered less trouble if we'd had this conversation with the others?"

"If we'd said half this shit to any of the others, they'd have fucking jumped out of the truck."

"Yeah, and what does that tell you?"

Sam glared at them both. "Do I need to be here for this conversation?"

"You *are* this conversation." Randy glanced at the clock on the dash. "You have one more minute of truth. Use it wisely, Peaches."

Sam turned to Mitch. "Do you want to forget this? Do you want to call it off? Because I don't want to do this if you don't want to."

He glared at Sam. "So you're going to ask *me* all the questions and give *him* the blowjob?"

Sam leaned into him. "Please, Mitch."

Mitch drew on his cigarette and tossed an angry glare at Randy. "You want to answer this one for me too?"

"Sure," Randy said, but there was no malice in his tone. "He wants this. He wants this so much it scares him. But mostly he wants you." He sighed. "He needs this, the three of us tonight, more than either you or I want this. And it scares him to death."

They pulled into the drive of the house. Sam stared at Mitch while he put the truck in park and turned the ignition off. "Is that true?"

Do you really want me? Do you need this the same as I need this with you?

Mitch stared back at him, his poker face down, his expression as naked as it had been the night of the storm. "Yes."

Sam's heart swelled, and he took Mitch's hand. "I need it too."

"You two," Randy said from behind him, "make me ill."

No we don't. We make you jealous. Sam realized how little time he had left with Mitch, and he found he was jealous too. He wanted more. He wanted this to go on forever. But maybe that was part of the magic, because their time together was so brief.

Would it make a difference if they didn't finish this game? Would it change him in the way Randy hinted if he did? Would it be more kinky sex? Would he be more or less able to stay with Mitch if he did this? Was this that important? Or was it simply sex?

The only way to know was to do it and find out.

Sam touched Mitch's cheek. "I want you to stop holding back. I want you to show me what you want to do to me. I want you to look at me like you did in the bathroom. I want to be your object—for the game. I want to be there because I feel safe with you." He turned to Randy. "And with you." He took Mitch's hand. "But I want you to show me everything you want. I want it raw and almost scary. I promise to tell you if it's too far— *before* it goes too far."

Mitch kissed him gently. Then he looked Sam in the eye and said, "Take out Randy's cock and put it in your mouth."

Sam kept his eyes down until he saw Randy's waist. He eyed the bulge there, small but growing. He reached for it, glancing up at Randy, but Randy only watched, his eyes dark and eager but also patient. Sam undid the fastening and pulled down the zipper. He tugged Randy's underwear down and his erection sprang up. He stared down at it, thinking about how it would taste, about how they would both watch him do this. About how Mitch had ordered him to do this.

About how Mitch wanted him to do this. About how *he* wanted to do this, for him.

Sam took Randy into his mouth.

He was still a little soft, but not for long, not with Sam's lips around him, not when his dick slid a few times to the back of Sam's throat. Sam shut his eyes and sank into his task, licking, sucking, bobbing, loving the soft-hardness of it, loving the feel of it on his tongue, between his lips, the tiny bits of precome he caught from the tip. He wormed his tongue inside the hole, carefully. He swirled the tip, took him deep, deeper, made a soft sound, and fucked himself on Randy's shaft. He fucked his own mouth for his pleasure and for theirs. He felt their hands on him as if from a distance, stroking his back, his arms, his hair, and Mitch slid his knee between his legs. Mitch unbuttoned him, taking Sam's cock into his hand and stroking him idly, as if he had all night to play.

Randy ended it abruptly, lifting Sam's head by his hair. "Slow down, Peaches," he rasped. "Or you'll get the Bellagio fountain all over again."

"I want you to come in my mouth." Sam dived for him.

Randy kept him away. "Yes, eager little slut, but I want to come on your face, and in your hair. And not yet. I'm not as young as you are, and I need to pace myself."

Sam let his head rest on Randy's thigh, clutching at the seat as Mitch continued to stroke him. "Can we go inside?" He sounded as if he were begging. He was. "Please?"

"What do you want to do inside?" Mitch's voice was low and wicked.

"I want you to fuck me. I want you to make me do things for each of you. I want you to watch me. I want you to do all kinds of things to me. Together."

Mitch's hand tightened briefly on Sam's erection. "What do you think, Skeet?"

"I think we need to take this boy inside and fuck him," Randy replied.

Sam shivered, and Mitch let go of his dick to slap his ass. "Get inside, Sunshine, and we'll play."

CHAPTER TWENTY-FOUR

THEY BEGAN IN the living room by having Sam undress.

Mitch made the suggestion, but Randy gave the directions, and Sam stood in the center of the room between them, eyes moving back and forth as he undid his jeans, pushed them down—"slowly, move slowly, Peaches"—and stepped out of them. He stood naked but for his underwear, and he let them look at him. He raised his hands as Randy told him to, turned, and came forward, hands behind his head so Randy could touch his body. Randy murmured appreciatively, telling Mitch what he liked, stroking Sam's belly, his thighs and his ass.

"Off with these." Randy snapped Sam's waistband. "Then bend over my knee so I can play with your ass."

Sam fumbled as he stepped out of his underwear. He tried to lean over Randy's legs, his cock humming in anticipation. But as he started to kneel, Randy's hand slapped him smartly on his bare behind.

"The other way, please, so Mitch can see your finer attributes."

Sam went around the other way, bracing his hands

against the floor, and this time when he bent over, his ass was aimed at Mitch.

Randy skimmed his hand over the bare globes of flesh. "Very lovely. Very sweet." He pushed them both together before separating them, so Sam felt the air on his hole. "Also lovely. Clench for me, Sam. Let me see your little pucker say hello." Sam swallowed and did it. "Very nice." Randy praised him as if he were a child performing a lesson. "Now spread your legs wider, and do it again."

Sam did, and Randy pulled his cheeks wider at the same time. Sam flexed the muscles of his ass, feeling strange and dirty and aroused. They were inspecting him. Thinking about fucking him.

"Mmm," Randy said. "What do you think, Old Man?"

"Looks good to me." Mitch's voice was husky.

"Come and take a sample."

Mitch had eaten Sam out before, but not while someone else held him open, not while Sam leaned over someone else's knees, spreading on command. Mitch had never been this slow, this maddening, as he ran his tongue up and down him, sometimes sliding over to lick Randy's fingers too. Randy pulled Sam tauter, forcing him open almost to the point of pain, and then Mitch entered him, slick and soft and wet, and Sam groaned and opened even farther, surrendering to them.

Randy was harsher than Mitch. Randy enjoyed talking, and while Mitch tongue-fucked him, Randy talked about Sam's hole, and how he wanted to fuck it, and how he admired the way he clenched, how good Sam looked. He talked about the toys he'd use on him, about how he'd tie him down on a bench, spread his legs wide, and spank him with a paddle with a dildo rammed deep inside him, fucking him with every blow. His words were sharp and hard, and some of them were scary and more than Sam wanted. But they were just words, he realized. That was Randy. He fucked your head as much as your body. He found the edges in your mind and tried to send you over them.

Mitch, however, was all about Sam's body. He said little because his mouth was fairly busy, but even when he went away and came back with lube, fucking Sam first with fingers and next with a series of dildos—Randy describing them in graphic detail, threatening to stuff one into his mouth because it looked so good with a cock inside—Mitch still remained silent, using Sam's orifice as a sort of sensory laboratory. What did this dildo do? How did it look? What noises did Sam make when he fucked him with it, or held it deep inside him, or teased him with the tip? All the while Randy ran his commentary on what he saw and how he'd improve things. Sometimes Mitch took his suggestions. Sometimes he didn't. They were a fitting team: both objectified Sam, but in complementary ways. Through it all, Sam remained pliant, spread and open for their use, and in the space between them, he found a strange, erotic peace.

When he complained his arms hurt, Mitch arranged Sam against Randy, arms around his shoulders, bent slightly while Mitch played with his ass a little longer. He used large dildos now, and Sam grunted and huffed as they went inside him. When he'd taken the largest and Randy had complimented him on how nice he looked stuffed and spread by the big black cock, Mitch led Sam to the bedroom with the dildo still deep inside. He whispered something to Randy as he helped Sam onto the bed, and Randy left the room. Sam lay on his back, bending his legs and arching his hips as Mitch lay beside him, toying absently with the dildo.

"I want to watch Randy fuck you."

Sam blinked, rising out of his fog. He looked up at Mitch, who watched him carefully. He waited for Sam to say it was okay, Sam knew, but Sam wasn't sure yet that it was.

"I want it, but I don't want you upset. I don't want you to think I'm choosing him over you." He stayed Mitch's hand, feeling awkward enough without being fucked while he confessed his insecurities. "I know it sounds stupid when I've let him do so much else. I don't know why this is different. But it is." He caught Mitch's wrist and squeezed it. "What's too far for you?"

Mitch put the dildo aside. He thought a minute, stroking Sam's belly while he did so. "Kissing," he said at last. His eyes met Sam's bashfully. "I'm funny about kissing."

Sam blinked. "Seriously?"

Mitch nodded. "That's all, just kissing. You could fuck six men in a row and let me watch or not, and I wouldn't care. To be honest, it really turns me on. I don't know why. Probably some twisted power thing— if you fuck somebody and come back to me, I must be pretty good. But it's hot too. I like to watch the way you move when another man touches you. You look so vulnerable, and so sexy, and then when you get nervous, you turn to me. Not them—me. I worried with Randy it would be different, that he'd charm you away, but if anything, you've charmed him."

He still stroked Sam's stomach, and between that touch and his words, Sam felt safe. He thought of what Mitch had said, about kissing, and he realized Mitch had avoided kisses initially, but now they kissed all the time. Not in public, not often, and never much when others could see. Kisses were private. Kisses were *theirs*. It was oddly charming.

"Did I kiss the man in Denver?" Sam couldn't remember.

Mitch shrugged. "You didn't know, and it's kind of a strange thing to be fussy about, so it doesn't matter."

Sam was crestfallen. "So I *did* kiss him."

Mitch's fingers skimmed low on Sam's belly. "Actually, you didn't."

Sam let out a breath of relief. "I won't kiss anyone else," he promised. "Ever."

Their eyes met, and their inevitable parting cut across them both.

Mitch kissed his forehead. "Not now, Sunshine. Don't think about that now."

"I won't kiss Randy."

"He won't try."

Yet upon their arrival, Randy had tried with Mitch. Sam looked up at him. "I want him to fuck me, but I want you to watch. And I want you to touch me, sometimes, while he does."

Mitch nodded and kissed him, gently at first, then deeper, his tongue stealing into Sam's mouth, luring Sam's into his own. The kiss was more powerful now that Sam knew what it meant to Mitch, and he sank into the mattress, opening not only his mouth but his heart and his soul, a lotus that kept expanding.

When Mitch rose, Sam lay there, sated and soft, but when he left, Sam knew what was coming, and he tensed a little, a virgin laid out for sacrifice. Randy came into the room with Mitch close behind, and the sensation intensified, but it turned him on as well, especially as Randy shed his clothes and knelt, naked, before him.

Sam lifted his legs for Randy, opening himself, inviting the other man in. He watched as Randy put the condom on and smeared himself with lube. He forced himself to relax as Randy probed him, first with one lube-slick finger and next with two. Then he fucked Sam with them, not roughly, but not sweetly, either. Sam looked into Randy's eyes, thinking about what was about to happen, about what he was letting happen to him. He saw the darkness, the lust in Randy's expression, and he loved it, but he feared it too.

When Randy pushed against him, Sam turned his gaze to Mitch. He was on the edge of the mattress, leaning on one arm and one hip, and his eyes were trained on the juncture of Sam's thighs, where his friend was entering his lover. *That's what I am,* Sam realized. *His lover. Mitch's lover.* This was Mitch's secret desire: to watch his lover be fucked by someone else. That was his edge, his danger, and Sam was giving it to him. As Randy pushed his legs up against his chest and thrust inside of Sam, Sam touched Mitch's hand. Mitch lifted it, not breaking his gaze, and kissed Sam's fingers and sucked them briefly into his mouth, matching the pulse of Randy's increasing thrusts.

Randy was rough, but he was smooth too, lulling Sam into a strange sort of trance. Soon Sam begged Randy to fuck him harder, to please move faster, and he became incoherent as Randy ignored him and did as he liked, rolling his hips, withdrawing, pushing deep, raking Sam's prostate with the same ruthless madness that he lived his life, until Sam was mad and raw with his own wanting. Just as Sam was almost there, when he was sliding over the edge, Randy pulled out, whipped off the condom, and came all over Sam's chest.

The spunk sprayed against his skin, a few strands hitting his cheek and mouth. He looked up at Randy, dazed, lost, and still so horny he thought he would explode. Randy smiled at him, proud of himself. Then he glanced at Mitch. His expression darkened, his smile widened, and Randy moved away.

Before Sam could cry out in protest, someone grabbed his hip, and the next thing he knew, Sam was turned over roughly onto his stomach. Someone gripped his hips again, this time with both hands, and roughly raised him up. When he tried to adjust himself, a sharp, strong slap on his ass stayed him. Sam gasped and held still, arms against the mattress, his head down, his eyes wide and staring between his opened legs. Mitch's jean-clad knees filled his line of sight, and he whimpered as Mitch peeled them away, freeing his dick to place a condom on it. As he entered Sam, Mitch wrapped his arms around Sam's waist and torso as he'd done so many times before, and Sam opened himself as he waited for what he knew was to come.

Mitch had never fucked him this hard. He had never made these kinds of sounds, like he was an animal, never had so little finesse that he was nothing more than rutting inside Sam. It was so possessive, so total, so incredibly arousing that Sam could only spiral up a short spike. He screamed into the mattress and came in a hot, almost adolescent spurt into the tangled sheets. Mitch thrust on, and Sam *bit* the mattress now, too sensitive to take this but too enthralled to make it stop, and then Mitch pulled out too. Sam shuddered into the mattress as hot come sprayed across his back. Mitch's erection tapped his ass, and his hand slapped it softly. Sam held himself still, spinning from it all.

"Jesus," Randy whispered from somewhere far away.

Mitch sank onto the mattress beside him, pulling Sam to him with a tenderness all the more stark for how roughly he'd just used him. Sam opened his eyes and smiled wearily as Randy came to lie on the other side beside him.

He was coated in spunk: Mitch's, Randy's, and his

own. He was sore. He was exhausted. And as the three of them snuggled together into a quiet embrace, he realized he'd never felt so sated or safe in his life.

CHAPTER TWENTY-FIVE

S AM HAD A great deal of sex the next few days.

Randy called in sick to the distribution plant and arranged for someone to cover his run to Reno the day after that. He had the weekend off already, he told them, but couldn't get out of anything past that. Mitch pointed out by then they'd need to be heading east.

"We'd best get started then," Randy said. And they did.

They were gentle with Sam the next day, the morning especially—at least, they were kind to the insides of his ass. Randy took Sam on a private tour of his kinkiest toys, some of which Sam recognized from the catalog at the Denver shop. Sam dismissed a great deal of them, but he was intrigued by the sex swing, and he fell completely silent at the spreaders and the paddles.

They did a lot of role-play, but also some general goofing around. Sam's favorite game was when Mitch hooked up his iPhone and fucked him to the entire repertoire of Kylie's Favorites: the *very* best was when they'd dressed him in a cowboy hat, boots, and nothing else, and had him take turns riding them while "Cowboy Style" played seductively on repeat. They had him wear an apron and fondled him while he served them. They blindfolded him and tied him to the bed, taking turns touching him, trying to get him to guess who it was, trying to trick him. Sometimes he got it right, but sometimes he couldn't tell.

They lingered in the house a lot. Randy cooked, and Mitch lounged, his fingers curled in Sam's hair as he surfed through the television channels. They ate, and they talked, about music, about where Sam and Mitch had been traveling, and Randy's adventures. They were careful not to talk about the future.

One night, after dinner, Randy introduced Sam to a spreader.

He began by bringing out wine and suggesting Sam take off all his clothes, because he felt like taking him to his room and giving him a good, rough spanking. Sam agreed readily, but once there, he balked. Waiting at the foot of the bed was a bench, and beside it were several cuffs, and a crop, and a long metal bar with closures on each end.

Sam almost bailed, and he probably would have, but Mitch leaned against the door, watching. He looked lazy, but Sam knew he was there to reassure Sam, to remind him this could stop anytime, but also if he chose to go forward, Mitch would be here to make sure he was safe.

It was enough. Nervous, Sam let Randy bend him over the bench, let him bind his hands beneath it, but he clenched his fists as Randy fitted his ankles into the spreader. It was strange to not be able to close his legs, and for the first few seconds he panicked and almost called out for the game to stop. But when Randy's hand slid down between his open cheeks, his touch gentle and masterful all at once, Sam went pliant and waited for what was to come.

It was, surprisingly, not bad.

It was nerve-racking at first, because he couldn't move, couldn't close his legs, couldn't even shift his position, but once they started touching him, he realized it was the same as always with them, except now his submissiveness was decided for him. They touched him, they probed him, and they talked about him, and Sam shut his eyes and lay there, letting it happen.

They blindfolded him, and that was the only time Sam spoke up, to say, nervously, he didn't want a gag, but Randy stroked his cheek and promised to give him other things to do with his mouth.

It should have been scary, should have been too much, too far, and probably for a lot of people it would be. But kneeling at the bench, spread, trussed, and blind, Sam found not just pleasure but a strange sort of Zen. What was there to be embarrassed about now? After this, what could make him blush? After letting himself become so helpless, what was there to fear?

He welcomed them both into his body, not always knowing who they were, though sometimes he could tell by the tenor of a touch or by technique who was inside him, who stroked him. Mostly, though, they blended together. They spanked him with hands and paddles. They nudged him open and filled him with God only knew what—toys large and small, vibrating and still, ridged and smooth. At one point, Sam did have a tail after all, and even in his sexual euphoria, he laughed.

They put themselves inside him too, first one at a time and then together, and when he finally came, it was with a cock in his mouth and another in his ass. He had become, he realized with quiet pleasure, his very own *Twink Kink*, though at no point was he unwilling in his capture.

On another night, Sam asked, "When the two of you were dating, who fucked who?"

Their embarrassed, awkward reaction was almost more fun than their answers. "We didn't date, we fucked," Mitch said, as Randy added, "That was always the problem."

Sam had to have this answer. "What was the problem? What do you mean?"

Randy's lip curled. "Why do you think we had to go and get a third?"

This confession led to stories of their myriad sexual adventures over the years, and as they all became aroused, Sam had a wicked idea. "Let me see you do each other."

They balked and made excuses, but Sam pleaded and eventually seduced them, drawing them together and sucking first one and then the other, kissing their stomachs and their chests, whispering how much he wanted to see them do it, of how hot it would make him if they did, and before long he had Mitch on his knees, Randy arranging himself behind.

He understood, as he watched, what they meant by saying it didn't work. They were the same ends of a magnet, neither one wanting to give. Both complained they hadn't done this in a long time and demanded the other take it slow. Both seemed more nervous at the prospect of being entered by the other than any reservations Sam had exhibited. But each wanted to do the other, and they dueled all the way to the end, each trying to have the fuck go their way, each trying to direct the other and the other angry at being directed. In the end, neither of them came, and Sam collapsed onto the mattress, laughing.

"Okay." Sam held up his hands. "I won't ever ask you to do that again."

Randy, who had cursed and complained the whole time Mitch plowed him, sighed in relief and moved away. "Thank God." He pulled the sheet over himself. "I don't know how you stand it, Peaches, giving or receiving with that bastard."

"I've never given." Sam smiled as he watched their awkward recoveries.

Randy lifted an eyebrow at him. "You mean with Mitch, or ever?"

"Ever," Sam confessed.

The game changed.

He didn't know why he was nervous about fucking them, but he was. He wasn't sure he could manage both, but they were eager for it to happen, and for all their hesitation at bottoming for each other, they were surprisingly eager to do so for him. They were unfazed when Sam fumbled with the condom, having never put one on himself, and they helped him. Randy was almost playful as he lay back, patient as Sam eased inside him, enjoying Mitch's help and whispered encouragement. Once he got over his awkwardness, Sam enjoyed it too. He felt oddly powerful, almost heady with his discovery, and soon he had Randy breathing fast along with him and clutching at the sheets. But Randy cut him off before either of them finished, saying he wanted to see the flip side too.

It was different with Mitch. Mitch flatly refused to be on his back, and Sam was glad because he didn't think he could do it if he had to look at Mitch's face. He wasn't sure he could at all, at first, which was even more awkward, because he thought it was probably some fucked-up head thing, and he retreated so much Mitch had to sit up and reassure him. "You were beautiful with Randy, Sunshine. It's okay."

"I feel silly." Sam tucked his chin down. "I'm sorry."

"You'll feel better for having done it." Randy nudged him to his knees. "Come on. Think of how good it will be for Mitch."

Randy was right. It *was* good, once he did it. When Mitch began to respond, Sam felt even more powerful than with Randy, and because it was Mitch, their joining was like a circle closing. He lost himself in his thrusts, braver with Mitch than he'd ever been, and to his surprise, he came. Still riding the high of his new experience, he jerked the others off, but as they drifted into sleep, he lay awake, staring up at the ceiling thinking, the smell of sex and man all around him. The next day, as they touched and joked in the shower and the kitchen, and as they dressed to go out, finally cajoling Sam into his sexy jeans, complete with the leather thong Mitch bought him in Denver, Sam acknowledged he thought of them differently too. He'd been inside them. Somehow that made everything different.

He was so used to being the one who got fucked he never thought about what it felt to go the other way. As they led him up and down the Strip, as they took him back to the Watering Hole, everyone seemed shocked to find not only Mitch and Randy but the *three* of them still together. Sam had affected them in the same way they'd affected him. They were all inside of one another.

But soon it would all end.

On Saturday, Mitch announced he'd arranged a load for Chicago, heading out on Monday. The announcement put something of a pallor on their evening, and they lingered at the house, ordering pizza, watching movies, and going to bed without anyone even suggesting sex. They did, however, all go to bed together.

On Sunday, they went to Zion National Park.

To Sam's complete surprise, they went on motorcycles. There were two in the garage, and in days past, apparently Mitch and Randy had driven them everywhere. That day they took Sam too. He clutched Mitch's waist and huddled inside his helmet against the wind as they rode out of Vegas and across the desert, all the way into Utah, to Zion, which Sam discovered was a dazzling array of rock and tunnel and vistas that took his breath away. As the sun streaked over the mountains, Sam stood at the top of a multicolored ridge, for once heedless of the edge, rendered speechless by the silent, brilliant, almost alien beauty before him.

Mitch came up beside him, and without a word, handed him a small plastic bag.

"What's that?" Randy asked, watching as Sam unzipped it.

"My mother." Sam took some of the ash between his fingers and let it go. He watched the gray dust drift down, then upended the whole of it they'd brought along, letting the cascade filter into the valley below. Mitch, who had placed his hand on Sam's back, stroked him gently, then turned and walked away.

When Randy finally spoke, his voice was tender. "I didn't know your mother was dead."

Sam nodded. "Four years ago."

"Good mom?"

"Yes." Sam felt more vulnerable than usual as he spoke about his mother. "I miss her."

"I'll miss you." Randy took his hand.

They were subdued on the return to Vegas, as they poked around a late dinner and made awkward conversation. It wasn't the way Sam wanted to end this, whatever it was. After some wine, he found the courage to ask for one more thing, one more adventure from them.

"I want you both to fuck me," he said, as Randy cleared away the dishes. He took a deep breath and added, "At once. In my ass."

Randy dropped a dish in the sink, and Mitch went still. Sam waited to hear what they had to say.

Randy leaned against the counter. "Well." His voice was a little unsteady. "It's been a while for that one."

"You have to be careful," Mitch said quietly, but Sam could hear his eagerness too. "We have to take our time. If it hurts, you have to stop, Sunshine."

"I want to do it." Sam's confidence grew now that he'd gotten the worst out of the way. "I want to do it with the two of you."

It was more difficult than Sam anticipated, and it almost didn't work. It took them an hour to prep him, with dildos and fingers and a dictionary full of dirty talk, and another fifteen minutes to sort out the position, which ended up being Randy on his back, Sam crouched over the top of him, and Mitch driving the entire business from behind. As they fumbled, Sam wished he hadn't brought it up.

Mitch pushed him forward, captured his and Randy's erections together and carefully nudged them inside. Sam's breath caught, his eyes rolled backward, and his whole world changed.

It wasn't just that what penetrated him was large. It wasn't that it was two cocks. It was that it was Mitch and Randy, and this was the last time with the two of them, the beginning of the end. Mitch had to be in Chicago by Wednesday, which meant two days of hard driving. Two days—that was all. So little left after so long, and though he didn't regret anything they'd done, not even the fights, it suddenly all felt squandered, as if only now he was truly aware of how precious it all was. Ten days. He'd been gone from Iowa ten days, but it felt like a lifetime. Ten days ago he was miserable and angry and lost. Now here he was, on his hands and knees, body buckling as two men who loved him, and whom he loved back, each in different ways, pushed their way inside him.

He let go. As they found their rhythm, as each of them got lost in the erotic connection, Sam let go as he never had before and suspected he never would again. He was aware of nothing, not the sounds he made or the way he moved or what he asked them for in incoherent, sexually charged tongue, but only how they moved inside him, how they touched him, Mitch gripping his hips, Randy sliding his hands up Sam's chest. He gave himself to them completely, with no guilt, no shame, no reservation, and in that surrender he found a quiet, shining pearl he had never known existed—himself.

He was Sam. He was Sunshine. He was Peaches. He was a hot twink fucked by two men at once. He was a male nursing student. He was gay. He was his mother's son. He was a fatherless boy. He was his aunt and uncle's awkward yoke to bear. He was Emma's friend. He was everything, simply, and with no more complications.

He was, as they fucked him, the boy who got off on

sucking straight cock in the school bathroom. He was the boy who liked comic books, especially stories with slight boys and men whose greatest attributes were cleverness and kindness. He was the boy who loved music. He was the boy who fucked deliverymen in the alley while he was supposed to be working. He was the boy who ran away. He was the boy who had been ogled and appreciated and sneered at and envied and seduced all the way across the mountains. He was smart, and he was a fool. He was handsome, and he was awkward too. He was kind, and he was cruel. He was an angel, and he was a whore. He was all these things.

As the two men fucked him, aroused by his body, his cries, his offering, his self, Sam realized, actually, it was all just fine.

He laughed, a deep, lusty, powerful sound which drew him out of the strange space and back into his body, where he wrapped himself inside the power and rode them as hard as they rode him. When his orgasm filled him, he cried out, half-bark, half-roar, and he came, bucking and shouting, across Randy's chest. Then Randy came, and like the end of a string of dominos, Mitch came after. Then he pulled them both out of Sam and drew them all down to the mattress together, where they tangled one more time in an indistinguishable nest of gasping bodies.

"Fuck," Randy whispered, when he was able.

Mitch grunted his agreement, and Sam smiled, resting in their arms as his body happily throbbed between them.

CHAPTER TWENTY-SIX

I T FELT STRANGER than Sam thought it would to leave Las Vegas.

It was odd enough to get into Randy's truck before noon, let alone to be heading with Mitch and Randy to what was work in one way or another for both of them. It was awkward to no longer be their third but a third wheel again as Randy clocked in and Mitch checked Blue over. Sam ended up sitting in a dingy lounge near the repair garage, surfing through his phone, where, finally, he started dealing with the reality of going home.

He texted Emma to let her know he would be home sometime on Wednesday, but that he'd call her sometime on Thursday, unless things went really bad with his aunt and uncle and he needed a place to stay for the night. He emailed Delia to say he was coming home and that he wanted to talk about where they had left things, and where they would go from here. He had no idea where that would be, but he figured he had fifteen hundred miles to find an answer.

He texted Darin and told him to get over himself, because he was done with pizza boxes forever. He didn't text Keith—he wanted to ignore that bastard in person.

He called his advisor at college and asked her some questions, and he called the financial aid office and asked them a few more. He did a search on Craigslist for jobs. He found a few that surprised him, and while he didn't call any of the numbers, he took notes. Returning to Craigslist, he checked for apartments in Middleton, cringing at the prices, but he searched the listings anyway, seriously considering them. Then he got out a pen and paper and made some lists, of what he owed, of what he had, and what he could get rid of.

Then, with all this swimming in his head, he played Sheep Launcher until Randy came and asked him if he wanted to go to lunch.

"Where's Mitch?" Sam asked, shouldering his pack and tucking his phone away.

"Supervising the load. He said he'd try to catch up." Randy pointed at a building across the road. "Mexican sound okay?"

Sam remembered Los Dos Amigos, so long ago. "It sounds great."

The food was not even close to as good as Los Dos, but it was hot, and it was food. Of course, Sam wasn't hungry at all.

"You doing okay?" Randy asked.

Sam shrugged. "It's weird to be going."

Randy wiped his mouth with a napkin and leaned back in his chair. "I never imagined I'd be sitting here with you, that day I met you." Randy's smile was wicked but wry. "I was trying so hard to get rid of you."

Sam let out a shaky breath. "Well, give me another hour."

"That's the trouble. Now I want you to stay." Randy squeezed Sam's hand. "Thank you, Sam."

Sam hadn't expected this. "For what?"

"Bringing Mitch here. He wouldn't have come, otherwise. Or, if he had, he'd have ignored me again. You were our big do-over, and it'd be nice to think we got it right because we're older and wiser, but we got it right because of you." He picked up Sam's hand and kissed it. "So, thank you for giving me back my best friend."

Sam withdrew his hand and poked at his taco. "So it will be old times, huh, when he comes back to town? The two of you, partying?" He poked the taco so hard he made a hole. "The three of you?"

"You honestly think after all this, after everything I *just said*, that he's going to go out and find another Sam? Because that's the bar now, you know. *You.*" Randy kicked him lightly under the table. "I know you're young, but don't be an idiot. Don't let him go."

"Randy, don't." Sam pushed his tray away.

"I haven't been around quite as many blocks as Mitch, but I know the real thing when I see it. Do not fuck this up."

"It's not that." Sam felt sick, and he wished he hadn't eaten anything. He rubbed at his face and slid his fingers into his hair. "I can't describe it. Please. Just let it go."

Randy pushed an envelope across the table. "Here. My number's in there too, and my email, and my address, the whole lot. Call if you need anything from Uncle Randy. Or if you're ever in Vegas and you need somewhere to stay, or if you need a fuck, say the word."

Sam opened the envelope and looked accusingly at Randy. "What the fuck is this?"

"Your two hundred." His eyes twinkled. "Every penny earned."

Sam fingered through the bills. "There's more here than two hundred."

"Have to take care of the college boy." Randy nudged Sam's tray at him. "Go on. Eat. Milk that youthful metabolism while you can."

Sam did eat, most of it anyway, and when Mitch never did turn up, they took takeout to him. Sam snagged a few bottles of Bohemia for later too. They found Mitch sitting in the cab of Old Blue, charts spread out over his lap and his cell phone in his hand.

"Sunshine," he said, distracted as he saw them walk up, "can I borrow your phone? I need to check something, and the 'net is down."

Sam handed it to him, then turned to Randy. He realized this was goodbye, right now, and that he didn't know what to say. Randy smiled, a rueful, Randy smile, and took Sam warmly in his arms.

"Goodbye, Peaches." Randy kissed Sam gently on the cheek and slapped Mitch on the leg. When Mitch didn't pay attention, he slugged him in the arm.

"Hey." Mitch glared down at him.

"I'm heading to work, Old Man. Am I going to hear from you in less than two years?"

Mitch put his clipboard and Sam's phone down and hopped out of the truck. He regarded Randy gruffly for a second before taking the other man in his arms. "I'll call you."

"You'd better," Randy said, and in unison, they kissed one another on the cheek.

Randy squeezed Sam's hand, and then he was gone.

In another twenty minutes, Sam and Mitch were too.

Sam set up some music and settled in his seat, tucking his feet on the cushion and hugging his knees to his chest, watching the desert expand before him. They took the same road they had to Zion, but it was different riding in a rig, and where they would have turned off to go to the park, they stayed on the interstate instead.

Utah was quietly, desolately beautiful, but Sam missed the fat, leafy trees of home. Even when they entered national forests and he saw grass and scruff here and there, he thought of Iowa, of the green cornfields and pastures, and the well-manicured lawns of Cherry Hill Estates, and he missed them. Utah was beautiful, but it was someone else's beautiful. Even so, when Mitch stopped at a scenic overlook for him to get a better view, Sam scattered more of his mother's ashes.

They drove all the way through Utah that day into Colorado, into the western plains, stopping for the night in Grand Junction. Mitch checked fluids again and refueled, and took quite a bit of time with the brakes. They ate at the truck stop restaurant, their conversation subdued and slightly sad. In the truck, Sam surprised him with the Bohemia, which he accepted with a smile and a kiss, and settled Sam beside him on the bed as he surfed mindlessly through the satellite television, never landing on anything at all.

They made quiet, achingly tender love and slept in one another's arms. But once again, when Sam woke in the morning, they were already on the road.

Mitch was more talkative the next day, pointing out landmarks and interesting things about the land they passed, particularly when they went through Glenwood Canyon. He told Sam about the natural hot springs and lamented they wouldn't have time to enjoy them. He told Sam about the Eisenhower Tunnel, and had him look up Loveland Pass on the map, and did his best to illustrate what a wonder and boon the tunnel was. He explained the engineering of I-70 through the mountains, of how it was the last of the interstate system completed, and how hard they'd worked not to disrupt the landscape.

"You like Colorado, don't you," Sam said, after one of the stories.

Mitch shrugged. "I like a lot of places. We live in this huge country with so many climates, so many different cultures, so much different everything. I've been driving it over ten years and I haven't seen it all, not even close. I wish I could get gigs in some of the more out-of-the-way areas, but I don't have networks there yet. I suppose I should go and make them. I know I'll die not seeing it all, but I want to do my best to try."

It was such a Mitch answer, but Sam looked into that life with sadness, because much as he wanted to have that experience too, he couldn't see a way to be a part of it without being Mitch's special delivery forever. "So nowhere is home to you, then?"

Mitch rubbed his thumb along the wheel for a second before answering. "Home isn't a place for me."

He seemed to be waiting for something, but Sam didn't know what he was supposed to say to that, so he settled in and watched the mountains go by.

They stopped in Vail, and Sam scattered more ashes, though not much. There weren't many left. He felt sad, even though he was happy he'd taken her along and spread her everywhere, because he knew she'd rather have taken a trip across the West than sit forever on Aunt Delia's shelf. But he realized she wouldn't ever sit on that shelf, not anymore. She was everywhere now, all over the whole west, and she was in so many rivers and flowers and valleys that she'd keep going, and going and going. The woman who had spent so much of her life tied down, by her situation or by her disease, would never be tied down again. Blinking back tears, Sam tipped the little which remained of her into the rainbow glass chest, and as the secret plan formed inside his mind, it filled him with joy and hope and sorrow all at once.

By afternoon they were in Denver. They didn't stop, though, until Sterling, and they weren't there for long. They pushed on, across the flat of eastern Colorado to the western edge of Nebraska, where the Platte River greeted them once again, and where oaks and ash and maples bowed over its banks.

That night Mitch parked them at a rest stop, not in a town, and he stopped early. He led Sam to a picnic table, which he decorated with a cloth—one of the spare sheets—and to Sam's surprise and delight, prepared for him a barbeque of steaks, potatoes, and at the end, roasted marshmallows, for which he had graham crackers and chocolate bars to make s'mores, though they ate several of the marshmallows simply plain.

Mitch popped another marshmallow in Sam's mouth. "I would have made tamales, but you have to have a kitchen for that."

"It was lovely." Sam kissed him in thanks.

They sat at the picnic table a long time, watching the sun set over the river. They were far from the parking lot, where the cars and trucks came and went, and in that square of space, they created their own world. When night fell and the mosquitoes came out, Mitch fetched a blanket and wrapped them together in it, and when that wasn't enough, he brought out a can of bug spray. He also produced a bottle of sparkling wine.

"I wanted you to have a good memory of our last night," he said when Sam commented on the extravagance of it all.

This saddened Sam, and he sank deeper into Mitch's arms. *I will miss you, so much.* He wanted to say it, but he couldn't. He could hardly say anything. Randy's admonitions echoed loudly in his ears, but Sam was more tongue-tied now than at the restaurant. He thought of Mitch's arms, so warm and steady wrapped around him. He didn't want to leave them, even for a minute.

He started to shake.

Mitch fumbled in his pocket before taking Sam back into his arms, pressing kisses into his hair. "Sam, you have to tell me what you want."

To stay with you. To never go home. To never finish school, to never look back, to have this moment go on forever. But those thoughts felt so childish, so wrong, even though he knew nothing about leaving Mitch was right. "I don't know." He buried his face in Mitch's shirt, then swallowed again. "You. I want you."

The arms came closer around him still, and Mitch's kiss burrowed deeper into his hair. "That you already have."

Sam wanted to sob, and part of him thought he should and would have to later, but right now he wanted to be in control, so he fought himself until he could speak again. "I have to go. I have to go back and face what I left. I have to finish school. I have to…" He clenched his fists and released them. "I have to grow up."

"For the record, you're more grown up right now, I think, than I am. But I know what you mean. You gotta finish what you started."

"I don't want to. But I have to."

There was a pause, and then Mitch said, "Do you want me to come with you?"

Sam lifted his head and studied his lover.

Mitch meant it, Sam could tell, and it touched him. Mitch really would drive around Iowa instead of cross-country. He would live in Middleton for Sam. Maybe, just maybe, Mitch wouldn't mind being tied down.

At least for a while.

With great reluctance, Sam shook his head. "I mean—I do want you to come. But you'd try to fix things I need to fix myself."

"Sunshine, you don't get points for doing everything on your own. Trust me on this one. You end up lonely."

"But I need to learn *how* to be on my own. I need to get my own apartment. I need to make sure I have the right job. I need to figure out how to pay for school and not let myself get caught up in my aunt and uncle's issues. I need to show *myself* I can do this." Sam felt heavy as he placed his hand on Mitch's chest. "I don't know. Maybe I'm being stupid again."

"You aren't being stupid," Mitch said, with heavy regret. "You're being smart. Smarter, in this case, than me." He tipped Sam's chin up and gazed at him with sorrow. "I will miss you, Sam Keller."

The threatening tears finally won, and Sam let them fall. "*Mitch.*"

"Hush." Mitch nuzzled Sam's nose and nipped at it. "And I believe I warned you about using that word."

Stupid. Sam half-laughed, half-cried. "Sorry."

"That's okay. I think I found the perfect punishment."

Mitch kissed him thoroughly, and when Sam wrapped his arms around Mitch's neck, Mitch pushed them slowly back against the table, knocking the remainder of their picnic and the last of the champagne to the ground. He laid Sam onto the sheet and knelt over him, pausing only briefly to tuck something into his back pocket. Then he smiled at Sam sadly and kissed him again.

THEY MADE EPIC love that night. They started on the table, then moved to the grass. They had an interlude at Old Blue, where they necked on the floor, and finally they ended up on the bed.

"Undress for me," Mitch whispered, and Sam did, slowly at first, and as Mitch's eyes darkened, he moved faster, but he fumbled. Mitch reached out to him, drawing him close, and he took over, shedding Sam's jeans and socks and underwear.

Sam cried out as Mitch kissed his chest, trailing his tongue down his sternum, leaving a moist path across his skin as he drifted toward Sam's navel and on to his groin. Sam clutched at Mitch's head as he took Sam into his mouth, but it wasn't long before Sam pushed Mitch against the bed, straddling him backward over his chest to aim his mouth at Mitch's belt buckle. He gasped when Mitch sucked him, fumbling with Mitch's zipper until he'd freed him too, and then he bent, aching, to take Mitch into his mouth.

He kept his eyes open, drinking in the sight of

Mitch's cock, long and pink and ridged with veins he knew so well, and Sam's chest tightened as he realized this might be the last time he ever looked at it again. He memorized every plane of Mitch's body, reviewing every part of him with eyes and mouth and hands, his head spinning and soul aching, because he could not imagine being without this man, not for a minute.

How? A sob mixed with his orgasm as Mitch thrust inside him. How was he supposed to let him go?

When they were both sated, Sam wrapped himself tight around Mitch and held on as if he meant to never let go.

"Wake me in the morning with you," he whispered into the hair of Mitch's chest. "Wake me up as soon as you are."

"I will," Mitch promised, and he did, as the sun was rising. They drank coffee together, nibbled on leftover steak for breakfast, took showers, kissed a little more on the bed, had sex again, and when there was nothing left to do, they were on the road for the last time. By noon, they were in Omaha, and Sam watched with a strange mixture of emotions as they crossed the Missouri and the sign on the bridge read, *Welcome to Iowa.*

By three, they were heading north to Middleton.

Mitch took him all the way into town, past the truck stop where he'd parked on their first date, down the hill into downtown, past the pharmacy and up into the developments. Sam watched it all as if through water, not believing he was back, unable to let himself think about the fact that Mitch was about to go. But at last

Mitch admitted he couldn't go any farther with the rig, and he parked Old Blue in the place Sam had first seen it, on the highway at the bottom of Cherry Hill.

It took Sam an hour to get out of the semi.

They sat on the bed awhile, kissing and embracing, and then, inevitably, they made love one more time. When they were done, Sam reached over to the floor, fished in his pocket and took out his phone and the charger. He handed them to Mitch. "I want you to keep Judy."

"I can't keep your cell phone."

"You use it all the time. You use it more than I ever did. You need one, and really, I don't. I never did. I just wanted it." He pressed it into Mitch's hand. "I like the idea of knowing you have it."

"But it's your phone. You pay for the plan."

Sam shrugged. "I'll get a pay-as-you-go. It's all I need."

Mitch grimaced, and Sam got ready to duke this one out, but all of a sudden Mitch relented. He got up, went to the front of the rig and came back with his own cell. "I'll take it, but you have to take mine, then, in exchange."

Sam took it gingerly. *Mitch's phone.* He was truly ridiculous, but he knew with this he'd never miss Judy. *Why am I leaving him again?* He cleared his throat. "What about your work numbers?"

"I never entered them. They're all in a book. Nobody calls me, but if they do, you can text them on to me." He held up the iPhone. "You sure you want to give this up?"

"Three people text me, Mitch, and I'll see them all in the next twenty-four hours." His stomach knotted, and he wrapped his arms around his chest.

Mitch sat beside him and rubbed his back. "Why don't I stay in town for a few days, to make sure you're settled?"

The idea was so tempting. "Don't you have to get to Chicago?"

He shrugged. "It'll only be a fine. It doesn't matter." Sam heard the unspoken, *not the way you do.*

Even as the yearning filled him, Sam shook his head. "It'll just be harder." Sorrow rose up and choked him, and he leaned into the warmth of Mitch's body.

Mitch held him. "You only have to call me, Sam, and I'll come. And you have to call me when you know what you want, even if it's to say goodbye. Obviously it's not what I want, but this isn't about me."

"Why isn't it?" Sam was starting to get confused on this point. "Why is it only up to me? Why can't I ask what you want?"

"Because you're the one who's twenty-one, Sunshine. You're the one whose whole life has turned crazy and who doesn't know where to set it down now. Everything you said to me last night is true. But me, it's all the same. There's just you or not you. I'll wait to see which it is."

"That doesn't sound fair."

Mitch chuckled into his hair. "That, Sunshine, is life."

They held each other a little longer, swaying softly side to side. They kissed again, so tenderly it nearly broke Sam's heart. Then, at last, it was time to go.

Mitch helped him down, fussed over his pack, and asked him if he had everything. "Your glass box," he said, starting inside.

Sam stopped him. This part took serious courage. "No. I want you to take it with you."

Mitch stilled. "You said that reminded you of your mom."

Sam's throat was so thick. "I put the rest of her inside. I want you to take her with you, to see the country. Let her ride along and soak it all up. Maybe take her out sometimes and let her see something pretty. She'll have so much more fun than sitting on a mantle or a dresser."

Mitch kissed him once more, and when he started to pull away, Sam stopped him, leaned in close to his ear and whispered, "I love you."

Mitch stilled, gripped him tight and kissed his cheek. "I love you too."

People in nearby yards and in cars passing by were watching them, people Sam knew. He didn't care, not when Mitch took him into a fierce embrace, or when he tweaked his ass, or when he pressed their foreheads together as they both fought off tears. He didn't care what they saw, not anymore. He hoped he never would again.

"Goodbye, Sam." Mitch stroked his cheek. "Call me soon."

Sam couldn't say anything, only screamed silently inside his head as he stood on the hill of his hometown, watching the man he loved drive away.

CHAPTER TWENTY-SEVEN

COMING HOME WAS both harder and easier than Sam imagined, and most of what happened after Mitch left surprised the hell out of him.

His aunt and uncle, as he knew they would be, were furious. Delia was, anyway. Norm sat at his computer, as usual. Sam didn't let Delia go on her tirade. He interrupted her to say he knew she was right, at least in part, and that he intended to move out as soon as he could find a place to live. He also gave notice for his job, giving them the option to fire him now for not showing up for thirteen days or asking him to work for two weeks to make up for his absence. But he had no choice on the money for school.

"There isn't anything I can do," he explained as patiently and as calmly as he could. "They offered me a few scholarships, and I intend to take them, but there's no way I can get loans from anyone because of the tax thing, because of your income. It's a dumb rule, but no matter what, they said they can't bend it. I talked to the bank too, hoping maybe we could work something out, but honestly, that's a no-go as well. And I know you don't like this, but I want to go full-time this fall. I want to finish, Delia. I want to move on with my life. I want to see things and do things. I can't do that if I'm living in your basement, taking so long to get through school I'm gray-haired by the time I get out." He sighed. "So I don't know what we do, but I'm open to ideas. I've turned everything I can think of inside out."

Delia sputtered, cycling through her old talking points, and Sam's heart was heavy, knowing that though he'd done his best, nothing here had changed. And then, suddenly, it was completely different.

Uncle Norm turned away from his computer. "I'll cut you a loan."

Delia gasped, but Norm ignored her.

"I'll find out what the rates are at the bank, and I'll match them. I won't collect until you have your first job, and we can work out payments then, but I will collect, so plan accordingly. Write me up a list of what you need for school, and books, and *moderate* living estimates. Then I'll write it up with my lawyer, and I'll cut you a check. Oh, and as for apartments, you can have your pick of any of ours."

"*Norman.*" Delia sat down. "What's gotten into you?"

"Nothing. But this is the most adult he's ever been, and if we don't reward him for that, he'll never become a man. And he'll never leave the basement." He looked at Sam over the top of his glasses. "The other part of the bargain, however, is that you will continue to work in the pharmacy. And if you're serious about it, I'll give you more hours as a tech, which is more money and better practice for school."

"Okay," Sam said, a little blown away. Delia stared at Norm, mouth gaping, but Sam sensed the audience was over and went to the basement.

He ended up moving in with Emma after all.

She'd hugged him in a flying tackle when he went over to her house to ask her—walking, because his car was still impounded from being left by the side of the road—and she asked him to tell her everything about the trip. He told her as much as he could, but he edited a lot, not because he was embarrassed, but because it was private, and it was still tender. He steered her to talk of the apartment instead, and within three hours they were touring one on the hill to downtown.

By Monday, they'd signed for it, and by the end of the next week, they were moving in.

He worked hard all the rest of the summer until classes started in August, and by then he had quite a bit of money saved, even with rent, and he ended up taking almost a thousand off his estimate for Uncle Norm. He paid his tuition in full, and he went to class full-time, and when Keith Jameson gave him a leer, Sam waved and walked on by. Darin followed him around awhile, but eventually he latched on to a slightly overweight first-year student who, by all accounts, not only held out on him until he cleaned up his apartment for real this time, but also got him to turn in enough homework to pass.

Things were looking up for Emma too, as by the end of August she and Straight Steve the Pharmacist were dating.

It turned out his hesitation was because Delia had warned him he wouldn't be kept on if he dated the techs. When Emma heard this, she nearly quit, but Steve told her not to, promising that if it came to it, *he'd* quit, because pharmacist jobs were thick on the ground even in Iowa, and he could get a job anywhere. They started to date, Delia decided to become blind as far as their relationship was concerned, and the next thing Sam knew Steve was practically living with them. He really was a nice guy, and he was good for Emma. He liked seeing her so happy.

Unfortunately, though, their relationship only reminded Sam of the call he'd promised to make to Mitch, a call which, by September, he still hadn't made.

He looked at the photos of the trip all the time, flipping through them on the internet album he'd loaded them to before he gave away his phone. Every now and again he texted Mitch to tell him someone had called or simply to check on him, to see how he was doing. Mitch always said he was good and Sam's mother was enjoying herself, perched proudly in a space he'd made on the dash. Always, always Mitch said to call him soon.

Sam wanted to, more every day. Life felt empty without Mitch, even as Sam put his life together as he never had. Every brick he put in place without Mitch felt hollow. Part of what he learned by being apart from Mitch was that he honestly did love him, that he didn't want Mitch to take care of him, that he wanted to be with him because life was brighter and more interesting with him in it. He understood, too, what Mitch had said about not getting any points for doing everything himself. He needed his uncle and his money, and he needed Emma to help with the rent and to remind him to eat.

The problem was he also learned he needed to work. He missed Mitch, but he didn't miss feeling like his piece on the side, the cute little boy who had come along for the ride. He was getting better grades now that he wasn't so distracted, and he was starting to get excited about doing this nursing thing for real. That was the *big* problem.

How could he get a job and still be with Mitch? Would it be better or worse to see him when he blew into town? Would Mitch, the self-confessed gypsy, truly be happy to stay put? He kept trying to write out a compromise in his head, but he couldn't make it work, no matter how he tried. And so he let time wear on and on, aching more and more with each day but not knowing how to make his misery end.

In October, Randy called him.

Sam hadn't known it was him, at first—he'd seen the number and not recognized it, and almost hadn't answered it because he was heading to class. But he had, and before he even had "hello" out of his mouth, his ear was full of swearing.

"What the fuck are you doing? Why the hell aren't you calling him, you little shit?"

Sam blinked. "Randy?"

"Peaches—seriously, what the fuck is going on?"

Sam put his pack down and sat at the kitchen table. "I don't know what you're talking about."

"You haven't called him. He's going crazy, Sam, and now he's calling *me*, and he's *talking all the time*, and he never does this, so I'm worried, and now *I'm* going crazy."

Sam clutched at the phone. "Randy, I don't know how."

"To use a phone?"

"*No.*" Sam told Randy all his reservations, all his fears and all his unworkable solutions, and then he sank in his chair, so depressed he couldn't straighten his spine.

For a minute Randy was silent, and then he said, "Peaches, I love you very much."

Sam ached. Even Randy could see this was hopeless. "I love you too, Randy."

"Good. Sam Keller, you are a fucking idiot."

Sam sat up. "*Hey.*"

"You by a computer, sweetheart? Get to one right now, go into Google and type in three words. Let me know when you're ready."

Wary and still irritated, Sam went to his laptop and fired up his browser. "Okay, what are the words?"

"Travel nursing jobs."

Hope flickered in Sam's heart, but he quelled it, thinking, *no, it can't be that easy.* But then he hit *search*, and he saw what came up, and his breath caught. Job after job after job, positions around the country, from six weeks to fourteen. Still disbelieving, Sam clicked on one site, and then another and another, and then, quietly, he started to cry.

"Personally, I'm a fan of American Mobile, based on the limited research I did," Randy said, when the silence went on too long. "But you need to make sure you get something with killer insurance, unless it works out that if you base out of Iowa you're covered on Mitch's wherever you go. Most of them really are good, though, for benefits. And, I might add, there are always a lot of openings in Vegas."

"You knew about this?" Sam couldn't stop crying. "Why didn't you *say*?"

"Because I didn't know you didn't know. Jesus, Sam, I figured they'd have posters taped to your head with this shit."

"I didn't know," Sam whispered.

"Now, calm down. Honestly, you're both hopeless. I have no idea what the two of you would do without me."

"Me either." Sam smiled at the phone. "Thank you."

"Call him now." Randy blew him a kiss and hung up.

Sam waited until he'd recovered, but his hands started shaking as soon as he dialed, and when it finally rang and his own voice message came on, he choked up again, and all he could manage to say was, "Mitch—please come home."

Then, because he was already late, he left so he could get to class. He kept his phone on even though there were signs in every classroom to turn them off, and he checked it every few minutes to make sure he hadn't somehow missed Mitch's call. At six o'clock, though, he still hadn't, or nine, either, or ten, or ten thirty, and when Sam woke up at five in the morning with the phone in his hand, there was still no missed call.

"Call again," Emma suggested, when he couldn't eat his breakfast because his stomach hurt.

"I waited too long. He's angry. I waited too long."

"Call him." Emma spread her books out across the table to do her homework.

Sam didn't have class until nine, but he couldn't do his homework, couldn't do anything but clutch the phone and pace the apartment, and when he couldn't stand that anymore, he stood at the window, looking down at Middleton with heartsick despair.

As he stood there, despondent and terrified at what he'd left undone, he saw a semi and trailer go by, right beneath his window, heading down the hill into downtown, a little bit faster than it was supposed to be going on Main Street.

The semi cab was blue.

Sam shouted in joy and dashed across the apartment, grabbed his shoes, and tore frantically down the stairs. He wore the boxers and T-shirt that were his pajamas. He didn't care.

It might not be him. You could be seeing things. But his heart was sick of reason and caution, so it didn't listen. It had to be Mitch. The truck was the same color as Old Blue, and Mitch had said he'd come as soon as he called. It was him. It had to be.

As Sam came down the hill and looked ahead to the pharmacy, he saw that, in fact, it was.

Old Blue blocked the whole right lane, her flashers going, and everyone on Main Street stood around, pointing and wondering what was going on. Sam ran faster, not caring that his lungs were so overworked they were liable to explode.

Mitch was here. Mitch had come for him. He stood on the sidewalk—until he looked up the hill, saw Sam, and started running too.

They met like a movie ending, launching into each other's arms, but unlike a movie, they banged together, hit heads, and came down laughing, not kissing, not at first. Then their mouths met, and though Sam knew all of Middleton would talk of this for *years*, he kissed Mitch back and wrapped his arms around his neck, fully intending to never let him go again.

"There's a job—" Sam stopped for breath. "A service, online—Randy found it." He kissed Mitch hard once more on the mouth, just because he could. "I can go with you, Mitch. *I can go with you.*"

"Is that why you've been waiting?" He tweaked Sam's nose. "I would have stayed wherever you were, as long as you needed to. And I will, until you're done with school."

"But you need to travel. That's who you are—you want to see the country. I can't hold you back."

"Sunshine, I've done nothing but drive loads up and down I-80 between Chicago and Omaha ever since I dropped you off. I couldn't go any farther, because I wanted to be close enough to come right away as soon as you called. You caught me heading *into* Chicago, so I had to dump my load first, before I could come back. I drove here deadhead because I didn't want to wait to pick anything up." He smiled at Sam. "Just you."

A police car pulled up behind Old Blue, and an officer came over. It was a guy Sam knew from high school. "Sir, you'll have to move your rig. You're blocking traffic."

Mitch held up a hand. "I only need one minute. Maybe two." He turned to Sam, looking nervous but determined. "You asked me before I left what I wanted, and I didn't tell you. Can I tell you now?"

"You can tell me anything, anytime. What do you want, Mitch?"

Mitch almost went green for a moment, and then, carefully, disentangled himself from Sam's embrace and went down onto the sidewalk on one knee.

Sam's head spun. *He isn't, no he isn't,* reason whispered, as his heart hoped, and then as Mitch's hand came out of his pocket holding two silver rings, Sam's heart soared, because he realized, actually, Mitch was.

With half the town watching, Mitch Tedsoe took Sam's hand. "Sunshine, will you marry me?"

Sam heard Emma's strangled, joyful cry from behind him. He saw his aunt's shocked face through the windows of the pharmacy. He saw them all, but mostly he saw Mitch and the beautiful, wonderful, better-than-he-ever-dreamed future expanding out before them both as a smile split his face so wide it hurt.

"Yes," Sam replied, his heart so full he was laughing. "Yes."

ABOUT THE AUTHOR

 Heidi Cullinan has always enjoyed a good love story, provided it has a happy ending. Proud to be from the first Midwestern state with full marriage equality, Heidi is a vocal advocate for LGBT rights. She writes positive-outcome romances for LGBT characters struggling against insurmountable odds because she believes there's no such thing as too much happy ever after. When Heidi isn't writing, she enjoys cooking, reading, playing with her cats, and watching anime, with or without her family. Find out more about Heidi at heidicullinan.com.

Did you enjoy this book?

If you did, please consider leaving a review online or recommending it to a friend. There's absolutely nothing that helps an author more than a reader's enthusiasm. Your word of mouth is greatly appreciated and helps me sell more books, which helps me write more books.

MORE BOOKS IN THE SPECIAL DELIVERY SERIES COMING SOON

HOOCH AND CAKE

All Sam and Mitch want to do is get married, but between their busy schedules and the judgment of a small town, it's not as easy as it should be. Then their best friend Randy shows up, and the wedding that almost wasn't is about to become the wedding Iowa never even dreamed to see.

DOUBLE BLIND

Randy can't stand to just sit by and watch as a mysterious man throws money away on roulette. The man's dark desperation has him scrambling for a reason—any reason—to save his soul. Ethan has no idea what he's going to do with himself once his last dollar is gone—until Randy whirls into his life with a heart-stealing smile and a poker player's gaze that sees too much. Soon they're both taking risks that not only play fast and loose with the law, but with the biggest prize of all: their hearts.

THE TWELVE DAYS OF RANDY

Randy and Ethan are ready to enjoy their first Christmas at home together, but when Crabtree ropes Randy into wily holiday antics, Ethan feels left out in the cold. When Herod's new owner discovers his husband only plays at being an imp to hide a Christmas spirit bigger and tackier than Las Vegas, Ethan vows to find a way to have his cake and eat it too. Especially if Randy's the one jumping out of the middle.

TOUGH LOVE

Chenco Ortiz harbors fierce dreams of being a drag star on a glittering stage, but when leatherman Steve Vance introduces him to the intoxicating world of sadomasochism, he finds strength in body and mind he's never dreamed to seek—strength enough maybe to save his tortured Papi too.

OTHER BOOKS BY HEIDI CULLINAN

There's a lot happening with my books right now! Sign up for my **release-announcement-only newsletter** on my website to be sure you don't miss a single release or re-release.

www.heidicullinan.com/newssignup

Want the inside scoop on upcoming releases, automatic delivery of all my titles in your preferred format, with option for signed paperbacks shipped worldwide? Consider joining my Patreon. You can learn more about it on my website.

www.patreon.com/heidicullinan

THE ROOSEVELT SERIES

Carry the Ocean

Shelter the Sea

Unleash the Earth (coming soon)

Shatter the Sky (coming soon)

LOVE LESSONS SERIES

Love Lessons (also available in German)

Frozen Heart

Fever Pitch (also available in German)

Lonely Hearts (also available in German)

Short Stay

Rebel Heart (coming fall 2017)

THE DANCING SERIES
Dance With Me
also available in French, Italian coming soon
Enjoy the Dance
Burn the Floor (coming soon)

MINNESOTA CHRISTMAS SERIES
Let It Snow
Sleigh Ride
Winter Wonderland
Santa Baby
More adventures in Logan, Minnesota, coming soon

CLOCKWORK LOVE SERIES
Clockwork Heart
Clockwork Pirate (coming soon)
Clockwork Princess (coming soon)

TUCKER SPRINGS SERIES
Second Hand (written with Marie Sexton)
(available in French)
Dirty Laundry
(available in French)
(more titles in this series by other authors)

Many titles are also available in audio and more are in production. Check the listings wherever you purchase audiobooks to see which titles are available.